I0663186

THE DEVIL AND PRESTON BLACK

JASON JACK MILLER

RAW DOG
SCREAMING
PRESS

The Devil and Preston Black copyright © 2012 by Jason Jack Miller

Published by Raw Dog Screaming Press
Bowie, MD

First Edition

Cover: Cover design elements and typography by Hatch Show Print, Nashville, Tennessee, a division of the Country Music Foundation, Inc.

Book design: Jennifer Barnes

Printed in the United States of America

ISBN: 978-1-935738-30-5

Library of Congress Control Number: 2012944447

www.RawDogScreaming.com

Heidi,
Thank you for the words, for the harmony, for the sweet notes
you sing to me. Without you, there is no music.

CHAPTER ONE

I wish I could say I found that record the first time I walked into the joint. But honestly, I'd been going into Isaac's Records every week since he'd hung his shingle out. Ever since I started giving lessons next door, at least. Killing time at Isaac's was easier than killing time with Mick's Strats and Twin Reverbs. The guitar shop had become too much like work, Mick too much like a boss. If I showed up early he always found meaningless little jobs for me to do, like tuning the Guilds and refilling humidifiers. If I showed up a minute late he was all, 'Get yourself a watch.'

So I'd hide out at Isaac's until my lessons arrived, soaking up the juju that dripped off the old vinyl like heat from a spotlight. The simplicity of an album, its lack of moving parts, spoke to me in a way CDs didn't. Vinyl had a tender, handmade feel that made me believe the music had been born into a more authentic era. Like a record could somehow be more sincere than a CD or mp3. But I knew all that was a load of crap. In the end, only the music mattered.

For me, walking into Isaac's gave me the same feeling some people get when they walk into a church or a mall. I can't describe it. Maybe enlightenment, but I'm not sure if I've ever experienced that feeling. Either way, all I had to do to soak up the collective wisdom hiding in all of those vinyl grooves was appreciate the music, and try to understand where the artist was coming from.

I swore if I browsed long enough I'd find whatever guidance I needed to get me through my paper-thin life. And since my own father ran off long before I ever learned how to hold down a G chord, I'd never have to worry about overdosing on guidance.

The guys my mom brought home didn't have a lot of wisdom to pass on. They all either wanted to preach to me or beat me. I didn't need a semi-employed union pipefitter around giving me shit when I had the Holy Trinity of John Lennon, Joe Strummer and Jerry Garcia steering me toward dreams of stadium gigs and gold records. Each of these guys came into my life when I needed them the most. And each left just like my own dad did—long gone before I ever had a chance to say goodbye.

But their lessons stuck. Joe Strummer taught me it was okay to throw a few bricks, and that a cop was something I really didn't want to be. John Lennon taught me if you were clever they hated you, and for a fool it was worse. Robert Hunter wrote it, but it was Jerry Garcia who sang the devil's friend sure ain't a friend of mine.

In hindsight, I should've listened to Hunter—or Jerry—I guess, because the morning I found the old LP that started all of this, I'd been browsing near Ozzy, a friend of the devil if the devil ever had one. Before then, I assumed lyrics were just lyrics. Didn't know they could be their own warning labels too.

Besides, the douchebags who worked at Isaac's treated me like I had the musical tastes of a ten-year-old boy. I couldn't help it I never heard of Black Flag or The Pixies growing up. My brother and me were pretty much forced to listen to whatever mom played in the car. Mostly country. Kenny and Dolly singing "Islands in the Stream." Garth Brooks, if we were lucky. Most people didn't have to dig as deep as me to find something they recognized in an old record or song.

And digging deeper was pretty much what I was doing the day I found my LP misplaced behind *The Blizzard of Oz*. On my way to return it to the BLUEGRASS section, the most beautiful woman I'd ever seen stepped out of the stacks in front of me. She smiled. I smiled back. She asked what I had in my hand. On the album cover a bunch of anonymous pickers sat in front of an old log cabin. The back of the record said *Uncle Mason's Front Porch: Best of the Blackwater Sessions*.

And on the track list, between "Pretty Polly" and "Hangman's Reel" was a song called "The Sad Ballad of Preston Black," written by E. Black.

I knew right then and there that if I could ever find the man who'd written that song, I'd have found my dad.

CHAPTER TWO

Pauly honked the horn and revved the engine like gas was free.

"David, what time is your mom coming?" I nodded at Pauly, who fidgeted impatiently in the Jeep across the street.

"I don't know." David set his guitar case on the sidewalk and blew his nose into his sleeve. The wind off the river blew me against the stickers and signs on Mick's glass door—Fender, Ernie Ball, Visa and MasterCard accepted, *No store credit, not even for Dino Michelino!*

"Here." I gave the kid an old Dairy Queen napkin. "Maybe call her or something? It's freezing."

Mick usually didn't have a problem with us waiting inside. But he'd just gotten the carpets steamed and didn't want salt and ash tracked all over. I tucked the Uncle Mason album under my arm, rested my guitar case against my hip and pressed my hands against Mick's glass door. *No sense letting all Mick's heat go to waste.*

"You're smearing up my dang door." Mick rapped on the glass. He slid his bifocals back up the bridge of his nose, then wagged his finger until I shoved my hands back into my coat pocket. "Hands off the door."

"Jesus," I whispered. Not that I worried about offending the kid with foul language or blasphemy, but I figured I probably should try to be a role model. From what I could see his own dad wasn't much of one. "You practice?"

David sniffed. "My mom makes me." He sat on the tiny ledge beneath the big plate glass window. In the display case behind him, Mick kept merchandise he couldn't unload. A pair of Korean Strat knockoffs—a black one, now faded to gray, and a red one that grew pinker by the month. Two cowbells, a tambourine, a chipped ride cymbal and a Mel Bay instruction book rounded out the motley assortment of junk Mick used to lure unwary consumers into the shop.

"You mean you don't just want to practice?" I asked, watching the Westover Bridge for David's mom.

David handed me back the napkin. "Not really."

"You keep it. Just put it in your pocket or something."

David dropped it onto the sidewalk I spent a frosty half hour sweeping this morning.

I shook my head.

David plucked the napkin up and held it like he'd hold a dead catfish. When he flipped open Mick's mailbox and plopped it in, I just shrugged my shoulders.

"I loved to practice, and I couldn't wait for Monday afternoons to show my guitar teacher how much I'd learned." The first time Jeff played "Crazy Train" for me would've been better than the day I lost my virginity and the day I smoked my first joint had both things not happened on the same day. "David, I practiced until my knuckles looked like marbles."

Because of Jeff, I learned to love music more than I ever loved Tony Hawk or the Teenage Mutant Ninja Turtles. I pestered him for more songs, more riffs, and more guitarists over the next three years. When the time came for him to pack up and leave for college I figured I had to strike out on my own. I just needed to know where to start.

Jeff said, "Start with the blues."

I bought a slide, an old Coricidin bottle like Duane Allman used. But when I tried to get into Elmore James and Muddy Waters, I ended up with a bunch of CDs I never listened to more than once or twice. For a white kid growing up in a patch house on the outskirts of Morgantown, West Virginia, the blues may as well have been N.W.A. or Public Enemy. I thought Jeff'd steered me wrong.

So I started hitting record stores like Charlie Watts hit Mick Jagger after that 5 a.m. wake-up call. I knew my personal thread through the music went deeper, and I was more than just an orphan who'd been passed around like a bottle of Boone's. Music made me keenly aware that I could be more than my guidance counselors ever expected me to be. I had my own roots and didn't have to buy into somebody else's past or culture to feel complete. I didn't know nothing about my mom or dad, but I knew I was conceived to *Led Zeppelin III* and I knew when I finally kicked it, I'd kick with a guitar in my hands.

David struggled to pick his case up from the sidewalk. I helped him tip it upright. The top came to just below his chin.

He said, "Sometimes I just want to play video games. Sometimes my hands hurt."

"Listen," I said. "With a guitar you don't need video games. You write your own stories. You can make girls fall in love with you. It's a cool thing you're doing. I didn't start playing until I was in eighth grade. What grade you in?"

"Fourth."

"Music lets you write your own checks. Don't ever forget that. You keep practicing and you'll be the only sixth grader taking an eighth-grade hottie to the Valentine's Day dance. Women love musicians."

David didn't respond.

"I got a phone number tonight in fact. In the record store just before your lesson. I think she's Russian or something." I wondered how I'd never seen her around town.

David could care less about Danicka Prochazka, the woman I vowed I'd marry. I'd practiced saying her name over and over just like she'd said it, with the same accent and everything. But David just stood there, stunned like Punxsutawney Phil right after he'd been plucked from his hole. I changed the subject. "Is Mrs. Vascheck still principal?"

"Yeah." David said. "That's where you went to school?"

"A long time ago." My mind drifted back to eighth grade. Back before things got bad. And before I could stop talking I found myself saying the kind of shit old people say. "Things were a lot different back then. No cell phones. No iPads." I gestured with the record to make my point.

"Did you buy that?" Too cold to take his hands out of his pockets, David tilted his head toward the record.

"Yeah, picked it up before your lesson." I blew into my hands. My fingers were already getting stiff. I slid *Best of the Blackwater Sessions* out of its brown paper bag and poked at my name. "'The Sad Ballad of Preston Black.'"

Seeing it there plain as day still gave me a bit of a start. "See that? E. Black. I think that's my dad. I've been looking for him since I turned sixteen and this is the closest I ever got, I think. But I'm going to find out." I waved Pauly over to see, but he had his phone in his ear.

"So... You don't know your dad?" David pulled away, like I told him Santa didn't exist either.

For a second I thought about what I should say. David had both of his parents and seemed like a really nice kid. The kind of kid who'd been to Disney World a few times. The kind of kid who didn't need a guy like me giving Mick a twenty every now and then to cover his guitar lessons.

But I didn't see the point in lying to him. So I aimed for tactful. "No, David. I never knew my dad. Or my mom. I live with Pauly and his mom. He's like my half-brother but I call him my brother. And I call his mom my mom. But she's not my real mom." And Pauly wasn't even close to being a half-brother. He'd be the opposite, whatever that was... *A full brother. A brother and a half.* "Maybe some of your friends at school have parents who've gotten divorced. Same thing."

"Oh," David said.

Realizing I was headed into a corner I couldn't back out of, I switched gears. "There's the song." I slid the record out of its cardboard sleeve and knelt on the sidewalk. "You guys have a record player?"

David shook his head.

"Me neither." Me and Pauly had an old, red and yellow Fisher Price record player when we were little. I wondered if Mom kept it. "The record spins around and the grooves make a needle vibrate, like a guitar string. Each line is a new song." I ran my finger across the surface, like it was some type of Braille that my finger could hear.

"Which one is yours?" David wiped his nose on his sleeve again. I pulled another napkin out of my pocket with my free hand and gave it to him.

"This one, right here." I flipped it over and held it up so David could see.

"It's all scratched."

"I know." Pauly'd probably say the same thing, and how stupid I'd been to waste money on it. "I'll download it later."

"Pretty Polly" and "Nine Pound Hammer" and the rest of the gang looked near mint. Like the record had been pressed this morning. The jagged grooves of "The Sad Ballad of Preston Black" split side B like a musical San Andreas. Like somebody gouged it out with a box cutter. "Just wanted to have the record, I guess. Thought it might be kind of cool. Maybe I was stupid to buy it." I ran my finger along the track, around and around, hoping I'd be able to coax a note or a word out of it before sliding it back into its sleeve. I couldn't tell if David cared or not, and I wondered why I tried so hard.

"Well, here comes my mom." David yanked on the handle of his guitar case like he'd been waiting his whole life for this moment to end. The case swung twice before smashing into the sidewalk like a fat kid on a see-saw.

Down at the bottom of University Avenue, a VW Touareg turned onto Pleasant. I stood, wiping salt and ash off of my knee.

"No!" David yelled as he stepped toward the curb.

I put my hand in front of him like a crossing guard.

David said, "Make Abby get in the backseat."

David's mother, all lipstick and Chanel shades, rolled the window down. "Thank you for waiting. I appreciate it. I would've been here sooner..."

"It's no problem, really. I didn't want to leave him by himself." The wind blew right through my thin coat. I suppressed a shiver and cinched my scarf. Besides, of all the kids I taught, only David's mom tipped me at Christmas.

"I promise I'll be on time next week." David's mom smiled. David, like every other fourth grader, probably thought his mom was the prettiest in the world. He'd be mostly right.

"David?" I said, "Hey buddy, listen to the radio and think of some songs you want to learn, okay? And practice your scales. The more you practice the less your hands'll hurt."

An apathetic 'okay' came from the backseat. David's mom gave me a smile and a wave. As she pulled away, Pauly whipped the Cherokee across the street like he was rehearsing a bank heist. The fan belt squealed as I flung open the hatch to put my guitar case in. "Let's move," Pauly yelled from the front.

"Unlock it. I'm freezing my ass off." I banged on the passenger door.

Pauly clamped an unlit Camel between his lips and reached across the passenger seat to get the handle. As I climbed in he moved the Snickers bar and bottle of iced tea he always brought for set break to the center console. "Well tighten your babushka then, grandma. What the hell was all that, anyway?"

When he smoked he only talked out of one side of his mouth. Reminded me of his grandfather, Papa Pasquale Oliverio. Pauly Pallini'd fit right in with his pap down at the Sons of Italy, playing bocce all weekend and bitching about the weatherman.

"What do you mean?" I put on my seatbelt even though we were just going a few blocks.

"You and that kid? All that Big Brother crap?" Pauly tore up Pleasant Street, caught a green light at High Street and barely made the yellow onto Spruce. "I thought the whole scene was kind of cute. Like you're trying to save West Virginia, one tone-deaf kid at a time." Pauly lit his smoke.

"Beats driving a delivery truck." I rolled my window down an inch. The dry winter air had already made my throat scratchy, but the smoke was worse. It wouldn't have mattered so much if I wasn't singing tonight.

"Yeah, driving a truck beats the hell out of being Mick's bitch any day." Pauly thought that was a good one, and laughed into the rearview mirror. "How many guitars you tune today?"

I ignored his jabs. "If we played more of my songs maybe we'd be able to make some real money. Playing Blink covers at frat houses and bars ain't gonna get us our own Graceland."

The Jeep's heater made noise, but nothing came out of my vent. I banged on the dash until a trickle of warm air finally huffed out.

"Your songs can get us the Fillmore? Didn't think so."

I shook my head and held myself back from saying what I really wanted to say. "Man, I can't help it you haven't been able to get your dick up about anything since high school."

Pauly got quiet because he was pissed. And he didn't get pissed because I dissed the band, he was pissed because he knew I was right. So he kept his mouth shut.

Tapping the radio dial for emphasis, I said, "I'm sick of puking up somebody else's greatest hits for a bunch of drunks. Man, I have a notebook full of songs. One of them could be the song that really matters to somebody. But that's not how we do it around here. We drink and whine about the gray skies and everybody says, 'Nobody from here ever makes it,' so nobody ever even tries."

"Wow. What in the hell has inspired you?" Pauly laughed. That was how I knew he'd heard that speech one too many times.

"Nothing. I don't know. I met a girl at the record store. Holy shit, she is beautiful. She had an accent. Like a Bond girl. You think it's all right that I invited her to come tonight?"

"You invited her to a frat house basement? She must be special."

"Yeah. She's amazing. Too amazing for me. We kind of started talking when I found the record. And I had to get to my lesson, so my mind was all over the place."

"You know, you fall in love way too easy then end up all jacked up. Remember Giana? She only wanted to be around you when nobody else would see. Wonder why? She made you park behind the fire hall and only called when it was convenient for her. And she always cheated on you with the biggest douchebags. Remember—"

"I get it," I cut him off. I took the album out of the paper bag and rested it against the dashboard. "Looky here."

"You collecting vinyl now?" Pauly said. He had the attention span of a cat.

"No, just look at track eleven."

"No shit. You and 'Eleanor Rigby' should hook up."

"C'mon, man. You don't think that means anything at all?"

"Here's how I'll tell you what I think—if you see white smoke then you know I picked a new pope. And if I'm drinking a Snapple then you know I don't give a shit." He picked up his tea, snapped the cap off and chugged a few times.

"You're a dick. You know that?" I tapped the album cover, tried to think of something else to say, then figured Joe Strummer never wasted time worrying about shit like this. Besides, I had bigger things on my mind than what Pauly thought. "I wonder if the songwriter's related to me. Like, maybe my dad wrote it?"

"Just keep that shit down around Mom." Pauly got defensive, like he had more of a right than me to get defensive about family matters.

"I know. But if I have a chance to find out about my real parents…"

Pauly had another smartass remark in the chamber, so he cut me off. "Didn't I tell you? I saw your dad at an A.A. meeting last night with his parole officer. Looked just like you, I mean exactly like you. No shit. Except his teeth were all fucked up. Worst case of meth mouth I ever saw. If you ever came to meetings with me maybe he could sponsor you."

"Fuck you, Pauly. Even Mick gave more of a shit than you. I've been looking for my dad for ten years. Hoping he'd show when we were playing or whatever. I went to hospitals to look for my birth certificate. Tried to find my baptism record. You guys always wanted me to give up, and I did, and now that I'm this close, I'm going to find him." I slid the album back into the sleeve, let it drop onto the floor. "Fuck you, Pauly. You know what? Sometimes I fucking hate you."

Pauly took a long drag and coughed. "C'mon, Pres. Just relax. You're overreacting a little, don't you think?"

I picked up the record and laid it on my lap. "I don't even know my own fucking birthday. Goddamnit if I can't try to get a clue to who I am. You're mean, Pauly, you know that. Fucking mean. You've gotten worse since you started back to meetings. I bet you don't treat any of your A.A. buddies like this. I may not be educated but I'm smart enough to know what your fucking problem is."

At the top of High Street, girls in short skirts made their way down to the clubs on Walnut for two-dollar well drinks and Jell-O shots. Parents in imported SUVs waited in front of apartments that were nicer than me and Pauly's for their sons to gather up two weeks' worth of dirty laundry, unaware or unwilling to believe that the stains came from binge drinking and bong water. A group of professors walked to their cars, picking up their pace as they passed a pair of football players, not because they were afraid, but because they knew no matter how hard they worked they'd never mean as much to the university as those special teams nobodies. No matter what all those people on campus had or didn't have, educated or not, they knew who they were and where they came from.

My phone buzzed and I dug into my pocket to get it.

<Talent and education don't take the place of persistence. There are loads of educated tossers out there.>

"Sorry, Pres." Pauly held out his hand.

I ignored Pauly and read the text again. When I decided I didn't know who'd sent it, I put my phone away. "Whatever, Pauly. Why do you have to be a dick on tonight of all nights? Why do you always got to take the spotlight?"

"I don't want Stu to go either. Maybe that's why I'm edgy. This is going to suck." My comment stung him a little, snapped him back to reality. He put out his hand and went back into funny guy mode, "Happy Birthday, huh?" Pauly watched the red light and offered me a Camel.

"I quit. Besides, my throat's already scratchy. And you know it's not my fucking birthday. Asshole." I let his hand hang like trailer court Christmas lights in July. Pauly knew the birthday was a touchy subject, especially since I didn't know the exact day. All I knew was that it came the week before Valentine's. *Next week*. And I was pretty sure I'd die sometime in the next year, so I sure as hell didn't feel like blowing out any candles.

I said, "With this 'curse of twenty-seven' thing hanging over me you think you'd be a little more sensitive. All the signs are there, man."

"What signs?"

"Hendrix and Cobain, Pigpen—all grew up in really unstable homes and used drugs or alcohol. I just have a feeling, man. A really, really, bad feeling."

"Those are some pretty non-specific signs. Besides, how do you know it's not your birthday, you bastard? You might already be twenty-seven. Mom said you were about three or four months old when your mom died, so it's right around this time of year. Let me sing to you tonight." He placed the offertory Camel next to his Snickers and tea.

I didn't say anything. If Pauly was good for anything it was squirming his way out of situations before he ever had to feel bad about anything. Even the judge gave him a slap on the wrist for his most recent moving violation. I had to spend a month in rehab and do community service for a year. For his road rage, Pauly got A.A., anger management and a job.

He said, "I'm sorry, Preston. Okay? I just don't want to lose you to an asshole nobody who vanished before you were born. So, maybe this guy is your dad. But why didn't he take custody after your mom died?"

"You know I don't know."

We hung a right on College Avenue and headed up toward the shitty frats by Price Street. Zeppelin came on the radio. "Trampled Under Foot."

"C'mon, man." Pauly fidgeted, his seat squeaking like a pair of mice going at it in a box spring.

Being mad about shit like this wore me out. But I knew my biggest problem was forgiving Pauly too easily. I loved him too much. "Say it then."

Pauly took a drag, stalling for words. "I thought we had, like, an unspoken thing between us." He cleared his throat and spit out the window. "People notice that… We're like—" Pauly tapped the steering wheel while he tried to think of words that meant something to me. "John and Paul. They were like brothers. Or Johnny and Joey Ramone."

"Jesus, Pauly. Johnny and Joey weren't even fucking related and they hated each other. Did you forget that or just never know? I can't figure out which is more disappointing."

"Whatever, man. You're my brother and I love you. Without you and the band, I would have been just another loser failing gym."

"And what else?"

"Dude, I'm Pipeline's Ringo." He laughed.

"Bullshit, Ringo wrote "Octopus's Garden." If anything you're our Steven Adler." I grabbed his Snickers from the center console and ripped open the wrapper. With a mouthful of caramel and nougat I said, "And you'd better fucking remember that."

For a second I forgot where we were playing. Just before reminding the crowd of Jackson's non-smoking Wednesdays I realized it was Thursday, and the Delts smoked as much as they wanted. They were a bunch of pussies—Pauly called them the Felts—but they liked us and paid us all right. And they always had a lot of girls there.

My throat wasn't cooperating. I knew the words and how they should've sounded, but they came out of my mouth like black smoke from a tailpipe. Besides, our farewell show was supposed to be twenty years from now. In a stadium.

After rushing through "Wild Horses," I retreated from the apathetic crowd to the open window behind my Marshall. By now we'd amassed quite a collection of beverages on the windowsill. Pauly drank cranberry juice and sweet tea and Stu drank the Bud Lite and Jack and Cokes. I sipped a vodka and Coke. I started the night with MGD that tasted like it'd been poured from a keg that kicked before the Sugar Bowl. The fresh air tasted better to me anyway.

"Can we get a few more drinks for my boys up here? And a pop for me?" Pauly yelled into the mic like he didn't really understand the mic's sole purpose in life was to amplify noise, specifically voices. "It's Preston's special day today."

"Don't do it," I spun in a rush, knocking some of the drinks into the driveway below. Flat beer and cranberry juice splattered across the hood of somebody's Toyota Camry. A spindrift of cups disappeared into the night.

"Happy birthday to you..." Pauly sang with all his might, as if volume alone would make me happier. He raised a palm to the ceiling, and the crowd sang along.

I wiped my face with an old bandana as I returned to my mic. Tonight belonged to Stu. And maybe Pauly tried his best to hold it together. Maybe this was just his way of releasing frustration, so I let him have it. One of the pledges brought a few shots right at "...dear Preston...." I passed Stu's over his toms. As the basement decayed into a drunken roar, I found Stu's eyes and raised my cup. "Here's to you, man. Be safe."

Jäger.

Like a drop-kick to my woozy gut. *I should've eaten something*, although I wasn't entirely convinced that wings and nachos were the cure-all I required. I took another look at Stu. My face got hot, my throat got full, like I was trying to swallow a ravioli without chewing.

I returned to my mic. "Thank you all for having Pipeline back one last time. We love playing here, you know that, right?"

Drunken woo-hoos echoed off the cinderblock walls. We never even filled the places we used to fill.

I couldn't make eye contact with the crowd, not while I was lying. I ran my finger along the chipped edge by my Tele's strap knob, the only blemish on the thing. "We have a lot of requests to get through, and we're going to keep playing until you hear everything you want to hear. Tonight's a real special night for us. And a little sad. Pauly and me are saying goodbye to Stu, you know."

I extended my hand to Stu without looking back at him. "He's taking a year to see the world with a really long stop in Afghanistan. Is that a government-issue haircut or what?"

Everyone applauded quietly giving me their first genuine response of the night. "Count us off, Stu."

I let the feedback grow before catching Stu's beat a half-step late. With my eyes closed, I threw myself into the riff. Our take on Weezer. But "Tired of Sex" wasn't really the way I thought I'd say goodbye to one of my oldest friends.

Stu kicked his bass drum so hard my ribs tingled. Each beat helped me to forget who I was and where we were playing. In my head, this band was for real. And a good band. I stepped up to the mic, eyes still closed, and sang. Sweat crawled down my forehead, onto the bridge of my nose, into my eyes where it stung like the ocean. An ocean of sadness.

"I'm tired. So tired..." I pounded the strings. The pick squirmed between my sweaty fingers. It was easy to get lost in the music. My body rocked to the wall of rhythm Pauly and Stu built. Squinting into the room, I didn't see anybody even really watching us.

Ever since I picked up a guitar, I counted down the days until I'd be playing my own stuff to of a room full of people who'd paid to hear me. But my timer would never reach zero. Fayette County, Pennsylvania, was the closest we ever got to making it out of West Virginia. Pauly nodded for me to take my solo, but it didn't feel right. Nobody out there gave a shit anyway. They were too busy dry-humping. Pauly looked at me. "What the hell?"

I skipped the last verse too. Pauly and Stu followed me straight to the outro. They were pretty good that way. Finding a good drummer until Stu got back would be tough. "Thank you," I said. "Thank you very much. We're going to take a ten minute break."

"What's that about?" Pauly pulled his squares from his jacket and tapped the setlist with his toe. He lit a smoke before he even had his bass in its stand. "We got requests to get through."

"Grab me a cranberry juice?" I asked, and began wiping the sweat off of my strings. "I don't feel good."

Stu patted me on the back as he came between his high hat and my cabinet. "Good call, Pres. I have to piss like a motherfucker."

"Anything for you, brother." I gave his shoulder a gentle slap.

They pushed through the crowd, the two of them, not afraid of anything or anybody. And the Felts stepped aside even though they owned the joint. Because nobody ever challenged Pauly Pallini or Stu Croe. Not because they were the toughest. But because they weren't afraid to give every last drop. Whatever it took to win.

Except for when it came to our music. I plugged back into the Twin and turned the volume up to 8.

Alone, on the stage, I strummed, playing to hear myself play. Soft, slow chords. Just my Tele's neck pickup through the old Twin's bright channel. It wasn't even a song, just some harmonic minor thing. I noodled with a few chord changes. Pauly waited by the bathroom door and watched. Since it seemed like the only thing left to do, I stepped up to the mic.

"Here's a quiet one for you all. But mostly, this one's for Stu."

I had notebooks full of songs and hadn't memorized a single lyric, title, or chord. Even though I'd be singing a lie, I leaned into the mic, closed my eyes and drew in all the breath I'd ever need. I whispered the first line to "Strawberry Fields Forever."

A few people clapped.

I ignored them. This song was too beautiful for this crowd, for this room. And as I sang, the true meaning of the song began to unfold like a map of the universe. I used to think Lennon meant that the people with their eyes closed just had to expand their consciousness or whatever, a metaphorical eye-opening. Start seeing with their hearts. But while I stood there, strumming somebody else's chords and thinking that Stu's departure meant the end to my time making music, I realized that *my* eyes had been closed.

And it wasn't that I couldn't understand the things I saw. The truth was, I was only capable of seeing misunderstanding. *I'll be doing covers forever.*

Stu came out of the bathroom and stopped. I found his face and shut out everybody else's. I knew it was a dream, and he knew that I knew. But the words I sang were words I needed to hear. Maybe more than Stu needed to hear them. But if Stu and everybody else thought I sang to Stu, I figured it was okay to go on letting them think that.

Nothing is real, I kept telling myself. Because we never built anything real. Like maybe I should've been trying to make something of myself instead of worrying about what Pauly wanted. People clapped though. For the first time tonight, somebody did something on this stage worth acknowledging. Stu pointed at me then saluted. If only he knew that I'd have done anything to keep him from putting that uniform back on.

Into the mic I said, "I love you, man. I don't want you to go," and I yanked the cable from the Tele's jack and let it drop.

Stu blew me a kiss and laughed.

His gesture snapped me out of my mood. "Who's going to take care of my boy?" I reached into Pauly's jacket for a smoke. Pauly waved me over to the bar, holding up my juice.

"Give me a second." I pointed upstairs.

He gestured at a group of DZs who were coming in through a side door. They were all blond, they were all wearing short skirts and they all had on jackets or hoodies with their chapter letters on the sleeve. But they were too young. I shook my head, snuck up the steps and made my way to the front. In my haste to split I forgot my coat, and could already feel the night chilling the sweat on my face and back. "This is how I end up with pneumonia."

The front door stood wide open to the street noise. The piggies making out on the couch didn't even notice. I picked up a Bic from the end table and pocketed it. As I stepped onto the porch I put the cigarette to my lips. "Fuck." Until Pauly quit smoking, I didn't stand a chance.

The lighter sparked on the third try. My hand shook as I raised it up to my face. I knew the last cigarette didn't kill you. I coughed on the cold and the smoke. But the rush of nicotine cleared my head. I shivered as my blood soaked up the drug.

I sat down on a couch that should've been torched back in November. Except Pitt won. More than anything I wanted to flick the butt into the street and finally quit again. I told myself this was the last one forever.

"Preston." A woman's voice came from the house. Probably a DZ Pauly sent up. Probably told her I needed cheering up.

But I didn't answer. I wasn't in the mood for Pauly's shenanigans. I took a long pull from the Camel. "If Pauly sent you up…"

Her heels clacked as she stepped onto the porch. "I thought I had an invitation."

I flipped the butt into the yard. Two drags too many. I looked over my shoulder. "Holy shit." I jumped to my feet and rubbed my palms on my jeans. In the few moments I'd spent talking to her earlier I memorized every square inch of her face, but still couldn't believe she'd come to see me. Now nervous, I hid my hands in my back pockets. "I'm glad you came. I really am."

She slid onto the porch like a bead of mercury across a glass plate. Knee-high black boots and a short gray skirt. All of it shivering beneath a gray wool trench. Her hair sat up on her head, like a librarian's. She wore eyeglasses with small, round lenses. "Are you hiding from somebody?"

She tapped a Lucky Strike out of a crisp pack tucked in her purse. I offered my new lighter.

"White? You should know better." She dug through her purse and produced an old Zippo.

When she moved real close to me, I smelled herbs, like anise and citrus and mint. Mostly I smelled cigarette smoke and was pissed that the smoke killed my sense of smell. "Just a little distracted tonight. That's all," I said. In my head I kept referring to tonight as our 'last gig' and it made my mouth dry.

She leaned against me, shivering. Her skin was fair like a dogwood flower, soft like Van Morrison. I'd been accused of falling in love way too easy, but this time it was real. And I barely knew her. All I had were ideas about how things could be. Ideas about who she was and what we could be together. Her dark eyes pulled me in.

She said, "I'm sorry tonight is your last show. Unless you have plans after, maybe we can go out for a drink and talk…" She pulled me into a small kiss, then said, "And then talk some more."

I forgot about the cold, about Pauly and the *Blackwater Sessions* record. Her kiss helped me forget why I'd been so sad. Like that kiss was the only thing I'd ever wanted. Like I'd been living my whole life for that kiss.

In the basement Stu banged his drums. Pauly yelled into the mic, "Preston Black, please report to the stage. Mr. Preston Black. That is all."

"*To je jak když hrach na zeď haze.*" Dani took a long pull on her cigarette and smiled. "I'll wait," she said, leaning against the railing.

I'd hoped for one more kiss, but she'd turned toward the street and pulled out her phone.

The lights were off, our gear was stashed and the brothers of Delta whatever were tucked safely into their beds. Pauly followed a group of girls up the street to get phone numbers. Purple streetlights buzzed. Falling icicles tinkled onto slippy sidewalks. We stood out there in the cold like we were waiting to be invited back inside. Stu ran his fingers along his scalp as though he'd been expecting to find a lot more hair up there. "Bring your girl, man. It's no big deal."

Up the street, Dani's silver car sat in the shadow formed by a big holly blocking the streetlight. I tried to see her through the dark windshield. Stu was right about my priorities tonight and he knew it. And he knew I knew. But I figured being on stage with him was a better goodbye than watching ESPN and eating greasy pepperoni rolls at Casa D'Amici. "Yeah, but what kind of goodbye is it with a sober Pauly?"

I pointed at her car up the street and said, "Besides, this whole thing is new. I want to make sure I'm taking all the right steps. She's too good for me. I'm not ready for her to figure that out."

Stu said, "Not to be nebby, but why didn't she come downstairs?"

"She came down. After that break?" It came out a little more defensively than I would've liked.

"I don't know. Maybe I missed her. I just kept seeing the same hoes over and over. I thought you would've pointed her out to me." Stu looked big tonight. Pumped up like an action figure. He said, "You going to call Larry up again? Is he still drumming in town?"

"Larry Benco? No, he's horrible. He couldn't keep time with a pair of stop-watches. Besides, he's a little old. And he has no idea who Rise Against are. I'm thinking about auditioning a few guys—younger guys—maybe trying to play with a few different people 'til you get back. Try to tweak our sound a little."

"Well," Stu said, "maybe you should just try to hook up with another band. Might be easier?"

"What about Pauly?"

"I don't know if his heart's in it."

"Bullshit. He's in it as long as I am." Then I thought for a second and added, "Did he say something to you?"

Stu avoided the question. "Well, you do what you want. What if I don't come back? I don't want you wasting your time waiting for me."

I got angry and scared. "What the fuck are you talking about? Don't say shit like that, man. You'll be back. I'm serious. Don't say shit like that. Ever."

Stu put his hands up, a surrender. "Dude, chill. I'm talking about staying in this time, not taking frag in Marjah. I'm thinking about having a career and making money."

"Don't tell me Pauly's in your head. He's all about the money. I tell him all the time we're good enough to write and record our own stuff but he doesn't listen." I started to shiver. "No, I'm holding your spot 'til you get back. Any drummer we get's going to know up front the gig's only for a year."

Stu didn't say anything for a long moment. He just looked at me. "Well, don't forget the packages. Beef jerky, Cool Ranch Doritos and Dairy Mart pepperoni rolls. I don't care if it all gets smushed and crushed. And magazines. I can't ask my mom to get them for me but a perv like you should have no problem."

"Same as boot camp."

"Exactly."

"You know, I still have all your letters."

"I knew you would, you sentimental fuck."

"You're looking and talking more like a soldier and less like my drummer."

"Like Charlie Watts said, 'I'm not your drummer. You're my guitar player.'" He laughed. "And I got to get back in the right frame of mind. That's all."

"You keep that part hidden from me and Pauly. But I see it when you're with the guys from your unit. I feel like the stories we have can't compete with your army stories—"

Stu cut me off. "That's bullshit and you know it, man. You think I tell army stories when we're in the shit waiting for a patrol to come back, or waiting for air support? Fuck no. I tell them about the road trip to Huntington when we told Pauly we were going to Seattle and how he didn't know the difference because he'd never been out of Morgantown. Shit like that."

He put his hand on my shoulder. "Listen, I tell band stories over there to remind myself what I'm fighting for. I tell army stories back here so I don't forget what it took to get all this."

"Sorry, man. I'm going to miss you. That's all." We both watched Pauly come down the hill waving his phone to show us the numbers of the girls who'd never take his calls.

"I know."

Pauly lit a smoke and said, "Let's go, bitches." He got into the Jeep and turned the key. Just before pulling the door shut he yelled, "Don't forget about Mom's water pump tomorrow."

"I know," I held my hand up. "Just give me a fucking minute here."

I shook Stu's hand. Really I wanted to hug him. "I had a lot more I wanted to say."

He smiled. "Put it in a letter."

"Last time you left, the weather was like this. We got pizza and your family came over. It felt different."

"Afghanistan is going to be a lot different than Iraq," Stu said. "But you'll see me before you know it." He let go of my hand, went around the Jeep and got in. Pauly turned on the dome light and lit a smoke for Stu. They laughed, and Pauly flipped the light off.

Slush, and old ashy snow crunched as they drifted down the street. It wasn't very often the two people in this world I felt closest to went off without me. I didn't like the way it made me feel. The future, which had once been full of shows and songs, now seemed quite empty.

My phone buzzed to life. *A goodbye from Stu.* But instead of his name in the display, it read *Unknown Number.*

The text said, <Bloody hell, mate, you write your future.>

I replied, <Who the hell is this?>

A small beep came from Dani's silver Mercedes, a car that looked like something the Sean Connery-era James Bond would drive. It sat in the intersection like a bullet just waiting to be fired, with its little round headlights and curved hood. Pauly and Stu weren't coming back, so I put my phone away, walked up the hill and got in.

Before I had my seatbelt clicked she took off, racing down University toward High, red lights suddenly becoming green as she sped beneath them. Old buildings collapsed beyond my window, neon signs little more than streaks of magenta and electric blue. Brake lights on the cars ahead of us were just propositions, which Dani ignored. She hit the bridge over Deckers like a fastball into a catcher's mitt. The Mercedes begged for third gear, screamed for fourth. Then, just as suddenly, Dani hit the brake to swing onto Dorsey, skidding on a little ice. She smiled as I steadied myself on the dashboard.

Forcing myself to look relaxed, I sank back into the leather seat. It felt more comfortable than my own bed. "Nice car. So you're not a student I take it?"

"*Tváří se jako by neuměl do pěti počítat.* You're sweet. I received the car as a gift. Payment, I should say. You don't want to hear about the paperwork just to get it here." She stroked the steering wheel like it was a sleeping kitten. "Maybe you can drive it when you're sober."

I knew Dorsey, but not many of these side streets. Always considered this a richer part of town, even if I'd never been around real wealth enough to know what it looked like. The wraparound porches and ivy-covered trellises and stained glass windows were a far cry from the patch house duplex I grew up in. I rationalized my feelings of unworthiness by telling myself I was an artist, and that some things were more important than money, and…. Whatever.

From Dorsey we made a right then another quick right. The blacktop ran out, and the little Mercedes bounced along on a brick-paved road. The *brrrrr* of the bricks shook my head, getting lower in pitch as Dani slowed to a stop. In the chilly glow of a dusk-to-dawn light I could make out the back of a large Victorian. "We're here."

"This is your place?" I shut the car door and looked up. The bulk alone amazed me.

"No," she laughed and gathered her scarf. "I rent a room."

I held my guitar in front of me and let her lead. Inside, the old house smelled like wood smoke with a hint of cloves. Heat from big radiators made me sweat. I unbuttoned my coat. The building felt safe, like the Fortress of Solitude. Nobody slammed doors or said filthy things in a house like this. Things were always *Pee Wee's Playhouse* and Laffy Taffy here. This was the kind of place I always dreamt about growing up in, although lately I confused dreams with wishes so easily that I kind of lost track of which I'd been doing.

We started up a flight of stairs. I said, "You never told me what you do for a living." My voice was afraid to do much more than whisper.

"It's boring. And you didn't come here to talk." Dani softly touched my chin with her thumb. In the mild light of a lonely floor lamp she smiled. "Not this late, right?"

Not sure if this was a trick, I hesitated.

The corner of her mouth revealed the tease. "I translate books and contracts. Taking words and twisting them into brand new sentences. English to Japanese. Czech to German. Mostly contracts. Not the long-lost Božena Němcová novel I dream of. My legacy will be rewriting small deals for little business men who want to be big business men." She led me up another flight of stairs, to a landing below a half-circle of stained glass.

While she fumbled for the key, I held her bag and turned toward the ornate semi-circle window. Venus de Milo rising from a scallop. "You should have a light up here. You'd feel safer, don't you think?"

She twisted my lame aside into a lesson, "Preston, I was born in Prague before the Velvet Revolution. I studied literature at La Sapienza and linguistics at La Sorbonne and received my Arabic to English certificate at NYU. West Virginia does not scare me."

I mumbled a frail, "Point taken."

She stepped inside, letting me hold the door for her. After dropping her coat on an overstuffed leather armchair, she tugged the pull chains of a brass bookshelf light and a nearby lamp.

Shades of stained glass and mica cast the room in a bronze glow. Large shelves held leather- and cloth-bound books with titles written in faded gold. It looked as if the ceiling were held up by books alone. I recognized a few names—Kafka and Dante. For every name I recognized there were a hundred I didn't. Joost van den Vondel. Jacques Cazotte. Josef Čapek. Charles Baudelaire. My lack of education would've been more embarrassing if Dani hadn't been so far out of my league. Somebody like Stu would've been out the door by now. Pauly wouldn't have made it up the steps.

"Did you think we came up here to read?" Dani took my coat and scarf. "Would you like to wash?"

She went into the bathroom, flipped the light on and told me to come in. An old pedestal sink sat across from a big claw foot tub. I set my record on the chair and followed her in. If I pressed my cheek against the small round window I could see the lock and the city around a bend to the north. The lights looked too far away. Not miles away, but years away. Like I didn't believe for a second I was looking upstream at the same city I grew up in.

"The lights of any city still amaze me. Travel was not convenient when I was young—Prague had many checkpoints. Only when I was twelve years old did I finally see the city at night." She flipped the light off, leaving me with the view of Morgantown and the lock and the Westover Bridge. "Would you like a drink?"

"Thanks." I joined her back in the main room, and said half-jokingly, "But I already had plenty to drink tonight."

She smiled, letting go of a little of the sternness she'd worn all night like brass buttons on a fancy coat.

I came around the large leather sofa and found her leaning against the counter holding a Japanese teapot over a pair of small glasses with heavy stems. She slowly dripped water onto a sugar cube that rested on a fork lain across the top of the glass. Little by little the sugar dissolved. "The water releases oils from the absinthe the same way the drink frees your mind. Like a metamorphosis, maybe?"

She rested her elbows on the countertop and put her nose right up to the rim of the glass. Like a little kid peeking into a Mason jar full of fireflies. She placed the tip of her finger into the liquid, then swabbed my lip. The smell of black licorice rushed into my nose.

Dani put her arm around my neck and pulled me into a soft kiss that lingered on my bottom lip. She handed me one of the little glasses. Cloudy green liquid sloshed up to the rim.

"*Na zdraví*. You only ever get one first sip." She held her glass up, and I imitated her. She took off her glasses and set them on the counter.

The drink was more potent than anything I'd ever put down my throat—whiskey, bourbon, tequila. The closest was this purple stuff a chemistry major made with Everclear at a New Year's Eve party a few years ago. I almost died that night.

Dani took another sip and smiled, then led me to the leather sofa, dark like coffee. She took a seat at the other end and put her feet onto my lap. "My little feet are so tired."

I put my glass on the floor. Her toes curled as I loosened her shoe's black leather strap and carefully slid it off. Little spots of pearlescent red danced beneath her black stockings, back and forth, like a cat about to nap. She held a sip of absinthe on her tongue before swallowing.

"Preston Black." Dani rested her cheek against the leather cushion.

"That's me." My old buzz, now reactivated, dribbled into my head, down my spine and through my limbs like splashes of dusty sunshine through the windblown leaves. It took a minute to realize Dani had been waiting for me to go on.

"Not much to say, especially if you've seen me play. Speaking of which, you didn't come downstairs and watch the rest of our set?"

"I went for a coffee," she said unapologetically. "You had been saying?"

"Oh." Her forwardness tripped me up, my mind drifted a second. "Well, anyway, I was born and raised here. Raised by Pauly's mother."

"And what about your parents?"

I picked my glass up and swirled the drink around in it. "Nothing like building up to the tough questions, huh? My mother died when I was a few months old. Car crash on her way to work at the mall. Sometimes I think I remember her, but probably… I was probably too young." All the sad talk distorted my mood. "She had me when she was, like, seventeen.

"And my dad? The bastard left my mom before I'd even been born." I laughed and poured a big swallow down my throat. "That makes me the bastard, I guess. But I think I finally found him, though. I have a bone to pick."

At the risk of sounding too angry I paused to rethink my next words. "But I don't know if I have a bone to pick as much as I just want to look at his face and see if I can see any of myself in there. Like, after so many years of not knowing, to wake up one day and finally know? For me it's like being able to hear after years without sound. And then, maybe after the newness wears off I'll get mad, thinking about how I've been cheated out of a big part of my life. You know, I'll probably want to yell and punch him right in the mouth. I don't know. But I just want to have that option. Sometimes I think Pauly'd like to take a shot at him, too."

While I talked I ran my finger along the arch of Dani's foot. Her toes curled like guitar strings pulled from tuning pegs. She crossed her legs at the ankles, an invitation for me to play with her other foot.

While waiting for her to speak up, I finished my drink. But the lull in conversation got to me. So I went on. "Pauly's my best friend, but I'm afraid things are changing fast. I always felt like he held me back musically but I stuck with him for all these years like I had to take care of him. Now Pauly's trying to get sober and Stu's leaving and I have ideas, a notebook full of songs we never played. I'm not sure when I'll play for an audience again."

"Just find another drummer, right?"

"I know. Except something tells me the credits are going to roll soon. I'm not sure Pauly's heart's in it anymore. He never loved it like I did. And because I didn't try to get myself a better gig I'm the one left out in the cold."

"You should remain hopeful though, right?" Dani let out a breath. "Growing up, I didn't understand the idea of Communism. When I think of Prague now, I think of all the colors and lights and the Žižkov tower at night and the red tile roofs. It's hard to forget the city's past. Without hope, my childhood is only winter—the gray Vltava and dark, quiet, streets and cellars."

She swirled the slurry of sugary liquid around the bottom of her glass. "They made us march in parades and we had to wear red scarves around our necks. So, gray and red."

In one swift motion she tilted her head back and drank the rest. She smiled and said, "I'll prepare another?"

I handed her my glass.

"Luxury things were rare. Later I learned that nobody had rich foods and fine things—not just us. I counted every penny and learned little by little to appreciate. You have nothing, then suddenly, you have a little. When I smell clementines I think of Christmas and my childhood memories get a little brighter." She returned to the couch. This time she sat closer to me, and after handing me my drink, shook her hair free from a pair of silver barrettes. "Back in Prague I knew quite a few hopeless young girls. That's where I learned all about those ugly qualities that separate a child from an adult. *Sranda jak v márnici.*"

I shook my head.

"It's like 'having fun in a morgue,' so, a little sad."

"Your parents didn't spare you from all that?" She'd diluted the absinthe even less this time.

"Prague was a very sad place when I was born. Thinking and speaking against the party was illegal. Living in the *Panelaks* was only a little better than living in a barn stall. But the people were always hopeful and remembered that life is short. Just after my mother had me, Prague said goodbye to the Communists. They came together, shouting 'This is our city.'" Dani told the story as if she'd memorized it from a plaque in front of a museum.

"And when I left…" Her stare drifted a bit. "All my life they told us the West was a horrible place and people died because they didn't have enough to eat. And I went west and thought, I'm the poor one, where are the others like me? It wasn't what I expected. Outside was so much more…. The *sestra* did a very good job of protecting us. Once I was out I had to make my own way and I guess that's why I stayed away."

"So your parents died in the revolution?"

She laughed like she had to shake away bad thoughts. "Of course not. You never heard of the Velvet Revolution? No, after I was born my father ran off to Italy to find a better job. My mother fell in love with a man who already had a family. She left me with Barnabite Nuns at the Church of Saint Benedict. Cabbage every day. But there I learned Latin and German and Russian. Somehow I got the idea that speaking many languages improved my chances of finding a family."

She looked into her drink. "When a man and a woman came to look for a child I would say '*dobré jitro*' and then '*dobroye utro*' and finally '*guten Morgen.*' That's how I ended up in Munich, a *holčička* turned *Fräulein.*" She switched accents like I'd switch chords. "It's easy for me to forget how very fortunate I was."

I almost interrupted to say something sympathetic, but she went on. "In the orphanage, we learned first to grasp the world through language—for us—the language of Bible. But the regime didn't approve. To release my frustration I conjured up demons to attack *StB* agents—*Státní bezpečnosta* secret police force in plain clothes. I enjoyed this very much."

For a long time neither of us said anything. Sometimes she'd rest her head on my shoulder, then she'd just swirl her drink, forever around and around. When she finally finished her drink she took my glass.

"No more," I said.

She stood and said, "One more," then returned to the kitchen. While she poured the drinks I took off my Vans and set them over by the door. She returned, handed me the tiny glasses, then she undid the clasp on her skirt and let it drop to the floor, exposing thigh high stockings and garters. She took her drink from me, then unbuttoned the top and bottom two buttons on her gray shirt. She tapped my foot with hers. I uncrossed my legs and she sat down again, this time leaning right against me. I rested my arm over her shoulder, and she took my hand into her shirt and placed it on her belly. Her smooth skin felt warm, like August at nine in the evening.

Her delicate fingers clasped my forefinger and made small circles around her belly button. Her cultured ways made me self-conscious. My fingers were calloused from playing and my knuckles were scabbed from scraping the track bar when me and Pauly changed the Jeep's tie rod the other day. Never in my life had I felt so strongly that I wasn't good enough for somebody. I forced the rest of my drink down.

Dani didn't seem to mind, holding my forefinger like a pen as she continued to write half notes between her belly button and the top of her panties, whole measures on the black lace whorls that separated my fingertips from her skin. When she slid my finger to her thigh I figured this was only the first verse. Her breathing changed. Half notes became quarter notes. She arched her head back, looking for a kiss. She wrote measure after measure until the staff was full.

I wanted to add a verse of my own.

"Not yet," she whispered.

Guiding the pen to the page, she continued to write. Little by little, the chorus revealed itself to me. And as she pushed me into her panties I wondered if we were headed toward the bridge. She arched her head back again and found my mouth, singing lyrics directly into me. She twisted, took my glass, mostly empty, and set it on the table behind me. One by one she undid my shirt buttons.

She straddled me, rocking and rocking before finally settling upon my still-buttoned fly. Gently, back and forth, establishing a tempo. Writing her song with her thighs, and with the in-between. Rocking still when she found my belt.

I undid the last of her buttons and slid her shirt from her slender shoulders. Kissing her neck, her throat and the soft skin above her breasts elicited a half smile from her thin lips. In the broken light of the stained-glass lampshade I found her eyes, pupils wide in a bed of amber. She pulled my shirt over my head, then my t-shirt. She guided my hand toward the clasp on her bra. The more she took off, the more I could see that she wasn't a goddess. She was just a girl.

Dani reached behind me and turned off the light. She slid off of me and stood— now the brightest light in the room. She whispered, "Are you going to let me rewrite your song, Preston Black?"

I kissed her neck and shoulder, gently tugging her toward her bedroom door.

"Preston?" Dani looked up at me with serious eyes.

"Yes, if that means you want to be with me."

She kissed my chin, then my cheek.

"It does." She slid her hands along my waist, pushed my jeans and boxers to the floor. Nothing left to hide.

Her room smelled and looked exactly like I thought it would, like nothing could ever go wrong on this big four-poster bed. Like clementine and mint and anise. She threw back a heavy, embroidered throw and down comforter, scattering little pillows, all purple and green with gold tassels.

I fell into a clump of over-stuffed pillows with Dani on top of me. Even before I could slide her panties aside she reared up, like a cat upon a mouse. Her breathing and focus let me know I had catching up to do. With the tips of my index fingers I unclipped Dani's thigh-highs from her garter and slid the panties off of her hips and down her legs. She lifted herself for a moment and found me again as she kicked them off of her ankle.

I focused on a window, seated at the end of a deep dormer, and tried to think about Duane Allman or the cafeteria from my high school. Anything to curb my excitement. She kissed my neck, my chest. She bit at my earlobes and lower lip. Beyond the window I could make out a few stars. "Slower," I said, my voice barely a whistle in the wind.

She never looked at me, but I couldn't look away. Her hips pulsed, fluid contractions that came from deep within her. She squeezed herself around me. I tried to assert myself and change the tempo. "Slower."

Her breath, like a huff of steam from a boiling tea kettle, blew onto my neck. The scent of clementine and mint and absinthe lingered beneath my nose. Dani angled herself further forward and pushed her hips faster. The smooth skin between her breasts glistened with a touch of perspiration.

I scolded myself for letting my focus drift and directed my attention back toward the window. The stars didn't seem to be moving fast enough. After all the insecurities I felt tonight, the least I could do now was hold on as long as I could.

Dani smiled, said my name, then muttered something in Czech. The sound came from her throat, from somewhere deep inside her. The tone sounded familiar, but the words were ice in the desert. The way she said them made me lose it.

Synapses fired electric light into my skin and bones. She raised an eyebrow, kissed me, then rolled her hips forward twice, almost like taking a bow. Then, letting go herself, she sighed a sigh that filled my head, her breath filled my lungs. She fell onto my chest.

"Preston?"

"Yes, Dani? Danicka. I like that better, I think."

"I like the way you say it." She pushed her hair behind her ear, then sat up without getting off of me, asking, "If wishes were real, what would you wish for?"

I didn't say anything, thinking maybe she was being rhetorical. I closed my eyes.

"Preston." She forced my attention, holding my chin in her hand.

"I don't know." I didn't feel like talking. This was time to sink into the bed, drunk on love. "What do you mean?"

"For example, how would you change things, if you could change things?" she asked very earnestly.

"Why're you asking me now?" I tried to put on a face that hid my confusion and rested against the headboard.

"Maybe I don't do this kind of thing very often and want to know you a bit better. Why do you need an explanation?" She pushed me back into the pillows.

"Really?" I wanted a quick shower and a long night to dream.

"Really. Before I say 'goodnight' I want you to tell me three things. Three things you would change." She laid her head on my chest. Her thick hair fell onto my neck.

"Three wishes?"

"No, it doesn't have to be a wish. Just something you want. Save wishes for things you know will never happen."

"I don't know." I thought about it for a second. My life had been changing so fast, I found myself wanting quite a bit. Too much to boil down into three easy statements.

"I wish I could find my dad, I guess. So I at least knew where I came from. That's easy."

Part of me felt afraid to say these things out loud, like not telling anybody what you wished for when you blew out birthday candles. But I wanted to feel safe with Dani, like she could be different and I didn't have to put on an act.

"Maybe I wish Stu'd come back. I don't care how he gets back, I just want him back. Because then all this uncertainty about the band wouldn't matter and Pauly'd see that we can take it to the next level and all the mistakes he's making if he gives up." I found the stars again, but not the same ones I'd seen earlier.

"And the last thing, I think, is that somehow I'd like to be a part of music forever. Real music, the kind people never forget. I'm afraid life—real life—like jobs and taxes will tear me away from what I love. I'm afraid if I lose music I'll be just like everybody else. And that scares me." I forced a laugh. "Is that too much to ask?"

"No, it's not too much." She laughed with me, gently pulling my face toward hers. "*Polib mě.*"

And we kissed again. If I didn't know any better, I would've sworn right then and there that she loved me, too. I'd never been kissed like that.

She didn't cover herself when she left the room. I sat on the edge of the bed while she went into the bathroom and ran the hot water for the shower. After a few minutes she called for me.

The steam went into my lungs easy, like a shot of Jameson. I wiped moisture off the mirror and looked at myself, not proudly, but not regretfully either. But when I saw the extra toothbrush and the bottle of Prada, I felt a little shame. I didn't know French, but I knew *POUR HOMME.*

Danika remained silent while we showered. She gave me a big, soft towel and told me to get some sleep while she dried her hair. She kissed me and said she'd join me in a few minutes. And when I returned to the bedroom I saw a hundred things I didn't see before—a pair of cufflinks and another bottle of cologne on the dresser. I cracked her closet door open and found a white dress shirt and a pair of neckties, one gray and one red. I probably could've found more, but didn't want to.

When she returned I pretended to be asleep. With my back to her I watched stars through the dormer window, still thinking that they were moving too fast.

CHAPTER THREE

Pauly met me down at Mick's. I hated leaving Dani's so early, but she had work to do and I promised Pauly I'd help him put the new water pump in Mom's car. He nebbed about Dani all morning. My head hurt too bad for his crap, but I tried to hide my hangover.

Pauly had a way of turning a two-hour job into an all-day thing. He lollygagged, going to three auto stores to compare prices before going back to the first one, which he knew was cheapest anyway. The whole time I forced ginger ale into my belly to keep from puking. When we finally got to the house he took his time at lunch, acting like he'd never eaten a freaking meatball before. Then he bullshitted with his pap while I finally went out and got started pulling the bad water pump out.

When Pauly came out he just kept giving me shit for being hungover. Besides the hangover, I felt cranky anyway. Instead of being able to sleep the way I wanted to, weird dreams hassled me all night long. Dani sleeping next to me should've been all the sedative I needed, but instead I had to walk Joe Strummer's dogs for hours and hours. I knew he was asleep inside his big house, about to die, and I was afraid to take the dogs back because I didn't want to be the one to find his body. When I tried telling Pauly about the dream he kept getting hung up on the fact that they were Joe Strummer's dogs and asked me how I knew.

By the time we'd gotten the water pump in we'd talked about English bulldogs and pit bulls and how purebreds were really inbred, and all kinds of other, mundane stuff, but never really about the dream, which was the whole reason I'd brought it up in the first place. When we finished and headed inside to wash up, I didn't have much left to say on the subject. Or any subject.

"You eat yet?" Mom already had her waitress apron on, like if we sat at the table long enough she'd fill up our coffee cups, pull out her pen and pad and take our order. Pauly's grandpap slept through the evening news in the other room.

Pauly said, "No time, Mom. I just came back in for my birth certificate. I got to bring it in with me tomorrow. We have to get to Mick's before closing time then I have to get ready for a meeting. My sponsor gave me shit for missing last night."

I said, "Did you tell him it was Stu's last show?"

I could've eaten, especially since I knew she didn't mean she'd be cooking. But ever since Pauly's child support and clothing vouchers ran out, dinner meant going to Mountaineer Doughnuts while Mom worked and getting her discount. I said, "What's your hurry anyway? Why can't we just run it up to Mick's tomorrow? I have lessons, so I'll be there all day."

"Rent's due, and I'm counting Stu's drums as part of what you owe me." Pauly pulled his coat on and stuck a Camel in his mouth. "My sponsor says I got to be on top of shit like this."

"Take it outside," Mom said, whisking him away like a dust kitty. "Don't you light that in this house."

"Yeah, anyway." Pauly grabbed the doorknob, lit his Camel with his free hand, and flung the back door open to the cold evening. A rush of February wind brought cigarette smoke and the buzz of the dusk-to-dawn light back into the house. "We're rolling."

"Sorry." I apologized for him and put my arm out for a hug. "I'll stop up later this week."

"You boys be good." She leaned in and kissed my cheek. "Remember, the devil is a tempter, and an enemy of souls."

"He sure is." I replied. I liked her better as a Catholic. As far as I could see, the benefits of being born-again hadn't kicked in for her just yet. I mean, she lived in a shit house, had a shit job and she sure-as-shit wasn't glowing or walking on water.

I buttoned my coat and followed Pauly out to the Jeep. My heart sped up when I saw I'd missed a call. I hoped it was Dani, but Mikey Kovachick, a former student, left the message wanting to see us about a gig. I put the phone away.

The driveway's cold gravel and old snow crunched beneath my feet. Beyond the city, spread out below like buildings from a model train set, the winter evening arrived with a smear of magenta and crimson gels. February fooled you into thinking winter would end soon. Each sunset felt like a little white lie, hinting at a spring that remained too far away. I told myself it couldn't look like this in New York or LA. I wondered if the only reason I liked this town was because I thought one day I might leave it.

"So Pauly, I've been thinking about the band." I pulled my sleeves down over my knuckles. My breath clouded the windshield, and I wiped it clear with my elbow.

Pauly tried his hardest to get warm air out of the cold engine. He pumped the gas pedal and twisted the heater knobs, each time holding his hand over the vent like he was using the old Jedi Mind Trick. Nothing ever moved fast enough for Pauly. Wheezy heaters, red lights and little old ladies were all the same to him.

I made my pitch. "Like, who says you have to be from L.A. to make it? Look at some of these douchebags getting record deals nowadays."

The Jeep lurched into drive. It needed transmission fluid. We drifted down the hill.

I lifted my collar and tried to hide further down into my coat. "You know, I would've died for Joe Strummer or Eddie Vedder. Those guys are legendary now because they're real. They aren't just guys who want merch money and pussy. Who's the realest band playing right now?"

I waited for Pauly to answer, but he focused on the road. Passion made me talk with my hands. "I say somebody like Radiohead. Or Wilco. But shitty bands still keep getting deals." I added my own exclamation point by chopping the dashboard with the side of my hand. "And we don't even do any originals. So what does that make us?"

Pauly turned onto Richwood, then made a left onto Darst. If there'd been more snow on the steep hill we'd be dodging sleds and snowballs. But anymore the winters weren't like the ones back in the day. Either too warm or too cold, but never the same.

"Like, what if instead of just looking for a drummer until Stu gets out, we get us another guitar player too? Get away from the covers and challenge ourselves and really try writing our own stuff?"

Pauly waited for traffic to clear before making the right back into town. Steam from the old buildings along High and up at the university rose into the cold dry evening. White puffs from brightly side-lit chimneys and smokestacks rose into the dark blue sky. Streetlights were as bright as the first stars that poked through the sunset.

"Even if we can't get both a guitar player and drummer one or the other is fine. I'll sing and play drums if I have to. Like Phil Collins. People like the covers, but maybe we could take a few weeks and reinvent ourselves or something, maybe kill Pipeline—at least 'til Stu comes back. And when Stu comes back I'll go back to playing guitar or whatever and we can start working originals into our sets. This time it can be—I don't know—an organic experience where we move forward as a band, rather than a group of individuals doing their own thing just to make money. We write and record, write and record."

I waited for Pauly to say something. Anything.

"Well, what do you think?" I asked after a few seconds.

He just sat there. I could've kicked him in the nuts right then, and he wouldn't have budged an inch. For a moment I thought he was thinking about what I'd said, but the look on his face said he wasn't thinking about it at all. He took a long drag, pinched the butt between his finger and thumb, then flicked it into the cold night. "Look, man. I got a job interview tomorrow."

It took me a second to process. "That's fine. I can take care of everything myself then. I'll walk up to the campus and start posting fliers."

"I have an interview. I'm getting a real job." Pauly's head nodded almost imperceptibly, like this was pretty much how he thought the conversation would go.

"Well, we can be flexible with gigs. That's what I'm saying." I made my counter-offer and turned toward him.

"Listen." Pauly stopped at a yellow light at the intersection of Spruce and Walnut. Some asshole in a Jetta laid on his horn as he zipped around us. "There ain't going to be a new drummer or guitar player. My sponsor says there ain't going to be anymore gigs for me. I'm done."

"But the band... Listen, Mike Kovachick called me and says he has a gig for us. We're supposed to go up and meet him tonight. We can't turn down a gig."

"Preston, grow up. Stop daydreaming." He slid another Camel from the pack, offered it to me knowing I wouldn't take it, then put it to his mouth and lit it with a snap of his Zippo. The flame illuminated his face. "There ain't going to be a band anymore."

He took a long drag, coughed and blew the smoke out the window. "At least not one with me in it."

"You don't think you owe me just a little more notice?"

He didn't say anything else.

"You talked Stu into reenlisting, didn't you? You probably said something about the money being a hell of a lot better than working at the beer distributor and playing in the band. Is that right? Shame on you, man."

But like I said, he was done talking.

I added, "Then fuck you, too."

Of all the times I'd ever been dumped, this hurt the worst. Pauly stood over by Mick's basses, mostly Fender Ps and a lone Thunderbird knockoff.

Unsure of whose side he was supposed to be on, Mick remained unusually quiet throughout the transaction. But he had worked out a pretty generous deal with Stu for his kit. If I had enough money I would've bought it and kept it for him until he got back. Mick finally asked, "So, what the hell's wrong with you two?" The old cash register flipped open with the clang of a bell.

"Pauly's going to be bringing his rig in, too. But I wouldn't be so generous with him if I were you, Mick." I crossed my arms and looked down at the holes in my

Vans. On my list of things I needed to survive, new shoes came below guitar strings and Cap'n Crunch. In a perfect world, rent and utilities, all the shit society tricks you into thinking you need, would be even lower.

One by one Mick slid twenties from his drawer to the glass countertop between a jar of Dunlop picks and a few bottles of Martin guitar polish. "Pauly, you throwing in the towel?"

"We can't all be Paul McCartney, right? So I guess I'm going have to bust my hump for a living." Pauly stayed at the other end of the counter.

Mick scratched his scalp, leaving wiry hair standing at a hundred crazy angles. "Have to keep the lights on, right? Who gets this?"

"Give him half," Pauly said. "Stu said to split it fifty-fifty."

I counted out my part of two months' rent and slid it back to Pauly.

"Thanks, Pres. I can buy you dinner now." He tried to act all innocent in front of Mick, like he hadn't been making a big deal about the money all week. He slid a gumband around his cash and put it in his front pocket. "I guess we're rolling." He shook Mick's hand.

"You go ahead. I'm going to hang out. Maybe see who's playing before I head up to see Mikey."

"Don't be an asshole. We can get a bite to eat." Pauly seemed genuinely surprised I wasn't caving.

"No. I'll find my own way."

"You're for real? Christ, Preston, one of these days you're going to have to give it up." Pauly zipped up his coat with a dramatic flourish. He put his hand into his pocket and dug for his keys, adding, "How you getting home?"

"I'll walk."

"Look both ways before you cross the street." With that, Pauly turned and left.

He waited on the curb for traffic to clear. He lit a smoke and stormed over to the Jeep. With the squeal of a belt he vanished up Pleasant.

Mick watched, too. When I laid Stu's drumsticks on the counter, he shrugged. "I know."

Mick slid the sticks back to me and waved his hand like a cat waves a paw at its own puke. He backed over to his stool, took his glasses off and dropped them into his shirt pocket.

I gave Mick forty back.

Mick said, "Preston, keep your money. Maybe those boys need to find a way to pay for their own lessons?"

"I can't, Mick. I want to keep it straight with you."

"Do those boys even realize you take care of them like this? They know you don't work for free, right?"

"Yeah, they're very appreciative. I told them they can pay me back when they get famous. In the meantime, I'll keep paying for the lessons." I peeled off another pair of twenties for tonight and put it into my right pocket, then slid the rest into my left. In bars and in bottles were the only places I knew I could get away from Pauly. I put my palms onto the countertop. "I don't know what the point is. Maybe I'm stupid?"

"Don't lean on the counter," Mick said, then without missing a beat added, "Stupid for wanting to make music?"

"I guess. I don't know how to do anything else. It's not like I can just go be a teacher or accountant. I wouldn't even make a decent bartender. When I drop into a groove with Pauly and Stu, no bullet in the world can stop me. I truly believe I was born to make music."

My phone vibrated in my hand. Without thinking I flipped it open. The text came from another unknown number. It said, <supposedly, authority comes from wisdom. you better become a sodding authority fast or the system is going to crush you>

I clenched my jaw. Joe Strummer said something like that in an article I read in *SPIN* after he died. I replied, <who the fuck is this? Fucking pussy.>

Mick watched from his stool, arms crossed. After a moment to let me calm down, he replied with sudden earnestness, "I suppose you have to ask yourself if it's worth it. You think I saw the Beatles on Ed Sullivan and went to bed that night dreaming about running a music shop? My band gigged five or six nights a week anywhere we could—roller-rinks, amusement parks. But you know what? I met a girl and had some kids. Now I have grandkids. I figure my life's okay. Not what I'd hoped, but okay." Mick stiffened as a pair of high school students came in. They headed straight back to Stu's drum kit.

"And at least once a day I ask myself, what if I'd have kept at it for another year more?" Mick waved me aside. Once his line of sight cleared he relaxed. "What if I'd have given it another year?"

I watched traffic rumble up Pleasant Street. Part of me secretly wished I'd see Pauly back out there. "So you think I should keep going?" I checked my phone. Dani said she'd call.

"You're going to fail a lot before you ever get it right, son. Your skin's thick enough and your head's hard enough that in a few years you'll know if it's time to give it up. Giving up too early leaves a pretty sour feeling. Might be the only thing worse than hanging on too long." Mick tapped each word of his last sentence out on the counter.

I waited for what seemed like an appropriate amount of time before asking, "Can I bring some of my old stuff down here and put it on consignment?" Asking him wasn't easy, especially after he'd just shelled out all that money for Stu's gear.

"I'm not a bank."

"I know, and that's why I said consignment." I pictured the most humble person I could think of and tried to say it like they would.

"This ain't a pawn shop either." Switching gears, he said, "Before you go running off I got something for you."

He rang the register open. He lifted out the cash drawer with a clang of nickels and pulled out a scrap of paper. He set it onto the countertop. "It's about that record of yours. A friend of mine from the university says the songwriter's from up in Davis. There's an old-timey music thing this weekend. My friend says you should start nebbing there for Earl Black."

"Earl Black?" I said, just as stunned by the name as I was by the news.

"Jamie says the E's for Earl."

"I don't know what to say."

"Then don't open your mouth and ruin the moment like a brand new puppy shitting all over the carpet. Be here tomorrow morning by nine. Jamie says bring your guitar."

"Thanks, Mick. I mean it." I shook his hand, then tucked the scrap of paper into my wallet.

As I buttoned up my coat to leave, Mick said, "I'm trying to look out for you, son. The devil haunts a hungry man."

When I left Mick's the air went into my lungs a little stiffer. The city, and my life, felt a lot smaller than I thought it would without Pauly in it, like this really was the first day of the rest of my cliché.

I stopped at Monongahela Brewing, an old roller-rink just down the block from Mick's. Sometimes people called it 'The Stink' because of the yeast smell, but really it was the smell of the river in the summer. Big silver vats sat where the skate rental used to be. The stage sat at the other end. It was a big place, and if nobody showed up you sure noticed it. When a band went on, Ted lit up *Lady's Choice* or *Shoot the Duck* depending on whether or not he liked them. I'm pretty sure Pipeline was the only band to play the joint as a roller-rink *and* as a brewery.

Onstage, Billy Club ripped through a set of generic southern rock. The song they played sounded like an obscure .38 Special tune but they passed it off as an original. On the floor, business casual women in crisp white sneakers boogied to slide guitar and lyrics about what happens at the end of dirt roads on starry July nights. Or whatever. Les Popovich sang to a pretty empty floor.

Les used to sing for Pauly and me until the strain on his poor voice got to be too much. It wasn't like we were asking him to be Freddy Mercury or anything. After he quit I took a Sharpie to a Sex Pistols shirt he'd left at our house and wrote 'I HATE' in big letters right above the band's name. I got the idea from Sid Vicious, but apparently I'm the only person in the whole wide world who ever saw that episode of BEHIND THE MUSIC. In the end Les's split benefitted me because I never would've started singing otherwise.

I ordered bourbon from a bartender who had tried to get with me one night after a gig at Squares in Sabreton. She ended up with Pauly instead, poor girl. She had great blue eyes and a nice body, so when she smiled, I smiled back and wondered why I hadn't taken the bait. After I made a few jokes she loosened up and started setting me up with doubles. I told her about Isaac's and my dad and the record and put my phone on the counter in case Dani called.

I drank two right quick while I spun my phone around and around on the counter. When Les left the stage for set break I gulped the rest of my last drink down and followed him. Out on University, brake lights set the cold evening aglow with electric warmth. On the track above, a PRT car rumbled with all the ferocity that an electric tram could muster. Les and his drummer each lit up a Marlboro Light.

"Pres, hey man. How's it been?" Lester's gaze drifted to his drummer for a second and they shared a look.

"You guys sound good." I lied and stuck my hand out. "Preston Black."

The drummer put his cigarette into his mouth then shook my hand. "Denny Meyers."

"Hey Les, you looking for somebody to play a little rhythm? I could do the whole Keith Richards thing for you. Maybe sing some two-part harmony?" I felt like a fucking encyclopedia salesman or Latter-day Saint. Begging for sales or souls.

"What happened to Pipeline?" Les laughed. *Still a douchebag.*

"Stu's unit got redeployed," I said. That shut him down fast. "And Pauly got a job."

"You still got Mick, right? Maybe you and him can start something." Les laughed.

I studied his smirk for a moment. "Whatever, man. Go fuck yourself."

I pushed between them and walked toward the intersection.

"C'mon, man," Les said. "Here's my number… Three. Zero. Four."

I turned around and walked backwards for a few steps. "You're still an asshole. And your band sucks. Way to pack The Stink. Maybe pass out free t-shirts next time."

Les flicked his butt into the street. He put his hand onto Denny's shoulder and pushed him toward the door. "Maybe we need a roadie? That interest you?"

Adrenaline rippled through me and I had to keep shaking out my fists. My face burned. If Pauly had been with me we would've rolled him into the river. Instead I waited for the light to change. High above, another PRT tram clacked toward the University Avenue station. Behind me, Walnut ran beneath an old rail trestle down to the river's edge. Cold waves lapped the gravelly shore as a tug pushed ten coal barges up the river. When all was said and done, everybody was going somewhere except me.

The cold had a sobering effect on me, and I didn't like it. With my phone in my hand I went up to High, crossed against the light and went a little further up the block. Back in the day there were a bunch of good clubs for live bands through here—the Shining Star, The Oasis, Rosewood and The Wooden Nickel. Johnny Cash supposedly played at the Nickel one time while running from state troopers trying to serve him with a warrant in Wheeling. Now dance clubs with loud music and cheap well drinks bookended The Nickel. They made playing there sound like playing in a blender. I paid my cover to a bouncer who didn't realize I always came in through the back door instead of the front.

I found a stool near the door, but far from the band. The smoke hung so thick I couldn't even really make faces out. Maybe I didn't want to. I set my phone on the bar and waited for the bartender. He flowed to a girl wearing fishnets and a Dead Kennedys t-shirt. The kind of girl who didn't know Henry Rollins from Harry Potter. An eight, but no Dani.

"Hey." I tried to get the bartender's attention. Then I recognized him. "Hey, Little Stevie Croe."

I stood up and shook his hand. "What's all this?" I reached across the bar and tried to grab his goatee.

"Hey, Preston. What the hell're you doing here?" Steve held onto my hand.

"Trying to get a job interview." I looked back at the band.

Stevie grabbed me in for a quick hug, then pulled three shot glasses from the counter. He grabbed a bottle of Jameson and filled the glasses. "Good seeing you, brother."

Stevie raised the glass, closed his eyes and we drank. It didn't burn enough, and that's how I knew I was making a mistake.

"This one," Stevie said. "This is for Stu. Doing his duty so we don't have to." He refilled us.

"Fuck duty," I said, throwing it down. My throat glowed. My chest glowed. My head felt like Christmas lights. And before I could get sad, Stevie refilled the glasses again. I said, "He'll be fine."

"I know. But every time he goes back his chances get worse. Statistics, right? Like playing the lottery?" His thoughts tripped him up.

"He's fucking bulletproof, Stevie. I'm not worried," I lied like Madonna at confession. The seed Stevie planted in my head grew like skunk weed.

"I miss him already, Pres. And he's not even leaving the country for a few more weeks."

"Me too. But we'll be doing this with him in a year." We drank again. For a second I felt like I was drowning and got a little freaked out.

"I know." He put the bottle away and asked, "Where's Pauly? I ain't seen him in a while."

"Pauly's busy. I'm flying solo from now on."

"Tell him I said 'what's up', okay? Want anything else?" Stevie wiped his hands on a towel.

"Maybe a little more." I pointed at the Jameson. "Maybe a Coke to wash it down? Who are these guys?" I pointed at the band. They tried really hard to sound like The Ramones, except instead of singing about sniffing glue they stole their lyrics from The Misfits. "...The devil knows what's in your brain." I tried to ignore them.

He said, "They're from Uniontown," like I'd know what that meant. Stevie went back to the *chica* in fishnets. I drank and watched myself getting drunker in the mirror. *More drunk?*

The band made me jealous, the roadies made me jealous, Little Stevie Croe, who'd no doubt get a hand up that short black skirt as soon as he made last call, made me jealous. I checked my phone again.

That Dani hadn't called me today only made it worse, so I put my phone away and had another Coke. When I finally stood up everything got real slippy, like I had ice on the soles of my Vans. I stumbled, and Stevie and the girl and the guys in between suddenly all looked a lot more sober than me. Stevie stepped to the end of the bar and I sat back down.

"Easy, Pres."

"Sorry, man. I'm okay." Every bartender knew that nobody was ever really okay, especially when they said they were. I tried to give him a ten.

"You're not driving, are you?" The way he said it made me realize how pathetic I must've looked. Like without a band or a girl, I crumpled. Like I was never meant to be a solo act.

"Pauly got the kids and the car in the divorce. I'm hoofing it tonight. The walk'll do me good. But we should get together and talk, man." I never said shit like that sober. For a second I almost told him about the record and the song. But that all seemed kind of silly now, so we shook hands, then Stevie returned to his project.

The goth girl dropped the coy act and smiled at Stevie like he was passing out free Gummi Bears.

I took my time getting up and went back outside. I shuffled through the semi-frozen sludge toward the Met, simultaneously nodding at and hiding from people I thought I might know. But my people left town a long time ago.

When I got to The Met I sat down and ordered a Coke. The Met was the kind of place I'd hang out at if I ever had time to hang out. We loved playing there. Lots of memorabilia on the walls—pictures of old local bands, vintage beer ads, LPs. Mikey caught me between songs and waved. He had reason to smile. His band had the place packed. People bounced at the edge of the stage. I sat for a few more songs then drifted toward the back of the crowd.

All around people smiled, texted. It'd been so long since I'd seen a show from the floor. I looked for people I knew, but the people I knew had gotten older, got jobs, had kids, moved away. Some of these students might think I was too old, but they had no idea how old you can get in six years. At the far end of the long bar I saw Dani throwing down a drink.

She leaned against a skinny rich kid in a nice shirt, tie and vest and a fat silver watch. Pauly always said bitches like Dani never craved Big Macs. She looked at the guy in the vest like a pit bull eyeballs a T-bone.

I looked down at my shoes, pulled out my phone and pretended to text. It took a long minute to shake my reaction off. The way she laughed and touched his arm didn't make it any easier. When the band ended their set I slipped toward the front door. Just before going outside I waited to catch Mike's eye.

He held up a finger. I nodded and pointed at the door before heading outside. Despite the house music kicking in, the night suddenly seemed too quiet. The streetlights kept me from seeing any stars. I waited against a lamppost, watching the crowd spill from the club.

After ten minutes Mikey appeared in the door. He spotted me and came over, smiling like the star of a flipping Dentine commercial. "What'd you think?"

"You guys sound good. Really good." I put my hands into my coat pockets and made fists.

"Thanks a lot, Pres. Glad you liked it." He was starting to lose his hair very prematurely but hid it beneath a New York Mets cap.

"I mean it. I wouldn't just say that."

"Yeah, I know. I was going to stop in Mick's and tell you, but didn't have a chance—" He got cut off by a pair of students slapping his shoulder. He turned and gave them each a 'what's up?'

Still beaming, he said, "We got a deal, man. A three-disc deal with Blindside…" He paused, like I knew how his sentence ended.

It took a second for me to respond. "That's amazing, man. Your mom must be happy."

"She's a little freaked about the tour stuff, but she's happy. She keeps asking me if I'm going to finish school, though." Mikey waved at a group of girls crossing High.

I looked at him, my jealousy replaced by concern. "Don't stop for anything, man. Once you get momentum you have to keep going. Don't ever pass up an opportunity. Joe Strummer said you have to be slightly stupid to make it anyway."

Mikey asked, "So, your band…"

"Yeah, until last night we've been gigging pretty regularly." A smoke would've calmed me. I needed a smoke. "I wish I would've been able to come out and see you guys sooner."

"I just heard about Stu's unit being reactivated. Sorry about that." His phone buzzed. He glanced at the number.

"Yeah… Off to fight the bad guys."

"If I hear anybody's looking for a guitar player I'll let you know. I kind of had an offer for you guys, but it doesn't sound like it's going to work out." He took his sweat-soaked hat off and wiped his forehead with his sleeve.

"What is it?" I asked.

"Well, we're playing at The Stink on Valentine's Day. A launch party kind of thing. Our A and R guy's going to be there and maybe somebody else from the label. I think he said they're sending a photographer and an engineer to record some stuff for an EP. I wanted you guys to play."

"I'll do it," I said with a genuine smile, probably a little too eagerly.

He laughed. "Who're you going to play with?"

"I don't know yet, but I'll work it out. Don't ever pass up an opportunity. Who famously said that just now?"

Mikey laughed. "Okay, but let me know if things don't work out. We'll back you if you can't get anything together."

"It'll work out. I'm really happy for you, man."

He gave me a real quick hug. I was about to tell him about Isaac's and the record, but he said he had to go in and help the guys start to load out. "Two weeks. Down at The Stink. I'll call you about sound check and all that stuff."

"Okay, man."

For a long time I just stood there. Like, I wasn't ready to go home and be alone. Being rejected by Pauly, Stu leaving, the record and the search for my dad, seeing Dani inside—the list of things that sucked got longer by the second. My feelings about Mikey's success started to itch and I wondered how a flaky kid like him could become the rock god I was supposed to be. My feelings embarrassed me, and at the same time I wanted everybody to know I was the one who taught him. The worst part about it was believing I could've had what Mikey had. I just had to want it bad enough. I started walking up to the apartment. While waiting for the light to change my phone rang. It was Dani. My first reaction was to ignore it.

"Hello," I said, not sure what to expect from her. My pulse picked up a few extra beats.

Without giving the slightest hint that she'd just been inside, Dani said, "Preston, tonight I finished a little later than I expected. You can meet me out on High. In front of the gelato place, if you'd like."

I walked back up the hill, past where Backstreet Records and Utt's Music used to be. After all the insanity today, maybe Dani's call felt like a win. A tie, at least. Her silver Mercedes sat against the curb, its diesel engine tapping Morse Code into the quiet night. I peered inside, but it was too dark to see anything.

I heard the click of the lock and pulled on the handle. A tiny light from the dash cast dim light onto Dani's high cheekbones. She had a dark gray wrap covering her neck, her hair fell over her ears. She had her glasses on. Classical music, heavy with shrill violins, spilled through the open door and splashed onto the curb.

She offered no apology or further explanation. And once we got up to her apartment, and had a few drinks, we barely talked about anything at all.

Jimi Hendrix coughs. Everything's dark except for a sliver of light from the streetlamp below, but there's enough light for me to know it's him twisted in the sheets. I stand in the corner of the old hotel room, afraid to move for fear of being caught. He's talking in his sleep, but I can't understand the words. It sounds like he's saying, "The author of all evils." He doesn't seem to be referring to anybody in particular.

As my eyes adjust to the dusty blue light, details appear like images on a Polaroid: a green wine bottle smashed on the septic white tile of the bathroom floor, plastic hair rollers scattered beneath the bed like cookie crumbs, a guitar case, latched and silent, standing in the corner opposite me. His white Strat's inside. Suddenly I know this is the night he dies. Jimi says, "The author of all evils," and coughs again. I wonder if it's from one of his songs. The scent of sour red wine makes me lift a hand to my nose. He's vomiting.

He needed help, but I couldn't move. I was like a camera on a tripod. If I could get to him I could roll him onto his side. He says, "She is the author of all evils."

Jimi is awake now, drowning in his bed sheets, clutching at the headboard. I think he's crying for help, but the long gurgle he expels doesn't sound human. His tongue clicks against his palate as he tries to form words. He puts his hand into his mouth. He's trying to clear his airway.

Now the camera is at the foot of the bed. When he touches me his hand is warm and moist and stinks like vomit. Instinctively I try to pull myself away, but can't move. He heaves silent heaves then snorts. Vomit trickles from his nose. I've only ever seen Jimi with half-closed eyes and a cat smile. Like from the Monterrey video. Now his eyes are white, rolling up like window shades while he tries to form words. He pulls at my shirt.

Jimi's eyes can't find me. They just make wide circles that take in the whole room. His lazy eyelids flutter like moths around a streetlight. Gurgles and clicks are the last song he'll ever sing.

After the dream, I went into the bathroom and splashed cold water on my face, but couldn't get Jimi out of my mind. The smell of his vomit wouldn't wash away. All night long Dani's bed had felt like a prison. I'd watch the clock, fall asleep only to wake up and watch the clock again. The dream had been the last straw. I lay on the couch until indirect sunlight finally filtered through the bathroom window. Danicka was still asleep when I went into the bedroom. I gave her a little nudge. She rolled over.

"Hey," I whispered. "I have to meet somebody at nine."

"Let me drive you," she said, pushing herself up on her elbows.

"I'm fine. Maybe I can call you if I get back early?" I kissed her on the cheek.

"How do I know you'll call?" she said, her sleepy eyes trying to stay closed.

I said, "I always call."

"Okay. *Zavolej mi.* Don't forget."

CHAPTER FOUR

In tenth grade I skidded into a real rough patch. That was around the time I figured out me and my mom weren't related any more than me and John Lennon were. I made sure everybody who crossed my path knew the world owed me something.

Growing up I always played the good kid. I got out of bed on Sunday to go to mass with grandma while Pauly slept in. I took out the trash without being asked. But in tenth grade I learned the Golden Rule was a bunch of shit. Doing good to others hadn't done good for me. Soon enough failing class and getting suspended got to be like falling off a bike. Teachers I used to like got on my nerves. Skipping class and starting fights became a lot more fun than going to mass ever was. Only problem was, getting kicked out of school didn't kill the loneliness and sadness I felt. I lost a lot of old friends that year.

By the time summer rolled around the depression got out of control and I thought about killing myself a lot. Like, I'd imagine schemes that'd cause the least trouble for Pauly and my mom. And of course, it had to be painless. So jumping off of the Westover Bridge in January always seemed like the way I'd do it, figuring if the fall didn't kill me the cold would. But Pauly told me anytime anybody stopped on the bridge for too long the cops were called, so I never did anything more than think about it. Back then, I drifted off to sleep every night thinking about shit like that.

It was either July or August. One of those nights when an open window and a box fan only made things worse. I sat on my roof, crying or something. Probably crying. I had Pink Floyd *Animals* playing over and over. A full moon crept up over the mountains, shining a dense blue light bright enough to make nighttime shadows appear. Without wind I could hear every cricket for a thousand miles. A couple of hound dogs had a raccoon treed down by Deckers Creek. And, for a moment, I felt like the only person on earth. Like all the loneliness manifested itself in the sudden disappearance of everything I'd ever known. The world, with just me in it, suddenly felt like a very cold place.

At some point the tape had flipped back to side one. "Dogs" came on, even though I didn't really notice it. And the humid air, an amplifier for all those non-human sounds, brought the crickets and the hound dogs right up to my roof. The moon came over the treetops, washing out the city lights below me. And the dogs—either the ones from the tape or real ones—got closer. The dogs were like a bridge between the tape and real life, and it became hard to tell which was which. Suddenly being alone really scared me.

Even though that phase of my life ended that night, the details will always stick with me. The way the moon and the city looked. Individual trees, and the leaves just scattering the moonlight like a chrome bumper scatters brake lights. The feel of the shingles and the slope of the roof on my bare feet. I didn't know if it was the most dream-like experience I'd ever had, or the most life-like dream, but last night, up in Dani's apartment, felt just like that night on my roof.

If last night had left me feeling the way I wanted, I'd still have been in bed instead of hoofing it back to town. But the choice wasn't mine. The Hendrix dream made me feel like I did when my mom finally told me she wouldn't help me find my dad, except sicker. I woke up feeling like I was responsible for Jimi's death. Had the dreams been about Dani, I would've kept my eyes closed for hours instead of wondering if finding my father wasn't something I'd regret later, wondering if I was better off never knowing.

I got another text. This game had lost a lot of its intrigue. I just wanted to know who'd been fucking with me. The message sounded like something John Lennon would say. <everything's proven until it's disproven, isn't it? who's to say your dreams aren't real?>

I deleted it.

An empty bridge was the only thing that separated the gray sky from the gray river. I let handfuls of snow melt in my mouth to moisten my hangover. Tugs idled above the locks, just like they had last night. Light snow fell from the milky sky. Every so often I looked back up the hill, taking note of my footprints falling away behind me. Memorizing the twists and turns that'd get me back to her. My cold feet produced cold footprints that disappeared like breadcrumbs beneath a cloud of sparrows.

Wind snapped through my scarf, the cold bit my fingers and toes. Lucky for me my ride waited for me on Pleasant Street. An older guy with a bristly gray mustache gave a tentative wave, then put his Subaru into drive to meet me by the stoplight.

"Preston?" He asked through a gap in the window.

"Preston Black. That's me." I said as I blew into my cupped hands. "It's extra nice to meet you this morning. Jamie, right?"

Jamie laughed as he took his wool outback hat from the passenger's seat and flipped the door lock. "Jamie Collins. It's a pleasure."

He shook my hand, a perfect handshake. A secret handshake. His hand had the same grip as mine. I recognized a fellow musician.

"Mick told you to bring a guitar?" He released my hand and turned up the heat.

"Uh, I didn't go home last night. But my apartment is real close. If you don't mind?" I was suddenly afraid of smelling like booze. But the shame warmed my cheeks, so I let it sit a little longer.

I led him up to Fayette, to a space right behind Pauly's van. Sneaking into the apartment felt like sneaking into a movie. I knew to let sleeping Paulys lie. I crept up the steps and slowly twisted the old knob. A pizza box sat on the counter. I flipped it open. Pauly had saved me half. Sausage and peppers and onions. I left it and continued down the hall. In my room I sat on the edge of the bed.

It didn't feel like my bed anymore.

I threw on an old Clash t-shirt, faded and thin like shirts from when you were a kid, worn to translucence because they had Darth Vader or Snake Eyes on them. Thinking about the cold made me add a layer. As I buttoned up the old flannel I looked for a hoodie and scrounged around my closet floor. In the pocket of an old gray sweatshirt I found a thin navy toboggan which I pulled over my ears. I threw the hoodie onto my guitar case and looked for gloves. But I couldn't remember owning any. I grabbed the record to show Jamie. As I tied my scarf I caught a glimpse of myself in the mirror. An ex-con if I ever saw one.

On my way to the door I grabbed something heavier, an old pea coat from the Army/Navy store.

"Asshole, is that you?"

I held my breath.

"Pres..." Pauly shuffled in his bed. The box spring squeaked as he got to his feet. I made for the door.

When I shut it behind me, it hurt. Last night didn't feel like the fights we had growing up, usually a few punches followed by a quick apology and a smoke. Maybe I'd let Pauly simmer a little longer.

Outside, Jamie had the hatch ajar and directed me to slide my guitar into a space he'd made for it. He had a few other instruments back there.

We stopped off for gas at the Dairy Mart along University Avenue. In middle school we'd score pepperoni rolls and Mountain Dew there. In high school it was forties of St. Ides. But no matter when I went in there it felt like fourth grade all over again and I got cravings for goofy shit like Big League Chew and Atomic Fireballs and Lik-A-Stix.

I offered to pay for half of his gas. Jamie said, "I'd be heading up with or without you. I have to make a real quick stop along the way anyway." I offered to buy him a pop or tea, which he readily accepted.

The bright lights in the Dairy Mart hurt my eyes. I stomped my feet on the mat. Ice and black slush fell off my shoes. I made myself two cups of Earl Grey and made a cup for Jamie. While they brewed I picked up a package of Hostess Ding Dongs. Then, by the register, I spotted Julia's Pepperoni Rolls and grabbed a pair. A breakfast that'd make Johnny Ramone proud.

Back outside I handed Jamie his tea while juggling my own. "I just put a little sugar in. I didn't know how you took it."

"Much obliged. Your old guitar case piqued my interest. I wanted to take a look, with your permission?"

"Sure thing," I said, perhaps with a little too much exuberance. Before I set my teas on the roof I offered him a pepperoni roll and he shook his head. So I slid the Tele out from between the other cases. The spring-loaded latches flipped open with a metallic rattle.

"Wow," Jamie said. "She's beautiful. What year?"

I liked the way he held it. One hand, beneath the neck. The way a mom would hold a newborn. "It's a seventy-one. Had a refret done a few years back. Everything else is original."

"Beautiful," Jamie said again as he slid it back into the case. "Bet it sounds real pretty through a nice old tube amp."

"I have an old Fender Twin. Sixty-seven. I had to choose between that or college." It was a joke for me alone.

"Can't wait to hear it." He paused, kind of biting his lip, waiting for me to say something different. "Mick didn't specify when he said bring a guitar, huh?"

"Specify?"

"It'll be all acoustic music today." Jamie let out a restrained little laugh as I pushed the Tele back in with the others. "I got you covered." He patted a big, battered old guitar case.

We got back into the car, the heat made me sleepy. After Jamie buckled his seatbelt and set his hat on the backseat, he said, "Maybe I will have one of those pepperoni rolls. The heartburn'll be worth it."

"Here, take them both." While he ate I showed him the record. He wiped his hands on his jeans and ran his fingers through the tracks. Then he slid the vinyl out and looked at both sides carefully before stopping on my song. He traced the track with his fingers, nodded, and gave it back to me.

He said, "Hmm. E. Black." And that was it. Like, after we exhausted all the small talk there wasn't much left to say. Or maybe he was waiting for me to ask the inevitable question. All morning I'd rehearsed how I'd say it over and over in my head. After leaving town and twisting and turning up old Route Seven, and waiting for the right moment, and hoping another subject would come up I finally spit it out. "You friends with Earl Black?"

"Well," Jamie began. Then, after pausing to get his words in the right order, restarted, "Acquaintance is a better word. I don't know him well enough to ask if he left a wife and kid down here, if that's what you mean."

"That's what I meant. Sorry about that." I shook my head to show him I knew how stupid it sounded.

"It's okay. I know it's not easy," he said.

I felt bad for being so nebby and went back to looking out the window and listening to Jamie's music. Violins and a man who sounded just like a raven when he sang. I tried to tune it out and fall asleep. At some point we turned onto a dirt road. The transition from asphalt to gravel woke me up. After about twenty bumpy minutes Jamie said, "Here we are."

Keeping my feet out of the mud while loaded down with instrument cases and mic booms was dang-near impossible. Up here in the mountains they had a lot more snow on the ground than we had back in town. All around us pines mingled with naked, gray trees sprinkled with long-dead yellow leaves. A stream of melted snow ran right down the middle of the driveway.

Jamie said, "I won't be offended if you wait in the car." He took a few steps toward the old house.

"No, I'm good." I scraped my muddy shoe on a crusty snowdrift, leaving a brown smear.

"It should be quick and painless. And May usually bakes. It'll be over before you know it. I wouldn't have even stopped if it wasn't unfinished business. Don't like leaving loose ends. People get older and you keep putting stuff off... These folks won't be around forever." He walked toward the house.

"When I started, most of the people I recorded lived a long ways off the grid." He pointed at his canvas bag with a stub of a pencil. "I'd take this little recorder and I'd run a line out to the car battery if I needed juice. Heard a lot of amazing music. There's not much of that left up here anymore. The grid got a lot bigger."

I followed his footsteps around the muddiest spots, up the hill to the old house. White curtains, thin like a hospital gown, hung limply behind gray windows. The house was really just a cabin with an addition, neither part built in the last hundred years. The chimney hung off to the side like a bent cigarette. Yellow coal smoke came out.

Jamie knocked on a thin door covered with only a sniff of paint. A sweet little voice said it'd be right there.

I stood off to the side while Jamie smiled and gestured with his hat over his heart. The skinny old lady stood there like Joe Pye weed poking up through snow in her rubber boots and thick-framed, un-ironic, Buddy Holly glasses. A quilted flannel shirt hung loosely over a flimsy floral dress and pale apron that had the dirt beaten out of it. Her hair was up in rollers, like after we split her day got even more eventful. She held the door while Jamie went in. I hesitated, and she gave my sleeve a good tug. With a big smile she said, "C'mon now. I hain't paying for to heat the whole county."

I let her pull me into the small kitchen. The table had a sparkly Formica top like the counters at Murphy's downtown back in the day. There were two wooden, straight-backed chairs and a metal chair with red vinyl padding that had been patched with black electrical tape. She pulled out that chair for me and said, "Jamie, I thought for sure you was going to forget about me. And this young man, it's been such a long time since I seen him."

Jamie hemmed and hawed with his gear, speaking without looking at the old lady like he didn't want to call attention to her error, "I'm sorry. May, this is a friend of mine. I'm not sure you do know him." He unloaded jars of jam and a few books from his bag and laid them across the table.

May said, "I feel like I should." She stood behind me with her hands on my shoulders, holding me into the chair.

"Well then, this is Preston Black, he's from town."

She pulled her hands from my shoulders and took a step back. She wiped her hands in her apron. "Well, I reckon I *don't* know him then."

I stood up to shake her hand, but she responded weakly, like I owed her money. "You know the song?" I asked.

"I heard it but I don't know it." She drowned a battered teapot in the stream of spring water that dripped from the spigot. "But that song hain't of no account and you can honor my hospitality by not asking no more about it."

Jamie watched the whole exchange like a wino waiting for his horse to place so he could get another drink. But when I looked at him for some kind of intervention he just shrugged. So I sat back down feeling a little embarrassed. I didn't care about the song—just the guy that wrote it. To cover the sting I tried to come up with something clever to text Dani, but ended up just sending out a <how's it going?> and watching my phone for a moment, like she'd text right back. I finally put it away and said to Jamie, "Give you a hand?"

He passed me a boom and pointed to a spot on the floor where he wanted it, then tossed me the mic cables. As soon as Jamie hit his recorder's phantom power switch the tea kettle screamed, ruining his sound check. He said, "At least I didn't have headphones on."

May didn't ask if we wanted cream or sugar. We both got our tea weak with a little honey. May said it was dandelion blossom. I sipped mine while Jamie tuned his fiddle, slid up to the mic and began sawing away. I couldn't take my eyes off his fingers, working the fretboard like a cat works a pillow before it lays down.

When she sang, May's voice wasn't even as sweet as the tea. It sounded dry and throaty, like a turkey call, and hard to listen to. Her words curled in, like old movie posters, and her lips didn't move very much.

During breaks, Jamie asked May about cousins and nephews, said he saw old so-and-so down in Elkins and Mary said thanks for the book and she'd call this spring. Since none of it pertained to me I took my phone out again. Somehow none of my texts ever made their way back to me, like fishhooks with no worms. I stood to stretch my legs, drifting over to the sink for a sip of water. The curtains were so thin I could see right into the yard and across the mountains. For a long time I watched the clouds scatter across the aquamarine sky like they were being chased by wolves. I looked for my house, then town, and couldn't find either. The music May and Jamie made didn't seem as bad when it was in the background.

Above the window I noticed a small square of wood with hand-written letters on it. The top row said SATOR. The next four lines were written so the vertical columns were very straight, so they could be read up and down too. The next row across said AREPO. The next said TENET, then OPERA. The last said ROTAS. I squinted my eyes and looked again.

```
S   A   T   O   R
A   R   E   P   O
T   E   N   E   T
O   P   E   R   A
R   O   T   A   S
```

I looked at Jamie and pointed to see if he saw it, but he shook his head for me to forget about it. May kept on singing like a sick little bird. She didn't even open her eyes. I stepped across the kitchen and looked into the other room and saw the same square above a window. I didn't need to see the letters to know it said the same thing. I started toward it and Jamie said—stopping me in my tracks—"You might like this next song."

I almost said, "I'm good" when he motioned for me to have a seat. "Last one," he said.

May sang a real sad song about a jealous girl who threw her sister into a river. I kind of got lost in the middle part, but the end brought me back. The guy that found her body made a fiddle out of her clavicle and used her finger bones for tuners and strung the bow with her hair. When he played the fiddle it sang the name of the murderer.

When they finished I said, "Are there any more like that? Like, ones that tell stories and all that?" I buttered a biscuit and slathered some sassafras jelly on it. The butter melted a little from sitting out for so long. The jelly tasted like root beer. I wanted to eat more, but only finished half.

Jamie wiped his strings down with a chamois. "They all tell a story, don't you think?"

All of a sudden I was back in English class, not sure if I knew how to answer. "I guess."

Jamie said, "Or, maybe you liked the little bit of magic at the end? That the narrative had little details like the fur hat and gloves to anchor it in reality. Then when the magic comes you are forced to believe it because the tone was believable up to that point." Jamie pulled the biscuits away from me and buttered one for himself. His mustache went up and down when he chewed.

"Yeah," I said, but inside I felt a little lighter because he had understood exactly what I meant. "Like, how, because everything was real, the magic seemed real too."

Jamie nodded and licked his fingers. I liked Jamie a lot.

May 'retted up' while me and Jamie talked. My grandma used to 'ret up' the house when we were little, and when she got tired of retting up, me and Pauly had to ret up.

Jamie had another biscuit then looked at his watch. Time had come for us to ret up too. Jamie had a particular way of coiling his cables and packing everything, so I played roadie and just held stuff for him. On our way out, May gave Jamie a big hug. I waited to see if I should shake her hand or whatever, but she just waved at me.

As soon as May's house disappeared from the rear-view mirror I asked Jamie about those little squares above the windows. Jamie made like he was thinking about it. He said, "Let's see how to put this…"

Then he took off on a different subject like a hound dog after a rabbit. "No matter how poor you are, you always have music. That is, until they find a way to tax it." Then he went on to say how West Virginia was special and he could show me places that had more in common with Switzerland and Germany than with Pittsburgh or Baltimore. He said that there were people up here who not only believed in magic, but practiced it.

The way he talked about everything besides what I'd asked made me a little tense. He was treating me like I just brought home a stray puppy.

When I stopped nodding my head and responding, he took a deep breath, and finally said, "People up here live on slow time. A good many of them fear the devil and rely on practices handed down from generation to generation to protect themselves from him. I can introduce you to fifteen people today who could give you firsthand accounts of running into the devil up here."

When I realized he had been answering my question all along, I asked him for a specific or two.

He said, "The specifics aren't mine to tell."

I thought about those words for a few miles, and just when I finally figured out exactly what I wanted to ask, he said "You ever come up for the Buckwheat Festival?"

I looked out the window at Kingwood's old buildings and gas stations and nostalgia took over most of the space in my head. "Yeah. Mom used to bring us up. Buckwheat Fest felt like a minor holiday and she'd give us a few bucks to play games. Pauly'd come home loaded down with prizes, no lie. Like, he could get the ring around the penknife or the ping-pong ball into the goldfish bowl freaking first try. I never won squat."

In my head it was 'I never won shit.' "So I ended up buying fried dough or cotton candy with my money. Always felt bad because Pauly spent his money so fast, so I'd share with him on the way home. Pauly was always win-win. Should've known then I wasn't lucky."

Jamie laughed, and said, "A while back there was a young writer from down Huntington way. Breece D'J Pancake. A mouthful, right? Supposed to be the next Hemingway. Praise like that doesn't get bandied about too casually amongst writers."

"I suppose." I didn't really know.

"Well, a while after *The Atlantic Monthly* published his first story, the boy shot himself. Now, you can say what you want, about luck and whatnot—"

"It's not like his truck stalled on a railroad crossing. Not sure what luck had to do with it."

"You're exactly right. But to kill himself two years after he gets his big break? Maybe he'd have been better off staying unpublished. Maybe it was the pressure of success and the high accolades. Either way, he couldn't use the good of his situation to find a reason to go on. Maybe I don't believe in luck, and maybe what I'm trying to say is don't go out of your way to make a good situation bad. Luck or no."

He held his finger up like there was more coming, then added, "Maybe a more straightforward way to put it is don't go digging up old graves."

"Sounds like you're trying to talk me out of something." I started drumming my fingers on my knee. "Man, I've been searching for my dad all my life."

Jamie put his hand over his mouth like the Speak-No-Evil monkey, then returned it to the steering wheel and said, "I don't think that's what I'm saying, son. Maybe it is. But what I mean is, if you're happy with the way things are, whatever happens today shouldn't change it. Don't go making bad luck for yourself, right?"

"I suppose. And I appreciate you making yourself clear." I took a long look out the window. These mountains made me feel little, like I'd been back in town living with a bigger idea of who I really was. But from up here I could see my whole world in a single view. Like all along I'd really been living too small for my own good, and seeing it all laid out down there just confirmed it.

I checked my phone for texts. No signal. If Dani called I'd never know it.

Jamie caught me looking and said, "You'll pick something up a little closer to town."

"I didn't mean to be rude."

He laughed. "You're fine. I'm not what you'd call an early adopter, but I like my tech. I'm converting all my old reel-to-reels to digital right now and remastering them. Some of those old tracks sound better than they ever did in my memory."

For a long time I didn't say anything. I just thought about what I would say to my dad. Like, I wanted to be his friend, especially since he was a musician like me. And I reminded myself a hundred times not to get angry or say something stupid. Just smile and nod. Smile and nod. I reminded myself that I'd been waiting my whole life for today.

I said, "Pauly used to look out the bedroom window so he could see his dad come up the road on visitation days. Then he'd leave and I'd be all by myself."

I knew I should've been content to look out the window and keep my mouth shut, but I couldn't. "Back there you talked about Earl Black like you knew something."

Jamie turned his music down then sighed. "Maybe I do. We'll just have to wait and see."

I nodded, and said, "It's cool. I probably shouldn't have put you on the spot like that."

"You have a right, son. You have a right. No need to dish your chances just yet, though." Jamie's voice trailed off and he leaned forward in his seat. With a new smile, he put on his turn signal. "I have to show you something real quick."

We wound through a thick stand of pines, across a little bridge made out of collapsed corrugated steel pipes and up a really steep hill that made all the instrument cases slide back to the hatch. Jamie stopped the car at the bottom of a big white and gray field with old fence posts poking out every few yards. At the top of the hill stood a barn, and next to it a house. The way the blank windows stared out across the field and down the hill gave me the same feeling you get when you're in the cellar by yourself and you know something else is down there with you.

Jamie said, "Look up on the barn there." He took his glasses off and rubbed his eyes like he had no need to see it for himself.

"Where?"

He put his glasses back on and leaned toward me. "The paint's really faded. At the top, just under the eaves."

"A pentagram?"

"Technically it's a hex. But that's what you saw at May's today. A sign. For protection. Magic."

"Magic?"

"Magic. SATOR Squares have been used for all sorts of purposes—removing jinxes, protecting cattle from witches. This one here didn't work." He pointed at the pentagram on the old barn. "Supposedly a witch lived here. Had a falling out with a cousin. Notorious feud about thirty years ago. Anyway, the cousin got a hold of some hair and used it to curse this woman. Her cattle started giving poisoned milk."

"Guess the hex didn't work."

"No, that's why a SATOR Square does." He was about to go on, caught himself then added, "Supposedly."

"The words on the SATOR Square are the names of the nails pulled from Christ's body. And palindromes can't be tampered with, not even by the devil himself." Jamie put the car into reverse, but I couldn't turn my back on that place.

"So they're to keep the devil away? Like an apple a day?" I tried to make a little joke.

Jamie said, "I guess you could say that."

"It that something I need to worry about?" I said it with a smile.

Without looking over, Jamie shrugged his shoulders. "I don't know."

The thin aluminum walls gleaming in the cold mountain air reminded me I'd traveled a long way from High Street. A sign on the side said, 'DAVIS VFD Enjoy Coca-Cola'. The fire hall's thin walls did little to mask the shrill twine of violins and banjos. The bluebird-blue sky didn't carry an ounce of warmth or moisture; I couldn't tell if the mountains I saw were one mile or ten miles away. I followed the music, and Jamie, inside.

Rows of folding chairs faced an AstroTurf-covered stage that sat beneath a giant bingo flashboard, a ginormous oil painting of Blackwater Falls and an American flag. Student art covered the wall, mostly handprint turkeys and Christmas trees from last year. A small picture of Jay Rockefeller, the governor, not the senator, hung less prominently off to the right, near a snack bar where blue-haired ladies sold Sloppy Joes and hot dogs for a dollar and hot dog sauce—whatever that was—for a buck fifty. If I had to determine where I'd landed based on my surroundings alone, my guess would be somewhere between South Middle School and 1977. I wanted a Sloppy Joe bad.

The music from the trio on stage sounded like The Chieftains without the flute and drums. A guy with white hair, wearing a camouflage jacket and coal dust-stained ball cap, played guitar next to his twin, the only difference between the two was the mandolin the twin played and the coveralls he wore.

The bulk of the music came from the girl that stood between them swinging her fiddle bow like a bucksaw. Her exaggerated mannerisms contrasted sharply with the men's stony scowls. Light brown hair streaked with hints of blond fell from a loose bun on her head. Each time she blew a strand away, her nose and mouth scrunched with annoyance.

When she finished, the audience applauded mildly. Not a single person stood up or even showed a sign that her playing interested them any more than the Sloppy Joes did. *These hicks*, I thought, *wouldn't know music if it knocked their daughter up*. So I set my Tele and Jamie's acoustic on the floor and clapped singular claps that punctuated the fire hall's dead air. "Whooo!" I yelled. People in the audience turned and looked, just staring, their eyes full of confusion and pity. Jamie picked up his case and clamped my shoulder. The violinist gave Jamie a little wave from the stage, then shrugged her shoulders. "I don't get it, man. She's phenomenal."

"Well," Jamie said, pulling me toward the back, "Katy plays here every week. And most of the people here in this room can tell, just by listening, that she's a little off this afternoon. Probably thinking about boys or some fool thing."

"Wait, what?" I couldn't pull my attention away from the stage.

"She's a little sloppy today. They've heard better from her. She's a student of mine, so I'd know."

"Wow. So that's sloppy? What does it sound like when she's on?"

Jamie said, "When she's on, she'll make you cry."

The trio on stage began another number as Jamie led me down a long hall. Doors to the right opened up into the big garage where the pumper and ladder trucks slept. Along the left sat a pair of rooms. The first contained a group of kids strangling violins while a big man in a wheelchair patiently begged them to stop. He had a heavy gray beard and wore a Carhartt jacket with a POW/MIA patch on the sleeve. He'd lost both of his legs near the knee. He looked like a mama bird fretting over how to divide one worm among a dozen chicks.

Jamie made a left into the second door. I followed him into a small, wood-paneled room containing a pop machine with old glass soda bottles trapped inside. Jamie hung his coat on the back of a folding chair as the three men inside tuned.

I waited anxiously for Jamie to introduce me to Earl. Before I could take off my jacket the banjo player, who looked too much like a turtle stuck halfway in his shell, said, "Is this the city boy?"

"Hector, be nice, now," Jamie said.

The mandolin player had wavy red hair and I knew right away he wasn't Earl Black. Jamie said, "That there's Tim." Rather than reach across Hector to shake my hand, he just nodded.

Jamie stood directly behind the guitar player and gave the big man a good pat on the shoulder, then said "This here's Carter O'Dell. Sit where you can keep an eye on him. He'll show you chord changes and whatnot. Hector, why don't you switch him seats?"

"C'mon. You know how I hate sitting with my back against the door," he said.

"He needs a clear run at the window in case his ex-wife shows up," Tim deadpanned. He clipped an electric tuner to his mandolin.

Jamie lifted his old violin out of its case. The delicate oak leaf and acorn near the bridge had been worn smooth where it rubbed against his chin. "I'll be right back. Have to find some rosin," Jamie said and flitted out of the room like a squirrel in search of a nut.

"Fiddlers and their superstitions," Carter O'Dell said as he tapped Jamie's guitar case with his foot. "What're you waiting for, boy?" He watched as I unlatched the clasps on Jamie's old guitar case. The smell of old wood, like my grandpap's attic, made a beeline to the part of my brain that missed Cap'n Crunch and Super Friends on Saturday morning.

"Wow." I held the old Martin, all too aware of how close the chairs were. "Never had much of an interest. I always wished my amps went up to eleven."

I sat on the folding chair, put my head beneath the soft leather strap, then strummed an E. The thick strings bucked beneath my fingers like an angry bull trying to throw a rider. The body of the guitar wriggled beneath my arm like a kid about to get his first hair cut. Switching to a D minor diminished the guitar's liveliness a little, but sonic waves continued to pour out of the wood and into my ribs.

Tim tossed me his tuner. "Get yourself straightened out there." He noodled while I tuned, piecing together a little something that sounded like "Blackbird" meets "Bron-y-aur." Hector plucked rebuttals to Tim's twiny chirps.

Carter O'Dell rocked back in his chair, lifting its front legs off of the floor; his big hands clamped his Gibson's neck like he wanted to choke it. He thumbed the low G and picked out a simple bass line, a little glue to hold Hector and Tim together. Carter gave me an exaggerated nod, my cue to come in as soon as I tuned.

I watched his fingers for a few measures then joined in, picking out bass notes on the E and A strings. The notes came right out of the Lydian or Mixolydian mode, and once I chugged right along with Carter he played the full chords while continuing to walk along with the bass. My brain figured out the simple pattern before my fingers did. Bass-chord-chord. *Bass-chord-chord. Bass-chord-chord. Boom-chuck-chuck.* Jamie's Martin thumped like a bass drum kick.

At the end of the measure Carter left me high and dry to play a variation on the melody Tim had started us out with. Carter's Gibson had a crispy tone, like wind chimes. Just like that Tim went from melody to rhythm, accentuating my downbeats with palm-muted strums. The sudden shift in dynamics—Carter's transition from rhythm to lead and Tim's move to percussion—made me think, *Holy shit, that's sweet.* I let a little smile slip out.

Carter took the melody and twisted it, building rooms onto his foundation, turning it into a house. He hammered-on to a minor fifth, and now Tim's melody sounded a little heavier. Hector put a metallic exclamation point on it by playing a droning minor chord. Tim picked up the subtle key change and chucked out the new chord. I looked at Carter.

"A minor," he said.

At some point Jamie came back. Standing just over my shoulder he entered the song little by little. The whining fiddle filled the space in our tune like rain water fills a rocky riverbed. Hector backed off just a bit, assuming a more rhythmic role to let Jamie take the lead. Where Carter's guitar, or Tim's mandolin had been able to change the mood from jubilant to melancholy, Jamie's violin added nuance. Taking a pick to a hunk of marble that'd been hacked at with a chisel for too long.

Tim's head bounced, his glasses slid further down his nose as he tore through a frantic solo. I switched my A minor to an A minor seventh to give it a slightly funkier sound. Beneath the volume of our song Carter mouthed the words, 'one more time'.

I attacked the strings with my Dunlop HEAVY pick. The fierce vibrations radiating from that old slab of wood shook my fillings, for crying out loud. I looked for the cue to end.

A false silence filled the room as all the strings were muted to a stop. Phantom notes kept my ears ringing just a bit longer. Residual echoes went out into the universe, putting a firm time stamp on this musical event.

"Not bad," Carter said. He ran through a few warm-ups, his fingers bounced over the heavy strings like water droplets falling from treetop leaves. I silently chorded an F. My hands had grown so used to an electric guitar that I felt kind of weak, like my pointer could barely keep the low E down. My calloused fingertips felt like they'd been living easy for too long.

"It's a little different being in the background," I said, mostly just to have something to say.

In a drawn-out, exaggerated kind of way, Tim said, "Leave rhythm for the drummer, huh? Then give him five bucks and thank him for the pizza."

Before I could defend myself Tim let loose another. "What about the kid who tells his mother he wants to play lead guitar when he grows up? She laughs and says 'you know you can't do both.'"

Carter said, "Har har."

Knowing I'd been busted, I laughed. "No, I'm having a hard time wrapping my brain around the dynamic. All this time I thought I knew music. Guess I have a way to go."

Jamie said, "Not always a bad thing."

Before I could add to my defense Jamie said, "Let's keep it going. 'John Henry,' key of G? One, two, three, one two three."

Carter kicked the door open with a bass-filled run. I watched his fingers, trying to decipher the transitions he used to walk from chord to chord. By the time I had "John Henry" down, Tim called out the next one, "Greenbrier River."

We went around the room like this for the next few hours—them shouting out tunes I never heard of, me trying to keep up. My hands throbbed, the old Martin reminding me song after song who was boss. And I forgot all about the Sloppy Joes and the beautiful girl playing the violin. I even forgot about Earl Black for a second. For the first time in years music coursed through me, rather than through an amp and away from me. My mind rewrote every song I knew, rearranging them with chords and bass notes. I tried to predict how it'd sound, just me and a guitar doing all the songs that we did as a band. I wondered if somewhere in the old notebook I used for songwriting I'd find my very own "I Am Trying to Break Your Heart" or "Story of My Life."

We took a break while Carter and Hector packed up their instruments. I stretched a little, standing to shake their hands and shake out my legs. Carter leaned in and said, "You might be more valuable if you come prepared to sing a few next time. Singers are a rare thing around here, and Jamie's niece says you can sing."

After Carter shut the door Tim and Jamie made the circle a little tighter. "Without Hector we'll be able to hear ourselves think. Let Tim and I play a few bars of this next one. Join in when you think you know it."

"Key of D," Jamie said. He slid his bow across the strings and began playing a melody that reminded me of the first warm day after the snow's finally all gone. Then Tim joined, and music crawled around the room like a vine that produced a little white flower every so often. I couldn't figure out where to begin.

I didn't enjoy this one as much. Without a crutch I kept falling over. Besides, my mind kept drifting back to Earl Black. I didn't want to miss him. And to make that point I stood up when the song ended. I flexed my fingers a few times, a not-so-subtle hint that my hands were achy. Jamie rested his fiddle on his lap and said, "I guess that's a wrap?"

"I have to get a move on, too," Tim said, wiping his glasses on his shirt. As he put on his jacket, he said, "Preston, it was really nice meeting you. I hope we'll see you up here again." After a bit of a thoughtful pause he added, "And I hope things work out for you today."

My eyes found Jamie's. He gave me a resigned look.

Tim patted me on the back as he stepped past. He shook Jamie's hand before slipping out the door.

The room seemed really big with just Jamie and me in it. I put his Martin down and slid the pick into the strings before shutting the lid.

Jamie asked, "You ready for this?"

"I guess so. I came all this way, right?" I had more to say, but decided to hold it. "What's the worst thing that can happen?"

"I know you've probably spent a lot of time thinking about this." He coughed into his fist, perhaps taking an extra second to find words. "Whatever happens, it doesn't change who you are. You have to remember that. The man I met this morning doesn't change because of what happens today, okay?"

He made such direct eye contact that I eventually had to look down at my feet. "I promise." I extended my hand. "And thank you. I mean that."

Jamie took my hand. His shoulders dropped, perhaps relieved to have had my word. He stepped into the hall, shuffled a few steps, then turned around. "You know, my son never had an urge to touch a musical instrument."

The long hallway had fallen quiet except for the music from a pair of violins in the main hall, intertwined like blackberry brambles. Jamie led me toward the music.

In the big room the snack bar had been shuttered. *No Sloppy Joes for me today*, I thought, my belly rumbling. All the folding chairs but one had been leaned against the wall in rows. A pair of basketball hoops had been lowered, the scoreboard glowed, HOME 0, VISITOR 0. Neither bonus arrow glowed.

In the center of the floor, the girl I'd seen on stage earlier faced the big guy in the wheelchair from the clinic down the hall. The girl stopped when she saw me and Jamie come in. Her eyes were the kind of blue Miles Davis must've dreamt about when he recorded "Blue in Green." The drums on that record sounded like raindrops on city sidewalks.

"Sorry to interrupt you all." Jamie put his hand on my shoulder, gave a little pat, then said, "I'd like you all to meet somebody. Preston, this is Katy Stefanic. Katy's mother is my baby sister."

She clutched her fiddle with the crook of her arm and slid her bow alongside it. She smiled, her big eyes seemed to glow a little. "Nice to meet you." Her hand felt warm and dry. Not hot, like Dani's. I didn't want to let it go. She put her violin into its case on the floor, then took the man's.

"I heard you playing earlier. You sounded really good." Saying it reminded me that I'd made an ass of myself.

Katy blushed, then softened my embarrassment by saying, "I started young." I could listen to her soft voice all night long.

My mouth dried up as the man turned toward me. I straightened myself and tried to stop my hand from shaking. I tried flexing my fingers a few times. I thought for sure I'd cry, and swore I'd hate myself if I did. But I could already feel it in my throat.

Jamie grabbed my shoulder again, then slid his hand to the nape of my neck to keep me from bounding forward. "Earl, this is the guy I told you about."

I leaned forward and took his hand. The touch sent a jolt through me. A jolt of what, I didn't know. Maybe a little anger, a little sadness. Joy. "Preston Black, sir. Nice to meet you."

He flinched a little when I said my name. I thought it was certainly a sign of guilt. A multitude of questions and accusations flooded my head. Before I could get any of it out Earl said, "Just like the song, huh?"

"Yeah. I brought the record along…" I handed it over to him.

He looked it over real good and slid the vinyl out, just like Jamie had. He said, "That's me, alright. I'd get up, but…" He studied my face.

I opened my mouth, a placeholder for the things I meant to say, but Earl cut me off.

"I'd get up," he said again with a bit of a stammer, rushing his words, "… but a little incident I had on a trip overseas keeps me in the chair. Something that probably happened long before you were born, in fact. But if I had a son he'd be a lot older than you are, ten years at least. Jamie told me that's why you're here."

I cringed when he said that.

"It's okay. I can see why you'd think that, with the song and all. When I left Vietnam, like this, I married my sweetheart. We didn't make it last, not without me being able to…. Served in Ninth Division, in Tan An Delta. Thought the leeches would get me, it was a booby trap. Spent a few years wishing it would've killed me."

I let my eyes drift to the big scoreboard. Still read HOME 0, VISITOR 0.

"I'm sorry, Preston," Jamie said. "I could've told you, but I think it's better to have seen it for yourself."

"No, I understand. It's all good," I said with a forced laugh. But my odometer had been set back to zero. "Hey man, it's nothing. When I saw the name, I just thought…"

Earl handed me back the record and said, "If Black wasn't such a common name up here I'd say we could've been related. Who knows, maybe we're cousins?"

"Yeah."

Earl looked at me like I just had my bike stolen. "I am sorry it didn't work out like you hoped."

Katy stood beside me. "No news isn't bad news." She handed Earl his black violin case, which he set on his lap.

"I suppose." I couldn't find much more than that to say.

"Thanks, Earl," Jamie said. Then the two of them headed toward the door. Katy lingered next to me for a second, then fell into step behind them.

"What about the song? I'd still like to hear the song, if you don't mind," I said, trying to get something to take with me.

"That was a long time ago," Earl said.

"Please, man. I don't have any family pictures, no birth certificate. You can give me something real."

Earl glared like a possum that'd been poked with a stick.

"Sorry. I'm not trying to provoke you."

"It's not my song. I didn't write it. I heard it from a great uncle fifty years ago and slapped my name on it."

He said, almost more to Jamie than me, "I can't drive a truck, can't mine coal or railroad. What was I supposed to do?"

The air suddenly felt thick and awkward, like sitting too close to a bonfire. Jamie shoved his hands into his coat pockets and wiped an invisible smudge off of the floor. Katy was about to push the door open for Earl when he turned around and started to sing.

"Preston Black couldn't eat and he couldn't drink, Preston Black couldn't eat and he couldn't drink," his frail voice wavered. "But he'd sit at the table all the same, waiting for handouts from wherever they came."

He cleared his throat, then finished the verse. "Preston Black couldn't eat and he couldn't drink."

I knew he wasn't singing about me. At least that was what I kept telling myself.

"Preston Black didn't have a ma or pa, Preston Black didn't have no ma or pa. Didn't know when he'd been born, didn't know when he'd die, didn't know nothing about the how or why. Preston Black didn't have no ma or pa."

I silently recited the verses, doing whatever it took to etch the song in my mind. I looked at Earl.

Earl looked at the floor. "Preston Black never sang in church, Preston Black never sang in church. Though he knew the words to every song, the preacher told him that he didn't belong. Preston Black never sang in church." He grabbed his chair's wheels and gave them a few pushes. And the dirgeful groan that came from his throat reminded me that I was getting everything I asked for by digging up old graves.

"Preston Black couldn't sleep the whole night through, Preston Black couldn't sleep the whole night through." He stopped and crossed his arms. "He'd lay in bed 'til the morning came, but the devil'd visit him just the same. Preston Black couldn't sleep the whole night through."

Right now I wished it was last Friday instead of this Friday and Pauly and me were good and I'd never found the record. And I wished it wasn't so cold.

The night sky looked bigger than I'd ever seen it. Stars practically dripped down onto the old wool in my hat. No wind blew, and the whoosh of the Blackwater River reminded me that even though the distance was less than a hundred miles, home was still very far away tonight.

My phone's blue LCD screen killed the bright starlight, ruining any wish I would've made. When I scrolled through my missed calls and saw I wasn't alone, some of my fear shrank. At the prompt I entered my PIN, waited for my voicemails and turned my back on the stars.

The metallic female voice said, "First unheard message received today at 9:47 a.m."

"Preston," Pauly yelled into the phone, "you fucking bastard. You got a lot of fucking nerve sneaking around the apartment. You're being a real pussy, you know that? How long 'til you grow the fuck up, huh? I ought to change the locks and rent out your fucking room. Call me."

Message deleted.

"Next unheard message received today at 11:32 a.m."

"God damn it, man. You're really going all in this time. Whatever. I'm on the road for a few days, so you can have the apartment all to yourself. Maybe when I get back we can sit down and talk about all this. Later."

Message deleted.

"Next unheard message received today at 4:42 p.m."

"Hello, Preston?" Dani's voice sounded so warm, like an April breeze that blows just before rain comes. Hearing it reminded me that winter would be over soon. "I miss you. I had a good time last night. I couldn't remember if we were supposed to do something tonight, so call me."

"Shit," I flipped my phone shut. Jamie and Katy chatted with Earl as he loaded himself into his van. Looked like they were waiting for me.

I made my way over to Jamie's old Subaru. Katy opened the back door.

"Take the front," I said.

"It's okay. I'm getting out first." She wore a hat with bright knit flowers on it and a scarf to match. Her brown hair framed her pink cheeks.

"Well, let me help you then."

She handed me her fiddle, a case so dainty compared to my guitar. She scooted in then reached for her instrument.

"Thank you," she said, smiling. Her pupils looked quite large in the dim glow of the dome light, making them seem like they were smiling too. She watched me for a long moment.

As soon as I sat down Katy poked her head between the front seats and held her mittens up, as if collecting phantom heat from vents that had yet to produce any. She smelled like ginger and vanilla. "Uncle Jamie, what's the deal with Earl and all that anyway?" She turned the stereo down until only the footprint of a song remained.

"Katy," Jamie cleared his throat, almost a tsk-tsk. "Maybe we can talk tomorrow."

"I'm heading back to town tomorrow. I won't see you... Maybe 'til spring break." She sniffled into a tissue.

Jamie squirmed, more nerved up than a rabbit at a dog show. He ran his fingers along his jaw a few times. I knew he'd never find a way to put it delicately. He jammed the car into gear and drifted through a break in a snowdrift on the berm.

I tried to help him out. "A few days ago I found a record at Isaac's."

Katy interrupted, "On Pleasant Street? I'm in there all the time."

"Really? I work at Mick's. You need to stop in some time. You a student?"

"Grad school. PhD. Mick always has to special order my stuff and always gives me a hard time about it. Anyway..." she said, like it was my fault the story wasn't progressing.

I said, "So I find this record with my name on the back. As one of the song titles. At the time it made a lot more sense, but I thought the guy might've been my dad. Like maybe the song was about me. Sounds stupid when I say it out loud."

"Preston," Jamie said, "it was a good hunch. And now you know. You don't have to wonder anymore."

"But eliminating Earl as a candidate means my dad is still out there somewhere." After a moment to think, I said, "You think Earl was holding something back?"

"I don't know. I'll take a look at my tapes and see what I can come up with. Either way, it's more than you had this morning."

We bounced onto a gravel side road. A light snow fell through the headlights, joining the old snow rotting along the edge. The dark blue night swallowed everything but what the headlights touched. Around a sharp bend we passed a pair of homes flanking a barn. From an old foursquare with a big porch, blue television images flickered into the yard, and I could see a single person sitting on a couch, watching.

Up ahead on the right sat another house, spotlights from the front porch shined into the old field between the house and the road. A pair of deer spotted Jamie's Subaru and froze.

Katy said, "You guys going to play any more tonight?"

"I suppose we could. You don't have to go home now?" Jamie slowed to a crawl at the top of the long gravel driveway.

"Did Aunt Izzy cook?"

"She said she made lasagna."

"I'll just have my mom run over and pick me up after dinner then. If that's all right."

Jamie sputtered, a typical Jamie move, I discovered. He glanced at me, then looked back in the rear view mirror before I could meet his gaze. "I suppose."

Katy chirped until we got to Jamie's. She went on like one long Facebook status update until Jamie rolled to a stop in front of a long, wide porch. She didn't stop until I interrupted. "If it's okay I'm going to make a real quick phone call."

Katy retreated into the back seat like a kitten from a vacuum cleaner.

"You might be able to get a signal out here," Jamie said like he really, really hoped it'd be different than the rest of his life, when a snowball had a chance in hell of getting coverage.

"Really? So, sometimes you can get coverage here?"

Katy chimed in gleefully, "Jamie was just being polite. You won't get a signal out here."

I shut my phone off, waited, then turned it back on.

Searching for signal.

Searching for signal.

"You can use the house phone."

But once we got into the house and I saw the phone hanging on the wall in the kitchen, I declined. Jamie said nobody'd mind, but I couldn't see myself trying to flow to Dani while Jamie and his wife and niece ate lasagna.

After dinner we all pitched in to ret up, then Jamie led Katy and me into the basement. Instead of the busted Craftsmen circular saws and old croquet sets we had at home, Jamie had shelves of sheet music and old cloth-bound books about music theory and artists. He had shelves of CDs, cassettes and old reel-to-reels resting above a row of vertically stacked LPs, with small tags sticking out like hitchhikers' thumbs to keep them in order. In the corner to my right Jamie had a 24-track digital recorder and mixing board. Neatly arranged booms, some crowned with condenser mics, some with vintage mics, all waited patiently for the music to start.

The biggest wall held a curtain of musical instruments—more than a few fiddles, a half-dozen banjos, a quartet of mandolins, an upright bass, an autoharp, a bouzouki…

And guitars. Man, the guitars. I walked right up to a pair of Gibsons. In a floor stand Jamie had another Martin, this one much smaller than the D-28 I'd used all day long. The varnish had faded to the point where it had all but disappeared, perhaps it had simply been played away. This was Jamie's tool shop. These were his hammers and screwdrivers.

Jamie ran his finger along the rows of cassette tapes, pulled a few here and there, then did the same thing with the row of reel-to-reels. He saw me looking at the guitars and said, "Help yourself."

I picked up the little Martin. The wood felt soft, like parchment or an onion skin. I ran my fingers across the strings. The finish was light and sweet, like butter pecan.

Katy watched. I hoped she wasn't waiting for me to impress her, because I learned a long time ago the challenge of trying to impress a girl this way. After a few bars she pulled a violin off of the wall, put her ear close to the strings to check the tuning, then began to play a Celtic-sounding melody. She tapped her foot to the time I'd kept, but seemed to want to rush the beat.

"Jamie, you going to jump in?" She dropped the violin to her belly as I kept playing.

"Go on. I'm going to put some of these tracks on a disc for Preston." He licked his fingers and flipped through the pages of an old journal. He took a pencil from behind his ear and made a few notes. Then he stood up, without really looking up from his notes, and went back to the shelf. "Why don't you show Preston the 'Wildwood Flower'?"

Katy got right into it without putting up any fuss. She blew her hair away from her eyes and began playing a melody as sweet and syrupy as berry pie.

"C," Jamie said.

I quickly fretted the cord and finger picked along. When the chord changed I pretty much knew what came next and slid into a G.

"G7," Jamie corrected. "Is your record upstairs?" he asked, then jogged up the steps without waiting for me reply.

The second time around I thumbed the bass notes like I'd learned at the fire hall. Jamie returned and sat down, put the LP on the turntable. A long-forgotten sound, the low hiss of a vinyl, rose from the speakers. He plugged in a set of headphones and held them up to his ear. After a minute or two he dropped the headphones into his lap, spun in his chair, and began to sing along with me and Katy.

"Oh, I'll twine with my mingles and waving black hair…" He pronounced 'hair' like it rhymed with 'fur'. Katy cracked up. When she laughed her hair fell back over her face. It'd been years since I saw somebody laugh like that. I laughed too.

With that, Jamie put his headphones on and spun toward the desk. I put the little Martin back in its rack and took the iced-tea-colored Gibson off the wall. It sounded louder than the little Martin, maybe even louder than the D-28. But it didn't come alive in my hands the way the 28 did.

"Sing something," Katy said.

"Like what?"

"I don't know. Something good. Something to wow me." I couldn't figure out whether or not she was being sarcastic.

I couldn't think of something that'd sound particularly good acoustic. My fingers slid into a Cadd9, and I inhaled. I strummed the chord, but before I could begin to sing Jamie dropped his headphones on the desk and spun his chair.

"Bingo. I have it."

"What?" Katy asked, her interest in my song thinner than a Chili Cheese Frito.

"The record. Even though his picture isn't on the front I recognized Jesse Currence's fiddle. He's not even listed on the inside. That lead me to a version of the song I recorded in 1984 up in Pocahontas County. When I thought Earl wrote the song I decided not to look at my notes. But the record—it's all on here."

"Really?" I asked, unsure if I wanted to hear more. What I'd already heard sounded bleak enough.

"It's a good news, bad news situation." Jamie looked at his notes like they'd done him wrong.

"Bad news first," I said, hanging the Gibson back up.

"I only have the same four verses Earl sang at the fire hall. The tape just cuts out. There's more to the song, but I either forgot to flip the tape, or… I don't know what happened. My notes say it's four minutes long, but there are only two and a half here." He looked like he genuinely felt bad about it.

"There's good news?"

"Yes, there is good news." Jamie's eyes widened. I'd only known him a short time, but never imagined he could get so animated. "The good news is we have provenance. Get ready for a road trip."

"Where to?" I said.

Jamie flipped his notebook shut, leaned back in his chair and folded his arms behind his head. "We know where Earl got the song from. And if we know the source, hopefully we can get the remaining verses. We're going to Pocahontas County to get the rest of the song."

He stood up and grabbed a fiddle. Just before he slung his bow across the strings, he said, "We're going back in time."

CHAPTER FIVE

I didn't sleep well, but at least I didn't dream. Instead of eating breakfast I had a few cups of tea. Jamie told me he had a few things for me, and led me downstairs. Last night, after Katy went back home, he put together a few more CDs. He said the songs were arranged chronologically, and I should listen to the CDs in that order to hear the progressions.

He set the discs next to a small stack of books, two or three years' worth of reading for me.

"Look here," he said, "some people think that a tree is the best way to illustrate evolution of a song. But it's really more like a flower bed. The roots are all intertwined, and a song that springs up in Braxton will sound different when it springs up in Lewisburg, and different still when it springs up in Virginia or Kentucky. The same seed stock begat each song, but different growing conditions change the final product. So a flower closer to the downspout gets more water, and maybe gets a little fuller and taller."

"And that's what these are?" I pointed to the discs.

"Uh, yeah. And then some that you just have to get to know. I couldn't stop myself." He grinned.

He put them off to the side, and then set the books on his lap. "Now these… I've noted important passages with note cards." He held the books up to let me see. "What you'll find interesting—at least I did—is the way the song is seeded."

Jamie got kind of quiet, kind of serious in a way that made me perk up my ears. He leaned in and lowered his voice so much that I had to meet him halfway to hear what he said. "Instead of coming from one seed, it comes from many. Like maybe it's been bastardized quite a few times. At least a lot more than most of the stuff I recorded. One version of your song goes back to 1229. Came from the *Codex Gigas*?"

He waited for me to acknowledge, but I shook my head.

"It's a famous book from Bohemia. It's said to have been written in one night by a monk who'd made a deal with Lucifer to avoid being walled up alive."

To show I was paying attention, I asked, "Bohemia?"

"The old heart of Europe. A region east of Germany and just north of Austria," Jamie said, then told me we'd know more about the song later in the week. The song really didn't mean that much to me, especially since I was just looking for my dad. Maybe Jamie's enthusiasm kept me caring.

When I heard Katy knock at the door I stood up and stretched and shook Jamie's hand. "Thanks for everything. I really mean it. And, you know, it's okay if this doesn't really end up being fruitful. You know, the search?"

Jamie handed me the bag of books and recordings, then slid his hands into the back pockets of his jeans. "We're pretty close. By this time next week we'll have everything we need to put this to bed."

"Yeah, I understand. But I'm just saying I think I got more than I expected." I didn't want to say that maybe I realized who I was didn't depend on a song or my father. "Like, maybe if I started to focus on music instead of thinking the universe has it in for me, maybe then things would start to happen."

Katy waited by the door, tapping out her impatience on the bannister.

Jamie said, "I understand. Would you prefer that I didn't set anything up for this weekend?"

"No. Let's see where this goes. You've done a lot for me, and I owe it to both of us to see what we can learn."

Jamie agreed and continued to lecture while I got my shit together. My books and discs. My Tele, which—compared to Jamie's acoustic—seemed lifeless without an amp and a cord. Jamie and Isabelle each hugged Katy before giving her a big care package to get her through another rough week in Mo'town. Jamie shook my hand.

"Thank you for everything," I said.

"And I'll call as soon as I find anything out. I'll be in town this week, so we'll leave from there. I'll bring the Martin for you." Jamie held the door while we stepped onto the porch.

"Thanks, but I have to take a look at what Mick has again. Maybe try to get something on my own."

"Nice. Let me know how that goes. If you want advice, just give me a yell, although I'm sure Mick'll have plenty." Jamie waved again, then shut his front door.

Katy slid into the driver's seat of her little Honda. I couldn't tell if it was silver or champagne from the salt crusted to the paint. On the back window she had a few stickers—*WVU*, of course, and *Mountaineer Girl*. There was a Black Bear Burritos sticker and one that said *YMSB*. I slid my stuff into the back seat next to her laundry baskets and groceries.

She backed the little car out of the driveway with all the grace of a tugboat pushing a barge through the lock. I tucked my hands beneath my armpits. We chit-chatted as we passed through Davis and then Thomas. After a few more miles of polite small talk I asked, "Would it be rude if I checked my messages?"

She shrugged. "It's fine." Her tone implied she minded.

"I can wait."

"No, really, it's fine."

I flipped my phone open, waited for a sign from her to see that she'd meant it, then dialed up voicemail.

"First unheard message sent today at 9:03 a.m."

Dani.

"Hello, Preston? I'm thinking about brunch. Call me if you are interested. Goodbye." She sounded sleepy. I struggled to recall her face and the way she looked at me.

Shit.

"Next unheard message sent today at 12:15 p.m."

"Maybe you didn't get my first call? I don't know. I have to go up to the library. Call me, or maybe we can meet this week. Goodbye."

"Shit." I snapped my phone shut with a bit more force than I'd meant to.

"Everything all right?" Katy said it like she'd take a little pleasure in hearing that it wasn't.

"I suppose. Keep missing somebody, that's all." Then I said, thinking out loud, "It's like the more excited I get about something the more I'm dooming it to fail."

"Sorry."

"It's fine. I should've waited to check. I didn't mean to make you feel weird. It's this girl—woman—I met this week." I watched the winter-weary landscape drift by. Fields that looked old, houses that looked even older. White mountains with a dusting of naked trees. With just a bit less color it would've been a black and white photo.

"Should've known it was woman troubles." She said it with excessive exasperation, mocking me.

I tried to laugh. "Are you making fun of me?"

"You think?" She pushed a strand of hair behind her ear, and went on, "I'm sure you have boxes filled with panties the ladies throw at the stage. We saw you guys play down at Mon Brewing a few times. Way to keep the Nineties alive."

"Ouch. Who pissed in your Cheerios?"

"You did. There are guys up here who would play you into the ground, but nobody's ever going to hear them because they aren't as pretty as you." She kept looking into her side-view mirror. At the speedometer. Anything to keep her eyes from drifting to the right.

I kept my mouth shut for a long time. Plenty of silent miles slipped by. I should've been okay to let it go. But that wasn't what happened. "You know, I work hard for what I have. And I'm not about to apologize for growing up in town instead of out in the boonies. So don't give me what for like you know what you're talking about."

"Don't be mad. I'm just playing." She turned on the radio, flipped through the static, then slid a CD in. "You're an easier target than I thought you'd be. I thought city kids had street smarts."

She looked at me, her blue eyes pleading, then smiling. "When I first got to Morgantown you played at the Nickel all the time. My friend, Chelsea, thought I had a thing for you. I always told her that you'd probably be arrogant. And here I was right all along."

"Lovely." We came past the waterslide at Marilla, all frozen and quiet. It felt good to be home.

"You guys playing there this week? Maybe I'll bring Chelsea down to meet you. Now that we've bonded and all."

"The band's done. *Finito*. I'm a solo act now."

"That's too bad. Well, if you ever get the itch to hang out with amateurs we're up at the coffee shop a few times a week."

"Starbucks?"

"You *would* think that. No, I prefer to patronize local businesses instead of filling fat corporate coffers. Mountaineer Doughnuts, up on Spruce."

"How high and mighty. But Mountaineer Doughnuts is hardly a coffee shop. A couple of gay guys putting in a stage and hiring baristas doesn't make it a coffee shop."

"*Touché*. Maybe there's a little more to you than I figured, Preston Black."

"That maybe Chelsea was right?"

"Never. I'd throw my panties at Pauly."

"Jesus."

"Where can I drop you off?"

"Mountaineer Doughnuts is fine."

"Okay. I made a mixtape for you."

"You serious? It's been years since anybody made me a mixtape, and this weekend I get two."

"Well, a CD. Just some stuff you may have never heard. Sara Watkins, Yonder Mountain String Band, Uncle Earl." She handed it to me with an apologetic smile.

"Thanks a lot. I'll listen to it today." I got my stuff from the back seat.

"Yeah, right." Katy tooted as she drove away.

I stood on the corner waiting for whatever would happen next. Walnut Street looked a lot different today than it did Friday night on my drunken stroll up High. The sidewalk felt a little slippy, so I shuffled my feet, my Tele acting like a counterweight to all of the material Jamie had loaded me down with.

I thought about heading straight to Dani's, but remembered she said she'd be up at the library. Pauly's message that he'd be on the road for a few days reminded me I had the apartment to myself. My stomach growled. The easiest thing would be to take it into the diner to see Mom. But she'd know I hadn't been talking to Pauly and ask a lot of questions and tell me how sin makes us a prisoner of Satan and all that. Seemed like a lot of trouble for a cheeseburger.

Pauly had parked the Jeep on the side. Even though I knew he wasn't home I crept up the steps anyway. My shoes thudded against the bare wooden stairs. The click of the old deadbolt echoed through the naked hall. On the day we moved in, August sunlight had warmed the wood floor, so the whole place smelled sweet, a lot like Isaac's. Like an attic full of everything you ever loved. The drafty window at the end of the hall let winter blow right in. Winter killed that smell.

The lights were off, the TV asleep. The heat hadn't been run in a while. The sink stunk like dirty dishes, and the pizza box from the other night sat in the trash with my half of the pizza still in it.

I tapped open the door to his room with my foot. A pair of shirts hung over the closet door still wrapped in dry-cleaning bags. The embroidery on the patch above the pocket said 'Paul'. He had a picture of the three of us tucked into the mirror above the dresser. Paul and Stu and me at the Fayette County Fair. We thought we were on our way to a record deal and a big tour. Like driving up to Pennsylvania for a show was a big deal.

The fridge was empty. Not only was he still on the wagon, maybe he'd started a hunger strike too. In the freezer a container of halupki waited like that baby mammoth they found—encased in ice, furry. Somehow we could never get fifty bucks together for a microwave. Always had money for Jack, though. Maybe when we're dead and gone somebody'll take a DNA sample from the halupki and try to clone it.

The second-best cure for hunger is sleep, so I headed back to my room. Pauly had cleaned out the Jeep. He'd made a big pile of my gear right in the middle of my floor. My Fender Twin, a Marshall half stack, two Chico San milk crates full of pedals and processors, cables, an EMG 81 I'd put into the Strat that I sold to get the Twin. Looking at that pile felt like looking at a museum exhibit.

Tomorrow I'd sell it all.

These things were no longer essential to the way I made music. Stuff came and went. I sold my Strat for a ring. An opal. I'd never seen an item depreciate so fast. A nine-hundred-dollar guitar bought a five-hundred-dollar ring that apparently wasn't worth the hand that had given it to her.

I sold my first car to pay a fine. Ironically, without the car I wouldn't have incurred the fine. And without the car the six month driver's license suspension didn't matter.

But all the effects pedals and amps and guitars were small potatoes. I'd sold my soul to play covers in a bar band. Might never get that back.

I undressed and kicked all my dirty clothes into a pile by the closet. I pulled Jamie's CDs from the bag, dropped one into my player and tried to fall asleep to the sound of fiddles speaking in tongues, their accents choked with mountain laurel and pine trees.

The fiddle buzzed like hornets in a soup can. A man's dissonant voice sang, "Preston Black couldn't eat and he couldn't drink. Preston Black couldn't eat and he couldn't drink. But he'd sit at the table all the same, waiting for handouts from wherever they came. Preston Black couldn't eat and he couldn't drink."

That first verse could've been about anybody else in West Virginia. I got all that stuff about metaphorical hunger. Like, maybe I hungered for affection, or I thirsted for spirituality or whatever. But the first verse didn't sell me on the song. Jamie must've felt the same way, because when Earl sang it back in the fire hall Jamie didn't pay it much mind. But by the time Earl finished the second verse, Jamie looked at me like he'd just seen Elvis.

Another instrument came in on the second verse. Maybe a banjo. Not a crisp, hard banjo, like the one Bela Fleck played. I could almost hear fingernails grazing the head.

"He'd hide in bed 'til the morning came, but the devil'd find him just the same. Preston Black couldn't sleep the whole night through."

I hit REPEAT and let it play over and over. After a few more listens I didn't just hear my name just at the beginning of each verse; I heard it in every malnourished note.

Almost like the devil himself was singing about me.

I hurried and pulled the glass door shut behind me but still managed to let a little winter into the vestibule. Red offertory candles shivered in the cold air. For a second I stood next to the holy water, wondering whether or not I should bless myself.

Figuring it couldn't hurt, I dipped my fingers then made the Sign of the Cross. "In the name of the Father, of the Son and the Holy Spirit. Amen."

Up front a small group of women prayed their rosaries. My grandmother used to be one of them. Their murmurs unsettled me when I was little, like they were saying something secretive and magical. When my grandmother died I stopped coming to mass, like maybe it wasn't so magical after all. The smell of the candles and the Stations of the Cross didn't mean as much to me now. The old church, pretty much unchanged since my thirteenth birthday, didn't seem to have the soul it used to.

Some people think talking about souls is old-fashioned, but that was the one thing I clung to after I stopped coming. The idea of a part of us that lives on after we die took away my fear and made the future seem a lot less scary. Like, even if Heaven or Hell didn't exist, I could buy into the idea of the soul being absorbed by the energy of the universe. As much as I liked to think I'd outgrown that superstition, I knew I wouldn't be here if some part of me wasn't still hanging on to it.

I slid into the pew without genuflecting. I didn't kneel and pray, and retrospectively got a little angry for crossing myself when I came in. Tried to tell myself it was just habit. Two people waited ahead of me for the confessional. The stained glass windows sparkled like fireworks. The low sun turned the tired window into neon emeralds and rubies. Cinema from a less-sophisticated time. If I looked long enough I could almost see Mary turn to me and smile. She watched over me while I waited. As soon as I went into the confessional she'd go back to looking at her newborn.

When my turn in the confessional came I got butterflies. After I pulled the door shut, in the dark, I said, "Hello?" I figured it didn't matter who spoke first, since I didn't actually come to confess.

On the other side of the screen the priest shifted.

"Father, I haven't been in here since—" I tried to think of a way to say it that sounded less like a lie. "I haven't been to confession since my confirmation. Sorry if I forgot how it goes."

When he spoke I realized the voice didn't belong to Father Turek. "That's not the best opening, but now you can just tell me why you're here."

"Why I'm here?"

"You know, the whole 'forgive me Father, for I have sinned' spiel."

I stared into the screen, trying to get a feel for the man on the other side. "Well, the thing is I'm not actually here to confess."

He said, "So you've been living without sin?"

"Ha. No, not exactly. But—and I know this sounds crazy—but I think I might actually have a bigger problem."

"Don't be so sure of forgiveness that you add sin to sin." His tone reverted, like he'd reminded himself of the serious business taking place in here.

For a while I didn't know what he was talking about, so I didn't say anything. But the darkness made the time pass like melting ice. Enough time to make me believe I'd made a mistake. "Sorry, man. I'm going to roll. I'm probably not supposed to be here for this kind of thing."

The priest slid the screen open. "Wait." He sat hunched over like he was three sizes too big for the small bench. The robe he wore looked funny because he was so young. "This isn't the appropriate place for a discussion, but we can talk in the office. You came for a reason, right?"

I didn't say anything.

"As soon as I hear confessions we can talk, okay? Promise you won't leave?" He used his youth pastor voice.

"I'll wait." I opened the door and went back into the church. But before I could sit he opened the door a hair.

"Were you the last?" He peeked through the small opening. The only other people were in the first few pews.

"Looks like it," I said, waiting to see what he wanted me to do.

He stepped out of the confessional and stretched. He had to be seven feet tall.

"Jeez," I said, a syllable shy of *Jesus*. "Basketball much?"

"I'm Father James," he said with a smile and a handshake. "Center at St. Vincent's in Latrobe."

I shook my head.

"What? Mr. Rogers' hometown?" He walked toward the stairs behind the altar. "Rolling Rock?"

"Yeah, Rolling Rock. That's right," I replied, wondering how a guy not much older than me could go the rest of his life without ever making love again.

"It's this way." He ran his thumbs along the outer edges of his purple stole.

"I remember. I served as an altar boy back in the day."

"For Father Anthony?" He nodded toward the women in the second pew. They were all deep in prayer. None noticed when he passed.

"No. Father Turek. I didn't last very long." Father James's height made me feel like I was ten years old again. We went around the altar and down the stairs to the basement. He asked me to wait in a wooden school chair at the old teacher's desk in the basement office. Returning to a scene that hadn't changed in seventeen years had the same effect as a time machine. I hated to admit it, but being in that building calmed me.

Father James returned. "Something to drink? Pop or tea."

"Tea sounds good." I took my coat off and laid it over my arm.

He filled an old teapot with water from a big plastic water cooler and placed it on a hot plate. "So, what could be a bigger problem than leaving the church? You may not like my tone, but I believe it's best to get to the point in situations like this."

"It's not the tone that bothers me. It's the way you talk to me like I'm in sixth grade. But I came to you for help, so I'm willing to put up with it."

He smiled and lowered his eyes. "You're right. I apologize. Usually I'm dealing with frustrated freshmen asking me to justify premarital sex and birth control. It's just an old routine."

He opened a cupboard and took out two mugs. "Cream or sugar? And it's skim milk, not cream. Don't know if that changes anything."

"Just a little sugar. Thanks."

He stood by the hot plate, waiting for the water to boil. He folded his arms and said, "So what's on your mind?"

Realizing that saying it made it real, I took a breath and started with the record and my dad and how those led to the song, which scared me because of the way it hit a little too close to home, especially the whole part about not having a mom or dad and not sleeping the whole night through. And then I added real quick a few lines about how I didn't really believe it, but I kind of did and I didn't know if it was real or if my mind just played tricks. I finished up by rambling about evil, hoping he'd get the gist of what I was saying without actually making me say it. I ended with, "I want to know about evil. Like the devil from the Bible. Like, does evil exist or do we imagine it?"

The teapot hissed, but the priest grabbed it off of the burner before it could scream. Steam rose from the cups and the priest tugged on the teabag strings to jumpstart the brewing process. He put a towel over the kettle, set a kitchen timer for four minutes and brought the mugs over to the desk. Instead of sitting across from me he sat in the other wooden school chair and stretched his legs. "St. Augustine said, 'I sought the source of evil, and I found no explanation.'"

I nodded appreciatively. "Maybe I should've been more specific. It's my fault for not wanting to embarrass myself. I was more interested in hearing about the devil. Specifically."

Without taking the same thoughtful pause he'd taken before, he said, "Evil is a very active presence, not just the absence of good. Evil infiltrates us, perverts our way of thinking. Sin pushes us away from God. That's when evil attacks." The timer went off and he removed the teabags from the cups. "God is the source of all life, and sin cuts us off from God. Sin cuts off our source of life."

"Sorry." I held my hand up just short of waving him off. "It's hard for me to say this without sounding stupid. But I really wanted to know more about Satan I guess. Like, does the church think he's real? Can we lose our souls to the devil? Make deals with the devil and all that? Specifically, does the devil exist? Is he on Earth now? I guess that's specifically what I'm asking."

He blew into his tea. His reply took a long time to get to me. "Saint Paul said the Devil was 'the god of this world' and Christians don't have to be concerned about just one, but many devils."

He leaned forward, clasping his hands and resting his elbows on his knees. "The Devil was there for mankind's original sin, and the Devil knows how to work his way into our hearts through temptation, through our libidos, our urges and wants. When we get jealous of somebody. When you see a young lady and think about hopping into bed with her before you wonder what her name is. Any of the dark thoughts we have before drifting off to sleep. When we get drunk and say crude things about other people, we are widening cracks that let the Devil in. We defend ourselves by arming ourselves against sin. Grace and innocence make us powerful. Jesus teaches fasting and prayer as a way to protect ourselves from the Devil's methods. 'Be not overcome by evil, but overcome evil with good.'"

I pushed my tea away and stood up. "Thanks a lot. I appreciate your time. I know that you have more important things you could be doing right now."

I buttoned my coat. "You know, I have no problem with good and evil and sin and all that. I know what you're saying. But fasting and praying won't change the record and the dreams. I don't need to know about penance and original sin. I need to know what I can do about this devil thing."

Father James didn't try to convince me to return to my seat. As I tightened my scarf he said, "In the desert Jesus kept Satan at bay by totally adhering to his Father's plan of Salvation."

"So you don't really know?"

"Church doctrine is cloudy. Almost like it's hidden in the same darkness that hides the Devil himself."

"So that's it?"

"I've answered your question as thoroughly as I can."

"What do you think? You personally? Man to man."

Father James stood, and walked over to the sink. He held his teacup over the drain and flipped it over, shaking out the last few drops. He rinsed the cup out, wiped it dry with a paper towel, then said, "I've already told you what I think."

Before I left the vestibule I called Dani. No answer. I hung up as it went to voicemail, then called right back. "Hey, Dani? This is Preston. Sorry I missed you, I didn't expect to end up staying down there so long. I found out a lot and I'd love to tell you about it. Give me a call if you want to get together again. Maybe I can meet you in the library, if you're still up there. All right? Goodbye."

The only way I could get to the library or anywhere on campus—except for some of the frat houses and the bars up on Sunnyside—was by starting from the Mountainlair. I bundled up and crept forward in that general direction.

With my head down and my eyes shut to the wind, I shuffled. I felt a drunk coming on. A whiskey drunk. I wanted to smoke. Marlboros. I could feel the soft paper against my lips and could smell the match come to life. I could feel the smoke catch in my lungs. Making me cough a little. I'd watch the paper flake, then disappear into the night. Somewhere in the middle of all those thoughts my phone rang. Like my sour little prayer had been answered.

I knew before I even got the phone out of my pocket that it was Dani.

Her old Mercedes didn't feel quite as impressive the second time around. The seats weren't as warm. The windows weren't as clear. The music a little harsher. The company a little colder.

"I'm sorry you had to come into town. I didn't know there were two libraries." Saying it like that seemed to validate her frustration. "I would've hopped the PRT up to Evansdale if I'd known."

Asking her to run by the apartment first so I could grab a change of clothes and my Tele made me feel even smaller. I apologized as I got out of the car and ran up the steps. I threw a few clean shirts into the backpack with all the books and CDs in it. Right before shutting my door I noticed the notebook with all my songs in it sitting in a milk crate. And the record. I threw those into the pack too.

By the time I got back to the car she'd softened a bit. She said, "I haven't eaten all day. Are you hungry?"

"Let me take you out," I said. "Someplace where we can talk?"

"It's late, don't you think? Tomorrow I am driving to Hagerstown." A demand disguised as a question. "I've already ordered."

I hoped for pizza or Chinese. She'd called Edo Mama's and ordered sushi. Still wanting to honor my offer to take her out, I ran inside to pick it up. Forty bucks for raw fish made my neck hot. Forty bucks was most of what I had left until I sold my Marshall and pedals.

Up in Dani's apartment old floors creaked a meek welcome. Worn Persian rugs purred beneath my socks. The old electric light bulbs glowed like candles behind their dusty shades. She took my jacket and my bag and set them on the couch. I followed her into the kitchen and put the sushi on the table.

"Please, just sit. Tell me about your adventure." She poured water into a black, cast iron teapot and turned on a burner.

While she measured loose tea from a small paper sack I told her about Jamie and the fire hall and the song. She set small teacups at each place setting, nodding. I could tell when somebody wasn't listening. When she returned to the cupboard I stopped talking about it altogether and asked her what she had to do in Hagerstown.

She composed a reply. "Nothing, really." Her voice trailed off, then picked right back up, like she'd talked herself out of feeling something. "More of the same. Contracts and deals."

I didn't say anything.

She raised her voice. "Translating books is not the only way I make money, Preston. I am free to choose whom I want to work with and the type of project. It may sound vain or proud, but I don't give a damn what people think when I take a job like this." The kettle whistled, and she slid over to the stove. She let the water sit a bit before pouring it through the tea leaves. She picked the teapot up by the handle with a cloth napkin and brought it over to the table. "I say let everybody write what she wants. Nothing at all matters until a writer puts it on paper."

She picked up a bit of eel at the end of her chopsticks. "Critics think they are like gods—like I have to be grateful for their breadcrumbs. A world without writers and literature is a sad place. A world without critics is most certainly not. I remind myself of this often so I don't become bitter."

After a thoughtful pause, she added, "If it is not written on paper it never happened."

I sipped tea and listened while she picked through bits of tuna and salmon with fish eggs and mayonnaise and talked about books I never heard of. I didn't have an appetite for anything but the tea.

While she showered I drifted back into the living room. Faint singing rose over the hiss of the water. Her voice crackled like sunlight through fog. I took my Tele out of its case and settled onto her couch. After running through exercises and scales, I tried to remember my song. But the phrasing and tone eluded me. It seemed simple—an A minor, an E, and a D. Or B7. Maybe the timing dragged a few beats; something sounded weird or off. As I played I sang, humming along, playing chords and variations of chords.

On the counter Dani's phone rattled to life, screaming like a baby with a dirty diaper. I stood up and looked at the incoming call. *Clay.* He must belong to the shirts and ties hanging in the closet. The guy from the Met the night I met Mikey. I told myself I didn't know her well enough to get jealous and went back to my guitar.

"Preston Black couldn't eat and he couldn't drink…" I sang, trying to get the rest.

Dani's singing from the other side of the door came to a stop. She let the door drift open. "Should we have something to drink?" she said, wearing a pair of white towels, one wrapped around her middle, one around her head. "I have a bottle of bourbon we can try. On the shelf by the refrigerator. Glasses are above the sink."

I got up and laid the Tele back in its case. She went from the bathroom to her bedroom, then back to the bathroom. I ducked into the small kitchen. Whiskeys, absinthe, schnapps and a scotch stood like kids in gym class hoping to get picked first. "Woodford Personal Selection?" I asked, giving each label a glance.

"That's the one."

I took two short, heavy-bottomed glasses from the shelf and poured three fingers into each glass. She walked in from the bedroom wearing dark blue pajamas, like a man's, but silk, and met me in front of the couch. She sipped a little, and said, "Mmm, it's very good? It is from a banker from Munich who invests for a consortium of horse breeders from Shelbyville, Kentucky. A very easy job." Dani looked deeply into her glass between sips. "Sometimes I don't feel good about doing so many contracts instead of novels, but it lets me stay."

I didn't follow. "Stay where? Here?"

"It's very important for me to remain invisible. If my name gets around then I am 'on the radar,' and I'm not so ready for that. Doing these jobs, where clients like to be discreet, lets me remain discreet."

"Like what?" I asked, "Immigration."

"Something like that." She sipped and savored the bourbon for a moment, then finally said, "Sundays always make me sad. It's guilt, I think." She tried to smile, but her thoughts got in the way.

"Sunday's when you're supposed to do nothing. Isn't that one of the big three?" I joked, but she didn't laugh. "Commandments?"

Disregarding my comment, she said, "First, we lined up in the coat room. During the winter the custodian kept the garbage cans in there so he didn't have to go outside. The smaller children needed help putting on their coats and scarves and mittens. In a line we'd go into the gray morning, happy to be outside. All of us in the same gray coats and scarves. The only color was our pink cheeks. Far below I could see Charles Bridge. I believed it had to be better on the other side."

Just listening to those few sentences made me realize how good I had it with Mom and Pauly. I muttered, "Singing was the only reason I liked church. I'd belt out all those old songs, especially at Christmas. The nuns told my mother I should be an altar boy. My mom didn't know for sure if I'd been baptized. Soon after she began inquiring, the priest asked her not to bring me back."

Dani smiled and went on with her own memories. She said, "Sometimes I miss the smells. Especially the candles. The beeswax smells like devotion, maybe? We always arrived early so the *sestra* could pray the Rosary. Always the same pew, always next to *Christ's face is wiped by Veronica*."

She took a moment to savor the memory. When her smile faded I asked, "What did they teach you about the devil?"

"The devil? Why do you want to know about the devil?"

"It's been on my mind. I can't seem to shake the song."

She accepted the challenge with a smile. "The communists believed it was unhealthy to tolerate thoughts of the supernatural. All state art abided by their doctrine of social realism, which was meant to transform the spirit of the masses in a way that reflected the ideological rebirth of our nation."

She stared at her books like she could get answers from them with just a look. "But I always believed the devil could exist one of two ways. He was either a malicious, magical force. Perhaps a formidable opponent to all but the most powerful saints. Or, maybe the devil is a sophisticate, one who leads a literate and lavish sort of life. You know, he prefers fine food and drink and art and rich fabrics."

Like you, I thought, then immediately felt horrible for thinking it.

She took my glass and went into the kitchen for more bourbon. "Some Czechs, like our president Václav Havel, defied the party and wrote what they wanted to write. Havel wrote *Pokoušení—Temptation*. It's like *Faust*?"

I shrugged.

"In *Pokoušení*, a scientist, Foustka, practices black magic. It is all very biting and satirical, but Havel meant to show how the people maintained their beliefs despite the regime's attempts to suppress them. The devil is an informer named Fistula— means, like a birth defect, but sounds like Mephistopheles. Foustka seduces Marketa with eloquent words he learns from Fistula. But to keep pursuing black magic he must lie to everybody by claiming to be an informer also."

Her hands poked and jabbed the air like a cat toying with a mouse. "When Marketa speaks up on his behalf, to protect him, Foustka does not defend her. He cannot take a side. He has no convictions. And when he falls, he finally understands, saying that he was arrogant and he thought he could exploit the devil without signing away his own soul. But he learned the devil cannot be deceived."

I asked, "How is that different than the original Faust?"

Dani replied, "Faust was not cast into hell because his intentions were not purely malevolent or selfish. That is how he sidestepped his contract. In *Pokoušení*, Fistula says if the devil exists, he must exist in ourselves. A very different ending. But still I admire Havel. He is an excellent choice for our first president. He is proud, just like Prague. He is artistic, just like Prague. He is an achiever, and he is admired, just like Prague."

She kept talking, and I watched her, afraid that if I took my eyes off of her for even a second she'd disappear. I stared at her, unblinking almost, until she fell asleep at the other end of the couch. Then I poured myself another.

Only after I finished that drink, and another after that, and then one more, did I finally fall asleep myself. At some point Dani got up and covered me with a warm quilt, then went into her bedroom to sleep.

"Remember, no matter who wins or loses, this is a game. ABC News in New York City confirms this unspeakable tragedy..."

Tender little rye seedlings poke up through cracks in the sidewalk. Waist-high rye stretches down Central Park West and down 78th, rustling as cars roll through.

Nothing is real. This is my statement.

All these little kids playing tag in the rye, stomping it into the concrete.

The seedlings tickle my cheek.

I'm sure the large part of him must be Holden Caulfield, who is the main person in the book.

The small part of him must be the devil.

Maybe he was the type of guy who could get a bang just buying a Charter Arms .38 Special revolver. Nothing like a few bullets in the back just to find out where the ducks went in winter. Nothing phonier than bleeding to death on a cold sidewalk while the city goes on like nothing happened.

Four bullets. Just to make sure I'm dead. Seems like three too many.

Like I ever stood a chance. They all thought my world ended on a cold rooftop above Westminster one January a long time ago. Better than a cold sidewalk, just steps from my front door. Holden Caulfield has to grow up some time. Sooner would've been better than later. This morning would've been better than tonight.

Somebody will cry tonight. A wife, a son, at least. Maybe more. Somebody will miss me when I'm gone. Somebody will watch a cop car roll by, wondering 'Will he make it?'

New York City. Bleeding where whores shake and kids make. Central Park West where I lay me down to sleep. So far from Mimi and Mendips.

Don't let me down.

When they run past me to the cliff, I let them all fall. Nobody bothered to catch me. Not even St. Luke.

"Hard to go back to the game after that news flash."

John Lennon couldn't eat and he couldn't drink.

John Lennon couldn't eat and he couldn't drink.

Nothing's going to change my world.

Dolphins win.

CHAPTER SIX

Cold water rushed down the drain. The ambient glow from the streetlights brought just enough brightness into the bathroom to let me see my face half-illuminated in a dusky blue light. I had to walk the dream off.

The cold NYC sidewalk on my cheek gave me a chill. I heard sirens, saw city lights reflected in the windshields of cars on Central Park West. Yoko screamed. I even felt them lift me into the cop car. All I knew was that we were headed to Roosevelt Hospital. Christmas lights and wreaths drooped from some of the poles, but not all of them. Then I woke up.

I felt a hangover steeping in my gut. I thought maybe I could make myself throw up. The sulfur from Chapman's bullets bit the back of my nose, stuck to my sinuses.

My breath came back to me in the living room. I lay on the couch to sleep. I didn't want to wake Dani up. But out in the kitchen I heard somebody rummage through a cabinet. I rubbed my eyes and stretched and went out to apologize to her.

"Preston," John Lennon said in a very narrow voice, "Have a seat." He poured brandy into a second glass and pushed it across the table. John looked just like he did when he played *Instant Karma* on *Top of the Pops*. His hair had just been cut short and he seemed agitated, like the primal scream therapy hadn't kicked in yet.

I almost asked what he was doing here and he said, "If you knew he'd shoot, why didn't you stop him?"

My reply got caught in my throat like a hiccup, and I took a quick drink to ease it out.

Lennon said, "If it was you on the sidewalk and me on the street I'd have let you know. It's the right thing to do, right?"

"But I didn't know. I thought he was one of us."

"Oh, I see." John took a drink. He held the glass by the stem and swirled the brandy around. "One of us, huh? Like you, me, us, 'one of us'? Or one of you 'one of us'? Big difference, you know."

"I know. I meant just one of the crowd. Like, as harmless as any of us."

"That's a bit like saying he's one of us murderers and thieves, only more so." He drained his glass and poured himself another. He held the bottle toward me.

I finished mine and tipped my glass toward him.

He went on, "We're all Hitler inside. We're all Christ inside. I'm not keen on the idea, but it's true, isn't it? We've all got a little bit of the devil in us."

"I guess. I always thought it was just me. Before the song and all this, it wasn't so complex. I played my music and tried to be decent."

I could tell by the way he leaned over the table he'd grown frustrated with me. He struggled to keep his voice low so Dani couldn't hear. "That's just it, though, what've you done besides just being yourself? If you'd have seen the gun would you have tried to stop him?"

"If I'd have seen the gun I would've jumped on him and held him on the ground. But I didn't see it. I wasn't even there. I'm sorry." I felt really horrible. Like I was personally responsible for his murder.

"It's too late now, isn't it? I mean, I'm over here, all... And you're over there, all..."

"I know. I wonder what it would've been like if they could've saved you at the hospital?"

"What it would've been like? Is that really what you mean? Or did you mean to say, 'would we have gotten back together'? That's all anybody wants to know. But none of it matters, I suppose."

He was mostly right, so I didn't say anything.

"Look, if you have to smile when you don't want to smile you do it, because nobody gets hurt, right?" He pushed his glass away, like he was finished, so I did the same thing. "But when somebody's going to pull a gun, or push your girl in front of a train or steal your mum's purse you have got to make a choice whether you want to get involved or not. It's not as easy as forcing a smile."

I nodded.

"Nodding is the same as smiling. It's easy. The hard thing would've been to have kept your friend Stu from leaving."

"I tried. I begged him, man. I went up to the university and got him info on the GI Bill. He'd made up his mind all ready."

"So you saw the gun, but didn't try hard enough to stop it going off. What'll you do when you have to stop a bullet from getting your brother?"

"Are you telling me something is going to happen to one of them?"

He scratched the stubble on his chin. "Let's just say I'm showing you the gun."

He stood up and pulled his scarf tight. I wanted to shake his hand but he walked by like I was going to ask for an autograph. I followed him to the front door. On his way out he said, "Do you remember what Jimi said?"

I didn't know who he was talking about.

"Didn't think so. What if you saw the gun and it was pointed at you?" His eyebrows went up above the rim of his glasses.

The steps creaked as he made his way down. He shoved his hands into his front pockets just before disappearing into the darkness.

I went into the bathroom, shut the door, and with the light still off, tried looking into the mirror.

After a few minutes Dani knocked.

"It's open," I said, afraid of my voice, and sat on the edge of the tub.

She sat down next to me without saying anything. For a few minutes she just rubbed my back. Soft strokes along my shoulders. When she got up to leave she held her hand against my cheek for a moment. She said, "I have to get ready."

I studied the septic patterns of spearmint and blue sky tiles in the floor for another minute. Thinking about the dream made me remember that I loved Pauly and had to call him. Sooner, rather than later, before the rift turned into an ocean.

Over the next hour Dani transformed herself from the girl I saw last night to the woman I met at Isaac's somewhere between Mudhoney and the Pixies. Dressing for the Lower East Side instead of Sunnyside. While she put herself together I threw on clean jeans and a new shirt and waited on the couch. I flipped through my old notebook and saw more than a few starts of half-decent songs, and one or two that may have been worthy of a revisit. They were honest and simple. I wondered how they'd sound on a record, if people would like them, if I'd be able to ever make a living playing my songs.

My phone buzzed, and since Dani was busy primping in the other room, I figured it had to be Pauly. The text said <music belongs to everybody. It doesn't always have to be a suit who decides how much it should cost. Remember what we talked about last night.>

I stared at the text. I knew who it was from, and it wasn't Father James.

I hit REPLY and thought of a way to ask without coming across as crazy. When I realized there was no easy way to do that, I typed <JOHN?> and hit send.

Dani's announcement that she was ready to go broke the spell. I carried her bag down the dark steps, and helped her into the cold car. I shivered the whole way to town. The air felt really crisp at seven a.m. Mountaineer Doughnuts was the only place in town open that early. Pearl, an older lady with a bad dye job, sat us at a booth that looked out onto Spruce. But the windows were cold, so we strayed to the warm end of the booth.

Dani whispered, "All women in Prague have hair the same color as her." She pointed at the waitress. "When I was little I thought this was strange. But a *sestra* told me that because of chemical shortages at the factories, this is the only color available. I wonder if there is a shortage here now, too."

I said, "Well, don't ask her."

When the waitress returned, Dani ordered egg whites and rye toast. I got buckwheats and sausage. She said mine looked better and helped herself to half. But I wasn't hungry anymore, and sipped my coffee. I asked if she'd have more tea.

She said, "I will have to leave soon."

"You can have dessert, right? Maybe a doughnut?" I wanted to ask her about the dreams.

But she didn't reply. Her weak smile, apologetic and endearing, reminded me that I already knew she had places to be today. Reminded me that I was not the only guy she spent time with. She said, "Tonight we can pick up here. I have a long drive. Unless the client gets chatty or the weather gets worse I'll be back in town this evening."

I nodded and looked out the window at the dark morning.

She checked her phone and said, "Perhaps the dreams are a way for you to move on? Your mind is clearing itself of the images and ideas it no longer needs."

"I suppose. But it wasn't the content of the dreams as much as the realism. I felt the cold sidewalk against my cheek."

"I stopped remembering my dreams when I realized my dreams would always be dreams. For me, not dreaming became an act of escape." She sipped her tea. "Out of spite, a *sestra* who thought I dreamt too much told me everything—how I was left in the *chléb košík*—like a bread basket? A small door in the gate with a bell, so a mother can leave a baby like a milkman leaving milk."

"That's a very sad story."

She changed expressions, forcing a laugh. "Who could be happy with so many memories hanging in the air like clouds? By nature, I am not a happy person. I wasn't raised to know happy, only right or wrong. Always asking myself, 'Is it a sin?' anytime I deviated from the sestras' ideals. But I want to pursue happiness." She checked her face in a small mirror she took from her purse. "If it hadn't been for the revolution I'd never have had the opportunity."

"Have you found happiness?"

"I am pursuing it." She smiled. "And I do not plan to stop pursuing it, even after I find it."

She pulled a crisp twenty from a thin black wallet, folded it lengthwise and set it on the table.

I said, "I feel like just as I get a glimpse of who you really are it's time for you to go." I stood and helped her with her coat and scarf then waited for a kiss. She cupped my chin in her hand and gave me a tiny peck on the cheek. Hoping for more, I followed her outside.

The cold poked through my shirt like the wind was blowing needles into my skin. "I guess you'll give me a call when you want to see me."

I held open her door. My fingers almost stuck to the handle.

"Would you like to see me tonight?" she said, with mock disinterest.

"Uh, yeah. I'd love to."

"Then I will call you."

"Be safe. And think warm thoughts." I shut the door and held my hand up.

Back inside, I spiked my coffee with a little creamer and took out my old notebook. The dry-rotted gumband that held it together broke when I slid it over the cover. I tried to knot it, but it broke again. My fingertips smelled like rubber.

Pearl refilled my coffee, saying something about taking a table 'from real customers.' As the sun got higher, students started to roll in and I kind of saw what she'd meant. At ten 'til nine she swiped the twenty and cleared the table of everything but my notebook and the cup of coffee, which I held in my hand. As I put my coat on, my mom came out from the back. Right off the bat she asked where the girl had gone.

"To work."

"Where's she work?" She tied her apron and put her pad into a pocket. "A bar?"

"From home. But she had to meet a client."

"What'd you do to Pauly? He called me and said you two had words."

"I didn't do anything to Pauly. Pauly needs to grow up."

"He said the same thing about you." She put her hands on her hips. She'd already picked a side.

"You really believe it was my fault. For a second I thought you were playing." I gathered my notebook.

"The devil's keeping you from getting saved. You can't pick the time when you can be saved. Think on that." She went into the kitchen before I had a chance to walk away.

The sidewalk along Spruce looked a hell of a lot sunnier than Walnut, so I walked that way. As soon as I crossed High, just up from the Warner Theater, I saw

Mick's Caddy sitting out back, shiny as a ripe apple. Chrome bumpers shined like salt couldn't stick to it.

I strolled down and rapped on the shop window.

Mick whipped around like nine in the morning was prime time for smash-and-grabs. He had a lot to learn about gangstas and meth freaks.

"Look at this precious little sunbeam," Mick said snapping the locks off.

"Lock it," he said as it swung shut behind me. "You hiding from the law? Can't think of any other reason why you'd be here this early."

"Stayed with Dani last night." I set the Tele by the counter and leaned my bag against it so it wouldn't fall over. I left my coat on.

"Dani's a woman? It's not Daniel?" He studied me over the top of his glasses.

"Danicka."

"She Polack?"

"Czech."

"Same."

"Said the Dago."

"How long you been seeing her?" Now that things had gotten decidedly less interesting he went back to his paperwork. He rifled through pink layaway receipts. Counting his eggs before they could hatch.

"I met Dani at Isaac's last week before a lesson."

"Well, call your brother and tell him that. Son of a bitch called me last night at home and asked if I'd heard from you."

"Sorry about that. I'll give him a ring."

"You hiding from him?"

"Why would I have to hide from Pauly? He's all wrapped up in A.A. and his new job anyway." I'd hoped for a better transition to ask what I wanted to ask. But without one, I went on. "I wondered if it'd be okay to bring a few things down to you today."

"What kind of 'things' are you talking about?"

"To sell. My Marshall and some effects."

"Jesus, Preston. Didn't we have this discussion? You know what things have been like around here." Mick set his glasses on the counter. "You hurting for money?"

"Jamie poisoned me. I've really been thinking about a new guitar."

"Let me guess: a Gibson Hummingbird. 1964. Natural finish. Four grand."

"Martin. D-28. Brazilian rosewood. I don't care when it was born."

"I got a goddamned shop full of Guilds you never even touch." He was mad. I'd have been insulted too if I had a room full of cats and all anybody ever wanted was a dog. "No, I don't want to take a look at your stuff."

"Just thought I'd give you first crack."

"So you're going to pawn it. May as well throw it in the river." He played with his receipts. "Don't expect a cent over fifteen percent below Blue Book. And when you little bastards make up and get your band back together don't ask for a cent less than what's on the tag. I'd only do this for you and my grandkids, and for you never again. This is a one-time deal."

"I do appreciate it, Mick. I really do. I wouldn't have asked if it wasn't important."

"Well, there won't be a next time. Do you even know what Brazilian goes for? You're going to need a lot more than an amp and some stomp boxes. Are you clean enough to sell blood?"

"I get it."

"I hope so. The least you could do is not interfere with my customers." He rapped the glass counter with his knuckles. "Let's get a move on before I open up."

I left, pulling the door shut behind me. A new guitar came with too many strings attached. Too many questions. If it hadn't been for the song and Jamie Collins, who Mick'd set me up with in the first place, none of this would even matter. Maybe the guitar felt important to me because it represented a new direction—a last chance to realize a life in music, a time when I wouldn't have to rely on anybody else to play.

Up in the apartment the only thing that had changed since the last time I'd been there was the note on the table. Pauly wanted to talk. *So what?*

In my room I took a long look at all the stuff piled on the floor, making two mental lists—the things I'd grab in the event of a fire, and everything else. It only took a minute to figure out the Tele and the Twin were all I needed. Everything else was sunroofs and leather seats.

All my pedals fit into a milk crate—the Crybaby, the Big Muff, the Boss digital delay, phase shifters, reverbs, tuners and all the rest. I carried it to the bottom of the stairs. Back in my room I eyed up the Marshall cab and head. Before I could talk myself out of it I rolled it down the hall, through the kitchen to the door.

After I backed it down the steps I sat on the curb, puffing a little. Cold air rushed down my throat. Mucus came from my sinuses to warm the cold air, making my cough worse. Pauly must've had a hell of a time getting it up the steps, meaning he must've been pretty pissed.

Rolling it down to High wasn't much of a big deal. I set the milk crate on top of the Marshall and started pushing. Up the wheelchair ramp and down the street. When the signal said WALK I pushed it onto the salt-covered street as fast as I could so gravity didn't pull it down Walnut through The Stink's window or into the Mon. I guess I'd seen people pushing weirder things down High. Couches mostly.

An upright piano once. A bunch of pro-life assholes pushing a coffin filled with fake blood and baby dolls.

When I got to the store Mick had a customer, a college student who kept trying to convince Mick to let him play a Custom Shop Strat. By the time I had all my stuff in the shop Mick had him sitting down with a Made in Mexico Strat.

"Give me a few minutes," Mick said as he rounded the counter.

While Mick tallied, I looked at the used gear on the wall like it was framed works of art in a gallery. Pauly's bass hung there like a taxidermied jackalope.

"Here's my offer." Mick slid the slip, face down, across the counter.

"Eleven fifty?"

"Two fifty for the pedals, four hundred for the head and five for the cabinet."

"Eleven fifty." That was how much a lifetime of saving, scrounging and collecting was worth.

"I'm not a bank, son. I've been as generous with you and your brother as I can be." Mick didn't act nearly as agitated as I expected him to be. "Business isn't personal."

"Sorry, Mick. Thank you. I'll take it." I held out my hand.

Mick gave it a firm squeeze.

"Still a long way off. I can always sell blood."

"Or sperm. Get paid for what you already do for free, right?"

"I guess. I'm going to run up to the bank real quick. I'll clean all this up and stock it for you."

"That isn't necessary." Mick started to fill out my slip.

"I know. But I want to show you how much I appreciate you helping me out."

"See if you think that when you see the mark-ups."

I went to the door.

Mick asked, "What do you need this guitar for? A guitar is just a hunk of wood somebody saw fit to take a saw to." He slid the check to the end of the counter.

"I know, Mick."

The door shut behind me, sealing out the cold. I never let the check hit my pocket. I never felt like it was my money. I asked for a deposit slip and let them have the whole thing.

When I got back Mick was on the phone again. *Must be a morning thing.* I grabbed his push broom and went out to sweep the sidewalk while he talked. But the cold made my nose run and I couldn't stand more than a few minutes outside.

As soon as the door closed behind me Mick said, "A buddy of mine has your guitar. Lou said it's a sixty-eight. Brazilian. An old lady played it at church once a week, fifty-two times a year from the day she bought it 'til the day she died."

"How much?"

He held up four fingers.

I nodded, and without thinking, asked, "How much would you give me for the Twin?"

"Jesus Christ, Preston," he stammered. "Not enough. Not what you're asking."

"What about the Tele then, too?"

"Absolutely not. I can't. You're throwing too much away. Sell it on eBay. I'm not going to keep signing checks for this. You're being irrational."

Mick watched the kid who'd been playing the Mexican Strat hang the guitar back on its hook. When the kid walked past he told Mick he'd be back, but Mick just kind of nodded, then folded his arms, and added, "Hotheaded like Pauly. This is a pound of flesh, is what this is."

"Well, I'm not going to push it then. Especially if it makes me seem ungrateful for what you've done."

Mick stared at me, his face empty of expression. Finally he asked, "I understand passion and drive, but I can't see where you're going with this."

"I've been thinking about that a lot myself. That gear meant something to me, but not enough to take with me if I ever made it out of West Virginia. For some reason I feel like things as I knew them are about to come to an end. Like, this situation, here in town, with Pauly and the same old places, will cease to be. I figure the universe is telling me nobody's going to pay to see a thirty-five-year-old nobody singing covers while they put down cheap PBRs. I have to make my own way now. I have to be able to put everything I own into a pack and split when the time comes. My dad's out there somewhere, and I'm going to find him. And I'm going to write songs that are going to make me famous. And I'm not going to quit until I make it, man. I can't, Mick. I let Pauly slow me down. Him dropping me was the best thing that could happen. It's scary, yeah. But it's mine. And I'm going to go down singing. I haven't been trained for anything else in this world except singing and playing a guitar. I can't build houses, I can't teach school and I can't write books. This is it, Mick. This is all I got. And you've been more than instrumental in helping me see the light. The hours I spent in that back room teaching kids pentatonic scales have been some of the best I've ever had. But I want more. Finally, I can say it. I want more than this world's given me. And I figure it's up to me to get out there and take it." My eyes dropped, like they sometimes do when maybe you let just a little too much of yourself out for everybody to see and you wish you could just take it all back.

"So you're serious? You're not going to stop until you make it?"

"That's right, Mick. I'm not going to stop." My phone buzzed.

"Then I'll lend you the money. Bring the Twin and the Tele down and I'll give you the difference for the Martin. But it's a loan and your shit is collateral. I want every cent of it back. Every cent. Hear me? And I want you to walk out of here with that Tele in six months. You have until August. Not September. Not October. That's your guitar. You've put such an imprint on it that I'd never be able to put a price tag on it. So you will pay me back. All of it. By August."

"I promise." I walked out, knowing it'd all be different the next time I stepped through Mick's door. It felt like graduation day all over again. Except today I wasn't going to end up laying in puke in an empty above-ground pool. I had a clean slate ahead of me instead of a resume of laziness and bad intentions. I had ten years' worth of knowledge and the desire to put that knowledge toward something more significant than the glorified karaoke I'd been practicing since eleventh grade. If it meant moving out of the apartment, out of the city and out of West-fucking-Virginia then that's what I'd do.

I checked my text. It was from Joe Strummer. Had to be. It said <if you're going to make it in music you have to be sodding stupid.>

And when I rolled that old Fender Twin back into Mick's he didn't say anything. He bent over, and rolled it toward the back room. But not toward storage, he took out his key ring and opened his office door. He rolled the Twin next to the tweed case that held my Tele.

"Can I get something real quick?"

I put the Tele case onto the Twin and flipped the latches open. The guitar seemed really quiet, like a body in a casket. I reached in and took off the leather strap Pauly had gotten me for Christmas. I rolled it up and put it in my pocket.

Mick let the lid fall, snapped the latches shut and stood it against the wall. I backed onto the sales floor, maybe trying to change my mind. Mick followed, and locked the door.

He said, "Lou's expecting us. Bring your checkbook."

I nodded quietly. Not because I'd lost my words. I nodded because for the first time in as long as I cared to remember, I was a guitarist without a guitar.

May as well have been dead.

I sent my four o'clock into the shop to pay as I wrote his lesson out.

"This kid getting any better?" Mick yelled from the front, smiling. It was his favorite joke. "Or should we start charging him double?"

I carried the Strat I'd used for the lesson out toward the counter. "Ha. No, if he practices more he'll be fine." I handed Matthew his lesson.

When the kid left, the guitar shop seemed suddenly empty. Mick went back to his newspaper. Across the street a Jeep Cherokee slid up to a meter. When the belt squealed Mick looked up. "Just take it in the back," was all he said.

Pauly waited for traffic to clear, taking a long drag on his cigarette before flicking it into the gutter. Pauly used to look like Freddy Mercury strutting across the stage at Wembley. Now he had his work clothes on. He'd gotten a haircut. He didn't look like Pauly. Now he looked like Freddy Mercury from the "These Are the Days of Our Lives" video.

I held the door open. "We'll go into the back," I said as he stepped onto the sidewalk.

"There he is," Mick said. "What do they got you doing now?"

"A lot of short overnighters. Kentucky a lot. Going to start making Nashville runs. The guy they hired with me made a furniture delivery out there and forgot to set his parking brake. Guess he destroyed a Waffle House." Pauly wiped his feet and stepped up to the counter. "The paper ran a story and everything. So I'm picking up a lot of extra hours."

I wiped Mick's Strat down with a chamois. Pauly shuffled along behind me, stopping to run his finger down the neck of his old bass. He flipped the price tag around.

He waited for me to put the Strat on its hook. "Where's the Tele?" he asked.

"Long story," I said, and led him into the back. I motioned for him to have a seat.

"Long story, like it's really a long story? Or long story, like you just don't want to talk about it?" Pauly leaned forward, resting his elbows on his knees, fingers clasped.

"A little of both. The main thing is that it's not really my guitar at the moment. Like that story about the girl that cuts her hair for a Christmas present? Maybe I don't remember it exactly."

"Well, sorry to hear that." He paused, for what must've seemed to him like an appropriate amount of time before changing subjects. "I came down here to talk to you about our situation. My situation, really. I guess I'm the one who threw a wrench into the works. My sponsor said I had to talk to you."

"Since when do you listen to him?"

"Since I really want to try to clean up. Since I'm tired of being a fuck-up."

For a second I waited for a punch line.

I said, "Just like that?"

"C'mon. Don't be like that. Scott said maybe I could help you. Like, I could invite you to a few meetings with me or something." Pauly looked like Johnny Utah at the end of *Point Break* after Bodhi realized he was a cop.

"Help me? You want to help me? Then you shouldn't have left me hanging like that, especially after I told Mikey we'd play that show. You know how it looks having to tell him I'm backing out? He's a student, man. And now he probably thinks I'm just a huge fuck-up."

"I am sorry about that. Scott just said I needed to stop putting myself in those situations if I was going to stay sober. He said that I could be in a position where I could really help you. He said I needed to stop being—"

"Jesus Christ, man. Listen to you. Can you even start a sentence without mentioning your sponsor?"

"Don't be like that. Seriously. I'm trying here. It's not easy. I got this job and I really want to keep it. I'm tired of Ramen and PBR two times a day. Being sober is like coming out of a fog. Food tastes different. I want you to know what it feels like."

"But what if I'm not an alcoholic? Did you ever think of that?" I tried to lose the edge in my voice. "You know what I loved, more than anything? Looking across the stage and seeing you smile. Seeing you with a nice buzz working those little fingers of yours. That's when I knew you were my brother. So I had what you're talking about. And I'm sorry if you didn't feel the same way because I thought you did. I thought we were in all this together."

"I'm sorry. How many times can I say it? I can't set foot in any of those places ever again. Jails, institutions or death are my only options if I pick up again. Look, why don't you come home with me tonight? You can come down to the church with me and I'll introduce you to Scott. He's a really great guy. He knows what he's talking about."

"I'm sure he's really helping you out. And I'm happy for you. I mean that. But I can't get my dick up for anybody who'd let you walk away from your old life and family. He doesn't know you. And what was wrong with the way things were? You weren't drinking at any of these shows recently and I wasn't trying to put a beer in your hand."

"Goddamnit, Preston. It was a lot of fun five years ago. But I'm seeing places and making money. I'm going to save for a house so when I finally meet the woman I want to marry I don't have to tramp up those shit steps into that shit apartment. I'm sorry this is so hard for you. But this is how it's going to be."

"Waffle Houses? Are those the places you're seeing? Truck stops? This is classic Pauly—you stomp around like Godzilla, but when it's time to put the brakes on you decide."

"Preston… Whatever. I'll see you around." Pauly stood, zipped up his coat and stepped into the hallway. "Look, I'm really sorry you had to sell your guitar. I know how much it meant to you." He went into the store, said goodbye to Mick then left.

When I got to the counter Mick said, "Preston, I'm afraid you're skidding down a long hill. But instead of slowing to a stop, I'm afraid you're going to burst into flames before you even get to the bottom. You need to find a way to keep that from happening, son."

Clouds moved in as we rolled over Cheat Lake. Really high clouds, pink and orange glowing from within, like fireworks in a fog. Dead mountains hibernated next to the dead lake. Ice revealed itself mostly at the edges. The rest of Cheat Lake may as well have been made of concrete. It didn't reflect. It didn't twinkle. If somebody jumped off the bridge they'd come apart without even chipping that ice.

We got off the interstate and Mick pulled up to a pump at the BP.

"Let me get this for you," I said.

"You just pump. I'm going to run inside. You want anything?" Mick adjusted his driving cap.

I could've downed a few pepperoni rolls and some Cool Ranch Doritos or a gas station kolbassi. And a pop. "You getting anything?"

"I'm getting a coffee."

"Then I'll have a coffee. Thanks, Mick." I walked around the big Caddy and flipped the gas tank open. A few tiny snowflakes fell lazily through the flat fluorescent light. They took forever to reach the ground. My teeth chattered. I put my hands into my armpits and pulled my shoulders into my body as I pumped.

"You have to pee?" Mick yelled across the parking lot and rows of idling cars. He had a coffee in each hand and held the big glass door open with his foot.

People watched, perhaps waiting to see if I did, in fact, have to pee. "I'm good. Thanks, Mick." The pump clicked to a stop. I shook the last few drops of gas out of the hose.

Mick got into the car. I hung the hose and rushed around the other side. When I pulled the door open Mick said, "You could've gotten the windows since I'm making a special trip all the way up here for you."

"Sure thing."

I was almost halfway to the squeegee when he said, "Just get in," with a laugh.

I put the coffee between my knees and pulled the door shut.

The Caddy rolled onto the shoulders of Chestnut Ridge, past small apartment complexes, through laurel thickets like the ones I'd seen on the way to Davis, around a magnificent horseshoe bend. We'd come this way for gigs in PA a few times. Stu always called the big crook Dead Man's Curve. In a few years the new highway would be finished, and I'd never have a reason to come this way again.

"The wedding soup line," Mick said. He tooted his horn a few times. "Feels like I'm going home."

"What?"

"You can get wedding soup in the Olive Gardens up here."

"Not in Morgantown?"

"No. Did you ever try? They act like you're asking for erbazzone."

"No. I don't think so."

Mick sipped his coffee. "You know what you get in Kentucky when you order a white pizza? Alfredo sauce."

"Savages," I said. "I almost said Royale with Cheese."

Mick laughed, mostly at the first part.

After we crossed the Mason-Dixon the road pulled away from Chestnut Ridge. The mountains stared down at me. Clouds moved in, obscuring the tops. Snow drifted across the road. Like gauze. All of a sudden, I felt very small, very alone.

I didn't say anything until we passed Rich's Farm. "Our permanent residence Thursday through Saturday from September up through Halloween. We played loads of 'scary' songs. Black Sabbath. Misfits. Some old Soundgarden and Metallica. The best part was watching members of the Mountaineer Maniacs making out in the parking lot while we ripped through 'Thing That Should Not Be.'"

I turned and watched as we passed. "Pauly hooked up with a vampire who worked the haunted hayride one year. Fishnets, jet black hair and a shit load of eye liner. She wore this shitty perfume that smelled like mangoes or something. Skin pale as baby powder. Almost translucent. By Thanksgiving I realized she wasn't wearing a costume. Of course she majored in Victorian Lit or something. Pauly said she freaked him out and he dumped her just before Christmas. The next spring we got a bat in our apartment, and I told him I detected the faint scent of mango." I laughed.

Perhaps trying to hang on to the memory for as long as I could, I said, "That was it, Mick. Our Fillmore. Our Madison Square Garden. Some of the biggest crowds we ever played to were in that parking lot." I didn't look back, afraid I'd turn into the Appalachian equivalent of a pillar of salt—a tree stand or an old Chevelle up on blocks.

Mick glanced at the rows of unsold Christmas trees, but held his tongue.

"We opened for Rusted Root one year. Remember them?" I gulped down the rest of my coffee.

"My family is from up this way," Mick said, like I wasn't even sitting there in the car with him. It wasn't so much that I intentionally tried to fill dead air for the sake of filling dead air, maybe I just wanted him to know that we had made money once upon a time. And that I could do it again. But once he changed the subject he never went back. "My grandfather came to work in the coal mines. Moved from Jersey about a hundred years ago. Worked for a nickel a ton. He lost two brothers on the same afternoon in two separate accidents. But my family stayed up in Uniontown for years. My cousins have a restaurant. They make amazing manicotti. And dandelion wine. They used to have dances. Made a killing on weekends. You'd have loved it. Day after day in clubs, in high school gyms and church basements just playing, playing, playing."

"How'd you end up in Morgantown, then?"

"Followed my wife. Her people are from down here. Met her at a dance at Shady Grove. It was this little trolley park with a swimming pool. She hooked me so she'd never have to pay to hear me again. Good thing I ended up down there, though. Uniontown's a one guitar shop kind of town."

"Is that where you met Lou?" I asked.

"No, met Lou at Duquesne. Tried to get a music scholarship. They have a group, the Tamburitzans, but you have to be Slovak. With a name like Dino I couldn't pass. So I got stuck playing Italian festivals all summer long. And that's where I met Lou. We were two kids way out of our element. But things are different today. Kids don't want to hear live music. I don't know how you can connect with a disc jockey."

"You can't, Mick. We tried adding a keyboard one year to diversify. Everything we played ended up sounding like Duran Duran."

Mick didn't say anything, and I kind of felt like I'd talked myself into a dead end. So I spent the next twenty minutes thinking about my new guitar.

Mick and Lou apparently both came from the old-school tradition of dubbing a business with their first name. Neon Fender signs and wall-to-wall guitars jammed the small shop. Basically Lou renovated a house and stocked it with guitars. T-shirts hung on a hook by the window, fading in the cold winter light. Just behind the sheet music a cardboard cutout of Yngwie Malmsteen hid a glass display case with a pair of beat acoustics and an old Jazzmaster. I looked for my Martin.

Mick led me past a counter full of strings and picks displayed like salami and capicoli. Mellow notes came from a hot amp in a back room, reminding me of the stuff Joe Negri used to play on *Mr. Rogers' Neighborhood*. The guitar had a sweet tone, like tea with too much honey.

"Hey, hey! Dino Michelino! Live in Uniontown, PA, for one night only." Lou put the old Gretsch on a stand and stood up. Mick held out his arms and embraced Lou in a big, manly hug with a lot of back patting.

"Tennessean," Mick ran his thumb along the headstock of the guitar Lou had just been playing. White purfling lining the f-holes really helped the old wood grain pop. A Bigsby tailpiece hung on the bottom like tail fins on an old Plymouth. "You've had this guitar put away for years, huh? What's the occasion?"

"Reducing stock. Who's your protégé?" Lou grabbed my hand. His fingers were big, calloused. Made my hands feel like a little kid's.

"Preston Black. Pleased to meet you."

He put his hand on my shoulder. "You should be famous with a name like that."

Mick pinched my cheek. "He's trying, Lou. He's trying."

Lou asked, "Presley or Costello?"

"Costello. Please."

Lou said, "That's what's wrong with this world," and made his way to the front of the store, squeezing between Mick and me. He came back with a blue guitar case that looked a little like a suitcase my mom had. The one time I was going to run away from home I filled it with comic books and my Winnie the Pooh. Pauly dumped Cherokee Red into it and mom had to throw everything away. Except for Pooh, who she threw in the washer. He came out more pink than anything else.

Mick said, "Well, stop sucking your thumb and crack her open so we can see what's in there."

Lou offered me the stool he'd been sitting on.

I set the case on the floor and flipped open the latches. My hands shook. It smelled just like Jamie's, like sweet wood, whatever that was.

Lou said, "Does he know what to do with it?"

Mick said, "You hold the skinny part with your left hand. It's called 'the neck'."

Lou said, "Those silver things are the frets. Those are where the different notes come from."

Mick said, "Try 'Mary Had a Little Lamb'."

Lou said, "'Twinkle, Twinkle, Little Star'. You know how it goes?"

Straight wood grain ran across the flat top. The finish was smooth like Stevie Ray's "Little Wing." Only up on the headstock, where the previous owner had tied off a strap, did the guitar give any indication that it had been around for forty years. The bridge hadn't begun to lift, and the intonation was perfect.

I touched my pick to the big E string and strummed. Sound boomed from the flattop. I chugged on the E, fretted an E7, then played an A. I barred a minor and played it up the neck, dropped down a string and fretted a minor 7 and played back down. I strummed a G really hard, then a C, then picked out the pedal point intro to "Friend of the Devil," played a verse, a chorus, then picked out the intro again.

Mick and Lou got bored real fast and drifted out to the front of the store. Somebody flipped on an amp, plugged in, and played a really loud "Funiculì, Funiculà." Mick yelled, "Sorry."

I turned my back toward the shop. Over my shoulder I heard Lou come back in, and I turned. Lou said, "Let me know if you need anything," and slid a pocket door three quarters of the way shut.

"Thanks, Lou." I put the Martin to the test. The Beatles, Clapton, Screaming Trees, Rise Against. I ran through fragments of scales, played some Randy Rhodes, some Django-esque chord progressions. I even played a little "Stairway" just because. The sharp frets felt like they'd cut my fingers if I pushed too hard.

I played some of the stuff from Davis, "Wildwood Flower" and my song. Imagining how the guitar would sound with a banjo, or Jamie's fiddle, wasn't easy. So I sang along, trying to imitate the range of the violin. I played "Blackbird," a semi-lame, acoustic "London Calling," and "Nice Dreams." But no matter what I did the guitar didn't feel at all like I wanted it to. I shook the needles out of my hands.

Pain in my wrists spread into my fingertips. After clenching fists and cracking my knuckles I hammered the strings, choked the neck and squeezed the body to get the sound I'd been anticipating. But nothing made this Jamie's guitar. I couldn't believe I'd given up the Tele for this. This block of wood and a set of strings. Just like Mick said. I wiped the neck off with my flannel, then put it back into the case.

From the other side of the door came the sound of guitar accompanied by a squeezebox. My ears rang a little from the Martin, but the amount of noise coming from the front stunned me. Lou sang, "...*Tu vuo' fa' l'americano, mericano, mericano...*" and laughed while Mick plucked crazy jazz chords.

Lou had all kinds of vintage stuff—a few Gibson archtops and acoustics, two Les Pauls—a seventies and an eighties, a Tele that could've been my Tele's sister. On the bottom row he had all kinds of unusual stuff. A few Peavies, an old Kramer and a pair of B.C. Riches. I pulled a square-shouldered Gibson acoustic off the wall and propped it up on my knee. It sounded like I'd pulled it out of a deep sleep. Like I was pinching its nose. I put it back on the wall.

Lou did have a few Martins on the back wall. A pair of cutaway acoustic-electrics, something made out of birch and a twelve string. Nothing that interested me.

I picked up the case and carried it with me to the front of the shop.

"You didn't break it, did you?" Mick looked up from a white Jazzmaster, the one I saw in the glass case when we first came in. His hair stood at wild angles; he looked like he'd just gotten caught making out in the backseat of his dad's car. His glasses had slid so far down his nose he nearly had to look up to the ceiling to see me. "What's wrong with it?"

"Nothing. It's just not what I'm looking for. It didn't feel right." I held the case out in front of me like it was a puppy I'd hit with the Jeep.

"Didn't feel right?" Lou seemed concerned. He took the case from me and set it behind the counter.

"It felt stiff. A little dead. I'd been expecting something a little livelier. I don't know. It just didn't feel like Jamie's." I put my hands into my pockets and looked at the other stuff he had on the walls.

"Well, come over here. Take a look in the case. I have another 28 in here, I think. It's either a 28 or a 35. Not too many folks around here willing to drop five grand on a guitar."

I said, "I'm not sure if I can bring myself to do it."

"It's a fifty-seven. Brazilian, of course." He took it out like it had been crafted out of uranium. "A few cracks… one here by the pickguard and one here on the back. It's been in here a long time." Lou apologized and blew the dust off the guitar's shoulders, then gave it a quick tuning.

The finish looked like it'd been dragged behind a bus then kicked a few times. The pickguard curled a bit at the pointy end. A huge chip on the headstock made it look a little lopsided. The finish on the neck felt thinner than Dani's thigh-highs. Where the other Martin had a few belt buckle scratches on the back, this one looked like it'd been hacked with a belt sander.

"Sit down." Mick pushed a stool over with his foot.

"'Whiskey in a Jar' on three. And a one, and a two…" Lou tapped out a quick tempo with his foot, then played a few droning notes on his squeezebox, making it sound a bit like bagpipes.

Mick plucked out a quick melody with his fingers, using triads and parts of chords in a way I'd never really seen. Like, he fingerpicked the notes really fast, but the sustain let the full sound of the chord materialize.

Chords boomed from the old wood like thunder from a mountaintop. The bass E made my carpals quiver. The percussiveness of the notes—no lie—made my heart palpitate. The guitar's neck felt hot, and it squirmed like a black snake in a five-gallon bucket. The body buzzed beneath the boom, maybe from all the cracks, but the depth of tonality sounded greater than anything I'd ever experienced with any guitar. The fucking thing sounded like it was plugged into a tube amp.

My ears rang. I had a hard time believing three people with only one plugged in instrument among them could be so loud.

"The kid can pick. He'll do all right." Lou put the squeezebox into the glass case and shook out his hands.

Mick asked, "This one 'feels' right?" He reached for it.

"I suppose it does."

Mick strummed a little, then picked out a few runs. "That's the ugliest guitar I've ever seen." He handed it back.

Something in the body rattled. I thought maybe somebody'd put a pickup in there, and took a peek for loose wires.

Lou said, "Rattlesnake beads. The guy who sold me the guitar put them in there. An old-timer from up by Indian Head with a really bad harelip got out of prison and needed a little cash. That's how the guitar ended up here. I thought they were kind of cool so I left them in there."

"What was he in prison for?"

"Accused of murder he swore he didn't commit. The judge released him when the supposed victim turned up alive out in Allentown. Sold the guitar because it was 'trouble.'"

I handed the guitar back to Lou. He wiped the strings with a chamois and set it in a stand on the floor. I said, "Give me a minute to think about it," and went into the back. I looked at my phone and saw that I'd missed two calls.

I called Dani back immediately. The phone rang six times, then went to voicemail. I figured she was in the shower and went back out to join Mick and Lou. Lou looked ready to deal. Mick strummed the Jazzmaster.

"You like it?" Lou asked Mick.

"It's beautiful. Where'd you find it?"

"Down in South Hills. A buddy of mine's closing his doors. Big chain store went in, put him out. Better hope they don't make it down your way." Lou tapped his pen on the counter to make his point.

"You buying that?" I asked, surprised that he desired something more than the world's greatest scaloppini. Making me think he made the trip just for me was pretty smart of him.

"I am, Pres. I loved my Jazzmaster. Have to show you pictures." Mick's expression said he was thinking about the good old days. "You ready to do some business?"

"What do you want for the Martin?" Haggling ranked up there with skiing and knitting on the list of things I sucked at. "It's in poor shape. A lot of cracks, may even need a neck reset."

"Yeah, but it's a lot older than the other. Age equals value and I think this one has a lot of character. Plus, you like it. You really like it. Blue book's about $9500, mint, which this one isn't. Tell you what… I can give it to you for what I'd have let the other one go for." Lou gave Mick a wink.

Mick watched to see what I'd do next.

I comically rubbed my chin, then countered, "How long's it been hanging there?"

"That's my boy," Mick said, clutching my elbow and shaking it. "Now you got him on the ropes."

I thought about it for a minute or two. "So I'd be doing you a favor?" The uncertainty in my voice killed my momentum.

"So close," Mick said. "The champ lives to fight another day."

Lou laughed as he set the case on the counter. "Blue book for an instrument in this shape is $4600. So $4450? Sound good? Call it a draw?" Lou pulled out a pad, flipped to a new slip and stuck the cardboard in between the pages just like Mick did. He took a pen from a Mason jar by the register and stuck it in his ear.

Pauly would shit if he knew how much cash I was about to drop. And no matter what Mick said, or what I thought, it wasn't just a block of wood. I wrote out the check and signed it. My hand trembled.

The guitar looked up from its case like a cat brought inside after a life on the street. Eyes all gummy, flea-ridden. I pulled the strap Pauly had gotten me for Christmas out of my pocket. I slid the soft black leather over the endpin before setting the guitar into the old case. The plush interior had been worn bare in some places by the years of use. Lou flipped the lid shut, and I rested my hands on the case.

After settling with Mick, Lou said, "Pleasure doing business with you boys. I'm always happy to take your money."

At the front door, Mick said, "You need to come down my way a little more often. Don't be a stranger. We'll go watch WVU beat Pitt." Mick tossed me the keys.

"Be careful going back. Watch for slick spots. And watch for deer, all right?" Lou walked us to the car. He grabbed Mick's door and helped him slide the guitar case into the back seat.

I put my guitar in from the other side, angled toward the back so it wouldn't fall. "Thanks, Lou," I said.

"Come back anytime. You don't even need to bring the old man with you." He backed onto the sidewalk.

I walked around the car and got in. After adjusting the seat and mirror, I pulled out, a little nervous with Mick watching my every move. I set my phone on the seat next to my leg.

"You expecting a call?" Mick asked.

"Dani…."

"Not while you're driving." Mick adjusted his seat, reclining a bit further. "Don't you watch the news?"

I crept up Morgantown Street toward a shopping center. Mick helped me find the toll road.

Once the city lights were behind us, he said, "Preston…" and turned toward the window. He waited a long time before finishing. For a second I thought he'd fallen asleep.

"I was unfaithful to my wife once," he said, his voice barely louder than the radio. "To say I was sorry, I sold my Jazzmaster and took her to Las Vegas."

I didn't know what to say, so I let the silence ride.

"I was twenty-seven years old. Curse of twenty-seven. Just like Robert Johnson." He sank into his seat and held his head in his hand.

"And Pigpen McKernan, Jimi Hendrix, Kurt Cobain. There's a bunch of them."

"My wife called it the Return of Saturn. She forgave me because it was the first time I had to be an adult. Being on the road, in clubs every night, she said it kept me from growing up. So she gave me a few weeks to get rid of the old habits. It wasn't easy, let me tell you. After that my head cleared up real quick, I stopped going on the road. I took my savings and bought the shop." Mick turned to the window again.

So I kept my mouth shut. While waiting for him to finish, my phone rang. *Dani.* Even though it burned my thumb to do it, I hit IGNORE and drove a little faster. Mick didn't even seem to notice. I looked over and saw that he'd fallen asleep.

I eased the radio's volume up. Mixed in with Nirvana and STP, the X gave me some Rise Against, some Silversun Pickups. When we got closer to the Mason-Dixon the X started to fade and I had to pick up CLG. I caught the very end of an announcement for Mike's show at The Stink. It reminded me I had to get a set together. If Dani was going to be there, and maybe Pauly, I wanted to do something spectacular.

I tried to wake Mick up as I got off 68. "Mick," I whispered.

He didn't stir, so I let him sleep longer. I turned the radio up, hoping he'd hear Linkin Park and wake up.

"I'm awake," Mick said, his voice low. "Maybe you can drop me off? Pick me up in the morning?"

"Take your car back to my place?"

"You're not going to steal it and drive to Atlantic City, are you? Tomorrow's the middle school."

"I forgot tomorrow was Tuesday. Sing-along with the kids. Yeah, I'm good to go." I turned up toward the old Mountaineer Mall. "What time?"

"After lunch. Can you take my purchase inside with you tonight? I don't want to leave it in the car, and I can't take it in with me yet. Bring it with you tomorrow. We'll jam a little."

"Sure thing."

"Thank you."

"Anything, Mick. I always forget where to turn."

He pointed to the right, and said, "You make it through your twenties and things will change. I promise you."

After another right I pulled up to his house, a big, two-story Brady Bunch-looking place. The Christmas lights were still in the shrubs. I got right up to the curb.

"Tonight was a lot of fun." Mick grabbed the door handle.

"Yeah, I had a great time. I'm going to be up playing all night, probably." I made a mental setlist.

"You're pretty good. I don't know if I ever told you that. Parents always have a lot of nice things to say about you."

All this nice stuff at once made me wonder if Mick knew something I didn't. So I replied as best as I could, "I don't want to disappoint you, or do anything that would hurt the business's reputation."

"I appreciate that." He got out of the car and turned around. He ducked his head back in, the glow from the interior dome light made his face look really tired. "You know what you could really do to help me?"

"What's that, Mick?"

"Promise me you won't quit until you make it out of here. Then I can tell people you used to work for me."

His wife waited for him just inside the storm door. She waved at me, and I gave the horn a quick toot-toot. She kissed Mick on the cheek and took his scarf and gloves. Mick gave me a big wave as she helped him with his coat.

I waited until I got out of sight before trying Dani. I figured if I got a hold of her I wouldn't have to go home. I dialed, and let it ring six or seven times, but she didn't pick up.

Maybe she's tired from driving all day.

I got back to Don Knotts Boulevard and tried again.

Maybe she's in the shower.

I got nervous wondering if maybe something had happened. Her car could be in a ditch up in Preston County somewhere. And just before my right at Walnut I made a really dumb mistake. I made a left and headed up to Dani's. She'd called me three times, she obviously wanted to talk. I didn't think that made me a stalker.

I crept up side streets, searching for her apartment. All the houses looked the same, especially in the glow of fluorescent street lights. All brick and ornamentation. She hid up there somewhere, like Rapunzel.

My phone buzzed and I hurried to answer. But it was a text. <it's arse about face to kill the shopkeeper because you're all out of fags.>

For a few minutes I thought about a reply, but ended up deleting it and dialing my voicemail instead. I put the car in park and crept up to the garage window on foot. A black Saab sat where her silver Benz should've been. When I heard her voicemail message I cleared my throat and called right back. "Just returning your call. If you want to get together just let me know... Good night."

On the top floor, in her apartment, there were lights on.

Guilt and jealousy washed over me, made me warm. I rushed back to the car, put the Caddy into D and rolled down the street. I made my way back to the apartment, radio cranked way too loud. "Sabotage." Beastie Boys.

I parked Mick's car under a street light where it was visible from my window and locked it, checked the doors again just to make sure, and took the two guitars inside. My footsteps echoed up the naked hallway. I didn't care. Pauly wasn't home.

My phone rang. I leaned the guitar against the table and answered it. "Hello?"

"Preston, I tried calling you so many times. But you never answered."

"I know. I'm sorry. I went up to PA with Mick. I didn't know—"

"You said that you wanted to see me. I specifically remember you saying that this morning, when you walked me to my car."

"I know." If there was something else I could've said to make her understand how sorry I was I would have said it.

For a long time she didn't say anything.

So I said, "Dani?"

"It has been a very long day. If I had known you were going away I would have gotten a hotel room for tonight. Driving over the mountains by myself made me feel very uneasy."

"Dani, I am sorry. Today was crazy, but I can still come up. Mick found me a guitar and we went up to PA…"

"It's fine. You don't owe me an explanation. We are not married. I had just called to tell you I was too tired to see you tonight anyway. So, maybe tomorrow."

"Maybe tomorrow?" I replied, but she hadn't asked a question. *Ask her about the car*, I reminded myself, but my throat closed up.

"Goodnight."

She hung up and my stomach balled up, twisting with anger or sadness or something in between. But I knew she was home, knew she was awake, and knew she wasn't alone. Knew it knew it knew it. Mentioning it would've made me a stalker. I held onto the phone, waiting for it to ring again. It took a few minutes to figure out it wasn't going to. That I was the other guy. I flipped open my guitar case and took out the Martin. I put the strap around my neck, shut off the light, and sat in my bed. Headlights and street lights from the top part of High came through the ice clinging to the inside of the window. I watched the lights through the ice and strummed the guitar for a very long time.

CHAPTER SEVEN

It had snowed all night. Long enough to coat the Caddy, at least. I cranked the engine and let it run while I brushed off the windows. Even after a few minutes the vents weren't blowing hot air. I ran up to get the guitars anyway.

Snow squeaked and thumped under the big car's wheels as I made tracks through the empty lot. By the time I passed the Wings Olé by the Westover Bridge it had started to warm up. The warm air made my mouth and throat dry.

When I got to Mick's he waved me in from the porch. Mick's wife, Anna, had made breakfast he said. I asked him what he wanted me to do with the guitar, and he said it'd be okay in the car for a few minutes.

Anna made an obscene amount of bacon and eggs but my stomach still rumbled like it was sick. It felt like I hadn't eaten in weeks. I threw a few cups of coffee down while Mick chowed. Anna offered me a Little Debbie Oatmeal Crème for the road, and I took it even though I didn't think I'd eat it.

Once we were at the shop, Mick's mood was pretty sour, so I drug an amp up to the counter and told him to get out his Jazzmaster. I grabbed Pauly's bass off the wall, and Mick told me to put it back and get another. We played for a long time, until right before lunch.

Then Mick said, "I'm not going to the school with you today. Make sure you tuck in your shirt. And don't swear."

"You okay?" I asked.

"Yeah, Anna's coming in for lunch."

"That sounds great, Mick. Well, I'll go now so I can run up and get the Jeep."

"Take my car. She's going to pick me up. We're going over to Colasante's."

I put my coat on. "Bring me back a stromboli? I'll pay you back."

Mick joked, "With what?"

I told Mick I'd see him this afternoon and to enjoy his lunch and hopped in the Caddy. I stopped at Dairy Mart to get a Mountain Dew. Almost bought a pack of squares, but figured Mick'd kill me if he smelled smoke in his car. Besides, I didn't want Jamie to know I smoked. I couldn't wait to show him my guitar. I reminded myself to get a few extra sets of strings and picks and all that kind of stuff just in case.

The drive over to the middle school gave me too much time to think about Dani. Like who she'd slept with last night. But walking into my old school, and smelling pencil shavings and cafeteria pizza weirded me out enough to push her out of my mind.

The kids weren't really into it this week like they had been other times I'd been with Mick. They wouldn't sing along and they wouldn't listen to their teacher. So I went rogue and taught them "Three Little Birds" and "Stir It Up." We did "I Want to Hold Your Hand" twice. As I left, the teacher thanked me. She looked tired and grateful. I told her I didn't know how she did it. I started thinking of stuff I could do next week. I told her I could type up lyrics and make copies. We could do "Buddy Holly" and "Island in the Sun." "Imagine." "Lucy in the Sky with Diamonds" had fun lyrics. I could think of all kinds of kid-friendly stuff.

When I got back to the shop Mick still wasn't there. I took out my phone and looked at the call log. Nothing since last night.

I closed my eyes and tried to sleep. The cold kept me from drifting off. I had a key, but Mick didn't want me using it unless it was an emergency. And I didn't want to run the engine in case Mick came back, he'd be like, "Gas isn't a buck fifty a gallon anymore." So I pulled my jacket tight and lifted my collar.

After a few minutes he tapped on the window. "Why didn't you wait inside? Might have sold something."

I said, "Can't win for losing," and followed him.

While we got settled, Mick said, "Heard you went off script today?"

"Yeah." I smiled. "The little kiddies had enough 'Battle Hymn of the Republic' and little houses made of ticky-tacky."

"Mrs. Defazio went on and on about you." Mick crossed his arms and leaned against the counter.

"If I didn't know any better I'd think you were proud of me."

"You represent me well. You want that to be a regular gig? You might have to get clearances from the state and submit a resume for them to keep on file."

"The school? Sure, it was a lot of fun. And I still get to play, so, yeah. That's awesome."

"It's just a way to get that Tele out of my back room faster. Did you take your Martin today?"

"Yeah, sure did. You want to get the Jazzmaster back out?"

"Later."

My next lesson came in with a huff of cold air. He rocked a leather coat and looked a little like Henry Rollins with a normal-sized neck. Part of me thought I should've been a little more like him back in high school. Maybe I looked at him as a version of who I could've been. Either way, Tuesdays with Aaron always went too fast. "You ready? You can go in back and plug in. Warm up a little."

Mick said, "You *are* in a good mood."

"Despite some girl trouble and some Pauly trouble things are all right."

"I thought you and Pauly made up."

"No, he doesn't get that the shit he does is wrong. He's a hypocrite, acting all uppity for going to A.A. meetings, but says stuff to rip on me, like 'I saw your dad at a meeting last week. He's a meth freak,' and crap like that." I fished for a Dunlop Heavy from the jar by the register.

"The other shoe doesn't always have to fall, you know."

"I know. Usually it kicks me." I followed Aaron into the back. We got settled, I played a few chord variations, putting together a little rhythm for him to play over. As soon as he really got going my phone buzzed. I apologized and we kept playing. Suddenly, what had started out as a fast-moving lesson began to drag. Intuition told me it was Dani.

By the time the clock hit four I was ready to go, but Aaron kept right on playing. He knew I didn't have a lesson after his, and he'd gotten used to just hanging out. With the same smile that helped me get through a lot of shitty nights doing Mötley Crüe covers out in Westover, I gave him ten more minutes.

To wrap up, I said, "Be thinking about some things for next week. Text me or whatever. Maybe more Django?" I flipped open my guitar case and laid the Martin inside.

He shrugged then strummed a few more times, like when you're going too fast on a bike and can't stop.

Guilt worked too easy on me. "We can hang out some more."

"No, I have to go anyway. There's a game tonight and a bunch of us are going out to the Fishbowl first. And I have a lab report to write up." He put his Les Paul back in his case. He told me it was his dad's, but I knew they'd bought it for him. "We're going to be in the playoffs. You want to come see a game?"

"Sure thing, man. That'd be cool. Haven't been up to the high school in a long time. You got everything?"

"Yeah, thanks." He stepped into the hallway. "Mikey said you guys are playing with him at the Met."

"Probably just me. I'll do some acoustic stuff, I guess."

"What happened to the band?"

"Stu got shipped to Afghanistan and Pauly got a real job."

"You going to start a new band?"

"I'm trying, buddy. I'm trying." I stepped back into my lesson room before he'd even started squaring up with Mick and scrolled through my missed calls. *Pauly.* I listened to his message.

He said, "Uh, I've been talking to my sponsor a lot from the road, and he thinks…" Pauly coughed and mumbled something before starting over.

"Well, I think it, too, I guess, that our situation with the apartment and all that— he thinks that I should tell you that some things need to change. Like you need to try to get sober or maybe move out." He mumbled again. Like it all wasn't coming out like he'd practiced it. Like he somehow deviated from his cue cards and couldn't figure out how to get back.

I could see him, leaning back in the seat, smoking or drinking a Snapple. Maybe even trying to put a look of concern on his face, to really sell it even though I wasn't there. "Yeah, so that's it. You need to make a serious attempt, like me, or move out. Or I have to look for a place. I can't live with you anymore if you're still drinking, man. I'm sorry."

"End of messages. For saved messages, press one."

I rubbed my temples. Part of me wanted to hear the message again. But I knew better. I knew it'd be the same.

I forced myself back into the store.

Mick watched traffic out on Pleasant Street. Salt-crusted cars rolling along salt-crusted streets. February needed rain like Strummer needed another twenty years. "Everything squared away back there?" he said, still not looking.

"Yeah. Everything okay with you?"

Mick said, "Why do you ask?"

I walked over to the door and leaned against the jamb. "I don't know. You seem a little distant or something."

"Just thinking, that's all. Might have to sell the Jazzmaster."

"You need money?" I asked even though I knew the question sounded pretty stupid.

"It's not a good thing to have around. Makes me think of what I did. You can head out if everything's taken care of in back."

"I can stay if you want me to. I don't have anywhere to be."

"It's fine. Go out tonight. Call that girl… Or better yet, find some place to play. Get a band together."

"Maybe want to grab a drink?"

"Thanks, kid, but no."

"Okay, Mick. Have a good one." I threw on my coat.

Mick asked, "When's Jamie coming in?"

"Thursday, I think. He hasn't called."

"I'll give him a ring. It's always good to talk to him. You tie up all your loose ends?"

"Rescheduled all my lessons. So, yeah, I guess that's it."

"Okay. Have fun. Spending a few days with Jamie will do you good."

"I hope so. Man, do I hope so. Thanks again for everything this week, Mick. I really mean that." I stepped into the cold and gave Dani a call.

Straight to voicemail. "Hey, Dani, this is Preston. If you want to get together, maybe have some coffee or something, I guess I'll be up Mountaineer Doughnuts. I am sorry about last night. I did tell you I'd be around, so... It is my fault, and I'm sorry. See you later, I hope."

I scurried up Pleasant to High and crossed on DON'T WALK. My breath left me in a cloud. Through big windows I saw a group of students on the stage at the back of the coffee shop. I put my face against the glass, using my hand to block the glare. A banjo, a few guitars and some kind of lap thing. Not a resonator, maybe a dulcimer. A pair of girls playing violins. One of them waved, but I couldn't see her face, so I waved back and went inside.

The transition from daylight to interior made me blind as a bat. I squinted and made my way toward the plucky sounds of the old-timey stuff we played up in Davis. But the group was only a quarter as cohesive as the group I'd been a part of in the fire hall. But I had it all figured out. The rhythm ran straight ahead, like punk, and there were never more than four chords. And like punk, it got better the more you drank.

Katy met me at the counter where the barista handed me my Americano. Caffeine was a pretty good appetite suppressant, and I'd been hungry all afternoon. If I remembered correctly, Katy was also an appetite suppressant.

She said, "Hey, Preston Black. Didn't think I'd ever see you here." She pushed a long strand of brown hair behind her ear. She had this shy, awkward thing going on. It threw me.

"Hey, Katy Stefanic, how's it going?" I tore open a few sugar packets and dumped them into my coffee. She watched me swirl the cup a few times, then add another packet. "Aren't you just a beam of sunshine on such a winter's day?"

When she smiled her eyes picked up a shade or two of the lavender in the sweater she wore. Everybody else in the place, myself included, wore black. But she looked like a tiny little flower in an asphalt parking lot. I smiled back.

"Thank you. I don't know if I'm more surprised that you remembered we played tonight or that you actually came down."

I looked to the big stage in the back—not really a stage so much as a riser—and watched the musicians slogging through some slow-tempoed waltz. A big guy with dreads and a Takamine held it all together. Nodding and keeping a sloppy pace. He closed his eyes like he was at Red Rocks halfway through his encore, a sky-full of stars and a crowd-full of cell phone screens coaxing him on.

"What if I told you I forgot, and I just kind of randomly showed up?" I said it with such a big smile there was no way she could miss my sarcasm.

"I'd say you really are an asshole." She returned the smile and played with her hair. "You coming, or what?"

She weaved between tables, I followed her to the back.

"Hey, guys." Katy pulled a chair right next to where she'd been sitting. "This is Preston Black. He's going to sit in if that's okay."

The circle seemed about as nonplussed as a circle could get. The big guy with the dreads mumbled something to the banjo player on his left with a dickish smirk. "Try to keep up, and just watch me if you get lost. And no Stone Temple Pilots, okay? The Nineties are over."

"Preston, this is Chelsea. I told you about her Sunday?" She gave a shy wave, but kept giving Katy a *Chasing Amy* stare.

The only thing I could really remember from the weekend was "Wildwood Flower," so I didn't even wait for the leader to count us off. My strings loved the wide room, hitting with a voice that coated anybody who listened like cigarette smoke. Katy played the vocal line on her fiddle.

On the second time through the clawhammer banjo player played the vocals while Katy plucked out the chords. Her high crisp notes were the jelly to my peanut butter. The rest of the circle felt totally extraneous, as far as I was concerned. If the rest of them suddenly split, I wouldn't have minded at all.

Katy's playing sent chills right through me—like she channeled gypsies or banshees or both. I considered myself lucky to be sitting right next to her, where I could watch her fingers work. We made eye contact, and I quickly looked back at her fingers. But she had to see me smiling. That was the last time I remembered telling Dani I'd call her.

When my turn came again I played a few slow, well-placed notes that were a direct contrast to the big guy's attempts to be the ring-leader. Almost anybody could play fast notes over chords. Maybe I wanted to show Katy, really show her, what I had in me. So I layered in something totally different, something that wasn't old time or traditional. I played a vocal phrasing twice, something that would be recognizable even in the context of this song.

On my next pass through Katy picked up on it. I strummed, adding a slight tweak to the chords for "Wildwood Flower." Then I sang a hybridized version of "(What's So Funny 'Bout) Peace, Love, and Understanding" about walking through a wicked world and all that.

Katy looked over her shoulder and mouthed the new chords to her friend as I sang, asking myself if all there was is pain, hatred and misery. I sang it with a big smile on my face.

My voice sounded good, better than it had in a while. Maybe shouting into a mic wasn't my thing. I heard tones in there I hadn't noticed in a long time. At the chorus Katy stopped, put down her fiddle, and in her best Elvis Costello voice, sang right along with me. The rest of the stuff we played was mostly G-C-D over and over, so I practiced barre chords, bass lines and picking out melodies.

When the party ended, the mandolin player asked if I was coming back. I took it as a compliment. Katy ordered a cheeseburger. For the first time in a long time I was hungry, and ordered one too. Her friend Chelsea hung out a little longer, but eventually saw that she was a third wheel and split. I asked Katy if she had to go, too, but she said she still wanted to play a little, if I wanted to.

For the next hour we kicked songs back and forth, trying to stump each other. Some of the people who had been studying in the café even took off their headphones to listen. Katy went first, throwing out "Norwegian Wood."

"Seriously?" I fired back "Nice Dream." Not only could she play it, but she sang it beautifully right along with me.

She hit me with the one-two punch of "I Will Follow You Into The Dark" and some Replacements that stumped me. "'Alex Chilton,'" she said.

We went back and forth—White Stripes, Wilco, Arctic Monkeys, Zeppelin. She stumped me again with Beyonce, her version of "Crazy in Love."

The only interruption came when our waitress returned and took our coffee mugs instead of asking if we wanted refills. Then somebody shut the middle row of lights out.

"Time to go?" Katy wiggled her fingers and rubbed her wrist.

"We can go someplace else. You want to get a drink somewhere? Or we can go back to my apartment and play?"

"I suppose I should get back. I'm meeting Jamie for lunch tomorrow before he goes back up the mountain. He said there's supposed to be a big blizzard this weekend."

"He didn't call me."

"He will. He forgets sometimes. Drives Aunt Izzy batty. I wanted to go with you guys this weekend. Jamie said no way, José. No girls allowed. Jesse Currence is an amazing fiddler, you know. Jamie said he's going to get Jesse to do a clinic in Elkins this summer, at Augusta, so I'll have to wait 'til then. You should come down this summer. It's a lot of fun. People dancing and hanging out all night." She pulled her coat on and wrapped a scarf around her neck until she no longer had a neck. We headed out toward the street.

After I didn't say anything she said, "You probably don't even know who Jesse Currence is, do you? You definitely don't deserve to go up there."

I said, "I probably don't. It'd be like if you were related to Jimmy Page or something. I'd be jealous. But I'm going up for a much different reason."

Evening had departed a long time ago. Late night, the time between Letterman and last call, had crept up like a stray cat to a Laundromat. Katy shivered.

"You want me to walk with you?"

"Is that a question or an offer? Because an offer comes from someplace nice and fuzzy." She sped up, her little black boots skipped along the salted sidewalk.

"Katy Stefanic, it would give me great pleasure to accompany you to your…" I pointed up High, toward campus.

"I'm in an apartment up by the Towers." She pointed in the other direction, to the PRT station. "Would've been nicer without the sarcasm."

"I'll ride up with you then."

"It's not necessary. Really."

I took her fiddle case, which allowed her to fold her mitten-clad hands into the arms of her coat. I would've put my arm around her, if I had been like that. Low clouds covered the city like a blanket. Stoplights, streetlights, headlights, neon lights from bars and places like Mick's, they all got tangled in the clouds, making me feel like we were walking in a giant snow globe. We headed down Walnut. If it wasn't so cold I would've slowed her down a little. But my ankles and toes hurt from the cold, like I was turning to stone from the bottom up. "It's not too often you get the city all to yourself."

She smiled.

The fluorescence of the PRT landing busted the snow globe, leaving us standing there in Morgantown, West Virginia, on a mid-winter night. All the water leaked out, and the only thing left were plastic snowflakes and plastic buildings. Suddenly the stuff I had to say didn't seem so clever, the night, seemed like any other.

We went up the steps, through the turnstiles. Katy hit the button for the Towers. I didn't have fifty cents, so I hopped the turnstile. A tram pulled up right away, so the transition of getting in kept us from settling into a groove like the one we had at the café. The rubbery whir of tires on corrugated metal filled the cabin. The car shimmied from side to side as it rounded the corner toward Beechurst. We'd run out of things to say.

Morgantown faded into the darkness as we passed through town and climbed up to Evansdale. The lights from Seneca Center were the last thing I saw as we crested the hill. I thought of a thousand ways to keep this night going, but in my head they all seemed dumb.

"Well, have fun this weekend." She stood up as the car creaked past Engineering.

"I will. It's not such a big deal to me now as it was up in Davis. I've kind of accepted the song title was just a coincidence. I don't believe it means I'll find my dad anymore." I stood up, too. "What did you think of the song?"

"I don't know. It's just a song. I've been hearing about old magic and charms and hexes all my life, so it's probably not as out of the ordinary for somebody like me. My grandma used to do all kinds of stuff to protect the livestock from the Lewis's spells. I have no problem believing that this song, in some way… But if you don't believe it, why are you going back?"

"I really like Jamie. He's kind of fatherly, you know? And I love music. If that's all I have right now then I have to jump into it. The year is young. Maybe by the time next February rolls around I'll be on my way… Whatever that means. Speaking of which, there's a show down at The Stink next week. I'm playing a few songs."

"Oh yeah? No covers?" She smiled with only the tiniest part of her mouth.

"Maybe one. I have to dust some of my stuff off. See what happens."

"If there's nothing else going on… Maybe I'll see if Chelsea's into it." She looked out the window. The tram decelerated.

"Or, you could come alone. That is, of course, if there's nothing better to do."

"That's what I meant. Let me know how it goes this weekend. Okay?"

"I will. Should I walk you up?"

"No, I'll save you fifty cents. It could be a long wait. Besides, I don't want to get a call from campus security to come bail you out of college jail." The tram stopped. Light from the terminal fell on her cheeks.

"Okay. You know, I have an idea. Do you want to head over to Eat'n Park for coffee?" My mind raced to find a way to keep her here.

She stopped and paused for such a long time I thought she'd accept. While she stared up at me I studied the curve of her cheekbones and the way the light reflected off her smooth skin. Just when I thought I might kiss her, she said, "I have to work tomorrow. Somebody has to read to the little ones so they don't turn out like you," rather quickly, then backed through the door.

"Goodnight, Katy." I followed her onto the platform and the tram door slid shut with a hiss. Just before she passed through the turnstile I grabbed her elbow.

She whipped around, her wide eyes studied my face.

"Hey…" All of a sudden my plan didn't seem like such a good one. I took a step toward her and my mouth got dry. I lifted my hand to her cheek.

She said my name and sighed before backing through the turnstile. She swiped her student I.D., hit the button for Walnut, then disappeared down the steps.

While waiting for the next car to pull up I watched her walk down the lonely sidewalk toward the Towers. She stayed on my mind for a long time. As the tram started down the big hill past Engineering the front of the car shimmied like one of the old trains on The Racers at Kennywood as they came back into the station. A coal barge crept up the river. When the tram rolled into the Beechurst station I stayed on. I didn't want to go home. My phone rang. I thought it might be Katy. I smiled.

Before I could even get out a 'hello' Dani started yelling, the only thing I could clearly understand was my name, like an exclamation point at the end of a sentence. She sniffled, slowed down, then said, "If I had known how you were I never would've given you a second look. You are ignorant, white trash. But to call me, and invite me out only to let me see you flirting with some little girl is cruel. Make no mistake, we are through. There will be no tomorrow for you and me."

She hung up.

My face got warm. When the tram pulled into Walnut I got out and went straight to the apartment.

I pulled out my keys and fumbled with the lock on the big exterior door then slammed it shut. I didn't care who heard or who it woke up. I hit the stairs two at a time. When I got to the top I saw light streaming from beneath our apartment door. The TV was on. Pauly was home. I stood there, key in my hand. I went back down the stairs, less authoritatively than when I came up. My mom lived on the other side of town, too far to walk. At two, the bars closed. I didn't have a hundred bucks to drop at the Morgan.

"I'm lost. Fucking lost." Like being at Murphy's Mart at Mountaineer Mall when I was five. I had on this Washington Redskins jersey that I loved and everybody else hated because it wasn't the Steelers. Mom got it at Goodwill or something. Some old guy found me and sat me at the lunch counter and ordered me a Coke. He waited with me while security paged my mom.

I didn't freak out then and I decided I wasn't going to freak out now.

I had a key to Mick's shop.

Past Yama, down Chestnut past the parking garage, across Walnut. I didn't know how I went from feeling so good to feeling so bad so fast. At least Mick's would be dark and warm. And I'd be alone. And after tonight, maybe I didn't need anything else. Or deserve anything else.

CHAPTER EIGHT

Morning came way before I wanted it to. Mick got into work whenever he felt like it anymore, so I had to cut early. There'd be hell to pay if he came strolling in at 8:30 and found me sleeping in the showroom. And since I spent all night worrying about what time he'd get in, I barely slept at all. I wanted a cigarette as soon as I opened my eyes.

I put my shoes on, zipped up my coat and took a look around the shop. Once I convinced myself no sign of my stay remained, I locked up and headed to the café. Maybe I thought I'd catch Jamie there with Katy if I hung out long enough. At the very least, I might catch my mom. Maybe I wanted to be warm and get fed. Maybe I just wanted a reason to stop running.

I stepped into the diner. Pearl said my mom didn't come in 'til later and, in a way, that relieved me. On top of everything else I didn't need to hear about end times and the devil. So I ordered coffee and hoped it would stimulate my appetite. My guitar case sat across the booth from me. I paid up, and asked Pearl if I kept my cup, would she refill it? When she said she would, I went to the back, found a sunbeam, sat down and opened up my guitar case.

I played for an hour or two at the edge of that little stage. Practicing songs I might play next week. Working on lyrics and melodies. I had one called "Kill Every Sparrow" I really liked. I came up with a riff that sounded like Keith Richards himself had handed it to me. I played it over and over, each time feeling like I'd been granted three wishes. I put it into my notebook. I didn't enjoy playing alone, but I figured I'd better get used to it.

My phone rang around noon. Jamie said he'd made it to Mick's, and I should come down when I was ready. The café had filled up. A few students, some dozing on their laptops. Old men talking about basketball, about how the Mountaineers got robbed of respectability because the Big East was such a strong conference. I wanted to say it had nothing to do with the conference—Seton Hall and Louisville still got lucky and beat them once every two or three years. I gave Pearl my cup and a few bucks. "Thanks," I said.

"Your mum thinks you're avoiding her. You should call her." Pearl put the tip right into her apron, and for a second, I thought she was going to slip the coffee cup in there too.

The high, bright sun melted the snow that plows had pushed against the sidewalk. Cinders mingled with ice, and when it melted the ash crept across the road in a tiny stream of water that would evaporate by one or two in the afternoon. At the leading edge of the stream a little white crust formed where salt had already been deposited. For the first time in weeks it felt like the thermometer might crack forty degrees. For the first time in months it actually felt like winter might really come to an end.

I rolled into Mick's through the front door, paranoid that he'd know I'd spent the night there. Like maybe he had a hidden camera in the back or some shit. But he didn't raise an eyebrow. He showed Jamie the Jazzmaster. I wiped my Vans really good on the mat and strolled back.

Mick said, "Here comes that ugly guitar I told you about."

Jamie spoke in a serious monotone to Mick, his subtle accent giving his speech the slightest air of sarcasm, "Oh, I heard all about it. About how Lou had been trying to give the thing away for years, how he even put it out in front of the store with a 'free to a good home' sign, like it was a box of kittens or something." He let out a little laugh. "Mick says Lou's such a wonderful salesman that he actually got you to pay for the thing."

"Wow." I smiled. "Why does everybody turn into a douche around Mick?"

Ignoring me, Mick said, "Crack that thing open, let the professor see it."

I slid a small wooden stool over with my foot and laid the case on it. Jamie bent over as I flipped the latches.

"Good thing you got here when you did." Jamie leaned over the case like he'd turn to stone if I didn't get it into his hands that very instant. "Mick was moments away from giving me a good deal on a used Tele. It's a seventy-one, Mick?"

Jamie lifted my 'new' guitar out of the case without even asking. He spun around, looking for another stool. When he plopped down he propped the guitar on his knee and took off his hat, which he hung on an empty hook.

He checked to see if it was in tune. It was, but he adjusted the tuning keys anyway. Then he went straight to the neck and fingerpicked out a light, lively version of "Sweet Georgia Brown."

"Oh yeah, she's real nice."

He pulled a coin out of his pocket for a pick and jumped into a fast, straightforward number that sounded like it had originally been written for the fiddle. His fingers worked the strings, knuckles straining to jump from fret to fret. He ran through it once more, paused, then said, "Really nice. I like it, despite what Mick says."

I asked, "What was that last thing?"

"That's the 'Clinch Mountain Backstep', son. Doctor Ralph Stanley? It's a banjo tune, and that's the only reason I can excuse you for not knowing it." He laid the guitar on his lap, inspecting the cracks and ridges that ran across the finish. His fingers grazed the lines, like a needle does a record. He looked in the sound hole, first at the serial number, then he shook the guitar gently.

"Rattlesnake beads," I said, helping him out.

"Really?" He smiled really big and tried to shift them toward the light. "Did you put them in there?"

"No, Lou said the guy he bought the guitar from put them in there. He said he just left them in—"

"Where'd the seller come from?" Jamie shook the guitar to see them, like my word wasn't good enough.

"I don't remember. Somewhere up in the mountains in PA. By Seven Springs."

"There's a strong fiddle tradition up by Dunbar, PA. So, I guess that sounds about right. Down here the old-timers put rattlesnake beads in their fiddles, too."

"Oh yeah?"

"Indeed." He handed the guitar back to me. "Do you have any idea why?"

Jamie let the question hang for a second.

"I don't know… Because it sounded cool?" Seeing Jamie put his stamp of approval on the guitar made it that much more precious.

Jamie stood up and blew his nose into a clean, white handkerchief. "Katy said she tried to call you this morning to join us for a brunch but you didn't answer."

"Aw, man. I left my phone for a second when I went to the bathroom. Must've been all the coffee. I would have loved to have joined you guys." I opened my phone and flipped through my MISSED CALLS. Sure enough, there it was.

"I suppose you'll be seeing enough of me over the next few days. When did you want to leave?" Jamie took his coat off, and hung it on a hook right next to where he'd hung his old fedora.

"I'm ready whenever you are. I just have to run home and pack a bag." I backed toward the door.

"Mick and I have a little catching up to do, and I have to make a quick trip up to the library. So two hours? Meet back here at two or three?" The way Jamie rolled up his sleeves it looked like he wouldn't be taking off any time soon.

"Sure thing. Is Katy coming up this weekend?"

Ignoring my question, he said, "Leave that guitar here, I'll keep it busy."

"Yeah. Sure." I zipped up my coat. "I wondered if I should get something for this guy? Like a token or something?"

"Not a bad idea. He likes chocolate." Jamie draped the strap around his neck and strummed a few chords. "And whiskey."

"All right. Mick, how you going to manage without me?"

"I'll just have to shutter the doors until you get back."

I hit the sidewalk almost running. It would've been nice to see Katy again before heading up the mountain. Would've been nicer to see Dani, but if that ship sailed, it sailed. I guess I wasn't a sailor.

I dialed her up. Voicemail.

"Dani…" I slowed my pace and tried to control my breathing. "I just wanted you to know I'm not playing games. That girl is Jamie's niece, okay? I met her last week up in Davis. I didn't know she'd be there. I just went up to look for my mom. So—I don't know—maybe we can give it another shot. I really like being around you. You make me really happy, and I don't think it should end like this. Look, I'll be away for a few days, but should be around later this weekend." That was pretty much all I had to say. "I miss talking to you. I'm sorry."

On my way to the apartment I hung a left and went down to Beechurst to pick up a bottle of Jack and a bottle of Knob Creek. For a second I thought about grabbing a pack of Camels to clear my mind. Especially since eating didn't make me feel better. But I left with only the booze and a pocketful of Atomic Fireballs. I figured if I could resist temptation a little longer, the cravings would go away.

At the top of the apartment steps I paused, listening at the door for any sign that he was even home. After convincing myself the place was empty I went in. On the kitchen table sat a big blue Alcoholics Anonymous book. Other than that everything looked exactly the same. I put the liquor bottles on the table and went into my room. My stash of clean clothes had begun to shrink. I put some of the freshest things in my backpack. My notebook sat right where I'd left it. The pile of stuff that remained important to me grew smaller by the day.

The only thing missing was the record. It sat on my dresser, right next to the mirror. I picked it up remembering the first time I saw Dani. She'd been there when all of this started. I pulled the sleeve out of the cardboard, and let the record slide into my hand. The cool vinyl felt smooth, flawless except for "The Sad Ballad of Preston Black." For a second, it all seemed too convenient. I put the record into my pack.

I got into the shower and let the hot water stream down my face. It seemed like I only felt warm in the shower anymore. And around Dani.

Pauly sat at the table. He was glowering if I'd ever seen anybody glower.

He said, "Aren't you a sight?" Pauly sat in the chair facing the bathroom door, the sun streamed in over his shoulder. He had his book in front of him. My bag of booze sat right where I left it.

Either unable, or unwilling, to speak, I grabbed the booze, walked back into my room, put my stuff on the bed and threw on a flannel. When I came back into the kitchen, Pauly said, "I wasn't going to touch your hooch."

For a second I thought about sitting across the table from him, but knew this conversation wouldn't last long.

Pauly tapped the table. "I want you out of here. And if you don't move out, I'm going to get a place by myself."

"You're a different person, like something from *The X-Files*. You know, I went to a few A.A. meetings myself, and I never came back acting like this."

"And you're still a drunk. If I wanted to wake up puking, with headaches, in jail.... I got to take this one day at a time until I get some time under my belt, then, maybe, I can lighten up. Relax a little."

"You don't seem very happy. I'd rather be stupid and drunk than whatever the hell it is you are. You got a permanent scowl, man. I haven't seen you smile since before Christmas."

He stood up and pushed the table away. "Because I'm trying to change! Don't you understand? Jesus, how stupid can you be? The clock's ticking, and if you don't do something soon you're going to end up a nobody. You're already a nobody."

He lowered his voice and lifted his hands out in front of him like he was holding a turkey platter or something. "Look, my sponsor says jails, institutions or death. That's it for guys like us. We don't get famous. Maybe I'm talking about just me, I don't know."

"No, you're talking about me. I'm not stupid. Maybe you got more to lose because you never really lost anything, but I came onto this planet with three strikes against me. All I got left is the short trip from the batter's box to the dugout. You're standing on third waiting for a sac fly. So don't give me any of your higher power, 'everything's going to be A-Okay' stuff. Your mom raised me, but she never treated me like her son. I know she was pregnant with you when my mom died so it's not her fault. But it's not mine either. I thought you were my brother. Now I see you were just the fucking guy I lived with."

I forced myself to relax a little by taking deeper breaths. I didn't want to dislike Pauly. "Really, man, I thought music saved you. I sincerely thought you loved it as much as I did. I'm sorry that's not the case. I have to keep moving forward with this. This is my job… My life. This is what I feel in my soul. I have nothing but this." I held my hand against my heart like pledging allegiance.

"C'mon, Preston. Maybe we should grab a coffee. We'll go to a meeting tonight. I'll introduce you to some guys. There's even a guy from Fairmont who plays drums. We talked about getting together and playing dances and stuff."

"What kind of dances?"

"You know, A.A. dances and stuff."

"Do you think somebody like me is meant to get married and get old? You made a joke about seeing my dad at a meeting—but it's not funny to me. I don't know who my parents are. I don't have cousins and that's why it's not funny to me."

Pauly didn't reply.

"Do you think I'm going to wake up and punch a clock and come home to kids and a pot roast on the table? For you maybe, because you know how it feels to be tucked into bed by real flesh and blood. I've lived on this earth for twenty-seven years and I've never felt that."

I stepped away from the table. "So don't preach to me. Like I give a goddamn about one day at a time. I *am* one day at a time—not knowing where I'm going to eat or sleep."

I couldn't think of the words fast enough. "I want a whole year, not just twenty-four hours. I want my twenty-seven years back. The only time I ever felt like I belonged was when me and you and Stu were setting up or driving to a gig. I know it's not your fault Stu went and re-upped, but you could've given me some warning before you jumped ship."

"I didn't jump ship, Pres… I'm trying to stay sober. I want to piece something together. I want to get married and have kids. I want to be happy. You had to know the band was done."

"You weren't happy when we were playing four or five nights a week?"

He didn't say anything.

I said, "I felt happy. And don't try to tell me that it wasn't genuine. I know how I felt." I leaned on the table, it seemed like the only thing I could do with my hands to keep me from pointing or pushing or punching. "You talk about this self-improvement, but you're the one who's leaving a trail of destruction in your wake. Like you can't do this without stepping on toes and breaking dishes. I scheduled gigs around your meetings, got us places that weren't bars. I tried. Man, I tried and tried and tried to find a way for this to work. Believe it, or don't." I went into my room and put the liquor into my pack.

I yelled out to Pauly, "Maybe your sponsor can find you another roommate. I hope the next one is as patient and forgiving as I have been because I always had your back. I lied to cops for you and kept you from getting your ass kicked a hundred times. I'll be gone until Saturday or Sunday. But I'm not moving out."

I zipped up my hoodie and pulled my wool cap down over my ears. Tucked into the edges of the dresser mirror were all the ticket stubs from the shows we'd gone to, pictures of me and Pauly and Stu at shows, and with girls after shows. A few guitar picks.

I picked up my alarm clock and slammed it into the mirror. The glass splintered and shards tinkled onto the dresser. I went into the hall, pulling my bedroom door shut behind me.

"Preston…" Pauly said. "Hey man, you're bleeding." He pointed to his cheek. I touched my face where he'd pointed. Bright red blood, a lot of blood, came off on my finger. I took a roll of toilet paper we'd been using as Kleenex from the counter and held it against my cheek.

By the time I got to Mick's I'd gotten myself straightened out. In other words, I got the bleeding stopped. In the end it didn't matter. Mick was talking with a customer, a real buyer in a suit and tie, looking over his Jazzmaster. I wanted to tell him he should keep it, but he'd just tell me to hush up. Jamie was ready to go anyway. When I joined him in the back I apologized for being late. He said I wasn't late, he got in early—he ended up skipping the library—and put my guitar back in its case. He looked at the cut on my cheek, which still stung, but he didn't say anything. I showed him what I had in the bag and asked if it'd be all right. He said it would be more than all right.

Mick wiped his cheek, like he was showing me I had pizza sauce on it or something. I said I'd tell him about it Monday. His brow dropped in the middle and his lips, which had been almost smiling, pulled back into a very serious expression.

"I'll be all right," I said. I couldn't blame him for not believing me.

Jamie didn't care about the cut or Pauly or my mother or Pauly's mother. He cared about music and storytelling and hearing good stories. In the car we talked about the relationship between punk and old-time. The way The Ramones were like a group of fiddling families from southern West Virginia. He wanted to know what I listened to, what new bands sounded good, what CDs he should pick up next time he came into town.

He told me all about Robert Johnson, about how he left Robinsonville for two years and returned a virtuoso. Jamie said Johnson probably practiced hoodoo and referenced it all the time in his songs. In "Hellhound on my Trail" Johnson sang about sprinkling 'hot foot powder' around a door to keep people away. He mentioned 'mojo bags' and 'nation sacks' in several songs. Jamie reminded me that Johnson even supposedly went down to the crossroads.

Right before we pulled into Jamie's driveway things got a little awkward. His tone changed. Grew somber. He put the car in park and let the engine run.

I reached for the door and he stopped me.

He said, "Remember our discussion at Mick's, about the rattlesnake beads in your guitar?"

The change in his inflection made me slow to respond. "I remember."

"The reason they do that down here has very little to do with sound, even though some people think the tradition may have begun that way. Anyway, I just wanted to tell you the whole story…"

"Which is?" I asked.

"The reason that people put the beads in their fiddles is to keep the devil away." He turned the Subaru off.

Not sure how to reply, I said, "Is, uh, that something I have to worry about?"

"I don't know," he said, his voice not quite as reassuring as it had just been. Then, like he changed his mind, or thought better of it, he added, "I don't believe it is."

CHAPTER NINE

Waking up warm, in a real bed, in a house where tension and anger—as far as I knew—didn't exist made me wonder if I even needed the rest of the song. If Jamie invited me to hang out all weekend and play music I could wake up on Monday a happy boy.

But Jamie really wanted to beat the blizzard—he had the Subaru warming up, and I'd already taken my stuff out. Ready for a real adventure, he handed me sleeping bags and pillows. I gave him a look that he must not have expected, because he could only say, "You'll be thanking me later."

Isabelle came onto the porch, crossing her arms and pulling her sweater tightly around her shoulders. Jamie hugged her, kissed her on both cheeks, and said, "We'll be back Saturday by dinner. As soon as the roads are clear."

"Be careful. If the roads are bad take your time. You boys look out for each other," she replied, waving like we were about to hit the Oregon Trail. The gray sky finally let loose some real snow. Like up until now, it'd just been teasing.

Jamie headed south, along roads I'd never seen, through valleys I never could've imagined. The mountaintops looked like different realms, like the trees and animals that lived up there had to be very different than the ones I knew. In the low areas, the dead, gray trees looked like the ones back home. But higher up, the trees looked jagged, like a row of teeth in a wolf's jaw. For as cold as it felt in the Subaru, I knew up there it was colder than I could imagine.

The highway twisted like shoelaces through a pair of Chuck Taylors. We went over ridges, along rivers with rapids and waterfalls like Deckers Creek on the way up to Masontown. After a half hour we crossed a ridge that had been cleared of trees. Jamie had been telling me about these big salamanders called hellbenders, when the road disappeared around a curve that sloped down as far and as steep as I could see. Jamie slowed the Subaru, dropped into first, and kept chattering as if this was an everyday thing for him.

I gripped the door handle and sank down in my seat. Snow blew against the windshield, up from the valley below. Visibility dropped down to a few hundred yards, but I could still see enough to know that nothing stood between me and a big drop except for a few inches of rusty guardrail.

Jamie went right on talking, about how he left Davis after returning from Vietnam, vowing not to stop until he saw the Pacific. He said his plans hit a snag in Morgantown when he got picked up for vagrancy. Mick witnessed the ordeal and offered Jamie a job to keep him out of the slammer. Jamie hadn't known much about music except for the stuff his family played, which he didn't much care for. Mick hired him because he felt a veteran shouldn't be treated like a criminal.

Once Jamie got into a real good groove with his stories I couldn't get a word in. But I didn't want to. Just hanging out with him made the trip worth it. I knew I'd let my mind get away from me, but I couldn't help thinking maybe my dad, if he was really out there, would be a lot like Jamie.

"This is laurel country, all right." Jamie paid more attention to the steering wheel than he had earlier.

"You want me to drive?" I asked. The look on his face made me a little uncomfortable.

"No, I'm afraid to stop." He pointed at the vehicle we were following, an old mail truck driven by Jesse Currence's nephew. We met him at the post office in Circleville, which looked suspiciously like a gas station to my untrained eyes. Jesse's nephew, also conveniently named Jesse, was working, but seemed to view our early arrival as a reason to close shop. A little guy with Little Guy syndrome, Jesse took great pleasure in ripping off his tie and putting a camouflage jacket over his government-issue sweater vest. He had teeth like gravel.

Jamie did a good job dodging ruts and grinnies for twenty minutes. We crossed a river Jamie called the Potomac, but I couldn't tell if he was messing with me or not. I was pretty certain the Potomac went through Washington D.C. Just up another hill Postal Jesse whipped his Chevy Bronco onto the berm. He backed up, grinding gears so bad we heard it with our windows up and a CD playing. Jesse stopped right next to us and rolled down his window. I rolled my window down.

"That there's the road up, but you're going to want to park here. Aim yourself downhill, that way, depending on how much snow we get, you ain't got to worry about backing around." He took a big swig from a gallon jug of sweet tea. "Get a ways up, that way if the county plow does come through you ain't buried."

"Take this up to him." He reached through the window, holding out a fistful of letters and junk mail—fliers and a few days' worth of newspapers. "This is so they know I's the one who sent you."

With that, he split.

Jamie looked at me, "This ain't nothing. I've been out a lot further in the boonies than this."

"How far is it?" I strained to see up the road, but it disappeared around a bend after about fifty yards.

"I don't know. I've never been here."

"I thought you said..."

"I know Jesse Currence from his trips to Elkins and Glenville and Charleston." Jamie put the Subaru into reverse and backed onto the dirt road. His wheels spun in the rocky mud. He tried once more, put it into park. "We walk from here."

I believed he was quoting Indiana Jones and the Temple of Doom.

The biggest challenge in getting out of the car involved jumping across the mud while avoiding the jagger bushes on the other side. At first I tried to keep my phone handy, but couldn't get a signal so I packed it. I humped my bag, a sleeping bag and a pillow under each arm, my guitar case in my right hand and a pair of mic booms in my left. Jamie laughed and said, "Don't waste any time up there. You're going to have to make another trip."

But he was joking, and by the time we set off up the road he carried only slightly less weight than me. He shoved as much as he could into his own pack and slung the old army-issue canvas shoulder bag around his neck. He balanced himself out with a fiddle case in each hand and a mic stand under his arm.

We walked uphill for a good five or ten minutes. The snow briefly turned into a drizzle that soaked us and most of the stuff we were carrying. I waited for Jamie, holding up the sleeping bags apologetically. He shrugged and said, "We can hang them out to dry." He managed a smile. "I hope."

The road leveled off, then dropped into a little stream valley. Old fields sat inside an anorexic barbed-wire fence where corn stubble poked through the decaying snow, maybe waiting for a fresh dusting from the dead sky. The driveway curved past a garage housing an old International tractor. Across the road sat a barn where a dirty cow stood in ass-deep mud next to a fresh bale of hay. The gap-toothed wood making up the barn's siding and roof only implied shelter from the elements. A big crater in the shingles had a bright blue tarp peeling away from it. The lane ended at a white, two-story farmhouse with dark windows. An empty dog house sat a few paces away from the front door. The chain ended at an upturned stainless steel water bowl.

"There's even an outhouse," I said.

"Did you pack toilet paper?" Jamie said, to get back at me. "If not, it's going to be a long weekend."

A split second from telling him no, I remembered the incident with my cheek and the mirror. When I held open my coat pocket for him to see the roll, he shook his head and chuckled. "City kid."

The cow wallowed in the mud, and Jamie spotted a man in an old windbreaker, on unsteady legs, breaking up a bale of hay. As we crossed over the creek another cow, this one half the size and twice as pathetic, ambled over. The old man yelled, "C'mon, Jake," and a third came out of the barn. The old man steadied himself on a fencepost and caught his breath.

We stepped out of the gravel lane and up to the barbed-wire fence, but the old man still hadn't seen us. Jamie coughed a little cough, then said loudly, "I heard there's a pretty decent fiddle player lives here."

The old man turned around, grinning broadly. His eyes looked toward us, but not quite at us. He wore an old trucker hat that had been handed out by a guy running for commissioner of Pocahontas County. Somebody had crossed out the silk-screened candidate's name with a magic marker. "You fellows here to play some music, I suppose?"

We shook hands over the fence as Jamie made introductions. I struggled not to drop my load into the snow and mud. Jesse's skin felt dry and thin like onion skin. "Go ahead down to the porch and I'll show you boys around."

The house sat in the hillside like eyes in a head. We passed over another small wooden bridge that crossed the rushing stream. The old planks flexed noticeably as we walked over it. Clear water danced around mossy rocks and, as pretty as it looked, I hurried right across because I didn't trust this old guy's handiwork. All around us birds sang. I thought it meant the end of winter.

Jamie set the mic stand and his recording gear down on a low bench next to a big stack of firewood and shook out his hands. Water dripped off of the roof along half-hearted icicles. Jamie took the sleeping bags from beneath my arms. Jesse trailed not so far behind, walking along the gravel lane with a fairly noticeable limp. When he made it to the porch he ushered us inside. The small, dark kitchen had a coal stove that rested in the corner furthest from the door. A red glow and a hot, sulfury breath came through cracks where the griddles didn't seat properly. A steady tinkle of water came from the spigot. Above the window over the sink hung a small SATOR square like I'd seen last week. There weren't any pictures on the plaster walls, and the only other thing of note in the big room was a shelf holding a candy dish and a cookie jar.

Stairs to the second floor began right next to the front door. A narrow doorway adjacent to the stairs opened up into a storeroom—walls of shelves stacked high and deep with jars of veggies. A few bags of sugar and flour. Cornmeal. Another SATOR square above a small window. Another door, this one closed, went beneath the stairs. Jesse helped us hang our sleeping bags and pillows over chairs by the stove to dry. He and Jamie went back onto the porch. I waited by the fire to get warm.

The ceiling creaked, and I jumped. Slow footsteps shuffled across the floor above my head. I ran to the porch, letting the screen door slam behind me.

Jamie waited for an explanation.

I pointed back at the second floor windows and shook my head as I caught up.

We followed Jesse through some thick laurel, back over the stream to the outhouse. The bridge to the shitter was a pair of railroad ties half-buried in the earth. This bridge looked a lot sturdier than the other bridge, but much narrower. An old, waist high stump at the one end was the only thing to hold onto. I figured when I fell into the stream and drowned Jamie'd have to tell Mick and Katy I was last seen running through the snow trying to 'hold it'.

Keeping my voice low, I said to Jamie, "Is this a good time to ask about the song?"

"No, or we'll be out of here faster than a pair of striped-ass jaybirds." Jamie waved me off like he was fair catching a punt. "Be delicate and tactful and don't rush it."

"Okay," I said, and stepped back in line.

Jesse showed us a chicken coop and plenty of scrawny white chickens. He showed us his bird feeder, which had been attacked by a bear earlier in the winter. Claw marks girdled the post and the feeder itself hung askew like a girl I once knew who drank way too much Boone's.

Looking back at the house made me glad to be away from it. Dark, empty second-floor windows suggested empty rooms. But somebody else was up there, watching. I studied the darkness, both wanting and not wanting to see movement behind the glass.

"Come on, now, Preston."

We made a big loop through pine trees and laurels back toward the driveway. The path snaked through more jaggers and over slippery, moss-covered rocks. The stream came really close to the path, and I had to use saplings like a handrail. Jesse was a talker, but there were times I could barely hear his low, soft voice over the rush of water in the stream.

Jamie paused for a second, letting Jesse get ahead a bit, and quietly pointed out a dead tree eerily porcupined with hundreds or thousands of needles and nails sticking out at all angles. Cut nails and roofing nails and tiny paneling nails. Some were galvanized, some had rusted nearly to dust. In some instances, two nails shared a hole. Some came straight up from roots that disappeared into the patchy snow. The highest were about the height of Jesse's raised arm, like he was the one torturing this old oak. Jamie said he'd tell me about it later.

Jesse pointed down into a field that disappeared over a hill. The surface seemed to squirm with a multitude of starlings. They sang and called out and jumped in the air at each other.

"I'll show you the pasture after we see the woodpile, if you want," Jesse said, and continued back down the lane toward the barn where we first met him. His woodpile sat just past the bridge on the left, between the barn and the house. It looked like a grand affair, a neatly stacked mass covered with a corrugated tin roof.

I recognized Jamie's show of astonishment as only mildly patronizing, but in the kindest way possible. "You cut all this yourself?" he asked.

"From God's ear, I did." Jesse balanced against the stack. The man shook like a goddamn house of cards. He pointed at me, "Give it a try."

I stood there, not sure what he wanted.

"You ever split wood?" he asked.

I pulled the ax from the stump. Jesse balanced a log with a finger then stepped away. Jamie laughed.

I took a huge swing, splitting the log on my first try.

"He's good at it, sure enough. Try again." Jesse put another on the stump. "Make sure you take turns," he said to Jamie, specifically. With that, he wobbled back toward the house.

"I think I got played," I said as Jamie put another log on the stump.

"A small price to pay."

I lifted the ax over my head. "You said you'd tell me about the tree?"

He pulled his fingers away and raised an eyebrow.

I brought the ax down on the log, splitting it neatly in two. "With the nails?"

"Oh, yeah. I guess I did say that." He put another log on the stump. "Well, some folks think it'll make a tree bear fruit—putting nails in it like that. Some think it'll stave off blight."

"That dead tree? Some of the nails were really new."

Jamie said, "I suppose you're right. Well, in Old England they drove nails into a tree to heal a toothache. Probably comes from ancient Egypt where nails signified prayers. You know, like transferring illness or problems to the tree."

"That makes zero sense to me. That's a lot of nails for a toothache or a missing calf or whatever." I rested the ax head on my toe.

Jamie put another log up. He had a hard time hiding his reluctance to continue. "The crown of thorns worn by Christ during the crucifixion came from the Thorn Jujube tree. Its leaves are said to be the best natural protection from demons. I suspect the Currences do it to attach the power of the devil to that oak tree up there. For protection."

"Why didn't you just tell me that in the first place?"

Jamie smiled. "I thought you might buy one of the other explanations."

We took turns with the ax all afternoon, and I built up a nice sweat. I took my hat and jacket off and steam rose from my arms and head. Once Jamie finally figured we'd done enough to keep Jesse happy for a while, we wrapped up. He said he had to 'cross the stream' before dinner, as he put it, so I headed back alone.

I sat on the porch for a few minutes, letting myself cool down, but really stalling because I didn't like being in that house. I picked up a few handfuls of snow and held them to my face, then let a bit melt on my tongue.

I pulled the thin front door open and stepped into the dark and stopped. Somebody sat at the table. I stood in the door, unable to say anything. He was a younger version of Jesse except for a bit of disfigurement near his right eye. Like Jesse's ghost. I couldn't speak.

The ghost said, "Who is it?"

My mouth got really dry.

Jesse came out of the spring house with a bag of flour, almost scaring the piss out of me. "Ernie, this is one of the boys I told you about. They come up to do some recording."

I stepped over to the table as the man stood. He grabbed the air, I placed my hand into his. He laid his left hand over mine and slid it up to my wrist, my forearm, my elbow, then finally my shoulder.

"Preston Black. Nice to meet you."

"Preston Black. That ain't a name somebody gets by accident." He let his hand slide over my collarbone and rested it on my chest, like feeling for a heartbeat. He felt for his chair before sitting back down.

I stumbled toward the sink. To make like I'd meant to do it I turned and started to wash. The spigot released a trickle of ice-cold water from a gravity-fed spring— the breath of the mountain itself. Then I beelined for the back room where I could hide. I threw on a dry shirt, grabbed the bottles of whiskey, and went back to sit at the table. "I brought you something, as a way to thank you for your hospitality. I didn't know what you drank…"

I held both bottles up to let Jesse choose. He said, "Thank you," and took them both. "We drink just about anything." He put them on the counter next to the sink and said, "Go ahead and shake down them ashes."

I went over to the coal stove and stood there, not sure how to shake down anything. Jesse talked me through it while tending to the red beans bubbling in a big old pot on the stovetop.

When Jamie finally came in and washed up for dinner I relaxed a bit. Jamie's introduction to Ernie was brief. Jesse cut it short with a really long grace, in which he blessed nephews, nieces, cousins, the departed, farm animals, his preacher and his deceased wife. By the time Jesse wrapped up and everybody else served themselves I was good and hungry. Pinto beans with ham and cornbread wasn't a T-bone, but I ate as much as I could, which wasn't much. I kept waiting for Jamie to steer the conversation toward my song, but they talked about everything besides. Things like the people they had in common, things that weren't there anymore. Ernie stared at me, nodding to the rhythm of his own chewing.

I'd hoped for whiskey, or music, didn't matter which. But after we cleaned the kitchen Jesse went upstairs to get his checker board. He whupped Jamie's ass, game after game. Jamie could barely get a king. Even after it got dark and they had to play by the light of an oil lamp, the games went on.

I fell asleep at the table. But it wasn't real sleep, their voices and conversations infiltrated my brain. I knew where I was and my mind never quieted. The smell of wood smoke reminded me I'd be sleeping a long way from my own bed.

CHAPTER TEN

Sleep without sleep.

Jamie snored. Jesse came down the stairs a couple of times to "shake down them ashes," and the old house made sounds of its own, like whispering, or some kind of murmuring. Like the old ladies praying the Rosary before mass. Maybe the wind had been blowing against the walls. Outside, branches snapped from the weight of the heavy, wet snow. And birds, just outside the window, whistled and screamed all night long.

The more I thought about it, the more it sounded like murmuring instead of the wind.

Halfway through the night, after Jesse tended to the stove the second time, I hovered on the verge of real sleep when my phone rang. I knew I heard it, and dug through my bag as fast as I could before it woke Jamie up. The phone had settled to the bottom, right up against the Pancake book Jamie lent me. I took the book and my phone into the kitchen. I pulled a few handfuls of cold spring water to my mouth from the spigot. Even in the dark I could see the snow piling up outside. It showed no sign of quitting.

I looked at my call log. *Dani. 5:37 a.m.*

This morning.

"Shit," I whispered. I tapped my foot while the phone struggled to connect. Sounded like when you hold a seashell up to your ear. But I kept listening.

Nothing happened. It never rang. I never got to hear her voice. I put my head on the table.

At 6:14 it rang again. "Hello." The ring seemed so loud in the quiet house. Adrenaline hit my veins like espresso.

"Hey." It was Dani. I stood up and went over to the window. She said, "I just wanted to say 'hi'."

I couldn't think of a reply. So I said, "Really? After the last time we talked?"

"I know."

I waited for her to apologize.

She said, "The snow makes me a little lonely. I just wanted to hear your voice." She paused. "You are on the verge of having the life you wanted." Her voice sounded sleepy and very far away.

I didn't say anything.

She said, "*Stýská se mi po tobě.* But you'll hear from me soon."

I said goodbye but she'd already hung up. For the longest time my ears rang with the echoes of her words. I wanted to text her or call her back, just to tell her how much I missed her. Thousands and thousands of things to say to her. I put my head on the table.

When it got light enough to read by, I cracked opened the Pancake book. I read the shortest story in the there, a story about a guy hunting squirrels. About how his brother ran off to form a church as far away as he could, leaving the main character all alone with his old parents. Pancake's character seemed real. Like me. And the farmhouse seemed real, like this one. I believed the story could happen.

I read another, "Trilobites," but liked the first one better and read it again before Jamie got up.

He crept into the kitchen, smiling as he rubbed his eyes. "Isn't this great?" he said, before going to the sink and splashing cold water into his eyes and onto his cheeks. "Katy would've just ruined the whole thing," he joked.

"How's the book?" He pointed at the Pancake.

"Pretty good, I guess." I flipped through the pages thinking the words might just fly off like water drops from a wet dog.

"I'd put on coffee," Jamie said, "but I don't see any." He opened the drawer to the firebox and stoked it a few times real good. "Did I hear a phone this morning?"

"Yeah, sorry. I got a call. Didn't think I'd get a signal here." I flicked the phone with my finger and it spun lazy circles on the table.

Jamie looked at me, like I was supposed to say more. I was about to apologize, and he said, "You getting a signal now?"

I picked up the phone. "Not anymore."

"Preston…"

I thought he was going to scold me, but he just sighed, nodded, then forced a smile. He took his time to think of his words, then went on like he'd changed his mind. "You ready for some music today?"

"Heck yeah. I was ready last night."

"Be patient," Jamie said, almost interrupting. "It'll happen today. With all that snow there's not much else to do. Did Jesse like the bourbon?"

"Sure did."

Jamie laughed, then hushed up when somebody shuffled upstairs. After Jesse's voice assured us he was awake, I said, "I wonder how long I can hold my pee. You look out there?"

Jamie walked over to the sink, "Holy macadamia nut, would you look at that. You bring snowshoes?"

"That's a lot of snow."

"That's a lot of snow," Jamie reiterated.

The steps creaked, but the creaking could've just as easily come from the old man's knees or hips. "How's that fire look?" he asked before he even fully came into view. "And how come I don't smell bacon yet?"

Jamie assured him that the fire was fine, and asked Jesse what we could do to lend a hand. Jesse went into the storeroom for cornmeal and a few eggs. Jamie asked me, "Ever make Johnny cakes?"

I hadn't, and that was how I ended up bringing wood in. The cold gave me a shiver. I had to stand next to the fire for a long time to get blood pumping again.

Breakfast lasted forever. Jamie primed Jesse for what would come later this afternoon, like previews before a movie. Even though he never mentioned my song directly, I knew it was coming. Jesse had plans for Jamie on the other side of the creek after breakfast. I was to go with Ernie to feed the cows, unless I wanted to kill and pluck two chickens for dinner, which I didn't.

I dressed warm and met Ernie on the porch. Ernie lead me straight through the yard, more or less following the footprints I'd made toward the outhouse earlier. When he got to the little bridge he didn't hesitate. He went across like a squirrel on a power line.

We got to the barn and Ernie dragged a bale of hay over to the stalls where the cows waited. The smell of manure filled my nose—the strongest thing I'd smelled in weeks. Ernie stripped the twine from the bale, and I helped him bust it up.

After a few quiet moments just listening to cows chew, he turned toward me. His eyes drifted up and toward the light, for the first time letting me see the full extent of his disfigurement. He said, totally without irony, "Preston Black, you don't say much."

It startled me a little, so my reply came out quickly and incoherently. I mumbled an apology—I didn't want to make a bigger ass out of myself by telling him I thought he was deaf-mute too—and said something about not being a morning person.

He said, "I have to keep an eye out for my brother, you know. He's all I have. People'd take advantage of a man like him."

"I understand. We have only good intentions." I grabbed a chunk of the bale and dropped it over the fence. "To be honest, I'm the one who got us into this. Don't get me wrong, Jamie loves this kind of stuff. But I'm looking for a song. I got it in my head that this song is important and personal to me. At first I thought it'd help me find my dad. But now I wonder if it's not more about me. I know that sounds stupid…"

Ernie just nodded.

"But I'm afraid learning the whole thing will change me." I didn't know if he was waiting for me to go on or not, because I really didn't leave much of a segue for anything else.

"It's just a song."

"I know," I said.

"You go to church?"

"Used to. A long time ago." After a few long minutes of watching Ernie feed cows I'd already fed, I said, "I hope this doesn't come off rude…"

He smiled, the first time I'd seen him smile since we got here. "Korea, 1951. Nothing exciting really. Caught the fast end of a loose cable. That's all."

A mixture of rain and snow really started coming down, so we finished and hurried back. The rush of water almost drowned the sound of the birds. I walked real close to Ernie, figuring if he stumbled I could give him a hand, but he crept through the heavy wet snow like he was on skis.

Back in the kitchen, Jamie had his mic boom fully extended and was checking the batteries in his digital recorder. Whiskey sat on the table. Jesse stripped a flour sack away from his fiddle. In a pot by the sink, two chickens had been cleaned and quartered, a feather near the stove the only evidence that a double homicide had taken place.

When I shut the door, Jesse, now rip-roaring and ready to go, said to me, "See that old spot on the wall right there? To God's ears, my shadow wore that hole in there from so much fiddle practice." He laughed, then said, "Where's that old guitar of yours?"

Jamie told me to tune to Jesse and gestured to take my time while he got his recorder running. Even I could tell Jesse sounded flat, so it must've been driving Jamie absolutely crazy. Ernie cracked open the bourbon, pouring us each a few fingers with a little spring water from the spigot.

We drank and played right through lunch, almost right up to dinner time, and never made it through any new or groundbreaking material. My untrained ear couldn't even determine if Jesse really sounded as good as Katy said. Even Jamie seemed a little disappointed. Every time Jesse started a new song Jamie'd sigh, and tell me the chords. He'd say, "'Forked Deer,' that's a D, G to A, then a dad, gad gad," or, "'Boatman.' D to an A7. There's a G in the second part, just listen for it."

At one point Jamie even turned off the recorder. Jesse didn't take any notice. He played right through like nobody's business. Then Ernie started giving suggestions. He said, "Stop acting the fool and play 'em something good, Jess. Play 'em that 'Yew Piney Mountain.' Sometimes at night I'd be in the bunk getting a little homesick, and I'd think about that song and cry myself right to sleep, so I did."

Jamie hit record and Jesse got right into it. We sounded like a sawmill tearing through that old kitchen. Jesse lit up, too, for the first time smiling instead of holding himself tight like a pill bug. "To God's ears, that's a good one," Jesse said when he finished. "I thought you fellows wanted to hear all them popular ones first."

Jamie said, "Anything you play is wonderful. But what we really like are the ones nobody wants to hear. Or ones you don't hear too often. You know 'Black Mountain Rag' or 'Old Sledge'? Maybe that old 'Ballad of Preston Black' even?"

I sat up straight and my cheeks got warm. Jamie gave me a nod and a wink.

Ernie interrupted, the tone in his voice stern. "That song ain't no good. Matthew says to get thee behind me, Satan. Thou art an offense to me, and if you believe in God, the devil ain't going to bother you."

My heart sank. Jamie looked down at his strings. Maybe he'd shot his cannon off a little too soon. Maybe that was why he said to bring the whiskey.

Ernie drank what remained in his glass. He poured himself another and said, "Play them that 'Cuckoo's Nest.' Used to be when Jesse'd play that 'Cuckoo's Nest' your feet'd come right up off of the ground."

Jesse picked it right up where Ernie told him to. Jamie could see my disappointment even though I tried to hide it. He patted me on the leg as soon as the song ended. He whispered, "When I get back home I'll start calling around again."

And it was over just like that. Jesse put his fiddle back in its flour sack and Ernie went over to the sink and started to get the chicken ready for the frying pan. Jesse said he had to run across the creek. Before he left, Jamie asked if he had a dulcimer. Could've been his way to keep the conversation going.

Jesse said, "I wouldn't swat a pig with one of those things," and disappeared through the front door.

Jamie shrugged his shoulders. "Your turn." He rubbed his eyes and set his fiddle in his case on the table. He shut his recorder off.

"I'd just as soon turn in to bed hungry and get going as early as possible." I said it loud enough for Ernie to hear, but not loud enough that Jamie'd figure out I'd said it loud enough for Ernie to hear.

Jamie poured us each another finger or two of whiskey.

I saluted him and threw it down. I whooped, and Ernie came over and said he didn't want us getting too far ahead of him, so we all drank another.

"Requests?" I asked Jamie.

"Play what you feel, son," he said.

"What I feel? That's a tough one. Let me try this on for size." I strummed a slow D and played the opening to "Grace is Gone."

Jamie nodded, eyes closed. After I finished the first chorus he accompanied me with his fiddle, playing just like Boyd Tinsley. When we finished he said, "That's a very nice song."

"Dave Matthews Band. Haven't played that in a long time."

"Give us another, maybe something I can sing along with."

Jesse came in, singing something else to himself, and helped Ernie at the stove. Jamie and I went back and forth, playing songs I hadn't thought about in years. Jamie was happier than a tick on a fat dog and he laughed easily. "The Rain Song." "Goodbye Blue Sky" and "Dogs." Israel Kamakawiwi Ole's "Somewhere Over the Rainbow/What a Wonderful World" medley. Old Jimmy Buffett. Some Beatles B stuff, whatever that means. "Mother Nature's Son" and some other White Album stuff. I didn't know as much Dylan as Jamie thought I should. I told him I'd work on it if he listened to more Wilco and Black Keys. Whenever either of us forgot chords or words we helped each other out.

Jesse lit an oil lamp and a candle to make dining more romantic, he said, but it just made the little room hotter. Almost reminded me of firefly weather. Even though the chicken looked good and greasy, I couldn't eat. The smell made me a little sick in the stomach. I tried to put down some red beans and a little cornbread. After dinner Jamie took his fiddle back out and even had his mic stand pointed and ready to go. Jesse said he'd play again, maybe, after he did dishes, so I chipped in and gave a hand to speed things up. But he really just wanted to play checkers. I'd been tricked.

Only two of us had any song left in us. Jamie and I sat at the wooden table, each facing a glass with a few fingers of Jack in it. Jesse went upstairs for his checkerboard. Ernie opened the bourbon I'd brought. He stopped putting wood in the stove some time ago, but the odor of wood smoke lingered.

The forest outside grew dark and distant as the rain continued to fall even harder. What remained of the snow had mostly melted. The icicles that had been hanging on the porch fell to the ground with splintering crashes like breaking glasses. Water dripped through the gutters in straight 4/4 time.

Jamie did his best to maintain the show of gratitude to our hosts, relaying anecdotes about other recording sessions with people Jesse and Ernie both knew, the whole time still working on getting the song out of Jesse. I strummed my guitar, going through scales and arpeggios and chord progressions I didn't even have to think about. The calluses on my fingertips grew harder and the playing had gotten much easier.

I stared at Jamie, trying to give the appearance that I'd been listening. He glanced at Jesse and Ernie and leaned in closer.

"Besides," he said, locking eyes with me and raising his glass, "it seems like the one song I always hope to get ends up being the most elusive."

Jesse dropped the old cardboard checkerboard and wooden box of checkers onto the table. I stood, partially because I had to make a trip to the outhouse and mostly because I couldn't take another evening of sitting around watching a game I didn't like to begin with.

"I'm going to go for a pee," I said. "You know, Jamie, it's all good. I think I need to let the song go."

"Sit," said Jesse. "Have another sip to warm up before you head out."

At that moment, thunder rattled the windows. If we'd have been back in town the lights would've flickered, the TV and refrigerator and furnace all would've kicked back on. But out here only the whoosh of more rain followed.

Jamie froze, holding his drink with his head halfway tilted back.

I looked at Jamie and Jesse. No one moved a muscle—all ears waited for whatever'd come next. Water continued to drip lazily into the sink.

"I better go before it really starts coming down," I said.

"Shh," Jamie hissed.

Just then rain pounded the roof with doubled intensity, like a thousand buffalo running down the hill and right over the house.

"Too late," I said and opened the kitchen door. The screen door slammed shut behind me with a bang.

I jogged over to the bridge. Cold rain rinsed sweat off of my face. Lightning flashed overhead, and before I could even begin counting 'one Mississippi, two Mississippi' the thunder boomed.

A reverberation coursed through me as I approached the stream, and it scared the hell out of me because it had a more ferocious tone than the rain. The stream spilled over its bank and spread through the yard. The stump next to the bridge sat a good ten feet away and half underwater.

I went upstream a few yards and found more water where yard had been earlier. Because of the whiskey I didn't feel totally confident in my ability not to fall. The stream rushed past so furiously I backed up to a tree and hung on like the flood might get hold of me.

In the muddy light I saw ripples and waves with white tips washing well over the railroad tie bridge. The high dark pines acted like funnels, pushing it all into the tiny stream. I backed away like I'd back away from a snake, and made my way down the lane to cross the creek there.

I walked with purpose. The cold rain gave me a shiver. I pushed my wet hair back from my eyes and coughed. When I crossed the lane's bridge over the creek I paused to watch the flood make its way down the hill. A silver ribbon widened then narrowed then disappeared with a boom that sounded like the water at the lock on the Mon back home.

Water lapped the edge of the muddy path that ran upstream, past the chicken coop and corn crib, to the outhouse. When I passed the tree with the nails in it the path got really narrow. The water covered the trail and I had to go around the tree to keep my feet dry. I stepped over the wet roots carefully, but still slipped. I put my hands on the ground in front of me and pulled myself up using the roots like rungs on a ladder. But there were nails in some spots, so I felt with my fingers to make sure I wouldn't cut myself.

I stood for a second next to the tree. I'd gotten tired of thinking about the devil and thinking that the devil had it in for me personally. Superstition and ritual wore me out. The feeling that no matter what I did, the universe had final say, defeated me. So I put my hand on the tree, found a loose nail and wriggled it free.

I paused, waiting for the lightning to strike me dead. The sky didn't fall. No limbs crashed down on me. So I shoved the nail back into its hole and went up to the outhouse.

The walk felt good even if the cool air didn't. My buzz faded, but I was still woozy from the whiskey. The noise from the birds made my head ache. They tweeted so loud—like they were just inches from my head. Even though I stayed really close to the buildings my feet still got wet. Up the valley lightning flashed. Across the stream I could see the house and its empty upstairs windows looking back at me. I couldn't make eye contact with the windows.

"Be a good time for a smoke."

Wobbly from the whiskey, I started back downstream. But I figured the chances of me slipping and getting washed into Virginia weren't worth it. So I cut into the trees and laurel to go behind the chicken coop and corn crib. A big jagger bush blocked the way, so I backtracked and went the long way around. The breath of the forest felt warmer than the air by the stream. In between drops I smelled spring.

Pushing through the trees made me sweat again. Water washed salt onto my tongue. But the dark night made seeing impossible. I tripped over rocks and roots and stepped away from the buildings to get better footing. Through the trees above I saw another flash, and waited for thunder, but the boom never came. I stopped walking and looked up to watch it.

The light shined dimly, and steadily, like headlights from a car coming around a bend. I didn't think it was the light itself that held my gaze as much as the idea that I'd gone without electricity for this long. It seemed like a novelty, and I went up the hill to look.

The higher I went the brighter the light got, like a spotlight from a police cruiser through the treetops. Shadows moved from left to right as the light circled. I couldn't hear anything other than the rain. No motor or electrical hum. Even the birds got quiet. When the lightning flashed again, the light disappeared. I stood there for a second, waiting for it to come back. I pushed the hair out of my eyes. Then I caught it, another sound blended with the rain, a shuffle that grew until there was no mistake. I thought Jamie had followed me out here.

"Jamie."

I waited, and the sound stopped.

"Hello."

I started back down the hill and saw another light, like a firefly this time. Maybe not as green. I squinted through the rain to see more clearly. I wished that I was sober.

Somebody pushed through the laurels behind me.

I walked as fast as I could without running. Suddenly the light seemed to be the least of my worries as the sound of the footsteps just a few yards behind me got closer.

I stopped.

A fraction of a second later I heard it. And ran.

Wet laurel and jagged pine branches clawed at my shirt and my skin. In some parts it grew so dense I had to hold my arm above my face and close my eyes. Small pine needles and dead leaves stuck to my cheeks and hair and arms. They got into my mouth and I had to spit them out.

Off to the left I heard the rush of water. I turned toward the sound and picked up my pace, shuffling my feet to avoid getting tripped up in roots and rocks. The stream stayed the same distance from me no matter how fast I walked. I began to jog.

With my arms crossed in front of my face I took the most direct route back to the creek that I could. In between rain drops and laurel hells I saw more of the fireflies. First two or three, then dozens throughout the forest all around me like spotlights off of a mirrored ball. They didn't move at all like fireflies. The sound of the water got more distant.

I panicked. At first it came like nausea, like I was going to throw up after a long night drinking. But the nausea was overtaken by a feeling like too much caffeine. Spikes of energy down my spine, through my arms and legs. I shook my hands out like you do when it's cold. My heart fluttered and it got hard to breathe.

The lights are just your mind playing tricks.

They were in the trees behind me now, glittering like sugar stuck to a donut. Pinpoints of almost-white light. I could imagine the house watching from the other side of the stream. Dark, empty windows staring into the forest while Jamie and Jesse and Ernie talked downstairs. I thought about Pauly and Stu and Katy, and for the first time got afraid I'd never see anybody again.

I told myself over and over it was all in my mind. I told myself over and over I had to ignore the lights and listen for the stream. As soon as I figured out which direction was downhill, I ran. The bright spots went by me like porch lights past a fast-moving car. I had to tell myself over and over that they weren't out to get me.

When the hillside flattened out I knew I'd made it. I pushed through the shrubs and came into an opening. Water came up over my ankles. The fear of being pulled downstream made me fall backward into the mud and leaves. I looked for the house and outhouse, but I must've come out too far upstream. With my hands clinging to branches and trees, I shuffled through the icy water. I placed one hand over the other, never letting go until I had something else to grasp. I slid my feet through the sand and mud and rocks making sure I wouldn't trip and end up face down in the stream.

Branch. Tree. Foot. Foot.

Branch. Tree. Foot. Foot.

The next light I saw was the light from the kitchen. I stayed cautious and kept both feet on the ground and tried to shuffle toward the bridge.

Branch. Tree. Foot. Foot. I began to shake. Whether the shaking came from the cold or nerves, I couldn't tell.

The water got higher, covering my ankles and creeping up my calf. But I couldn't let go of the tree I'd been holding, and retreated to the shore. When I passed the outhouse I didn't waste any time heading back to the lane. Back to the corn crib and chicken coop. The water ran higher now, pushing me right up to the buildings. Splinters from the old door caught my palm when I steadied myself. I scratched a few out and held my hand in the cold water.

At the rise where the nail tree stood I reached ahead of me to feel for roots. I kept one hand on the ground and the other feeling the air ahead of me. When I found the nail tree I pulled my hand back like it was an electric fence.

The tree felt like a clean shave. I got my feet under me and pressed my hands into the bark. My fingertips read the tiny holes, where the nails and pins had been, like Braille.

I slid my hand down the tree's roots and found thousands of nails on the ground instead of soil and snow and stones.

I picked fistfuls up with both hands, then dropped them back onto the ground. I wiped my hands clean on the tree. The holes had closed. The bark felt smooth as the skin of an apple.

I took three big steps away from the tree and ran toward the lane. Maybe Jamie was right and I was just a stupid city kid. We only ever camped up Jenkinsburg with beer and take-out from Wings Olé. I ran the whole way to the house.

When I stepped onto the porch I took a minute and tried to think of what I'd say to explain what took so long, and made up my mind I wouldn't say anything at all unless asked. The rain picked up again. My teeth chittered from the cold.

The heavy kitchen door remained propped open, just like I'd left it. Murmuring escaped through the old screen along with hot air from the stove. Jamie sat right next to the door. As soon as he saw me he turned, and put his finger up to his lips, then pointed at his mic. Candlelight threw long shadows on the walls and ceilings. The bottle of whiskey, almost empty now, sat on the table. Jesse had his chin resting on the heel of his palm. I caught the door so it wouldn't make any noise when it shut. Ernie sat with his back against the stove. A halo of sparks drew my attention to his face, his mouth in particular. He hummed the melody, and softly clapped his hands. The tune, dissonant and disjointed as it sounded, was still immediately recognizable. Ernie just happened to be between verses.

With a voice that reminded me of sulfur matches, he sang, "Mmmm, now old Preston couldn't sleep the whole night through, told Preston couldn't sleep the whole night through…"

I leaned against the wall and listened. Jamie scribbled lyrics down in a notepad.

Ernie went on, "He just laid in bed 'til morning came, but the devil she'd visit him all the same, now old Preston don't sleep the whole night through."

His words came out at odd angles, like when a dog's hair gets all bristly because he's angry. "Now old Preston Black went to the crossroads, he did, Preston Black went down to them crossroads, tried to make the devil a deal but the devil she said he ain't got a soul to steal, Preston Black went down to the crossroads, so he did."

Ernie's dirgeful version sounded a thousand miles away from the version Earl Black sang last week at the fire hall. Ernie sang with a voice full of pity and remorse, singing about a body rather than a person. Or better yet, singing about a person rather than a fictional character. "Preston Black writ his own sad song, so he did, Preston Black writ his own sad song, none of it mattered in the end, after his body went floating 'round the river bend, Preston Black writ his own sad song."

After a moment of silence Jamie shut off the recorder.

Ernie shifted in his chair and asked, "How much did he hear?"

I replied, "Just enough."

CHAPTER ELEVEN

Rain came down so hard I started to wonder if we were going to get another thirty-nine days of it. The little creek had been up over the lane at least once during the night. The high water stripped leaves and snow from the bare rock, recording the event, almost flaunting the way isolation had made me a prisoner.

Jamie loaded as much of our gear as he could into a few garbage bags. I asked Jamie if he wanted me to try to back the Subaru up the hill and he said, "Not if you want to spend another night here. Just start her up, get the heat going."

When the only things left on the Currence's kitchen floor were my guitar, Jamie's fiddle and his digital recorder, he launched into a ceremonious goodbye. He gave Jesse and Ernie the things that he'd brought with him—jars of jam, apple butter, honey and a box of chocolates—cream centers, no nuts. Jesse smiled, and told Ernie, "…lookie here."

And even as we were heading onto the porch Jamie reminded Jesse about the workshop this summer. Told him about pickin' on the porch, Saturday night contras, walking downtown for ice cream, watching the Perseids over campus. The more he talked, the more it sounded like something I'd be into. Only the smallest part of me noticed when he mentioned Katy taught a beginner fiddle course.

Jesse shook my hand and told me to stop by any time, like I'd just happen to be in the neighborhood. The only thing Ernie said to me was, "That old song don't mean a thing. The devil can't do nothing to you if you have faith."

Jesse said "Don't pay him no mind."

I tried to let his words go on the trek back to the car. I really did. But birds squealed their goodbyes, making it hard for me to focus. They hung in the trees, dense like a fungus. And as soon as Jamie put the car in gear I asked, "What did you think about what Ernie said?"

After a moment, he asked, very earnestly, "Did you make a deal with the devil?"

I felt a little dizzy, like the first time I got busted for underage drinking. My face got hot.

"Hey," he said, slowing the car to a near stop. "Easy, son. I'm just kidding."

But I didn't recover so easy. Not after last night.

He said, "It's over now, isn't it? You got your song, your guitar, and a hell of a great story to tell. Hopefully you learned a little about yourself."

"That's not fucking funny," I said, forcing a look of anger on my face.

"Aw, Pres…"

But I couldn't hold back my smile. "Serves you right."

He smiled and slapped my knee, then let the car drift toward home. He didn't say anything else until we hit the highway. "Ain't many left like them, Preston," he said, switching topics like a snake changes skins. He revved the engine and hit the concrete at the speed of light compared to the slow two days we'd just spent up on the mountain. "Wires are going to kill what's left of guys like the Currences. Phone lines, power lines, TV cables and fiber optics. Mark my word, in another twenty-five years you'll only be able to read about guys like them in books."

When I thought about it my eyes drifted to the side view mirror, like any minute now one of the Currences would come strolling down the hill and give me a dire warning about heading back to the dangers of the modern world.

Jamie went on, "And what technology doesn't wipe out, the goddamned coal operators will. They'll blast the top right off this mountain and bury that entire valley. It's happening in the south and it's only a matter of time before they bring their destruction up this way."

Hearing Jamie so fired up threw me, so I held my tongue for a while. Finally, to show empathy, I said, "So basically all of it will return to the earth unless somebody writes it down? Sounds like something Dani said the other night."

Jamie opened his window to let his anger leave the car and said, "Dani's the girlfriend? The one on the phone this morning?"

"No, she's not a girlfriend. I wanted her to be, but…"

"But?"

"It's difficult, but it's not going to work out," I said, too aware that I was talking to Katy's uncle as much as I was talking to my friend. Words raced through my head, just not the right ones. And I didn't want to talk about Dani with Jamie. Not if I wanted to see more of Katy. So after a minute, I said, "I wonder how trilobites like the ones Pancake wrote about managed to make their mark. They were basically bugs, right? If I died right now any record of my existence would be gone in a matter of years. Not centuries or decades. Music is like my hobby because I got nothing to show for it, man. Unless I do something to positively affect another soul my time here would have been better spent flipping burgers or pouring Slurpies."

Jamie seemed to silently note my shift in interest and went along with it. "You're young. Maybe creeping up on thirty is getting to you?"

"I don't know, man. I just don't want that song to be the only thing left of me." We rushed through the colorless world. Rain washed salt and ash from Jamie's Subaru as it stripped the landscape of snow. Brown rivers and streams flowed past gray houses and fields.

Jamie tried to make me feel better. He said, "Songs connect people to parts of themselves they didn't know they'd lost. They hear a few notes and it reminds them of Christmas Eve or their senior year in high school. Songs keep track of who we are when we can't keep track of the time ourselves. Whenever I hear John Denver, the sun is shining and I'm bringing my son home from the hospital."

On the other side of the window I saw a world that hadn't stop turning while we were away. Electricity still hummed through overhead lines. As we climbed up the big mountain past Seneca Rocks Jamie said, "Look, you're playing Friday, right? That'll be an important night for you. Get some of your material out there. See how people react to it."

"You think you'll be around Morgantown Friday night?"

"Hadn't planned on it. But I hadn't planned not to be. If you're inviting me I'll do my damnedest to be there."

"Well… Don't go out of your way or anything. But if you are in town…"

"You seem nervous."

"You can't bomb with material that's been tested and proven. There's a reason somebody yells 'Freebird' every time we play. Even if they are trying to mess with us." I rolled my window down a hair to let some air in. After I finally built up a little courage I tried to get Jamie to talk about what'd really been bothering me. "What do you think about what Ernie said? About the devil?"

He turned the radio volume down. "Preston, belief is a powerful thing. It can heal the sick, keep folks alive long after they're dead. Like Elvis. Look, I once met a fellow who told me playing fiddle was forbidden on the Sabbath. Said if you made music after midnight the day before Sabbath the devil'd get into the fiddle and it'd play all by itself. The only way to get it to stop is to burn it. So every single week, for the rest of his life, he made a big deal about putting the fiddle away early so God would know he still honored all the commandments."

"I can buy that, and it's not the belief I have a problem with. But that's not what I'm asking. I want to know what you believe, deep in your heart. Do you feel the devil's real? Is he a trickster or a demon with horns and a split tongue or what?"

Finally, a question he couldn't answer so easily. He let his reply slow-roast, like a Thanksgiving turkey. After a minute, he said, "I have to think about all that I've seen and experienced. One time I saw a guy on the railroad chop off a blacksnake's head. It crawled away and squirmed and didn't die until after the sun went down, just like the superstition says. And I swear I remember seeing my great-grandmother get milk from an ax handle when I was a kid. I remember that day on the farm like it was my birthday."

Jamie let a quarter of a mile slip by before going on. He said, "The devil... I suppose the devil is whatever it wants to be. Like the Bible says, the devil's like a pissy cat looking for the next mouse he'll devour, though not in such certain terms. The devil's an unclean spirit working within the children of disobedience. The Bible says the devil leads men to sin then opposes all of God's efforts to save them from sin. He tempts those who lack self-control and when he fell to earth he hit with nary a splash."

"Nary a splash?" I said, trying to ease Jamie into a lighter mood.

"With nary a splash," Jamie said. "Supposedly Satan was lifted up because of his beauty. He has the power of death. Satan is the deceiver of the whole world. Sorry you asked yet?"

"No, it's all good. It's all just Biblical warning and all that. None of it means anything."

"Well, let me help you out then. We know the devil is beautiful, the devil tempts with sin—drugs, alcohol, food, wealth, sex. The devil probably doesn't have horns, wings or a tail..." His tone grew angrier.

I shook my head to let him know he could stop. And I thought about what he said, because I respected him and I knew he wouldn't mislead me. My mind worked his words over for a really long time. Finally, I said, "Maybe I did make a deal with the devil. I don't know anymore."

By the time we got to Davis I was pretty nerved up. My shoulders hurt and my stomach knotted. My mind took to worrying, about Pauly, about Mick, about Dani. The song stuck with me a little more than I'd let on.

Jamie's wife had a late lunch on the table for us so we didn't go to the fire hall hungry. But I couldn't eat, and asked Jamie if he minded if I went downstairs to play instead. Jamie's studio felt like Mick's shop minus the responsibility. My mind ran through lyrics and snippets of the stuff I'd been working on while Jamie and his wife talked upstairs. I pulled out my notebook and wrote down every single thing that came into my head. I wished Pauly was with me.

Jamie came down after a bit, set up the mic and started tuning his fiddle. He said "You got chords there?"

Somewhat stunned by the offer, I shared my notebook with him.

He said, "Let's play each one twice, the second time we'll roll tape."

We ran through "Kill Every Sparrow" first. I wrote it about how people didn't have control over the stuff that happened to them. The lyrics needed work, so before putting it on tape Jamie helped me with a few tweaks.

We did two more numbers. The next one didn't have a title, but I wrote it about a girl I used to know. About how I'd cut out pictures from old magazines and put them into notes I'd give her between classes. Pictures of beach houses or the New York City skyline. Jamie said I should call the song "Trilobites," because it sounded like the Pancake story.

For the last song I wanted to do something else from my notebook, but Jamie objected. At first, he politely said I had better songs. When I said I didn't follow he started getting specific without getting specific. He said, "Maybe something from this weekend," and, "Is there something more relevant, more personal?"

I shrugged.

He said, "We have to record the song. You have to put a stamp on it, son. Make it yours."

"I can't, man."

To his credit, he let it go. Maybe he was right, and maybe I knew it, but now wasn't the time. So we did my third song, which I called "Twickenham." The mediocre mid-tempo riff sounded too much like Social D. I wrote it about George Harrison after seeing the abuse he put up with while recording *Get Back*.

I considered doing the Preston Black song as a fourth cut, but by the time I changed my mind Jamie started transferring files and fiddling with levels and all that, so I figured we were done. He burned me a disc, then said we'd leave in a bit.

When he said that Katy would meet us later the knots left my belly. I went upstairs and threw on my cleanest dirty shirt. After a quick trip into the bathroom to wet down my hair and brush my teeth I felt ready. But when we got to the fire hall I didn't see Katy. Jamie took his time talking to folks, shaking hands while I strolled to the back and peeked down the hall. I wandered back over to Jamie and lingered, waiting for him to tell me what to do next.

But I didn't get very far before running into Katy, her bright pink cheeks a sign that she'd just come in from the cold.

I said, "Hey, you survived the storm."

"It just rained, mostly. How was your trip? Was Jesse phenomenal or what?" She slid off her mittens and shoved them into her pocket. When she pulled her hat off static brought some of her fine brown hair right along with it. I wanted to push the loose strands back behind her ear, but shoved my hand into my pocket to make sure I didn't.

"I'll tell you all about it. Where were you planning on settling in?"

She smiled. "Anywhere you are."

I wanted to take her hand. Instead, I said, "Maybe someplace less crowded?"

She found one of the firefighters, a guy she either went to high school with or went with in high school, and asked if we could go into the garage. A defensive lineman-looking dude wearing coveralls and a WVU hat opened the door. He looked right at me, said, "Don't touch anything," then, "Katy Bear, let me know if you need anything else, okay?"

"Thanks, Alt." She pushed the heavy door shut behind him. A tanker and a ladder truck sat with their backs to us. Helmets and heavy coats hung along the back wall like a Broadway theater curtain. A faint smell of wood smoke mingled with rubber from the tires and the scent of moisture in the air, perhaps from all the rain outside. Light streamed in through the garage doors' big windows.

She ran her fingers along the edge of her case, and said, "Do you feel like playing?"

While we tuned, she asked about the trip, was it far, about what Jesse was like, she didn't know he had a brother, she couldn't wait for Augusta and I should come down, even if I didn't take a class, and a bunch of other words that came flying at me like bowling balls at duck-pins. Then she asked about the song, asked me to sing it. I said, "Not now. Maybe I'll practice it for Friday."

She asked what else I'd play Friday, and we ended up running through my other songs together. Where Jamie played parts of jigs or reels that kind of fit, Katy played parts that sounded like a synth, or the low drone of a bass to accent what I wrote without trying to tie it to traditional stuff. Her playing sounded more like what I had in mind when I'd written them. Between songs we discussed ideas about bridges and interludes and intros. Then we played them each again, incorporating the new ideas. Eventually I had to pull my notebook out and start writing stuff down so I didn't forget.

After a while we took a break to stretch. She went to the bathroom and I bought some hot chocolates. I waited for a few minutes before deciding I looked foolish standing there with a Styrofoam cup in each hand. She came into the garage a minute or two after me, saying Chelsea'd been texting all afternoon. And that Jamie wanted to grab pizza. She said we should meet him over at Sirianni's. I handed her a cup of hot chocolate.

The rain had finally eased. Across the street I could hear the river rushing full speed ahead, almost as loud as the cars that went by. The gray sky created premature evening as streetlights hummed to life. Jamie waved at us through the window. The low lights gave the interior a golden glow. A haze of frost on the glass, and the angels cut into the screen door, gave the scene a cinematic quality.

We sat down at a table for eight, and were—despite the sign that said *No joiners*—eventually joined by some of the guys from last week and some new people from the fire hall. Twelve total when you counted Jamie, Katy and me. I drank Arnold Palmers as though I'd been wandering Moab for weeks, and listened to friendly sarcasm and condescension fly round the room like bats trapped in an attic.

Katy and I made our own fun, inching our chairs toward the big picture window at the front. She kept asking me about groupies. I thought she was messing with me just like the rest of the group had been doing to each other. So each time I replied with a joke she found a way to rephrase the question. Finally she said, "There must be one special girl amongst the hordes, right?"

It took me a while, but I finally saw what she had been getting at. It stunned me a little. I thought about Dani and the way she treated me. Disposable, like trash. I said, "'Hordes' is a bit strong. There had been one… I thought it would go somewhere but she broke it off. So, no, there's nobody."

Something about the way she looked at me changed. She leaned in, unfolded her arms and dropped her eyes a little. "This means you owe me a real date then."

When the check came we just split it twelve ways. Then Katy suggested we head over to the Purple Fiddle for drinks, but Jamie said we had a long day and ought to be getting back home. Katy asked me, not Jamie, if I'd be up for something else.

I waited for Jamie to approve before accepting.

Katy sang Elton John all the way to Thomas. I laugh the whole time. We swung through town, but couldn't find a parking spot, so she pulled into the post office lot down the street and locked up. "You just want to leave our instruments in there? I thought…"

"They'll be fine." She grabbed my hand and led me onto the big front porch, past the kayak and stuffed moose head and show fliers and the sign that said 'Hippies use back door.' String band music came through the walls. We went through the crowd, straight to the back, past old glass cases filled with t-shirts and books. Katy procured us a pair of Hornsby's Ciders.

She stopped and said hi to the guys in the band then snaked past tables of dreadlocked trustafarians and locals. I followed, part of her little 'here I am' parade.

"The locals seem easily impressed by Katy Stefanic," I joked.

"Jealous much?" She slid into an old wooden booth near the front door.

I sat across from her.

She came and sat next to me. "Mr. Touchdown City doesn't like to share the spotlight, huh?" She smiled and leaned until her arm touched mine.

"A few people you know from high school does not a spotlight make." I smiled back.

The more we talked, the less I missed Dani, and realized maybe there wasn't ever all that much there between us. Dani and I both mourned for a family we'd never had. Katy had never known a life without family. The way she spoke, the way she looked at people without assuming they were out to get her, the way she forgave and forgot—these were all things I found myself falling in love with. With Katy I didn't feel like I had to rehash disastrous childhood events. Caught up in the emotions I'd been feeling, I asked her, "Is there someplace quieter we could go?"

We settled our tab and went outside. The air smelled like spring and sat heavy in my lungs. Each breath contained equal parts mountains, river and water dripping over moss. An enormous moon bounced light off of the puddles and melting piles of snow. It was either that big moon or Katy herself that made me believe I could jump and not ever have to worry about coming down.

Deer lined both sides of the road on the trip back to Davis, so she drove cautiously. Jagged pine trees on the ridges of distant mountains stood out like shadows on a sidewalk in June. Instead of going back into town, Katy made a right onto the road that went to Blackwater Falls. "You said you wanted to go someplace quiet."

"I meant get a coffee or something. Maybe pie?"

"Trust me."

She made a left just before a gated road, toward the lodge. Dense forest blocked out the moonlight here and there. When we came around a bend with a wide view of the sky, it almost looked like we were driving into full sunlight.

"I think we just passed the lodge." Lights from the parking lot disappeared down the road behind us. When all traces of civilization had vanished she pulled over on a wide shoulder. The trees fell away, exposing a thousand shades of blues that changed with distance. Cobalt, navy, sapphire, cerulean, midnight, indigo and colors not yet named tinted mountain ridges lined up like records in a bin at Isaac's. The rush of water drew my eyes to the canyon floor where a thin sliver of moonlit river wound its way between the steep walls. I shut the door and leaned against the hood.

"You're a long way from home, Preston Black." She slid up to me, almost like the breeze had blown her. "Sometimes I dread Sundays, knowing I have to leave this."

"Won't you have better luck finding a job in town?"

"There are schools everywhere. Once I finish my PhD I'm free to go wherever." Her arms brushed mine, sending fire into my belly and down my legs.

"Morgantown would seem empty without you. Like a playground without kids." I gave her a nudge with my elbow, but didn't pull it away so quickly. "Why do you want to teach anyway?"

"I didn't know what else to do, so I kept going to school." She put her head on my shoulder. "And it's safe."

I could smell her hair, feel the soft skin of her forehead on my chin. My heart went from "Dazed and Confused" to "Since I've Been Lovin' You" faster than people forgot about The Yardbirds after Atlantic released *Led Zeppelin*.

"Besides, you haven't given me a reason to invite you back up yet, have you?" She twisted toward me, looking up into my eyes. Moonlight left half of her face in shadow, but I could see her sincerity. Wind blew hair across her face. I gently pushed it behind her ear with my finger.

She leaned forward, lifting her lips to mine by standing on her tiptoes. Her eyes were closed. All I had to do was lean forward.

When I touched her lips I heard a new song. As I put my hands on her tiny waist, slid them down her skirt then beneath her jacket, I forgot it. She wrapped me in a tight embrace, then leaned away, studying me. Her wide pupils locked into mine. She touched my chin, gently tracing my jaw and my cheek with her fingertip. Her delicate lips pursed at the corners, like she was reading a novel. I smiled, then laughed.

"What?" She pulled away and covered her mouth with her hand.

"You look like you're about to burst into flame."

She smiled and kissed me again, unzipping my jacket and laying her palms flat on my chest. "Should we go to the lodge? Or there's a B and B in Thomas?"

I kissed her forehead, taking a second to lay my cheek against her soft hair and skin. I knew what I wanted to say, but couldn't think of a way to say it without sounding like a seventh grader. "Not tonight."

She stiffened. "Why not? What's wrong?"

"Nothing at all. I just don't want this to end. The breeze, the sky, the sound of the water—I couldn't have imagined a more perfect scene. Besides," I said, holding her head against my chest. "I like you too much to take you to a hotel for the night."

And when she relaxed again and sank into me, I closed my eyes. For once, I'd meant what I'd said.

CHAPTER TWELVE

I washed my stubble right down the sink. When Jamie asked if I'd like to join everybody for Sunday lunch at his parents' house I knew I had to look presentable. I'd woken up feeling really shitty, like a hangover without the alcohol. But then I remembered where I'd woken up and things got brighter. The guy in the mirror looked like a new person. Cleaner and more well-rested than I'd seen him in a while.

Katy and her mom were late getting there, so I got to hang out on the couch with her grandpap. John Henry Collins seemed like the type of guy who'd disapprove of any guy his girls brought home. That's what I told myself anyway. It made it easier to accept the strained silence I got. Katy's grandma, Alice, was far kinder. She made sure I had something to drink and showed me pictures of all her kids and grandkids. She reminded me a lot of Pauly's grandma.

I asked Alice if she needed help and ended up peeling potatoes. When Katy got there I drafted her too. She introduced me to her mom, Rachael, a beautiful woman with half a smile, just like Katy's. When Rachael mentioned Katy'd never brought a guy home from school, I endeared myself to her with the awkward joke, "I didn't really have a choice."

We hung out until about four, playing Scrabble, which I sucked at, and filling our bellies. Katy asked me when I wanted to leave, and I said I didn't have a reason to rush back to town. So we walked back to her house to load her car. As we dodged mud puddles she showed me important places from her personal geography—stone walls where blackberries grew in the summer, an old pavilion where they used to have family reunions. I told her, "We barely had a yard."

After a quick tour of the house we went up to her room. Pink walls and white bookshelves filled with high school yearbooks and pictures of her as a younger girl made me really, really look at her differently. She was a girl I barely knew, but wanted to hang onto. She handed me a few bags and a laundry basket and went toward the stairs. Katy said, "For a long time I couldn't figure out if I wanted to stay here or leave forever. I still don't know."

Then she handed me a silver coin. "Mom wanted me to give you this. It's from Ireland. A knot to keep the devil away."

I didn't say anything.

Katy said, "Jamie told her. Sorry."

We drove back to her grandparents' house and said our goodbyes. Alice gave me a delicate silver chain and pendant. She said, "Our Lady of Medjugorje. You need to wear it."

Katy kind of rolled her eyes apologetically.

I thanked Alice, and hugged her. She said, "Be careful."

Rachael kept her distance, putting her hand on my shoulder and asking about the coin. I patted my pocket, and she mumbled something I couldn't quite understand.

I shook Jamie's hand, and told him I couldn't ever thank him enough, not necessarily for the song, but for the confidence and peace of mind the weekend had given me. He said he might be down Friday, but wouldn't make any promises. Right before leaving Rachael gave me a hug.

In the car I asked Katy what her mom had said when she asked about the coin.

"*Go mbeannai Dia duit*. It's Irish."

I said, "I thought they spoke English in Ireland."

She laughed for the wrong reason, and said, "Gaelic. Means 'God bless you' or something like that."

"Like when you sneeze?"

She smiled. "It means they're worried about you."

"Oh."

We drove home under the spell of a quiet sadness, like the weekend ended just before it could've gotten real good. We sped through the little town of Davis in a matter of minutes—the fire hall, the pizza shop, Jamie's house, they were all just memories if I never made it back up here again. We dipped into Thomas, down a one way road that'd take us home. The Blackwater got smaller as we crept toward Backbone Mountain. By the time I caught a glimpse of the big windmills, the river disappeared. As we crested the mountain, Katy turned on her phone. Almost on cue, Chelsea called.

"We can get a signal here?" I asked.

"Yeah. Back in Thomas really, but I consider this the border of the outside world." Katy hit ignore and put her phone into the cup holder.

"Mind if I charge mine?" I had to dig through my stuff to find my charger. I plugged in and waited for the buzz that meant it was done hibernating. The LCD screen glowed, a tiny little hourglass told me to be patient. After getting a few seconds of juice my phone rang to life. I had voicemails.

I asked Katy if she minded. She said she didn't.

The lady said, "Please enter your password."

I obeyed, like I always did.

"First unheard message, sent Wednesday at eleven twenty a.m."

Dani. I put the phone to my other ear so Katy couldn't hear. She said, her voice as low and soft as I'd ever heard it, "I may have overreacted. All night I thought about you, wishing that you were here. I may have made a mistake. Please call me."

Shit. I guess that was a no-brainer. I deleted it.

"Next unheard message, sent Thursday at ten twelve a.m."

"Preston, this is Pauly..." He didn't say anything for a while. I could hear him sobbing. "Stevie Croe just called me." He set the phone down for a moment. "Stu's dead. He's gone, man. His Humvee flipped into a flooded drainage ditch. The driver got out and Stu didn't. Never even made it off base."

Then came a really long pause. "Maybe we can ride down to the funeral home together? Call me, man. I need you here right now. Please call me back."

My head dropped. I rolled down the window. "Please pull over," I whispered.

Katy slowed down and rode the shoulder for a hundred yards. A sign by a turn-off read CATHEDRAL STATE PARK, but the road had been blocked with saw horses. I opened the door and took a few steps away from the car. Katy killed the engine and got out, her jangling keys like a bell around a cat's neck.

"Preston..." She put her hand on my shoulder, "Hey, Preston, look at me."

I couldn't do anything but stare at the ground. She pushed my hair away from my eyes and kissed my forehead. "What is it? Are you okay?"

I looked at her. My lips parted, but my throat hurt to say it. My head hurt to comprehend it. "Stu's dead. Pauly said Stu's dead."

I dropped to the road, aware of my knees in the mud and grit on the berm but not caring. I grabbed a fistful of icy snow and pushed it into my eyes. But it couldn't stop my head and throat from squeezing shut. Katy knelt beside me. I fell into her, and I let it all go.

"Stu, oh man. My brother." Tears slid down my cheeks. "My brother.... It's not fair, Katy. It's not fair." I wiped my nose on my sleeve and then noticed my tears had gotten on Katy's sweater. She pulled me closer.

"It's not fair," I yelled into the trees. My shoulders shook. I coughed. I wanted to throw up. Katy cupped a little bit of clean snow in her hand and held it to my lips.

A car rolled by on the highway and caught us in its headlights. I must've looked like an asshole on my knees in the snow.

Katy helped me to my feet, but my knees felt weak. She guided me back to the car and brushed off my knees with her hand.

I tried to speak, but couldn't.

Katy rested her head against my chest and squeezed me in her arms. "He knew."

"I didn't want him to go back. I told him every time I saw him. I don't know why he re-upped. I don't know what made him do it." I looked for last night's moon. The sky had clouded up. It felt like rain again. "I begged him. I did everything but get on my knees. Man, I have to see Pauly."

"Do you need me to stop somewhere? Do you want something to drink?" She took my hand.

"No. Thank you."

She kissed me. A different kiss than the one I took last night.

I led her around the front of the car, its four-ways clicking. The light threw our shadows way out on the road ahead of us. I helped her in, and shut the door for her.

I wiped my eyes as I came around. Some kind of resolve welled up in me, and for a second I had myself convinced it wasn't true. It couldn't be true. I sat down and clicked my seatbelt. My phone had fallen on the floor by my feet. Katy pulled onto the highway, turning her four-ways off, and gently accelerated around a bend. I wiped my phone's screen off. I had more messages.

I showed her. "Do I even need to hear anything else?"

"Yeah, you need to check the rest. See if Pauly called you back." She bit her mitten and pulled it off with her teeth. She dropped it into the center console, and went to work on the other one.

"Next unheard message, sent Friday at three thirty-five p.m."

"Where the fuck are you?" Pauly screamed into the phone. He was drunk. "Stevie asked about you, his mom—everybody did. I spent all fucking night telling everybody I didn't know where the fuck you were. You'd better be fucking dead."

"Next unheard message, sent Friday at four forty-five p.m."

Dani again. I deleted it.

"Next unheard message, sent Saturday at seven seventeen a.m."

"They're burying him this morning. Call me if you want a ride."

"Next unheard message, sent Saturday at eleven fifty-five p.m."

"Preston Black, this is Jennifer Kaminski, from Ruby Memorial. I'm calling from the emergency room about Paul Pallini. You are listed as his emergency contact. I'm sorry to tell you there's been an accident. Please call us as this is urgent."

"End of unheard messages. Check skipped messages."

"Katy," I said, "Could you take me up to Ruby? Pauly was in an accident."

We stood in the hallway. The TV glowed softly in his room. Nobody ever looks good in a hospital, patient or visitor. I said to Katy, "If you want to go you don't have to stay. I know you have class tomorrow."

"I'll do whatever you want. If you want me to stay I can wait down by the nurse's station." She pointed her little finger down the hall.

"That means a lot to me. I don't know how long I'll be or how it's going to go. Maybe I don't want you to know how white trash I really am." Maybe I said 'white trash' to represent the sick, ugly way I felt inside. I didn't mean it.

"Preston, you're generous and you have no idea how talented you are. I've been waiting for you, you know that?" She wrapped her fingers around mine.

I held her and stared down the long, bright corridor.

Katy looked at me and said, "This weekend was nice. Maybe you'll want to go back up next week?"

"Friday night's my show."

"I know," she said, almost interrupting, "I mean after. We can leave right after. Maybe Jamie's right. Getting you out of town is better."

"Why would Jamie say that?" I asked.

Katie shrugged. But she knew.

Next weekend was a long way off. I didn't know what would happen tomorrow. I still wasn't a hundred percent about tonight. "Do you want to get together sometime to play a little? Maybe grab a bite to eat or coffee or something?"

She seemed to relax a little when I committed to getting together again. "Sure."

I thought about Stu. And Pauly. My old life gone, like that. I needed somebody to save me. "I have a few lessons tomorrow. Text me after class."

I held her, and kissed her cheek and forehead. She laid her head on my chest. I stroked her earlobe, then a line down to her collarbone with my fingertips, the tiny hairs on her neck were just like dandelion seeds blown by a July breeze. "Want me to walk you to your car?"

"No," she said earnestly. "Your brother needs you. Get in there and see him." She zipped up her coat and pulled her mittens on. "I'll see you tomorrow, Preston Black."

"I'll see you tomorrow, Katy Stefanic."

She closed her eyes for one last kiss. I gave her the CD of the songs I recorded with Jamie, then watched her walk to the elevator. When it arrived on the floor, but before the doors opened, she turned around. She smiled, perhaps a little surprised to see me still standing there.

I watched her get in and disappear before going into the room. Gray and blue TV light flickered into the hallway. The keyboard intro to "Baba O'Riley" buzzed faintly over ambient hospital noise. I knocked on the door jamb and stood there. "Pauly?"

I waited.

"Here." He raised his hand.

The blinds were up. The football field took up most of the view. The big scoreboard waited patiently for September. Some of the apartments on the hill still had Christmas lights twinkling in their windows and wrapped around their balconies. I looked for the Coliseum, but it sat too far to the right. On the TV Roger Daltrey strutted across the stage. "*Isle of Wight*?"

He didn't reply.

I had a hard time looking at him. Low light from the dim fluorescent bulb over his bed let me see how beaten and bruised he was. He had a black eye and his arm hung in a sling. I pushed a chair over to the bed and sat down. "Was Mom here?"

He just stared at me for a really long time. I couldn't tell if he was giving me the silent treatment or putting something together. Then his eyes got wet. Tears ran along his nose. He raised his good hand to wipe them away. "A few months ago he asked me what he should do, man. What the fuck could I tell him, huh? I said we needed to start thinking about what came next."

His shoulders shook, and I could see he tried to keep them as still as possible. He clutched his ribs and took a few deep breaths. A nurse came in with no introduction or regard for Pauly's emotions or our conversation. She set a small paper cup with several pills in it on the tray by Pauly's bed. With his good arm he put the cup to his mouth and swallowed all the pills at once. She gave him a small cup of water. She asked, "Are you family?"

Pauly spoke up. "He's my brother."

She jammed a thermometer into his ear without warning him it was coming. "Do you want him to take you to your meeting? You have about ten minutes."

"He'll take me."

"Very good," she said as she checked his temperature. "Somebody will be back to help you into your chair."

"She's a delight," I said with a whimper of a laugh.

He went back to staring out the window.

"Pauly, whatever you need, let me know. I'll do whatever. I didn't come down here to judge you. Shit happens. You know I've done dumber shit than this, same as you. Some of it we got nabbed for, some of it we didn't. You have to forgive yourself. You didn't do anything wrong. I'll be more supportive. I thought I was telling you what you wanted to hear. I'm really sorry, man."

"I almost had ninety days put together. My sponsor didn't think I could do it. He said I needed to get serious about getting sober… He said I needed to find a new sponsor."

"You know I don't think you're an alcoholic anyway. Everybody drinks. A lot of people fall off the wagon."

He cried. I grabbed his good hand and laid my head down on his arm.

After a few minutes he sniffed and tried to compose himself. "I left the cemetery… It was raining. All those *God Hates Fags* people were there and I got so fucking mad. If I had a gun I swear I would've blown somebody apart. I even went to a meeting and went to lunch with my sponsor. He said I needed to remember what was good about Stu, and when he left I fought to remember Stu. Like, I couldn't see his face, so I went out to Squares to see if I could remember what it felt like playing there, even though I knew Scott meant something totally different. Being in that room, I could feel Stu, man. I'm telling you I could feel him. He fucking spoke to me. Well, Casey asked if I wanted a drink. I told her to give me a Sprite. Then she asked if I was okay and before I knew it I was crying and drinking. Casey cut me off and called a cab. But I didn't want that humiliation on top of everything else, so I split."

He put his hand over his eyes. "You know that big curve coming in past the waterslide? I almost took out the Kwik Mart. This little silver car came right at me. I swerved and hit two parked cars. Thank God and Mary and Jesus and all the saints nobody was in the lot because I would've killed them."

He tried to catch his breath. "You know, I never connected with anybody in A.A. like I connected with you and Stu. Like, the people there don't know what we had. Part of me is wherever Stu's at. I swear to you I could feel when it happened. He's our brother, and it feels like…"

"It's okay, man." I grabbed his hand.

His tears came faster. "When am I supposed to start living? What do I got to do to get married and have a house and kids? What the fuck do I have to do?"

"Were you ever as happy as when we were playing?" I should've stopped. "Life's too short to spend it doing something you hate. So what if you get a little hung-over every now and then? We've calmed down a lot. And I miss you. And I just want to hang out and tell you all the crazy stuff that's been happening to me. Like, I think I found my purpose, and if you believe getting sober is your purpose I'm there, whatever you need I'm there. But you just got to be happy. Money doesn't matter, things don't matter. You have to ask yourself, what's going to make you happy?"

He pulled his hand away. "Don't do this to me." He pointed at me. "Last time I volunteered. Now my sobriety is court-ordered. Now I don't have a choice and I don't need you putting stuff into my head. This hospital is going to be my home for the next twenty-eight days."

"I'm sorry, man. I really am. And I won't ever do anything to disrespect you again."

Pauly turned his head away as a man knocked on the door. He said, "Hey, buddy. If you want to give us a few minutes I'll get Paul ready to go downstairs."

The nurse had huge arms and a Kenny Rogers beard. He helped Pauly to the bathroom. I just kind of stared at my feet for a few minutes. When the nurse wheeled him out he asked, "Do you know where you're taking him? Elevator to first floor, make a left and look for Addiction Services. It's just past the chapel. Bring him right up after, okay? Tomorrow he gets transferred to Inpatient Treatment. Visitation will be restricted. You'll be able to visit for an hour or so after the meeting tonight, but when he goes over to Inpatient, visiting hours change."

I processed everything the nurse said, but all that I could get out was, "Addiction Services."

As I started Pauly down the hall he asked, "That the girl from last week?"

"No. The girl from last week went Courtney Love on me. I was her white trash slum fuck." I stopped Pauly right in front of the elevator doors and hit the down arrow.

Pauly chuffed, but that was about it.

The ride down and the search for Addiction Services felt like a movie scene. Two hours ago I'd been in the car. Two hours before that I ate dinner with Jamie and Katy and her mom. When we finally found the room I asked Pauly where he wanted to sit and if he wanted me to stay. He said anywhere and it didn't matter.

But I didn't want to leave Pauly. I went to the bathroom across the hall and washed up. When I came back I poured a cup of bad A.A. coffee for each of us and got nestled into a corner. There were a few empty chairs in front of me. I couldn't tell if physically distancing myself from the group had the effect of making me more, or less, anonymous.

After my stint in rehab I'd gone to a few meetings a week when I could. But everybody was older than me. Their experience of losing jobs and family members because of drinking was something I couldn't relate to, having been just a kid who got in some big trouble. Nobody ever invited me out for coffee after. Nobody ever called to check up on me. The whole experience left me feeling very lonely. That probably had a lot to do with the way I felt now.

The secretary spoke. An old guy, wiry with a bushy beard and a grease-stained railroad engineer's cap said, "Good evening fellas, welcome to the regular meeting of the Keep on the Sunnyside Group of Alcoholics Anonymous. My name is George, and I *am* an alcoholic." He emphasized the 'I' by pointing at himself.

Everybody said 'Hi, George' but me.

The Serenity Prayer, the Twelve Steps. Slogans, prayers and routines, nothing had changed. Except for the lack of smoke. Afraid of violating anybody's anonymity, I threw my coffee down and went out the side door when they pulled out the Big Book and started reading "How It Works."

The time went by real fast. I stood by the door, nodding at doctors and nurses. Sometimes averting my eyes if the same person came by more than once. At about 7:50 I heard applause, and knew Pauly picked up his chip for twenty-four hours sober. I wondered if I should've been in there for that.

I listened for the Lord's Prayer, and when I heard the group chant, "Keep coming back! It works if you work it," I snuck back in. Pauly looked real small in the wheelchair and his hospital robe. He had people giving him pats on the shoulder, shaking his good hand. He grabbed his right wheel and spun, looking for me.

I took a nervous stroll across the room and said, "I can hang out if you're not ready to go up yet."

"No, I'm ready."

I pushed him toward the door, half nodding at some of the people standing closest to us. A clink make me stop. Pauly's twenty-four hour chip rolled toward the coffee table. I took a step, stopping it from rolling away with my foot. When I handed it to him he grabbed my arm and pulled me down to get close to my ear.

"Remember how I said I saw your dad at an A.A. meeting?"

I nodded.

"See that tweeker with all the tattoos in the quilted flannel shirt?"

I looked, saw the guy Pauly meant, and nodded again. He kept picking at some scabs on his face and looked more jittery than a cat trying to cover crap on a marble floor.

"That's him. And I'm pretty sure he is your dad."

I didn't want to look, not when there was a chance I could see myself, a chance that Pauly could be right. As soon as I saw his eyes I knew.

When the only feelings I could muster were pity and disgust, I couldn't decide whether I'd won a twenty-seven year battle, or lost.

CHAPTER THIRTEEN

The cold tile made my toes curl. I sat on the edge of the tub because I knew if I stood up I'd be sick again. My head ached like it'd been beaten with a skillet. I put some toothpaste on my finger and spread it over my tongue and teeth.

I didn't remember exactly how the hell I'd ended up here. Dani called a bunch of times while I waited for Pauly's A.A. meeting to wrap. Then I wheeled him back up to his room, and I started telling him all about Katy and the mountains. We had a real good talk going. Probably the first real talk we had in two or three weeks. Maybe a month even. I told him about the song and the devil, how it'd been fucking with me and all that.

My phone rang and I answered without thinking. I told Dani I was at Ruby with Pauly and didn't have time to talk and hung up. Then on my way through the lobby to catch the PRT, I saw her waiting. She said she'd give me a ride home. But I didn't end up at home.

I didn't sleep with her. At least, I'm pretty sure I didn't. I got sick in the middle of the night and I'd woken up on the couch. On the counter sat an empty bottle of bourbon, the one we'd started last time. And a bottle of absinthe. Thank God it was still half full. The absinthe did this to me. Bourbon usually made me feel better.

All night long I dreamt the same dream over and over. I stood right in front of Stu's kit while he pounded the skins and laughed. I tried to warn him, just like John Lennon said to. But he couldn't hear me. All night long, trying to tell Stu not to go.

I needed to get the fuck out of here.

All through the night I thought about Katy whenever I couldn't fall back to sleep. It was summer and I was back up in her mountains. The fields and hills were crazy green, like an old photo hand-tinted Mountain Dew green. Or Jolly Rancher green. It was hyper-emerald, a velvety, deep green that absorbed light almost like night does. Blackberry blossoms fell like snow over the old stone walls she'd showed me. We were on a blanket right next to the wall, but the wildflowers were so high nobody could ever know we were there. She had on a little old-fashioned sun dress, with tiny buttons all the way down the front. Her skin felt soft and had grown tan from afternoons in the sun. My Martin and her fiddle were on the blanket with us. Thinking about her made me happy.

The living room was still very dark. Only a tiny sliver of outside light remained once I closed the bathroom door. Still woozy, I felt for a different shirt in my bag. I'd been recycling clothes for two days now. With my foot I tapped out a silent Morse Code on the floor. *My shoes. Find my shoes.*

My head spun from the booze, and whenever I bent over I felt nauseous. I heard Dani in the bedroom. I jammed my shoe on, figuring I could tie it downstairs. Or never. As long as I got going. My hands and feet felt like they were made out of swamp ash. I fumbled with the cinch on my bag and grabbed my guitar case. I threw my coat over the crook of my arm. Light flooded the room. I turned around, lifting my hand to shield my eyes.

"Where are you going?" she asked. Her sleepy voice grew cold and clear.

A lie came faster than I expected. "I know you have to work. I didn't want to disturb you. But call me tonight."

"Come back, come back," she pleaded. "I cleared my appointments to have the whole day with you. We can talk and take it slow." She glided across the floor so fast I barely had time to take a step back.

"Well, I have a lesson at two, so... But Mick wants me to come in early to help him with inventory, so I have to go in early."

"You should have told me. I will have to stay home tomorrow instead. I suppose it doesn't matter. I can rearrange some things. But let's have tea before you go, please?"

Having used my only good trick, I stood there, still holding my stuff. "Just a cup. I don't want to be late."

The water took forever to boil. She went into the bathroom to wash up, then changed clothes. I waited for her while the tea brewed, then dumped half of my cup into the sink. I refilled it with cold tap water. Before I sat back down I noticed her phone on the counter. I flipped through her call log.

Clay. Anton. Clay. Andrei. I heard her closet door close. I snapped the phone shut and sat back down. When she came out she asked if I wanted to eat.

"No, I'm going to finish this and go."

She talked about how much she missed me, her hands clamped firmly onto my wrists so I couldn't gulp the rest of my tea down. And when I said I really had to go she pouted. Her lips sagged and puffed, her amber eyes wouldn't look at me. She said, "It's not my fault. You said you would call me. I waited and waited."

She was right. It was my fault I didn't call. But things had definitely changed. I said, "And here I am now. We were together last night, right?"

"But you were so sad…"

"Jesus Christ, Danicka. One of my best friends is dead and Pauly's in the hospital. And if that was my dad… You know, you said some nasty things in that voicemail." I buttoned my coat.

"And I said how sorry I was." She pushed my arm to the side and sat on my lap. "Do I have to show you?"

She drew her leg across my lap to straddle me. She leaned in for a kiss, and I turned my head to the side a little, so she went after my neck.

"Please, don't. Dani…"

She put her cheek against mine and whispered in my ear. "I didn't get to touch you, Preston. That's all I wanted."

Muddy thinking made me force a bad lie. "Tonight. Just wait until tonight."

"Is that a promise? Will you call me or should I call you?" She collapsed onto my chest, her hands clasped behind my neck.

"I'll call you. After I finish my lessons." I gently pushed her away.

"Kiss me before you go."

I gave her a flat peck on the lips.

"Kiss me." The order came from her eyes.

I leaned in. She locked her elbows behind my neck. Thinking about Katy and this stupid half-lie made my face hot. Knowing that I could lie to Katy so easy but not tell Dani the truth made me feel weak. I knew I had to kick Dani to the curb and get over it.

Dani wrapped her legs around me. I set her on the table and pushed her away.

"I'll be thinking about you all day. Call me when you can." She stood up, put her hand on my shoulder. Her amber eyes looked right into me. "Let me drive you."

"No, I need to shake this hangover." I zipped up my coat and took a few steps toward the door. I picked up my guitar case and my pack, and turned, "By the way, where's your car? Was that a rental last night?"

"Body shop. I had an incident Saturday." She folded her arms, leaning her head so that a few long strands of hair fell across her face.

"Incident or accident?"

"Does it matter?"

It did. She always said exactly what she meant to. Words, to her, were like hundred dollar bills. "Saturday, huh? Was anybody hurt?"

"How should I know? You know my situation. I could not just wait for the *policie* and give them an interview."

"What are the chances?" I mumbled, going for the door, shoes still untied.

Stomping down the old wooden steps made my head throb. I went through the big wooden interior door, slamming it behind me. On the bottom step I tied my shoes then texted Katy. I couldn't remember if she had class or worked at the daycare. It didn't matter. I just wanted to see her. Almost bad enough to call and cancel my lessons. But that would've been dumb. I started walking.

The river looked really high. I could see it through the bare trees. Water gushed over the dam at the lock, a huge heap of debris circled in the pool above it. I stopped at Dairy Mart and had enough cash on me to get a few pepperoni rolls before heading to an ATM and back up to the apartment to put in a load of clothes and sleep off my hangover.

But when I woke up the chilly air almost sent me back under the covers. I went over to the thermostat and cranked it up, and listened for the click of the furnace. "Fucking landlord."

I settled for a really hot shower and got dressed. On the closet floor, next to my shoes, sat Stu's drum sticks. I saw them and cried. I wiped my eyes on one of my newly-washed shirts.

Thinking about Katy was the only thing that made everything feel okay. Even if the snow never melted, and the sun never came back out, I had something with her.

Which meant I had to get this Dani thing resolved tonight. And fast, like pulling off a Band-Aid.

Before I left the apartment I took a minute. My shit was gone. Pauly's shit was gone. Like nobody lived there anymore. I took Stu's drumsticks with me.

When I got to Mick's, he was on the phone. I nodded. He nodded back. No 'How was your weekend?' or anything. I went straight to the back. All through my lessons I thought about two things—seeing Katy and tidying up my affair with Dani. But mostly seeing Katy. She texted during my lesson.

So I rehearsed my speech to Dani in my head while I ran through pentatonics and minor chords with students. Really, I didn't even need to see her. I could've done it over the phone.

When my last lesson left I went out to see Mick. He offered sour criticism of my early arrival and shorter-than-usual lessons. I said, "Say what you want, but you ain't going to put the kibosh on me today."

He said, "You're playing with fire."

I just smiled at him. Katy had texted.

When Katy showed up I grew two feet taller and lost my headache. I asked her to come in to meet Mick, figuring he'd believe it when he saw it. He treated her really nice—nicer than he ever treated a customer—and gave me a slap on the shoulder on our way out. Sooner or later he'd see I was okay.

Katy asked if I wanted to eat before we practiced, but I really wanted to see Stu and asked if she minded. I told her I'd take the Jeep except Pauly totaled it. She put her hand on my knee, and said, "Anything."

On the drive through Fairmont the sun finally came out. Just one of the many magical qualities of I-79. We talked about the guy at the meeting. The one Pauly said was my dad. We talked about the accident and Stu. A warm breeze blew up from the river. I opened my window a crack and let spring blow in.

Katy studied while I drove. But I did a poor job of letting her do her thing. Every time CLG played something we covered I had a story to tell. Johnny Cash came on and I told her about the time we played "Ring of Fire" at a gig in Fairmont a day after a hurricane came through and dropped three inches of rain. The fire chief ordered us to pack up and get out if we didn't want to swim home. Stu bought us water wings at a dollar store before we went on stage.

Then CLG played Alice In Chains, which reminded me of this one New Year's Eve show in Albright. I had the flu and brought a bottle of Robitussin with me. The security guard at the fire hall accused me of Robitripping and called the cops. When a county sheriff showed up he asked Stu, "And what are you hanging around here for?" and Stu, quoting Johnny Cash, said, "For whatever's about to go down, that's what for."

Then they went to a commercial break and my mind drifted until Katy squealed, "That's your show!"

I cranked the volume and caught the tail end of the spot for Mikey's show on Friday, "…Get your heart on! Sponsored by Blindside Records and WCLG, Morgantown's home for rock."

When it ended I asked, "Did you hear it? They said my name? What else did they say?"

"I didn't hear."

"Holy crap. Wow." It hadn't seemed real until now. Totally caught up in the moment, I asked Katy, "Why don't you play with me? You know, like we did Saturday?"

She put the cap back on her pen. "Because it's your night. Didn't you say there were going to be label people there? Besides, I've never played in a bar for that kind of crowd."

"And I don't want to go on alone. I'm not a solo act."

She bit her lips. "They won't like the music I play."

"Katy, as long as it get people on their feet it doesn't matter. That's about the only thing on this entire planet I'm certain of."

She said she'd think about it, and I drove the rest of the way down in silence for fear I'd talk over the radio spot again. Clouds moved in once we got off of 79. I said goodbye to the sun and rolled my window up. When we got to the National Cemetery I pulled off at the information kiosk. By the time we circled around the big cemetery to find the right section I forgot all about the radio, like it wasn't ever real to begin with. When I finally pulled to a stop, Katy asked if I wanted her to come with me, or if I'd rather be alone. "Of course I want you with me."

White, knee-high tombstones stretched along the hill like spokes from a big wheel. I felt lost and small and selfish for not committing myself to something greater. Like I had less to die for than the guys lying in the ground here. My life was exactly the kind of life that should've been given up for the greater good. I could pass through the universe like ripples on a pond with nothing, not even a memory, to note I'd been on Earth.

I told Katy this, and how I felt like a coward for not following a higher path. When it started to rain I gave her my scarf and she tucked her little hand into mine. As we walked, I looked at the names and dates of birth on the headstones. Most of them were old men who died at home with wives and family by their sides. I based my assumptions on the seventy or eighty years between the days they were born and the days they died. And I looked at the names of the wars.

World War II.

Korea.

Korea.

Vietnam.

World War II.

Iraq.

I touched Stu's stone.

Fresh flowers wilted against the weather. Reds and whites faded to black and gray. A soggy flag hung its head. I took Stu's drumsticks out of my jacket and laid them in the newly-placed sod. The soft earth gave beneath my knees. I sank a few inches into the wet soil. I couldn't believe he was down there in a casket. The letters carved into the headstone didn't tell his story. I touched the date of his birth. In a month he would've been twenty-six.

I looked at Katy and said, "Look at you, getting all wet. We can go."

"I'm fine, Preston. Take your time."

I stood. "I'd feel really bad if you got sick."

She took my hand and led me back to the car. Once we got in I cried. For a long time. It seemed like a long time anyway. Maybe a half hour. Then Katy's phone rang. She apologized and ignored the call, but the mood had been broken.

Just outside of Clarksburg we stopped at a little diner. It had a jukebox and Formica counters. The booth cushions were red vinyl, and on the menus were a bunch of ads for local businesses. My favorite was Frida's Curl Up and Dye Salon.

Katy got a cheeseburger and a strawberry milkshake. I got a double with extra pickles and a Coke. We split an order of fries. They were cut real big and came in a red plastic basket lined with paper, like French fries used to. Drenched in Heinz, the taste reminded me of the lunch counters they used to have at the drug stores on High. I ate like I'd never eaten before.

A couple of old guys kept playing Willie Nelson and Patsy Cline songs. Katy sang in a really deep voice, "Crazy…" I laughed. The lights came on in the parking lot, and Katy asked if I was ready to head back. I wasn't, but I knew she had things to do and felt guilty for keeping her out all day.

When she went to the bathroom to freshen up my phone buzzed. <if you enjoy doing nothing, then you aren't doing nothing, right?> I read Lennon's text and smiled.

The ride back didn't take as long as the ride down. It never did. Katy drove a little faster than I would've. When we got off of 79 by the Sheetz she said, "We aren't going to be able to practice tonight."

I looked out the window. I'd arranged to meet Pauly at his meeting but I didn't really want to go. "Don't you live around here?"

"You have to work for that. You may have fooled Jamie, but I'm a firm believer in a two-week waiting period."

"Isn't that just for handguns, or something?"

"You are not a handgun. More like a pellet gun. Maybe even a slingshot." She slowed down at a crosswalk near Ruby's main entrance. "I have a big day tomorrow. Valentine's party at the daycare. Have to bake three dozen cookies."

I hung onto the door handle like I could drag this moment to a complete stop. "See you tomorrow, then?"

She said, "Sure. I can't have you screwing up my big Touchdown City debut. I have my peeps to think about." She put her hand on my knee and leaned over. "Tomorrow."

"Tomorrow," I said.

She closed her eyes and kissed me. I kissed her back. I said, "I don't want to say goodnight."

She said, "Say goodnight, Katy Stefanic."

"Goodnight, Katy." I grabbed my guitar out of the back. She gave a tiny little wave, then drove up Stadium Drive before disappearing around a slight bend.

I stood in the cavernous entryway and faced the hospital's bright lobby. Addiction Services sat right where I'd left it. I took a quick peek inside, but Pauly wasn't in the room yet. I went to the gift shop and got a Snapple and a Snickers bar for him. Then I went into the bathroom and washed my hands and face. My phone buzzed. *Dani*. I hit ignore and went back into the hall. A nurse walked past. I thought it was the same guy from last night. I mumbled something about the patients from the inpatient treatment unit. With a total lack of joy, he said, "They come down at eight."

And when he saw that I was about to ask a follow-up, said, "And we take them up right at nine."

"Thanks," I said, shuffling away because I didn't know what to do next. I'd gotten there way early. At the end of the hallway I turned around and shuffled back.

After twenty minutes a group of guys walked toward the door. They nodded at me. The secretary from last night, George, asked if I was going in. He had a Pittsburgh accent, saying 'down' like it rhymed with 'pawn'. "Sit down, get a coffee, friend. Maybe listen for a bit."

If I learned one thing, it was never trust anybody who called you 'friend.' I said, "Sorry, man. I'm not an alcoholic. I'm just waiting for my brother. He's the alcoholic."

The old man laughed. "Son, I'm not saying you are or you aren't. I'm just extending an invitation. Saying it's okay to grab a coffee and wait for a spell."

"I didn't mean to get defensive. Maybe I will then, if it's okay? To sit?"

"Our primary purpose is to stay sober and help other alcoholics achieve sobriety. If that means helping your brother out, so be it." He held the door for me.

I took a seat right by the door like last time. As soon as I talked to Pauly I was gone. I sure as hell didn't want to see that fucking tweeker again.

"What you got in there?" George blew into his coffee cup and shoved his other hand into his front pocket.

"Martin. D-28." I flipped the latches.

George whistled. "Got a few miles on her." More people came in. The coffee table was getting crowded. Still no Pauly.

"Yeah, but I've only had it for a week. Sold everything I owned to get it." My voice sounded really loud. I didn't want him thinking I was shouting.

"Sold your soul?" George said it kind of fast, and I didn't quite catch it.

"Huh?"

"Nada. My brother had an old D-35. Used to play a lot down by Fairmont, Weston, Sutton. All over. When I railroaded we'd play four nights a week."

"You play?"

"The devil's instrument." George nodded at somebody, then turned around and shook hands with a skinny black guy wearing Moon Boots and a raincoat.

I almost told him about Katy and Jamie and all that, when George cut me off to say he was going up front to get settled.

Figuring I'd catch Pauly in the hall, I waved and thanked him, flipped my case closed, and stood up real fast.

A man blocked my path to the door. The PO from yesterday. I stepped to the side to get around him as another man came in. When I saw the tattoo sleeves on his arms, blues and reds running together into a mass of blotches I knew it was the guy from last night. Up close I could see dried blood bumps and scabs formed over his ink. The only teeth he had left looked like the black licorice nubs from Good & Plentys.

"That your guitar in there?" he said. He got real close, and I took a step back, but he kept moving toward me. Close enough to see all his shitty tattoos.

He said, "I knew who you was the second I saw you. That Dago bitch told me you died same day your mother did. But I know flesh and blood. I know it." His breath smelled foul. Sulfurous and acidic. Matches and acetone.

On his forearm I saw a heart with an arrow through it. My mom's name was in the heart. *Carlene July 16, 1966-September 1, 1983*. The lettering looked like it'd been written in black Sharpie.

And right below it I saw an angel, and in the angel, the words *Preston February 13, 1983-September 1, 1983*. .

I shoulder checked him and threw the door into the wall with a bang. At the end of the hall the elevator doors were sliding shut. Pauly sat in his wheelchair, waiting for a staff member to push him down to the meeting. He held his hand up, a defeated wave.

I shook my head and ran to the lobby, past the gift shop and lists of donors and directory maps, under the quilts that hung from the ceiling like giant leaves falling from hidden trees. I didn't stop until I felt that cold February air on my cheeks. The stadium sat on the hill ahead, a chorus of birds cried out from beneath the stands. The concrete sloped in such a way that it projected their noise into the night like an amplifier. I looked for the Towers. All I knew was Katy lived by the Towers. I'd call her when I got there.

"Now old Preston Black went to the crossroads."

I walked faster, trying to stay out of the mud along the berm. Past old frats and a run-down hotel, down to University where I crossed by the McDonald's. But the more I walked the more the song dug into my brain. Like a tick on a dog. "Tried to make the devil a deal but the devil said he ain't got a soul to steal, Preston Black went down to the crossroads, so he did."

When I saw Seneca Center and the river below I knew I screwed up. The road got steeper. The Towers were back over the hill and I hadn't seen Katy's car. Somehow I'd ended up on Eighth instead of Riverview. My head spun. "Preston Black went to the crossroads…"

Yeah, I met the fucking devil. If I'd have known I was looking for the devil all along instead of my dad, I would've put that record back in the bin and walked away. I wanted to walk into traffic. I wanted to rest on the bottom of the cold Mon. Sink in the mud, let an icy lullaby end it all like the song said. I turned around and went back up the hill. I stopped on University and realized how stupid this was.

"… tried to make the devil a deal but the devil said he ain't got a soul to steal…"

I took my phone out. Twenty-five after. I'd been walking for a half hour. *Three missed calls.* I checked my call log.

Dani.

Dani.

Dani.

I needed to hear Katy's voice. I needed to hear Pauly's voice. I needed Mick or Jamie. I needed my mom. I needed Stu. The phone buzzed in my hand.

Dani.

After all the rehearsing I did this morning and after the quality time I'd spent with Katy, I figured I'd get this over with. Use the anger I had building up in me for something positive. As soon as I took the call I knew I should've taken time to prepare, but being mad and lost made it hard to follow my own thoughts. "Hello?"

"Preston, all night I tried to call you—"

"I know. I said I'd call. Look, I'm on the other side of town, so I don't think I'll be able to make it over. I wanted to talk to you about some important things tonight anyway."

"I made dinner for you. It's cold now, but I can put it in the oven, or we can get something else. Where are you? Are you walking?" She sounded like she'd been crying.

"Yeah. I am." Like walking wasn't humiliating enough.

"Let me come and get you. You will get sick."

"No. Definitely not."

"It's silly to walk. Tell me where to pick you up. You said you wanted to talk to me, right?"

The universe had begun systematically taking things from me. Maybe this was what Mick meant when he said I was skidding down a long hill. Maybe he meant I had to take control. Besides, I was tired of living with all this hanging over my head. "I'll be waiting in the Seneca Center Parking lot. Down at the—"

It came out of my mouth before my brain could deal with it. "Down at the crossroads."

Light danced at the end of the match. I held it up to my face, eyes squinting at the brightness. All I had to do was breathe.

The inward puff drew the flame to the tip of the cigarette. Tiny curls of white paper caught fire, turned to ash, then disappeared. Smoke coated my tongue, my throat. It crept through my bronchial tubes, forcing a cough. It settled in my lungs, a golden nicotine tingle that dripped into my heart before spreading into my torso. I felt it in my fingers and legs.

I'd fucked her. As soon as we got to the apartment almost. On the steps, just inside the big outside door she kissed me. For a second I fought it. But I knew when I answered her call it'd go just like this. By the time we got up the steps to her door I'd surrendered completely. She fumbled with the lock. I would've kicked the door down. We fell onto her couch. Cold leather against my back. Her hot skin against my front. I told her to slow down, I didn't want to go too early and she rode me harder. Her tiny knees pushing into my ribs. She bared her teeth. She bit my neck, my ear, my shoulder.

After, we drank. I went into the bathroom to pee and clean up, but she wouldn't let me put even my boxers back on. She turned the thermostat way up. She put a heavy comforter onto the couch and kept pouring drinks. She tapped a cigarette out of a new pack, and I asked for one. She said she thought I couldn't smoke, because of my voice. I told her it didn't matter. I really wasn't all that great a singer to begin with.

When the alcohol made me sleepy she took my glass and set it on the floor. She said it was too early, and pulled the blanket off of me. I told her I was done. Her moist lips changed my mind. Needles of pleasure rippled through my skin, like I could pinpoint the location of every single nerve ending in my body. I arched my back, but her teeth wouldn't let go of me. Her amber eyes looked up at mine. She grinned.

She pushed me back against the couch and sat on me again. To be inside her, almost able to feel the bum-bum of her pulse, put me into a trance. Maybe because

I realized, at that moment, she could give a shit about me, or what I thought and believed, or what made me get out of bed in the morning. Just like I told Pauly, I was her white trash slum fuck.

We shared a cigarette and showered. She left all the lights off in the bathroom. Steam clung to the large half-circle window that looked out over the good part of town and the river. Steam entered my lungs, for a second I thought it could clean out my insides too. Maybe wash away the shitty things I'd done.

Was doing.

But her wet skin, so hot and smooth, replenished my store of indecent values from the inside. She pulled my hand toward the tiny, wet curls below her waist and fell into me, leaning against me, hot water between her skin and mine made it feel like I was wearing her. She guided my hand with her hand. Her long wet hair clung to my neck and chest. She breathed steam into my face. I began to sweat.

When she finished she shut the water off, and pulled a heavy towel from the towel bar. After a minute or two she went back into her bedroom. I stepped out of the big tub and fumbled along the tile on the wall for a light switch. I found myself a small towel in the linen closet. I shut the light off and dried myself while looking out the window. I wiped the steam away with my elbow, smearing all of the lights on Beechurst below.

When she finished drying her hair she said, "You can sleep on the couch again, or join me in bed. Whichever you prefer."

I crept into the bedroom, if only to keep from feeling like a whore. The dry pillowcase and sheet felt lovely against my clean skin. She put her arm around me and fell asleep without any chitchat. She didn't even say goodnight.

For an hour at least, I just laid there. The heat made it hard to breathe. I sweated into the sheets then threw them off. Any time I got close to sleep I dreamt vivid dreams about Pauly's hospital room. A heart monitor bleated out a steady stream of whiny beeps. It took me a while to realize it wasn't Pauly's room. The heart monitor didn't belong to him.

I sat in a chair, in the dark. Heavy shades were pulled across the window. Bright sunlight dampened by a few layers of material. It was hot outside. I had on jeans and a t-shirt.

I didn't recognize him without his glasses. He looked really big in his hospital gown. He snored real loud. They had the covers pulled up over his belly.

I knew it was a dream, like all those others. And I waited, instead of reacting. After a long time, Jerry finally said, "You can steal from the devil, you can steal from your friend, but the devil's always going to get his in the end."

When I figured out where I was and what was going to happen I tried yelling for a nurse, I tried getting up and throwing open the window. A weight pushed me down into the chair. Like somebody poured concrete over me while I slept. John Lennon told me to intervene, and I knew I couldn't let Jerry Garcia die.

Jerry was the most fatherly of all my fathers. Like, I could see him coming to pick me up from school in that faded black t-shirt, maybe even driving a shitty old Jeep like the one me and Pauly drove. Jerry-as-my-father never said anything unkind, and when I fucked up he disciplined me firmly, but never harshly.

In my wishes he taught me to play the guitar. He'd watch patiently as I fumbled through scales, my mind fighting for control over my fingers.

Jerry sang a few lines over and over, looping like a digital delay. He sang, "I went to the levee but the devil got there first, said you can run all night but you can't outrun a curse."

I thought he was talking about my dad. I asked him what I should do.

"The accuser of brethren doesn't want us livin' Godly lives," he said, wiping his hands on his black t-shirt. For a second it felt sunny and cool. I assumed it was Marin County because the light was the same as the light in all those old Grateful Dead family pictures. May as well have been heaven. He pulled his beard and said, "He don't want us living patient and lovely lives."

He was talking about my dad, so I listened, waiting for him to get to the good part. But after waiting a long time, knowing morning would be here soon, I got direct. "Is the song true? Should I be worried?"

Jerry strummed a banjo. As he plucked he said, "Satan's already been defeated, he just don't know it yet. He'll soon get all he has coming to him. Woe to my children for the devil's coming down on you with great wrath, because he knows that he ain't got but a short time."

In the hospital room the air kicked on, chilling the sweat that had formed on my skin. I folded my arms over my t-shirt, a shirt I had when I was little. Optimus Prime held up a laser pistol with one hand. With the other he waved with a half pointed finger, like Bumblebee and Bluestreak would appear on the horizon any second to kick Megatron's whiny ass.

I asked, "What do I have to do? To save myself?"

Nurses and attendants came and went, but they all ignored me. I figured Jerry didn't want to give me my answer while they were in the room. Then the sun went down. The room got colder. Light came from the hall through a tiny sliver beneath the door. Steady blue light from his heart monitor illuminated his silhouette on the bed. I got really tired just sitting in the chair waiting. I stopped paying attention to what went on in the room and my mind drifted other places. By the time I realized his heart monitor had stopped making noise it was too late to do anything.

When I felt the wetness of the tears on my pillow I woke up and wiped my eyes. Dani still had her arm clamped over me. I slid out from beneath it and went into the bathroom. I didn't turn the light on. Getting dressed and going home seemed like a good idea. But I went back into the bedroom. To a warm room. To the warm bed. Dani asked what was wrong.

"Just had a bad dream."

I waited for her to ask me about it, to ask if I wanted to talk about it. She said, "I know what will make you feel better."

She rubbed against my back. I didn't know if I was fully awake or not. She kissed my neck and shoulders. Her kisses were warm and wet. I rolled over. She found me with her hand. I didn't think any of it was real.

CHAPTER FOURTEEN

In the morning Dani drove me up to Mick's. She'd been on the phone with the body shop, and said she had to return her rental. She asked if I could pick her up before I went over to the middle school. I told her the Jeep had been totaled, and she said maybe I could pick her up in Mick's car. I told her I had to think about it, but I really meant no. My phone buzzed.

She said, "Who is that?"

I didn't know, but I said, "That's my business."

When she drove away I checked it. <I think I got an answer for you, from the Tibetan Book of the Dead. Trust the clean white light of the universe. It is your home.>

When I got to Mick's he told me I smelled like smoke, and needed to go home and change. I apologized, told him they smoked at Pauly's A.A. meeting. Mick said that wasn't an excuse for smelling like smoke this morning. So on the way back to the apartment I stopped at the old GC Murphy's on High and bought a pack of Camels and a handful of Atomic Fireballs. I had to ask for matches. Out on High I lit one up. It didn't feel as good as the one last night. But it didn't feel bad either.

I got another text. <this is jerry again. you always pick the lesser of two evils and you're never going to end up with anything but evil.> I deleted it.

When I got back to Mick's he gave me a twenty and asked if I'd get gas in his car. I left a little early so I wouldn't be late to the school. As soon as I got into the car I called Dani to find out where she was. She gave me directions. The god damned body shop was halfway to Fairmont.

When she got into Mick's car she asked what she was going to do the whole time I was at the school. I said she'd have to wait. She asked if I could drop her off at the mall. I said I was already late, so she suggested dropping me off and taking the car. I said, "No way. Absolutely, no way."

But when I got to the school it was five after, so I gave her the keys and said to park it and wait. I apologized to the music teacher ten times. She said it was fine, and the kids settled down once we got started. She asked about the lyrics I said I'd type up last week, and I told her I'd forgotten. I tried explaining that my brother had an accident, and she said it was okay even though her facial expression didn't quite agree. I tried to make up for it by writing "Lucy in the Sky with Diamonds" out on the board. Before we could start I had to explain what 'marmalade skies' and 'Plasticine porters' were. I had to admit I didn't know what Plasticine was.

I felt like I had pretty much made up for being late and forgetting the lyric sheets. I assured the teacher I'd be ready to go next week. She smiled, but I wasn't really sure what kind of report Mick would get.

I left, defeated, and took a quick look around the parking lot for Mick's Caddy. I called Dani, but she didn't pick up.

Motherfucker. I screamed it over and over again in my mind since I couldn't say it out loud while standing in front of my old school. My anger roiled. I wanted to smash my guitar against the fucking curb. I couldn't do anything but stand there. The halls were filled with kids going to lunch. Two minutes later I called her again and started walking. I told myself I'd call her one more time, and if she didn't pick up I'd call the cops.

She pulled up behind me just as I got halfway down the driveway. She leaned over and unlocked the passenger-side door like I was going to let her drive. I threw the rear driver-side door open, shoved my guitar case into the back seat. "Move over."

She said, "Don't be mad."

That was when I turned and noticed the magnificent gash along Mick's rear quarter panel. "What the fuck... What the fuck is this? What the fuck is this?"

"I said don't be mad, Preston. I—"

"Fuck you, Dani!" I slammed the door shut then ran my finger along the splintered paint. Part of the trim had been pulled away from the body. The scratch ran in two directions, like she hit something, then tried to pull away from it. "What the fuck happened!"

"People can hear," she said, sliding across the seat.

"I don't give a fuck who can hear me." I slammed the door and drove. "Fucking tell me what happened!"

"I don't know," she said. Her eyes got teary. "It was like this when I came out. It must've been a snowplow—"

"It's not even fucking snowing! Do you think I'm stupid?"

She looked at herself in the mirror and sniffled. Her tears disappeared like free Kool-Aid in a dollar store. "You are responsible. You shouldn't have let me borrow the car."

"I didn't let you borrow the car. I told you to sit and wait the fuck here." All I could do was shake my head. "I should make you walk the fuck home."

I cranked the radio and tried to think about what I was going to say to Mick. At the bottom of Pleasant I made her get out. Cars beeped at me, but I put it in park. She opened the door and laughed. "Should I call you or will you call me?"

"Fuck off."

"So you'll call me. I knew you would. See you tonight, Preston." She placed two fingers against her lips and kissed them. She slammed the door then put her fingers to the glass, smearing the two tiny patches of red lipstick she'd left.

I pulled in behind the shop and shut the car off and sat there. I didn't know what to do. Nothing I could ever compose in my head came close to making it okay. My phone rang.

"Where are you?" Mick was mad.

"Out back. Coming in now." I was about to say something else, but he hung up on me.

I didn't even get through the back door and into the show room before he started yelling. Ignoring a customer, he said, "Where is your head?"

"They were filling potholes over in Westover. I got hung up for a few minutes—"

"Mary Vascheck called me. What song did you teach them?" His face was red. I worried he'd pop a valve.

"I taught them some Beatles. 'Lucy in the Sky.'"

If it weren't for the counter Mick would've taken a swing at me. "She said it's about dope and getting high and taking acid. She looked it up online."

"What the hell? Lennon said it was nonsense. He wrote it for a girl in Julian's class. But now that you mention it... If it's not appropriate I can work on something else for next week." I put his keys on the counter.

"No, there will be no next week. I've gone above and beyond for you, Preston. Above and beyond." He took his glasses off and stood up. "After all that with the Tele? I want you out of here. You don't work here anymore."

I shook my head. I'd been disowned. "C'mon, Mick. Man...."

"From now on you're just a customer. Call your lessons and make sure they know. I don't want anybody coming in expecting to see your face. Tell them I'll find somebody else by next week." He took his car keys off the counter and put them into his pocket. "I'll give you three months to get your shit out of my back room. If you don't settle by June I'm selling it."

"You said you'd give me six months."

"End of May," he said.

"Mick... Please." I zipped my jacket up.

He wouldn't look at me.

I walked to the door and said, "Somebody sideswiped your car at the school today."

The door swung shut behind me. I left the shop, headed up Pleasant and lit a cigarette on the corner of High.

Negativity flooded my brain, leaving no room to think about anything good. I walked down High towards Dani, then turned around and walked all the way up to campus.

I finally ended up at the café—one of the few places I had left—I found a booth way in the back. I figured I could buy Katy something to eat before we started playing. I sent her a quick text. My mom came over, notepad out. "Everybody asked why you weren't at the funeral. You even see your brother yet?"

I didn't look at her. "Yeah, I saw Pauly, and I went to Stu's grave yesterday. I was up in the mountains for a few days. I didn't get any messages until Sunday night."

"I told you if you went sticking your nose in places it didn't belong you were going to get bit. Why don't you listen?"

"I have a right to know where I came from."

"Pauly said you found him last night at the hospital."

I didn't say anything.

"I could've told you Kevin Black was a rapist and a thief."

"But you didn't. You could've said he was no good. You could've taken me out and showed me what type of person he was and told me why I needed to stay away. All my life I believed he might be something special." I zipped my coat up. "You ever preach to Pauly like this?"

She put her pad back into her apron. "Peter said be sober and watchful. You are neither. Maybe after you stew and suffer God will restore you and strengthen you. You better get wise, boy."

"Maybe I should go."

"Don't trouble yourself, Preston Black. My shift's over. I'm going home. Stay as long as you'd like."

But nobody ever came over to take my order. I looked out the window; cars zipped by on Spruce. Maybe if the Jeep had survived I would've gassed it up and split. Went to New York or LA. My head thumped like an old Ampeg bass cabinet just thinking about it. After I got my own coffee, I found a quiet corner on an old sofa in the back and took out my guitar. But it wasn't in me to strum a single chord, let alone work on any of my songs. I went outside to smoke.

When I got back in I put my guitar on my knee, but could only stare out the window. I never even touched my coffee.

At four, Katy finally texted. She was on her way.

I went into the bathroom to check myself in the mirror. I popped a fireball into my mouth. A lot had changed since I last saw her. I didn't know why I couldn't hang on to thoughts of her when things got shitty. All I would have had to do was go home and lock my door instead of getting into Dani's car.

If it came up, I'd tell her about my dad—the devil I'd been worrying so much about. She'd say things that could help me move past it. I knew it. The Dani thing messed with my head, but if things worked out with Katy the way I hoped, Katy'd never have to know. I didn't get into Dani's car because I needed to fuck her. I got in because I was weak.

Katy showed up with her roommate and I rushed to the door to meet her. But she acted different than yesterday. She didn't smile or kiss me. It felt like her main motive was keeping everything we had between us a secret. I'd hoped to tell her what happened at the A.A. meeting last night, about my dad, but couldn't see myself discussing it with her roommate too.

Chelsea kept bringing up people and topics that were totally foreign to me, like frat guys and professors. Katy acted like she had an obligation to entertain her. When Chelsea finally got up to go to the bathroom I jumped in with everything that happened last night. I said, "Things didn't go so well at the hospital, at the A.A. meeting—"

"As soon as we walked in I could tell something was wrong." Her tone stung like sunburn.

I tried not to give in to the defensiveness I felt. After a deep breath I said, "I'm sorry. In my mind today played out a little differently, that's all. When I saw you walk in with her it threw me off."

"Preston." Her tone softened. "It's the same as last week. There will be a bunch of people here. Every Tuesday for a hundred years it's the same thing. If you wanted to be alone you should've said something. We could've gone someplace else. Did you think everybody'd just stay home tonight?"

"Sorry. I assumed we had an understanding that we'd go over stuff before Friday. I didn't realize you wouldn't be alone. I forgot all about today and what goes on here. I'm sorry. Sitting around playing the same songs over and over isn't going to make Friday any easier for me."

Chelsea returned, and despite the fact that we were smack-dab in the middle of something, stood there watching.

Katy, for once, didn't say anything.

"Look, Katy, I don't want this to get worse. I really don't. Being with you was the best part of this weekend and it's selfish to want you all to myself. Maybe I should split because I'm kind of freaking out right now. I don't think I can be part of the crowd tonight." And even when I put my coat on I expected her to say something to give things a chance to change directions. But she let me put my coat on and leave. Outside, I lit up another smoke. I put my guitar case on the sidewalk and rubbed my eyes.

The noose kept tightening. I felt it with every breath. My throat got a lump in it that just wouldn't go away. I should've gone home. But we had no heat in the apartment. Nothing to drink. Mick's was out. Forever. Pauly was out. Never thought I'd see the devil at an A.A. meeting. I started walking. I went down the hill to Beechurst. It always seemed easier to just go downhill.

I made a left to go past The Stink but I didn't have enough cash to get drunk. And it was stupid to count on free drinks again. I looked at the bulletin board by the door. *Drummer Wanted. Melodic Punk band needs bassist.* Everybody in the world played the fucking guitar. I was nothing special. A small note card at the bottom said the pub needed somebody to wash dishes. *Finally*, I thought, *something I'm qualified for.*

Our big poster hung on the door. In big letters at the top it said *QUARTERSTICK Friday, February 14*. The next line said *With Special Guest PRESTON BLACK*.

I wanted to feel good about it, but figured I wouldn't be around to see it—like the devil or the song had total control over me no matter what. Like I wouldn't even live to see my next birthday.

I wished Jamie was here to see that I was right. With no place to go I made a right onto the Westover Bridge to watch the river. Brown water crept beneath my feet.

The fall would be the worst part, knowing the whole way that you could never put yourself back on the bridge. Bones broken by the surface growing numb in the cold below. I wondered whether light or sound would disappear first. I wondered if my mind would stop rambling. I wondered if I would be reborn and have a shot at a real life. I wondered who would miss me.

I got a text.

<don't be blinkered, being alive is a hell of a lot better than being dead>

A million thoughts ran through my head. I tried to pick one out and make it coherent. I texted back <you think? Do you see what's going on?>

I stood there in the cold. The text broke the steam train of black thought screaming through my head. I stepped away from the rail and turned back toward town. The light just changed, and I hung my head to avoid eye contact with the cars coming from the intersection.

Joe Strummer texted back. <I squatted in a dumpster for three years. like i said, you got to be sodding stupid to make it in this business>

I replied, but I swore to myself it'd be the last time. <I don't know man. shit seems a lot heavier than that right now>

My phone buzzed as I walked back to the corner. <music is your soul brother. and right now you ain't got none>

Heavy traffic pushed into the intersection. I had to wait for the light to change before crossing in either direction. While I waited my phone rang. I thought it might be Strummer again. Traffic came and went all around, fencing me in. It was Dani. I answered.

She said she had her car back, and would pick me up.

I didn't tell her not to, and let myself get good and angry.

This would be my chance to tell her we were through and I rehearsed my lines the whole time I waited. But back in her apartment we picked up right where we left off. She had my pants off by 5:30. By six I had a good buzz going. And when Pauly called at seven and again at seven fifteen I'd gotten so drunk that hitting IGNORE got to be as easy as hitting snooze on my clock radio.

CHAPTER FIFTEEN

Any time I dreamed anymore, somebody I admired died. By spring I wouldn't have any fathers left.

I'd seen my unalterable future. Saw the cheap tattoos, the speed bumps all over his arms, the meth mouth. Now I just had to accept that I couldn't escape my white trash dreams. *Meant to say* genes, *but they both fit*. Seeing my dad confirmed it.

"Good morning," Dani said as I stumbled out of the bathroom. I washed, showered and still couldn't get the sick off of me. She worked at the kitchen table, laptop open, papers spread all over. "I made you a tea." She said it like she'd given me a kidney. "Of course it's cold now."

If I accepted misery as my destiny, then Dani became one of the best things that ever happened to me. I sat down.

She put a pen to her lip, and leaned back. "Preston," she said, "Do you think you're in the right place now?"

At some point last night Dani looked on my phone and saw Katy's number and some texts. Too pathetic to be mad, I told her all about Katy, where she came from, where she worked. I was very drunk and stupid. Part of me thought Dani was gloating. My will evaporated. I said, "If you say so."

"Don't be sad," she said. "Or maybe getting caught with your fingers in the cookie jar has embarrassed you, hmm? It doesn't sound like your little bluebird will be sad for long."

The small table felt like a prison, like doing homework in grade school.

"If it's any consolation, I've been fucking somebody else, too. We aren't exclusive, right?"

"I wasn't sleeping with her."

"You should've been." Dani blew me a kiss and went back to her work. I went back to not existing. She yelled into her phone and banged on her laptop's keys. I sat on the couch with my guitar next to me. But I just flipped through my notebook. All my songs sounded silly now. I'd never be Springsteen or Robert Hunter or Jeff Tweedy or Kurt Cobain. I could never come up with anything like "Blinded by the Light" or "The Weight" or "Sweet Melissa" or "Jesus, Etc."…

I didn't even know if I had a *hey-ho, let's go* in me.

My life had become a Chinese take-out fortune, a receipt for a guitar that cost way too much money, a thirty character text, a name on a faded concert flier stuck to a light pole with rusty nails, footprints disappearing with the melting snow, a black and white picture in a high school yearbook. I'd never been to Europe, never tasted wine that didn't come with a screw top until I met Dani. I actually thought a Big Mac tasted good. I liked to watch TV, when we still had cable. I thought *Theater of Pain* was a good record. The only book I ever read on my own was *Hammer of the Gods* back in high school. I wore Dickies or Carhartts from Sears, flannel shirts from Gabe's. I cried when I heard Mr. Rogers had died. There was nothing special about me. I wasn't extraordinary in any way. I wasn't the best at anything.

My belly started to rumble. I went into her kitchen and helped myself to red wine. She asked me to play something. So I sang her "The Sad Ballad of Preston Black" the whole way through. Hearing my name over and over like that, from my own mouth, had the same effect on me as a eulogy.

By four Dani finished working, putting her papers and binders into neat piles on her desk. She brought the bottle of red in with her, and we finished it. She said we should eat somewhere. I told her I should go see Pauly after that.

We ate at the classy place on High. It used to be a tapas bar. Now it was just out of my range. She asked why I didn't have a lot to say, and I told her I wasn't dressed right. It didn't require a jacket or tie, but I knew I didn't fit in. I didn't even know what some of the things on the menu were so I got a steak. She ordered beef Carpaccio and asked if I wanted to try it. I didn't. We had more wine.

Dani dropped me off at Ruby just like before. I told her to give me an hour. She asked for a kiss. The way she looked at me made me believe she really loved me. My heart softened a bit, and I kissed her. I got my guitar out of the back seat to show Pauly. It was the only thing left. It anchored me to the world and I realized it'd never left my side since I'd gotten it.

Coming into the lobby from the cold night felt like jumping from February into August. I unbuttoned my old pea coat and loosened my scarf and headed to the gift shop to get Pauly a bottle of tea and a Snickers bar. When I got to the room where they held the meetings, I went right in and sat down. When George came in I nodded.

He returned the gesture, got himself a cup of coffee and went to the center of the room. At about five 'til an attendant pushed the big door open and flipped the doorstop down with his foot. A couple of guys from Pauly's ward came in, the identification bracelets on their wrists the only thing separating them from everybody else in the room. The attendant wheeled Pauly in and placed him right next to me.

"Hey man," I said, "Sorry about last night..." As I fumbled for an excuse Scratchy Black came in with a big, down-to-brass-tacks looking dude. Scratchy Black looked at me, but I put my head down and got real close to Pauly.

"You smell like booze, you know that?" He gave me a look of disappointment.

"Dani took me out to dinner just now."

"So you just ditched the other girl? The one from Sunday? Just like that?" He shook his head. "Why don't you wheel me up to the group before the meeting starts? If you're here after we can talk about it."

He spun himself with his good hand. I pushed him up to the end of a row of folding chairs. Before I sat back down I slid my guitar case flat beneath my seat. Like clockwork we got the Serenity Prayer then the Steps and Traditions. When the secretary asked for new members or out-of-town guests, Pauly's head cocked a little, like he wanted me to introduce myself.

At about quarter after my phone vibrated. I ignored it for a moment, figuring it might be Dani. Then I figured it might not be, and I'd better make sure. I slid my hand into my pocket to check it. *Katy.*

I stood up and bolted for the door. "Hello? Katy?"

But she wasn't there.

I went into the bathroom across the hall and called her back, and it rang and rang. When it went to voicemail I hung up, figuring maybe she was leaving a voicemail for me. I waited for the new voicemail alert, and when it didn't come I called her back. Straight to voicemail. "Katy, please pick up. I don't know what happened yesterday, but I need to see you. Things are crazy, something's happening and I can't explain it. I need to talk about this. Please, please call me back. I'm pretty freaked out, to be honest with you. You're the only person I can talk to. Please...."

I hung up and felt really empty. Like I should've fucking jumped into the river yesterday. I splashed cold water on my face, the closest I'd get to drowning tonight.

I went across the hall and slowly turned the knob to get back into the meeting, closing the door as quietly as I could. Somebody was sharing when I sat down. Pauly held his head in his hand, listening, thinking. George leaned back, his empty Styrofoam cup clasped in his hands. Scratchy Black wasn't there and I almost laughed, like I no longer felt the presence of evil or whatever. But his parole officer sat on the other side of the room, texting somebody or playing Tetris on his phone.

I knew the bastard would see me when he got back from the bathroom, so I tried to make myself small. I listened to the speaker, but couldn't settle in. My mind replayed the seconds like they were a skipping record. If he'd been in the bathroom I would've seen him. It didn't make sense to me that the parole officer would just let him come and go.

My heart stuttered and I couldn't figure out why. With every muscle twitch I knew it. I felt for my phone and my wallet. The guy next to Pauly turned around. I mouthed, "Sorry." Figuring I'd just go wait in the lobby, I leaned over for my guitar. It was gone.

My guitar.

I slammed the door wide open and bolted down the hall and through the lobby. I ran into the parking lot. Milan Puskar Stadium greeted me with its hands outstretched. Crows screamed from beneath the concrete stands. A steady rain of noise filled my head. Big lights lit up the green field.

He'd go toward town. I had to be right about this or I wouldn't have anything left. I knew he ran toward the Coliseum past the old frats and their beer-soaked couches. I followed, head down, fighting to keep the cold air from making me cough. I got down by University Avenue and panicked. I stopped. That guitar was my way out of here.

I went up University for a block then made a right. He couldn't have gotten this far. I had to be faster than him. I cut across a parking lot and ran toward the PRT station, looking for a guitar case in the big field between the Towers and the rec center. At the PRT station I turned around and followed the tracks back toward the hospital.

I ran my hands along my scalp and spun around.

On the track above, a PRT car rolled from the Towers up toward Medical. I watched it roll away.

And when I saw him I couldn't believe it at first. He cut across the tennis courts right next to the Towers, staying close to the building and creeping real slow. I picked a small river rock out of the landscaping by the sidewalk and followed him at a fast clip. Confident he'd shaken his tail, he moved casually. He turned a corner back toward University, and I ran after him.

He heard my footsteps and turned as I came around the corner. He dropped my guitar case right before I hit him. He raised his arm causing the rock to glance off his forehead. Blood dripped down the bridge of his nose, and I hit him again. He fell onto the guitar case.

White light flashed in my eyes, my brain ran hot. No thoughts. No remorse. I cut my fingers on his broken teeth and tossed the rock aside. A couple of students came around the corner. One said, "Oh, shit," and egged me on.

I stood up and kicked Scratchy with my heel. I kicked him again and again in the same spot. Cars slowed down on Evansdale Drive to watch.

One of the kids said, "You proved your point, man. Let him up or I'm calling the cops."

I was going to tell them what Scratchy'd done to me. How he left my mom, how that fucking meth freak stole my guitar for a fix. But when I took a step they each took a step back. "Stay the fuck out of it," I said.

I kicked him again.

From one of the cars on Evansdale I heard my name.

My breath came in loud rasps. I never looked up.

"Preston!" Dani's passenger-side window was down. "Get in."

The top of my guitar case had a depression in it from Scratchy's fall. I pushed it into the back seat of her car and she drove away fast. Down University toward downtown. A campus police car, lights ablaze, came up University from town.

"What was that?" she asked.

I tried to catch my breath. "That was my dad. The fucking devil. The song said I'd meet the devil and I met him. I looked right into his face and saw myself. All these years I've been thinking he'd be something great and he'd save me or whatever." Adrenaline made my stomach a little sick.

She pulled a Lucky Strike from a new pack, lit it, and blew smoke out a sliver of open window. She offered me one.

The first thing I did when we got back to her apartment was set my case on her table and flip the latches. The top of the guitar had a crack running from the neck, through the sound hole down to the bridge. The force on the strings yanked the bridge up and away from the top. I told myself it was an easy fix.

When I pulled the guitar all the way out of the case the neck hung limp. When Scratchy fell, the neck must've acted like a lever, cracking the top and blowing out the rosewood at both sides. If I pushed the neck forward far enough I could read the serial numbers through the back of the guitar.

The cracks continued into the rosewood near the strap plug at the bottom. The back had been splintered and crushed a thousand different ways. I put the pieces back in the case. There wasn't anything else I could do.

Dani gave me a drink. Rye whiskey.

She sat next to me, but didn't touch me or say anything. She just sat there and lit a cigarette. I had to ask for one. When she finished her drink she said, "You still have a key to Mick's."

I took her glass and went into the kitchen for refills. I put four fingers in my glass, put it down with a cough and refilled it. After I handed Dani her glass, I said, "I do. I forgot to give it back to him," and threw my third double down.

It finally occurred to me what she'd been implying all along. "Fuck. I'm not going to rip Mick off."

She took my glass with her into the kitchen. She refilled only mine. "You don't think it was unfair that he fired you?"

"I'm not going to steal from Mick."

"You don't have to, you know. Isn't your old guitar there?" She gave me back my drink.

I dropped it and said, "I have to go."

"Again?" She smiled and leaned back into the couch. "Like a little boomerang."

"Goodbye." I picked up my guitar case and left.

I carried the guitar all the way across Deckers before I realized how stupid I was for carrying a corpse around. I threw it into the dumpster behind Black Bear Burritos. But before I even crossed Pleasant a wave of remorse hit me.

Holding my breath to keep the smell of garbage and old food out of my nose, I flipped the lid open. I set my guitar case in the alley and snapped open the latches. Tears started to come, and I forced those back, too. I held my throat shut until my jaw hurt. I held my breath until I thought I'd pass out. I took the strap Pauly got me off of the guitar, closed the case and threw it back into the dumpster.

As I made my way up High I pulled out my phone and started to compose a text. My hand shook. <Joe you there?>

I kept my phone in my hand while I walked.

The apartment was dark and cold. I could see my breath. My bed remained unmade. I laid down and tried to call Katy. She didn't answer. I got undressed and tossed all of my clothes into a pile on the floor. I went into the bathroom and started the hot water for a shower. Steam rushed into the hallway, into the kitchen.

Water scalded me. I turned the cold water up a hair. I hung my head and waited. No music remained in me. "The Sad Ballad of Preston Black" had taken it out of me. In two weeks I'd lived a whole other life. I'd tried for so long to just be decent. Maybe I should've set my goals a little higher.

When the hot water ran out I stayed in the cold. The steam disappeared. After a few minutes I shivered, my arms felt little, my shoulders curled inward. I took a towel off of the rod and threw it around my shoulders and went to lie down. When I looked at the time on my phone I saw I had a message.

I dialed voicemail. Katy said, "Some woman called the daycare and said I was sleeping around with married men. I don't want to dislike you, but you're not making it easy."

I called her back immediately. "Katy, I just want to talk." The words fell like snowflakes when I needed thunder.

I tried to compose myself and called her back. "Katy, being with you and making music with you gives me faith. The few hours I had with you made me believe. You converted me. You made me feel like my music meant something. I never wanted to disrupt what we had, but the circumstances are bigger than me. I don't know how I ended up here. It all goes back to the song. That day in the record store is the day everything changed."

My time had run out. I turned the light on and stood there. I'd sold everything. After twenty-seven years, I had some clothes and some CDs. My notebook. Stu's letters from boot camp. The record. I pulled it out of my bag.

I slid the record out of its sleeve and snapped it in half. I ripped the sleeve in half. I broke each of the halves into quarters. I broke one of the quarters into an eighth. I ran my finger along the sharp edge down to the tip.

My phone rang.

I threw the shard onto the floor and went to my nightstand, and flipped open my phone. <You are a bastard, aren't you? only a bastard's going to make it>

The record and the song were easy to blame for the stuff that'd been happening. But inanimate things didn't give you opinions or suggestions.

My phone rang again. <when you blame somebody else you get nothing. blame yourself and learn from it.>

I typed, <Thanks, Joe> and hit reply.

I sang, "Tried to make the devil a deal but the devil said he didn't have a soul to steal."

My brain screeched to a halt. Thoughts disappeared. I found the tiniest little bit of myself hiding in a dark corner of my head. I grabbed my notebook and a pencil and fell back onto the bed. Inside the front cover, at the top, I scribbled *Preston Black wrote his own sad song.*

CHAPTER SIXTEEN

My notebook lay open on the floor. I'd ripped all the old songs out. There were only blank pages left. My fingers hadn't touched guitar strings in days. "Yeah, Mike. I'm pumped, too. I have all kinds of new stuff I've been working on." I lied.

Mikey said, "Come by early. We'll be there all day. Our A and R guy is taking us out for drinks after, but I want you to meet him before the show. I've been telling him all about you so he's coming in early for your set."

I barely caught that last part. I half-paid attention, and half-wondered what the hell I'd even play tomorrow night.

Mikey said, "Sound check at five?"

On Thursdays Mick usually rolled out by five. I told him, "Make it 5:15?"

"Sure thing. Dude, this is going to be big. You stoked?" Mike's voice crackled like it was streaming out of an old Vox AC30.

"I will be. I've been a busy man." *Writing songs. Plotting to steal a guitar. Trying to win back my true love.* "I'm happy for you guys. No matter what happens I want you to know I'm proud of you. You deserve your success."

Mikey said, "We're going to do a bunch of spring break things in Florida and Arizona. Hopefully we generate enough buzz to get an invite to a festival. Maybe the small stage at Bonnaroo or Coachella. That might sound ambitious…"

"No, man. Don't settle for small potatoes." *Like I did.*

"I appreciate it. I don't know if I ever told you this, but the lessons and hanging out at Mick's got me through some tough times. Maybe you don't remember those hours like I do, but my lessons were sometimes the only good hours out of the entire week." His voice got mellow and sweet like a Butter Rum Lifesaver. "And I know you paid for all those lessons. Maybe this is just a way to return the favor with interest."

"I would've done it all for nothing…" I put my notebook down and gave him my full attention.

"I know, man. It's all good. I just wanted to tell you." I thought he was going to sign off, but he said, "You know, sometimes I wished you were my dad. Or my dad was more like you instead of a rampaging drunken asshole."

His bluntness made me nervous. "Man, don't say that. I would've been a horrible father."

"That's not true," he said. "You always told me those Sub Pop bands didn't sit around waiting for somebody to deliver them. You said they went out and did it themselves. You always said '...tonight in cities all across America the next big thing is meeting in a garage for the first time.' Well, I listened to you."

I didn't remember saying any of that. "You worked hard for what you got." I almost hung up, then said, "Mikey, I'm running a little late. Having some guitar issues."

Mick's key hung on my key ring. My Tele sat in Mick's office.

"It's cool. Whenever. See you when you get there."

Sun streamed through my window, covered my bed. I'd been out for a little over twelve hours. For a long time I sat there with my empty notebook open. I'd scrapped every lyric I'd ever written down. Stuff from all the way back to junior year in high school. And to make sure I didn't dig them out of the trash I ripped the pages into tiny bits. Two new Dixon Ticonderogas that I sharpened with a steak knife sat between me and the empty notebook. "Just like the first day of school."

I needed to write something, if only to get the momentum going. So I wrote out the lyrics to "The Sad Ballad of Preston Black" as neat as I could in printed caps. I made minor tweaks where one word sounded better than another, or where the old-timey dialect got in the way of what the song said. Or what I wanted it to say. When I finished I reread it, like I'd read a poem. I tried not to sing it. I decided that the song could still be tweaked. It had to be. It was my song.

So I went to the next new page and started writing down snippets of lyrics I'd been kicking around in my head for the last few days. Little phrases that had a cool cadence or imagery.

The first one I wrote came to me when Jamie and I were recording. He said I should call the one song "Trilobites," but it didn't actually have the word in it. So I wrote the words *thinking about trilobites keeps me up all night*. Then right below it I wrote, *I wonder if I'm ever going to see the sun again*. I didn't know if that was a song yet, but it was something. There were about thirty other snippets like that, so I gave each one its own line. When I finished I had about two and a half pages worth of stuff.

I went out to pee. The clock on the stove still flashed twelve from the last time the power was out. If I'd have had my blinds down I wouldn't have known if it was noon or midnight. I had to get a move on. I had more to write, but figured I could work on that later. I rolled my notebook up and tucked it into my coat pocket. After I put all of my clothes into my pack, I saw the necklace Katy's grandmother had given me on the dresser. I put it around my neck. The coin Katy's mom gave me was still in my pocket. The last item I packed was the bundle of Stu's letters from boot camp. Once those had been put away, the room sat completely empty. Like the day I moved in.

I didn't leave any lights on when I left. Somehow I didn't think I'd ever be back. As soon as I hit the sidewalk I knew tonight would be different.

I got down to the shop and saw Mick's Caddy sitting out back. But the longer I stood out there, watching from a half a block away, the less I thought I'd be able to go through with it. I kept telling myself I'd be able to get the guitar back in his office before he noticed it was gone. I promised myself, making that the only way I even considered it.

When Mick finally came out the back door I pressed myself against the bricks of the kung fu studio next to the downtown PRT stop. He propped the back door open and went back inside.

Fifteen minutes later my phone rang. It was Mike. He said, "Where you at, man?" with a laugh, trying to make a joke out of it.

I took a deep breath and slouched against the wall. "I told you I'd be a little late. Give me a half hour."

He took a long pause. "I'm supposed to meet my girlfriend at six, though. So—"

I interjected, "Is the back door open? Can I come in through the back?"

"Man, I don't know. I'll check."

"Thanks. Catch you in a bit."

A few minutes later Mick came out again, pointing out the gash on his back quarter panel to a pair of state cops. He raged and ranted and seethed. I pressed myself into the shadow like I was Snake Eyes hiding from Destro. Mick circled the Caddy like a turkey buzzard around a dead fawn. I pulled myself away from the wall and made my way back up to High.

My phone rang. It was Mick. I wanted to shove it right back into my pocket and pretend I didn't hear it. But I couldn't. I owed him.

"God damn you, Preston!"

I closed my eyes, bracing myself like I was at the dentist or about to get punched.

"You know who I just talked to? Do you have any idea what I've been dealing with for the last twenty minutes? I'm being accused of a hit-and-run." He spit some nasty words into the phone. Things that would've hurt me if they hadn't been true, and if I didn't already know they were true. It was the hellfire way he said them that let me know there was no going back. That I'd burned a bridge.

When he finished ranting he asked what I planned to do about it.

I told him I was taking care of it right now.

He said, "You're broke. You don't have a goddamned thing in this world and I don't have any idea how you're going to be able to scrape two thousand dollars together. Goodbye, Preston. You're not welcome here anymore."

Another dead father. Maybe I was nobody's son.

The air felt heavy for the first time this year. For once it didn't dry out my nose and throat like it had all winter long. In the moisture I smelled snow melting up in the Currence's fields, I smelled a touch of iron from Deckers Creek. I thought, and I knew this sounded stupid, but I thought I could smell flowers in the ground on the verge of bursting through the soil. I thought I could smell t-shirts and jeans instead of coats and scarves. Even the sunset seemed like more than a sunset. A halo of clouds padded the hills beyond the river.

On the long slog up the hill to Dani's apartment I thought of what I'd say to her. In a perfect world she'd just write out a check. But wishing for a perfect world doesn't make the world perfect. When I saw her car in the garage my fists clenched. The heavy exterior door was unlocked, so I pushed it open and went in. Sunlight flooded the rich lobby and settled into the thick plush carpet like dust. I stomped up the steps so she'd know I was coming.

"Like the little robin returning in the spring," she said when she opened the door without waiting for me to knock. "Do you want a drink, or are you here for some other reason?"

"I'm here for your part of the damages to Mick's car and the car you hit." I blew past her on my way to the kitchen.

She disregarded me and walked toward her work at the table. "It wasn't my fault. You should tell Mick to get an attorney. Or maybe you need the attorney?"

"I'm telling you!" I picked a bottle of absinthe off of the counter and smashed it into the sink. "You did two thousand bucks worth of damage. I'm not leaving without a check."

"Or what?"

"What do you mean, 'or what?'"

She slid to face me. "You sounded like you were about to make a threat. I'd like to hear it. Or will you break another bottle?"

I chuffed and looked at the floor.

She faked a pout. "Aw, it's okay, I still like you. But you can go now. I have so many things to do. Unless you came for something else?" She stood up and pushed the chair toward the wall. I backed against the counter. She draped her arms around me, put her left leg over my right and slid down a few inches. "You are here because your little bluebird isn't chirping?"

I pushed her off. She fell against the table and tried catching herself. But she kept falling, pulling the table onto her. An avalanche of papers slid across the floor. Her laptop hit the refrigerator. The screen went blank, then blue.

She screamed a string of curses at me, spitting Czech with the fury of Tom Morello and the blunt ugliness of Lemmy. Hair fell across her dark eyes. "Look at this! You did this." She used a chair to help herself up, then swung it at me. I caught it by the leg and twisted it out of her hands. She spun and picked her laptop up from the floor. She pounded the spacebar with the butt of her hand. Her blue screen didn't respond. She yanked it from the wall, the cord broke away from the socket with a snap. She lifted it over her head and heaved it.

I stepped aside and it smashed through some of the pictures on her bookshelves. Glass tinkled to the floor. She launched an mp3 player. I batted it casually and it fell onto the couch. "Throw it all. I'm not leaving without the money."

She fired a bottle of Irish whiskey. I batted it down with the chair. She yelled, "You fucking mouse. You ignorant fucking mouse. Mouse!" Spit flew from her lips. She wiped her mouth with her arm, smearing lipstick across her cheek.

"Two thousand dollars."

She clenched her fists and screamed. "You don't tell me," she said and heaved a bottle of wine. It hit her bedroom door. Red wine ran down the white paint. "Nobody tells me."

"Dani." I tried to remain calm. "I'm not leaving without the money."

She drew a breath like she was about to launch another round, but I cut her off. "Write the check or I'll call Clay and Anton and Andrei and tell them everything I know about you. Yeah, I got their numbers out of your phone. I'm a paranoid asshole and I'll spill every stinky detail of your pathetic life. How everything you do is illegal. I bet you all those guys you fuck over don't want the FBI calling them. I know I wouldn't. I'm uneducated, but I know if I call them and tell them I called the FBI it wouldn't look good for you."

She paused for composure, nodding slightly. "Preston, I'm not sure you'd know where to begin or perhaps you'd have called by now. I'll see you tomorrow. You go on at seven? You want me to wear something sexy?"

Dani pushed the hair out of her eyes and kicked aside the forms and documents that buried her purse. She slammed her wallet on the counter. With violent, angry movements she pulled out crisp hundreds and counted out twenty. "This is how much a good whore should cost anyway," she said, shoving the cash at me. "Do you know what I think? I think in less than forty-eight hours you'll be back."

"Bet you I won't." I went straight for the door. Before I put my hand on the knob, I said, "You were at the record store that day, too. This whole time I thought it was the record, but it was you. You kept making all these little suggestions and filling my head with all of your crazy bullshit."

"I'll wear something nice tomorrow, so you can tell everybody I'm the girl you fuck. Or maybe I'll bring somebody with me, I don't know yet." She followed me for a few steps. "It will be a surprise."

I slammed the door on my way out. As I went down the steps I heard a few loud bangs from the apartment. A chair, furniture, more bottles maybe. I didn't know and I didn't care.

I called Katy as soon as I got outside. Streetlights hummed to life. If there had been birds singing and bugs buzzing I would've sworn it was April. She didn't pick up.

"Katy," I said after the tone, "Ask Jamie to tell you what's going on. He'll tell you about the song and how it's—"

I didn't know how I could say it without it sounding like a paranoid delusion. Every verse read either like my personal history or prophecy, like that record had sat in Isaac's for years just waiting for me. Maybe Dani put it there, I didn't know. But it was my song. I started to sing it into the phone. When my time ran out I called right back, singing where I'd left off. After I sang the last verse I called her one more time. I said, "Please, ask Jamie. He'll tell you. I'm not trying to shirk responsibility for what I've done. Katy, I believe the bad things are happening for a reason."

Preston Black writes his own sad song. "Or something's making it happen," I said just before hanging up.

I left Dani's, heading toward Dorsey Avenue and the old Mountaineer Mall. Putting miles between myself and town filtered out some of the crap clogging my brain. Songs came to me like coal barges up the river. They came from down around the bend. If I kept walking they'd catch up to me eventually.

I walked down to Hite, past the tech school and all the ball fields. Me and Pauly smoked a joint in the woods behind the t-ball field the day I met my first girlfriend, Mallory. It was August, the week before school started. Mallory was Stu's cousin, and he didn't like her talking to me. The first week of school he came up to me in the cafeteria to check me out. We ended up in a pushing contest that got us two days in the box together. By then Pauly had found out Stu played drums. When the bell rang at the end of our first day in ISS I asked Stu if he wanted to start a band. So for most of the second day me and Stu passed lyrics back and forth.

I wondered what kind of song we'd write today. He never said much about his time over there or what he saw, but I knew he had nightmares and woke up crying a lot. One time I asked him if his first tour sucked so bad why he would even consider going back. He said he didn't fit any place else. If he was here today I'd tell him I'd carry his gun so he didn't have to worry about it anymore.

I flipped to a clean page in my notebook and wrote. It took more walking to figure out I had a song, but the rest came easier. I sat on the guardrail across from the Bluegrass Estates trailer park and wrote. Greenbag Road was a poorly lit, curvy place. The cars zipping by could give a shit I was putting my heart onto a scrap of paper. I wrote about wanting to know what Stu knew, and being afraid of what the knowledge would do to me. Maybe it wasn't a song, but it would be. I waited for traffic to clear and crossed the street.

When I got up to the trailer, Stevie Croe was getting into his car. Stu's old neighborhood looked pretty much the same as when I was sixteen. Maybe a little bleaker. The same Big Wheels and rusty bikes sat out in the same yards. The same dogs barked at the same ghosts. Stevie turned when he heard my feet crunching through the gravel in the driveway. He waved, but didn't get out of the car.

"Hey, Pres." He reached for my hand when I got up to the window.

I shook it and took a step back. Guilt wouldn't let me make eye contact. "Steve… I'm sorry, man. I'm so sorry."

"I know, Pres."

"I was away when it happened."

"That's what Pauly said." Steve just sat there. I handed Stevie all the letters Stu had written from boot camp. "I just wanted your family to know. I love him. I'm going to miss him."

The wind picked up. The sky looked really, really blue. The moon looked like a shiny nickel. Stevie started flipping through the letters one by one. Like, maybe he hadn't gotten many letters from Stu. I said goodnight and started back down the driveway. Stevie asked if I wanted a ride into town.

"I'm good." I took a deep breath. "Stu aways looked out for you. Don't know if you knew that. One time Stu saw Austin Forsythe talking to Kelly while you were on the field. Stu made him get down on his knees in back of the concession stand right before halftime. The whole band saw it."

Stevie laughed. "Using a hammer to kill ants. You should come up over spring break and we can talk. My mom wants to see you."

"Maybe. I did some things and I'm not sure what the consequences will be. But if I make it through all this I'll be up." I waved, and headed back out to the road. Stevie started his car. He pressed the gas, put it into reverse and crept out of his driveway. When he passed me he rolled his window down. I leaned into the car and said, "I don't think there was much more to Stu than what we all saw. He was real and that's what's great about him. You could spend five minutes with him and know his life story."

Stevie nodded. I stepped back and he drove away.

On the way out I walked past Stacy Kent's house, where I met Jeff, my guitar teacher for the first time. I made a right onto 857 North. Thoughts bum rushed my brain, then my head emptied just as fast. After twenty minutes I passed Byrd Elementary where I went to kindergarten and first grade.

Just below the Mileground I crossed 119 and made my way toward campus. When I got down by the Mountainlair, I thought maybe I should catch the PRT at Beechurst and just take it up to Ruby. But the miles seemed as important as the words. The air felt good in my lungs even though I knew residue from my last cigarette was still down there somewhere. Maybe the moon made me feel like I had some reason to keep going. If it could create tides surely it could uplift me just a little. Maybe the city, and her bright lights, whispering 'it's okay' to me over and over kept me from hanging my head.

The hospital's dusk-to-dawn lights called me to Pauly. I crossed the big, lonely parking lot as a helicopter landed on the roof. For a long time I could only sit there in the empty lobby. I went to the bathroom, washed up, then returned to the big soft couch. I may have even slept for a while. When I got up I went to look for Pauly's floor. I just wanted to see him and talk to him. Locked door after locked door drove me back to the waiting room. So I sat, pencil poised and ready to go. The moment my pencil hit the paper it took off, skipping through metaphors and rhymes, verses and bridges. I reread it a few times. The words seemed a little stiffer in bright light and warm air, like the cold breeze and open sky had kept me honest. In some ways it was just another song. That was probably why it mattered.

I went to the information desk and asked how I could get it to him. The nurse gave me an envelope. I dropped the song in, licked the envelope shut and said goodnight.

When I left the hospital I went toward the Towers to look for Katy. I had one more song to write.

Down at the intersection the Coliseum glowed, prettier than any church I'd ever been in. I went the other way, toward the Book Exchange then cut across to University. All the houses looked like faces in a crowd. At Riverview I kept on toward town instead of searching the same area over again. Shivering and sweating both, I went up into apartment complex parking lots and down alleys looking for Katy's car. I could see the big tower by Seneca Center down by the river. I turned around and went back up the hill, made a right on North, and cut up Jones to go back toward Ruby through an apartment complex parking lot. The first car I saw upon entering was Katy's. I could tell by the stickers. My scarf still sat on the back seat.

I sank onto the parking block, leaning against her back bumper and keeping my hands under my armpits until I was actually ready to put words on the paper. But they weren't coming so easy. Humming didn't work. Singing other people's songs distracted me. I put my head on my knees.

The only thing that came to me was, "Hey, hey little bluebird, why don't you stay? I thought I heard you singing, I thought I heard you say, that you loved me...."

I wrote it and signed it with my first name, folded it and put it under her windshield wiper.

I needed time to crawl to a stop. I needed morning to stay away like it had for so many weeks. I needed a way out, a way to not have to go to Mick's, but waiting only made the inevitable that much more difficult.

My *Preston Black Fucks Up Again World Tour* had one last stop. Mick's key burned a hole in my pocket like it was uranium. I kept telling myself all I had to do was let myself in and lock up on my way out. I believed if I played it right I could have my Tele back in the office before Mick ever noticed.

"When have you ever played anything right?" I asked myself. Then I thought, Mick's going to notice. "He's going to fucking notice."

I walked, hoping morning would beat me to Mick's. I shuffled past The Mountainlair, past the library. High Street slept. I shuffled past the apartment. Past the pawn shop and Cool Ridge. When I made the right onto Pleasant I checked the time again. When I got to Mick's I stared at the shop's back door. The heavy steel wouldn't keep me out. I was a schemer. A liar. *A mother-fucking bonfire.*

I swore every car that rolled up Pleasant was a cop and I wished one would just pull up and ask what I was doing. I wouldn't run or lie, just hold my hands out and let them cuff me.

I held the key over the lock. My heartbeat thumped in my ears. I slid the key in, thinking about what Mick always said. How "One 'oh, shit' can wipe out a whole stack of 'atta boys.'"

I twisted the key. The door swung right open, but it didn't feel like I was walking into any place I ever knew. It felt like walking into a trap. I pulled the door shut behind me and left the light off.

The old backroom smelled like cardboard. I weaved past Mick's back stock, past my lesson room and out to the office. The door didn't even squeak when I twisted the knob. Before I knew it, I was toe to toe with my guitar. I ran my finger along the frayed tweed on the edge of the case. I flipped the light on. Because I was acting purely on blind impulse I didn't feel the need to worry about fingerprints anymore. I put Dani's cash on Mick's desk. I pulled a Post-it off of the pad and wrote, *for the car*. I pulled my keys out of my pocket, threaded Mick's through the ring and laid it on the cash. Before putting the pen down, I scrawled, *I'll take care of the rest, too. You were like a father to me, and I'm sorry I ruined that. Preston.*

I picked up the amp, checking to make sure I still had a guitar cord tucked away. I rolled it into the showroom.

My Martin rested against the Tele. Somebody must've rescued it from the dumpster. I set it on Mick's chair and flipped the latches up. The smashed Martin rested in the cushioned case like a corpse. Seeing it made me angry, then sad. I dropped the lid and leaned it back against the wall.

I grabbed my Tele, then pulled the door shut behind me. Blood pumped in my eardrums as I left. Adrenaline tingled down my legs then right up through my core, like a weak electrical jolt. As soon as the door shut behind me the reality of my deed hit me.

I kicked it and pounded it with my fists. I threw my shoulder into it. But I'd burned my boat, so I directed resentment toward the guitar and amp sitting on the concrete at my feet like they were a pair of wet puppies that'd followed me home. "They're yours now, sport," I said to myself. "Pick them up and get the hell out."

Down at Beechurst I crossed over to The Stink, stopping for a second to look at the posters in the window. Since shit flows downhill, I went around back, beneath the PRT rail and down to the river.

I sang the words to my song over and over again, like praying the Rosary.

If it was your song you probably would've been singing it too.

"…none of it mattered in the end, after his body drifted 'round the river bend…"

CHAPTER SEVENTEEN

The sun rose, but the air got colder. Fits of shivering made me smaller, hands tucked into my sleeves, collar up. The sun rose and the red and green navigation lights on the Westover Bridge faded into morning. A gray sky and a stiff wind made me wonder where I'd hide next. I had a few hours before the cops came looking for me. I couldn't go home. Couldn't go to the café.

Rain came at about eight. A fog settled over the river, preventing me from seeing across. I moved up to the bike trail and sat beneath the Westover Bridge, now living and breathing with commuters and students.

If I ever get another shot at life I'm going to be one of them. I'm going to be like everybody else. I didn't want the spotlight anymore. I wanted to be anonymous. I wanted to be scenery. Like the fog that settled over the river.

At ten I went up the hill. A produce truck unloading at the Stink blocked Walnut. Ted, the Stink's owner, startled me when he came from behind the truck and said, "You're up early, sunshine. Getting up or just getting in?"

"Both?" I joked, but he really didn't hear me. When he looked up from his lettuce and potatoes I said, "I didn't sound check last night. Maybe I can hang out, rehearse a little?"

"The furnace guy will be in there banging and running in and out. There's no heat right now."

"No problem. I don't care, if he doesn't mind the noise." I stepped back to get out of the truck's exhaust.

After Ted agreed I spent a few minutes helping him stack produce crates onto a dolly and followed him through the back. Then I spent a few more minutes helping him unload it. When we finished he said, "There's coffee behind the bar. I can make you a few eggs?"

"Thanks, Ted." I made myself a cup and passed on the eggs.

The big room watched me walk to the front all by myself. I felt judged by all the empty chairs, like I was living my own Tom Sawyer funeral fantasy. I set my guitar and amp up on the waist-high stage along with a wooden chair I'd grabbed.

Mikey had a sweet pair of white Les Pauls in stands next to a pair of Marshall Plexi stacks. A beautiful black Gibson archtop rested in a rack with a white Explorer like James Hetfield's. Pedal boards were splayed across the floor near his mic. Mikey ran it all through a giant rack of digital processors and compressors.

I found a little space in the center and pulled the cord from the back of the Twin. I plugged the amp in beneath the drum riser and took a pick off Mikey's mic stand. When I flipped open the guitar case's lid I felt guilty for savoring the sweet scent. I put my strap back on the Tele, plugged it in and strummed a little. The old tubes crackled as they warmed up. The strings and neck felt tiny compared to the Martin. My hands flew from fret to fret, jumping octaves, skipped through arpeggios and runs like a hummingbird through a flower garden. I didn't know whether to face the empty room or the empty stage.

I put my notebook on the amp and folded it open. I wrote out the chords for "Twickenham." But it would be a new song by the time I finished. I jotted down what I remembered from the song I wrote for Stu. I wrote in big bold letters that I could see while standing. When it seemed more like a song than just a bunch of lines, I stood up and gave it a try.

And I didn't know if it was because the song was about Stu, or if it was because I'd never played a note of anything I'd ever written myself on stage, but I started to choke up. I stopped, refocused and played it again, stomping my foot like a platoon walking into battle. My own drummer. The tempo changed, becoming more than the bluesy punk riff I'd conceived when I wrote it down. The riff got angrier—made me want to kick something. I ran through it two more times, each time tweaking a few lines or words. When I finished, I nodded. *That's one in the bag.*

At the top of the next page I wrote "Twenty-Seven" real big. I pieced together the rest from memory, rearranging any snippets I could remember from the song me and Katy played. I kept the chords simple. C, F and G7. The lyrics suggested a metamorphosis, but I was no butterfly. Maybe a frog. I ran through it a few times and even though it needed work, it sounded like my opener.

And I went through the next four or five like that. Writing down the lyrics I remembered. Piecing together what rhymed, what flowed, or what imagery told the best story. I put down chords or riffs for a few different songs simultaneously.

When I got to "Preston Black" I picked out the melody with just a few, simple notes and a lot of spring reverb trying to sound like T-Bone Burnett. I played it through, accenting the heavier parts by moving up the neck and playing minor sevenths. I didn't sing it, though. Those weren't words I wanted hanging around my head all day. I played it a few times then went and got more coffee. I wanted to ask Ted what he thought, but he was on the phone. By now I had seven songs. Lucky seven.

I plugged backed in, eased the volume up and went through my set again. The songs changed the more I played them. I worked on arrangements, phrasing lyrical sections. And if I had another hand to take notes I could've written seven more songs.

In the short time I had the Martin I learned about subtlety and volume control. I learned how to make individual notes count, so I wasn't just hammering everything as hard as I could. I didn't just strum through these like I'd strum through "All Along the Watchtower." These songs represented my life and I knew how they were meant to be played.

My hands cramped and my eyes hurt. I went to get another coffee, but we'd emptied the pot and Ted was still with the furnace guy. I put another pot on and waited, watching traffic out on Beechurst. Just up the street, Mick was probably doing the same thing. Maybe wondering how he could've been so wrong about me. I owed him more than a song. I went back to the window while I drank a cup, then refilled and went up onto the stage.

This time through, I eased the old Twin's volume up a bit. The crackle of hot tubes breathed new life into the room. I took my jacket off. I should've told Ted to send the repair guy away because I was going to burn the place down tonight. Laughing, I turned away from all the empty chairs and closed my eyes.

I barely remembered the last time music made my heart race and breathing accelerate like this. Maybe it was up in the mountains. Either at the fire hall or Jamie's studio or the Currence's kitchen.

Halfway through my setlist, I realized "Twenty-Seven" and "My Own Drummer" were in the same key and tried to build a segue. I changed my setlist on the fly, playing around with a few bars of an extended outro, tweaking the chord progression to add in an A minor and an E. I hit the chords a little harder and doubled the tempo each time through. By the time I got to the verse the new song was running hot. The speakers crackled. I sang so my voice crackled, too.

I broke into a sudden, unexpected bridge, stomping my foot so hard my knee hurt. When I finished my ears rang. I'd always figured I'd be deaf by thirty if I wasn't dead anyway. As the ringing subsided I heard somebody clapping. I spun around.

Mikey was standing in the back. Mick always told the kid he could be my little brother, which Mikey loved. Tonight he filled up the room like a giant—I glowed in his white light. I flipped the amp off and leaned the Tele against it, then jumped off the stage to meet him. I said, "This is it, man. You did it."

Mikey took his jacket off and laid it over a chair. His white shirt and skinny black tie made him look like a waiter. He said, "Not yet. The tunnel keeps getting longer and longer. I heard there's a light at the end somewhere."

He said, "This is what you been working on?" The rest of the band and the girlfriends trickled in one-by-one behind him.

I asked, "One amp, one mic... I guess that's okay?"

"Yeah. It's good. It'll be easy enough to mic the amp." He changed his tone, like he knew he couldn't go on without getting some business out of the way first. "Hey, man... Stevie told me about Stu. I didn't know him, but I heard him play with you guys all the time. Guess you had a rough week."

I shrugged. *I guess I did.*

"Well, what I heard sounded phenomenal, man. Not sure who you been channeling, but it sure as hell sounds like you're channeling somebody." Mikey leaned against the stage, surveying the chairs, the bar and the big floor.

"I think it's all me, for once."

We made small talk until the rest of his guys came to the stage and Mikey introduced me. While they soundchecked I went out back and sat on the deck, just watching the river for a while. The rain came back, bringing heavy fog with it. My hands had taken to shaking really badly and I wanted whiskey. I folded my arms, tucking my hands away.

Around seven I forced myself to go back in. The bar was filling up and people spilled onto the floor. I did a lap, looking for people I knew, but nobody offered me a drink, nobody slapped my shoulder. When Mikey went to the front door to meet a pair of guys wearing sport coats and jeans I bolted to the bathroom and hid. I assumed they were from the label.

"This is stupid, man." I mumbled it over and over. My hands wouldn't stop shaking. I cursed myself for not shaving. I washed my face and fixed my hair in the mirror, patting it down with wet palms, and ended up splashing water all over my shirt. Blotting it with a wad of paper towels didn't make it any drier. I curled my toes and paced, but I couldn't shake my jitters. I gave myself a pep talk in the mirror, then went back out. "This is stupid, man."

Mikey waved me over to the table. I must've said 'excuse me' a hundred times. I don't know if this many people had ever come to see us play when ribs or chili weren't being cooked competitively. I shook the suits' hands and downplayed my excitement. I laughed at their jokes and put on my best smile. But I never for a second believed shiny industry-types like them would be able to do anything to make my life better.

One of the suits said Mikey told him I could play. He said he wanted to hear me sing. I promised him a good show and shook out my hands. I wouldn't have been more freaked out if the Grant Town Goon had been standing in front of me.

"What do you think?" Mikey cracked open a Red Bull. "Half hour?"

Thinking about it made me stutter. I said, "Sounds good, man. I need a little air," and bolted for the front door.

Rain came down at a good clip. University was clogged with cars heading out toward 79—kids heading back home to the mountains for the weekend. Their brake lights reflected off of the wet road. The sidewalks sizzled with the hiss of water running off of the old building's eaves. I pressed myself against the posters for tonight's show as people filed in. The PRT rolled by on the tracks above. I shivered.

Students walked down Walnut from the clubs above High. The college girls looked young. I didn't have the confidence to make eye contact with any of them. They all giggled and shared jokes. I knew I'd disappoint them. People came from the garage up University. People came from Pleasant Street. A man and a girl came down the sidewalk and crossed with the light. She wanted to walk faster, but he was holding the umbrella. She swung a small instrument case. I wanted it to be Katy. When I saw they were coming in I held the door, figuring it was about time to get myself ready. And when I realized it was really Katy and Jamie I couldn't hide. I knew that if they were coming past Mick's they knew about last night.

Jamie shook my hand and looked me over. He gave my arm a squeeze. He said, "I knew the minute I saw you that you'd been dealing with the devil."

I closed my eyes and let my head fall back against the window. "I haven't, man. I swear. Of all people—"

He cut me off with a raised hand. "'Dealing' isn't the word I meant. Cavorting? Associating? I knew that you didn't know. That's why I tried to keep you out of town as much as I did. All the signs were there."

I looked at Katy to see her reaction, but she had her poker face on.

Jamie said, "You went two or three whole days without touching a scrap of food the weekend I met you. The way your skin was always cold to the touch. And I don't know if anybody ever told you this, but you talk in your sleep. Said some pretty crazy things. In the end, the phone call that night at the Currences' kind of gave it away."

His words hung there like exhaust from a coal truck.

He said, "I'm going to grab myself a stout. What's your tipple?"

Katy shook her head. She was wearing a little red dress that buttoned down the front. She had my black scarf wrapped around her neck.

Jamie wished me luck like he really, really meant it, then ducked inside. He had his canvas bag and a mic boom with him.

Katy looked up with eyes that didn't waver. Whatever she thought, she thought. She had total confidence in whatever decision she'd made. She finally said, "We just came from Mick's, you know. Jamie and me went halfsies on your guitar and amp."

I rubbed my eyes.

She handed me the receipt. It was Mick's handwriting. The payoff amount for the Martin loan. "Yeah, Jamie said he warned you he'd buy that old Tele. Mick said we had to come down here to collect it from you." She didn't say it with a smile.

"Why would you do that?" I said. It was barely a whisper.

"I don't know, Preston. I really don't have a freaking clue." She looked up at a tram on the rail above. "Jamie said it wasn't your fault. He said you were 'under the influence' like I'm supposed to know what that means."

I laughed defensively.

"And he said you needed this." She handed me the rattlesnake beads that had been in the Martin. "He said to put them in your pocket and don't ever take them out. Ever. Jamie convinced Mick you were all right, for the most part. He said you just needed a kick in the ass to get through all this."

I gave the beads a little shake.

"And this is from me." She wrapped a violin string around my left wrist. "Silver," she said. "To keep the devil away."

I held Katy's string to my cheek. It was warm. "Katy… I barely know you guys. I haven't done anything at all to prove I'm worth any of this." I rubbed my temples.

She turned toward the street and looked up at the low clouds. "I know you haven't. Maybe we just like you."

"Well, I'll pay you back, every cent. I swear."

She looked at me like she'd counted to three and made up her mind. "I don't want any money. Preston, I can't believe I'm about to say this…"

I waited.

"You're going to be huge, right? That's the plan." It wasn't a question. She said, "Maybe you're meant for more than all this. And maybe I want be a part of it. Like I really want a PhD in child psych or whatever. So consider it collateral."

She took my hand. "Jamie believes you can make something of yourself. He says you have a gift, which is total bull because he told my mom the same thing about me and look where I ended up."

I didn't know what to say, not that she was giving me a chance to speak.

"I'm not convinced you're anything special yet. I want you to prove it to me. Right now. Mick said I could call the cops immediately after the show if you blow it."

"Katy, I have to tell you everything that happened. There has been some crazy stuff going on."

"I don't want to hear about it. Not now anyway. Jamie told me everything I needed to know."

As soon as she finished her sentence Stevie Croe and his girl stepped onto the curb. "Hey, Pres." He grabbed my hand for a quick handshake, then hugged me, and nodded at Katy. I put my hand on Katy's back, just above her waist. We followed Stevie and his girl inside.

While Katy hung up her coat I went to find Mikey. I asked about a second mic and told him what was going on. I looked for Jamie, but didn't see him. As I pushed my way to the stage he materialized at the sound board, tightening the arm on his boom. I wanted to tell him how much his help had meant to me. But he nodded like he knew. When the house lights dropped, I lost him. The crowd noise grew from a simmer to a boil.

Mikey pulled a second mic over to mine.

"Ladies and gentlemen!" The crowd responded with a staccato burst of applause. It was too early for drunken applause. Mikey said, "You all know we're here tonight because you put us here."

Somebody shouted, "Play some music, douchebag!"

Mikey laughed and said, "And my mom's here, so... Watch it."

That he wasn't a great front man seemed funnier to most people than the words themselves. I pushed toward the stage. In a moment of panic I realized Katy wasn't with me. I spun to look for her and almost knocked her down.

"I'm right here," she said. She looked tiny in between all those people.

Mikey said, "Tonight's a really big night for us. You all know we're hitting the road. Maybe we'll see some of you guys in Panama City or on San Padre over Spring Break. After that we're heading out west. When we get back to town in August we'll be bringing a new record with us."

The way he smiled reminded me of the time he learned Randy Rhoads' "Dee" all on his own. He sat down and busted it out note for note in that little practice room at Mick's. And when I told him what a phenomenal job he'd done I saw that same smile.

"We have copies of our demo for sale back at the merch table. We have t-shirts, too, and stickers, so make sure you help us out. Eric doesn't want to run out of gas or Dr. Pepper somewhere in West Texas."

I stood at the edge of the stage and surveyed the crowd. The faces looked so different than the people we always played for. I didn't know if I'd be able to connect with them. I looked for Stevie. When I found him I looked for Jamie. Instead, I saw Dani at the bar. She was rubbing up against the guy from the Met. She had her hair up and wore a gray dress open almost down to her belly button and had on high black boots. It wouldn't be a party without *her*.

Turning my back to Dani and the crowd, I took my phone out of my pocket and scrolled through my texts to look for the last one John had sent. I hit OK, then scrolled down to CALL.

It rang.

When the ringing stopped I expected John to say something. When he didn't, I said, "Just wanted to let you know I'm going to be okay. And I wanted you to hear this."

I said "Don't hang up," then set my phone on the floor in front of a monitor.

Katy watched me and raised an eyebrow. She said, "You'll tell me later?"

I shrugged. "Tell you later."

Mikey went on. "When I knew we were kicking off our tour here there was only one guy in this whole town I wanted to play with. You've seen this guy everywhere, mostly rib cook-offs, for some reason. He's the one who flipped you off when you yelled 'Freebird!'"

Ted lit up the Shoot the Duck sign. Seeing that brought a big smile to my face.

I got real close to Katy and raised the mic up to her violin. "The first two are in A minor. You tuned up?"

She looked at me like I'd sprouted antlers. "Please."

"Just like up at the café. I have a cheat on the floor. Chords and lyrics."

"Yeah, I got this. I actually listened to the CD you gave me." She smiled. I got caught up in the moment and wanted to kiss her, but didn't.

Mikey said, suddenly a bit more seriously, "This guy saved me. He gave me music, so I guess you could say he gave me my soul. My life. I don't know what I'd be doing without him. Please welcome my good friend to the stage, Mr. Preston Black."

The crowd responded with a round of polite applause. I knew how I felt about opening acts, now I knew what it felt like to be one. I picked up the Tele, plugged it in and fired up the Twin. My belly fluttered and my hands shook. I suddenly had to pee real bad. I took a deep breath and stepped up to the mic.

"Thanks, Mike. You really shouldn't give me so much credit, though. Everybody in this room knows that there aren't many bands that make it as far as you have."

I strummed a few times, then flipped the pickup switch to the neck. "Well... I've played in a band for so long I didn't think I could do it alone. So I've asked a friend to join me tonight. Please welcome Davis, West Virginia's own Katy Stefanic on violin."

She got some hoots and a few whistles as she joined me at the second mic. I turned the Tele's volume knob up a hair and gave her a G. While she tuned, I lowered her mic a little, then said, "I don't plan on saying much tonight. But I want to let you all know how I ended up here."

I gave her a D. She stepped back from the mic and nodded.

"A few weeks ago I found a record at Isaac's up on Pleasant. I was flipping through LPs and found this old record that had been pressed the same year I was born. On the back of the sleeve I saw my name. As a song title. I thought it meant something. I thought, maybe the songwriter was my dad just because we had the same last name. So I bought the record even though my track looked like it'd been worked over by a horny alley cat."

I plucked an A.

"So I started looking for the song. I had to know what the lyrics said."

From an open D string I hammered onto the E, then picked the C before strumming a few times.

"In the process I found out a little about the place where I was born."

I took a deep breath and picked out a slow, soft "Wildwood Flower." At the 'I will dance I will sing' part Katy stepped up to the mic and joined me.

Right then and there an amazing thing happened. In these kids who threw down Jäger by the pint every Friday night, I managed to induce images of the buckwheat cakes and the lonely hollows they went back to every Saturday morning. I had to let them know that I *knew*, and playing that song created a common ground. They were mountaineers not just in the hoodies and ball caps they wore to football games. That's why they sang "Take Me Home, Country Roads" every week at the top of their lungs. The hall stood frozen, like in an old photograph. It was so quiet Katy could've played unplugged.

I dropped the picked melody and played a variation of the chords, and sang, "In a picture I saw what we used to be, and wondered, where did that life go?"

I turned toward Katy so she knew I was singing to her, too. "When did I wake up in another man's clothes? A John Doe?"

She smiled and stuck with me like powdered sugar to funnel cake, playing like she knew what I had in mind when I wrote it. By the time we got to the chorus we found symmetry in our new song, neither of us trying to outplay the other. At the end of the final chorus I started to segue like I'd practiced this afternoon, but thought things might fall apart if I couldn't pull Katy along with me.

When we got to the breakdown I stepped away from my mic and got right next to her mic like we were sharing it. The time I pounded out with my foot got a little louder and uglier. She got right into the mic, her delicate notes growing angry like they knew we were about to make it rain.

I kicked out the time, the hollow wooden stage bounced like a big bass drum. When I went to my own mic to launch into "My Own Drummer" she abandoned the violin-as-accent approach she'd taken so far and grabbed her share of spotlight.

Shrill squeals fell from the sound system like Tomahawk missiles. She picked up on the symbolism in my lyrics and played quarter tones that mimicked an Islamic call to prayer. It was angry and sad and she let it get wild like Johnny Rotten in a stolen Camaro, pushing the intensity, convincing me to get louder and uglier.

I tried to get her attention. "One more time."

In a weird reversal of roles she was the virtuoso and I was the rhythm section. I was Pauly and Stu, holding it all together while she ran wild through the room punching out windows. I hoped Jamie was getting this all down.

When we brought it to an end I stepped back from the mic. And I didn't hear anything. For a second I thought I blew it. I thought it was only great in my mind. My ears rang. I had to actually look into the audience to see the wild response, the mouths opened wide, screaming for more of what we were throwing down. Stevie held his girlfriend. His head was down and I couldn't see his face. Katy bowed and for a second I thought I was at Red Rocks or Central Park or the Gorge.

"Thank you," I said. But I couldn't hear it through the monitors. "Thank you very much."

After the noise simmered I got up to the mic and said, "That song was for Stu Croe. He died in uniform serving his country."

My lips were dry. And before I could let it all get into my head and screw with me I launched into the next song. "Teeth without teeth, laws without claws…"

Katy looked down at my cheat sheet on the floor. After the first verse I gave her a sign. She joined me for the second measure, playing a slow, deep trill, a lulling undercurrent to the steady dirge I beat out of my guitar. Out in the audience a few people closed their eyes and rocked back and forth.

"Two foot tall, not a man, nothing at all."

A couple of kids texted. I saw the blue glow shining onto their faces.

"Sticks and stones, break my bones, not a clone but you can't fight DNA…"

I wasn't playing for the kids on their phones. Maybe I finally learned I couldn't change the world with a song. We kept this one short. The applause wasn't as focused as it was the first time, but it felt appreciative. I figured I couldn't ask for more. Not on a night like tonight. I looked for Jamie. I looked for Mikey and his band and their A and R guys.

Dani had pushed her way into the middle of the room.

I said, "Thank you. That song's about the night I found my real dad. You can probably figure out it wasn't good."

We caught our breath. It all happened too fast. Afraid I'd never get to feel this again, I dragged my feet. I flipped the page in my notebook with my toe. Katy looked down at my cheat sheet.

Into the mic I said, "But I found love, too." My light, little chords tinkled like sleet onto a sunny window. It wasn't "Layla," but then again, neither was anything else Clapton ever did. I sang, "Now, Alice couldn't climb out of the rabbit hole. Dorothy couldn't ride another tornado back over the rainbow, and I can't go back to a world without you in it."

I listened for Katy to join in because she hadn't yet. When I turned I saw her violin tucked neatly beneath her arm. Her head was tilted toward me so hair fell across her cheek. She was listening.

"What if I could go back to the day the music died, and send the plane away with no one inside? Would you give me another chance?"

I looked for a response from Katy, but I figured her presence was her response. I turned toward her and sang the chorus. Like I said, it wasn't "Layla." But it was mine. It was something new.

"Hey, hey little bluebird, why don't you stay? I thought I heard you singing, I thought I heard you say, that you loved me…"

It was an apology and a confession. Maybe something from mass had stuck with me after all these years.

"Went down in the morning, to where last I heard your song, the sun came up and then the stars, and I knew that you were gone."

It felt good to confess, to be rid of all the shit I'd been carrying around. It was about time I took a fresh start.

"I never said I love you, I know now that was wrong, I don't know where to find you, I hope you hear this song."

The last few verses, even though they were symbolic, didn't really seem to matter to anybody except me and Katy. I'd planned to play this long, instrumental interlude thing, but seeing the audience fade made me cut it short.

At the end I took a little bow.

I started to get scared. My heart palpitated, my tongue might've even gone numb. I felt I'd lost the crowd to make things right between me and Katy. I decided to cut out the middle and go straight to the end. A big end.

I let the air leave the room. It was still mine for a few more minutes. I said, "A funny thing happened with the song from the back of the record," I said, looking for Jamie. "A friend of mine did a lot of research to track down somebody he thought could help us with the lyrics to 'The Sad Ballad of Preston Black.' And from the second this guy started singing I knew the song was about me. My life in verse. The song said I'd made a deal with the devil."

I wiped sweat off of my brow with my forearm.

Looking for Dani, I said, "All kinds of bad stuff came raining down on me. And just like the song said I would, I found the devil herself."

I looked over at Katy. Her fiddle was propped on her shoulder like an AK. She was ready to go.

"I'm going to sing that song for you now, the song that kicked this crazy journey off."

I took a deep breath.

Maybe it was cliché to start soft and let it build, but that was what worked. "Stairway." "Everlong." "Two Step." I didn't really see myself having a choice. So I sang the first verse a cappella. Just like Ernie Currence sang in his kitchen, except in tune. I slapped my knee with my hand and sang, "I never knew my mom or a dad. No, I never knew my mom or dad. Didn't know when I was born, didn't know when I'd die, didn't know nothing about the how or why. Preston Black didn't know his mom or dad."

The ironic thing was the way they ate it up. Their attentiveness was obvious, because I'd seen a lot of crowds who could give a shit. And I wondered how many of them believed my story, and how many of them thought it was bullshit, but liked it anyway.

I continued without strumming my guitar. Beneath my vocals Katy squeezed a dissonant drone from her fiddle, something like fingernails down a chalkboard. She twisted the minor key, giving the song a gothic stain.

"Preston Black couldn't quench his thirst. Preston Black couldn't quench his thirst. But he'd go to the bar every night and be dry again by the morning light, Preston Black couldn't ever quench his thirst."

Katy built on the song's melody, playing notes complementary to mine but never the same note. Her tones and my words filled the space above the crowd with strange, new chords. Smothered them with noise.

While Katy played I turned around and eased the Twin's volume up. I looked for the sound guy, maybe trying to tell him I was about to drop bombs. When he nodded I got ready for the next verse.

"Preston Black loved to sing in church. Preston Black loved to sing in church. Though he knew the words to every song the preacher told him that he didn't belong. Preston Black loved to sing in church."

At the end of that verse I started picking out the melody. The Twin's hot tubes gave me a little fuzz. But I wanted more. I pointed to Katy's mic and pointed up with my thumb. The sound guy nodded.

I took a deep breath, then let it out slowly. I sang, "Preston Black couldn't sleep the whole night through. Preston Black couldn't sleep the whole night through. He'd lay in bed 'til the morning came, but the devil'd visit him just the same. Preston Black couldn't sleep the whole night through."

At the end of that measure I slid up the neck and pounded out an A minor 7, putting an exclamation point on the melody. I did the same with the E, strumming so hard I cut my right pinky and ring fingers on the strings. Just like Joe Strummer. The hot tubes released their fury into the composition.

Katy responded by playing an Irish-sounding reel to compensate for my lack of delicacy. It surprised me a bit. I looked over at her and smiled.

I yelled more than I sang. My voice strained and cracked like my old amp. "Preston Black went down to the crossroads. Preston Black went down to the crossroads. Tried to make the devil a deal but the bitch said he didn't have a soul to steal. Preston Black went down to the crossroads."

I stepped away from the mic, absolutely beating music out of my old Tele. Sweat dripped onto the stage. Katy's bow sawed the air, her head bobbing and dropping with dips and shifts in the riffs she plowed through. Maybe she had demons of her own to exorcise.

I came back to the mic and took an extra beat or two to catch my breath, hacking out the A with staccato chops of my fist. I closed my eyes and spit out the last verse. "Preston Black wrote his own sad song. Preston Black wrote his own sad song, he knew if he didn't do it the devil would, and she'd already taken everything she could. Preston Black wrote his own sad song."

I jumped away from the mic like it was a crate full of black widow spiders. Katy turned toward me, her fiddle screaming like a mother over a lost son. Screaming like a cougar cornered in a wild hollow. Screaming like a storm pushing its way over her mountains. The wailing bursts from her fiddle pushed light away from the stage, brought time to a halt, infected my blood with a tinge of something Jamie called 'chills of hilarity.' It felt like I mainlined the song straight into my blood.

I looked for Dani through all the fists in the air. The light from the stage cast the audience in an orange glow. The movement from the crowd had the same effect as a bonfire. I found her dark, unblinking eyes and I improvised.

"Preston Black went toe-to-toe with the devil..."

I stopped playing and muted my strings, letting Katy's wild creation run rampant through the hall all by itself. "Preston Black went toe-to-toe with the devil."

A wave of feedback caught in the old Twin's tubes. I let it boil and bubble. As the teapot screamed I sang, "If I don't have a soul to steal then we sure as hell don't have a deal. Preston Black went toe-to-toe with the devil."

I kicked the mic stand off the end of the stage and slid right up to Katy. But she didn't back away, throwing wild jabs with her bow to keep me back. She wasn't about to let me put her in a corner. She came out swinging haymakers.

I gave Katy a nod. One more measure. A whole life for a few notes. And when I hit the last chord the train stopped so fast the caboose didn't know what was coming. I yanked the cord from the Tele and dropped it to the floor. I slung the guitar behind me and yanked Katy out of her moment. She put her arms around my neck, violin in one hand, bow in the other. She kissed hard, like a bee stings. She looked up at me. I pushed a loose strand of hair behind her ear with my finger.

The noise from the floor blew like a nasty wind coming down Cheat Canyon. Like a semi through my bedroom. I'd never heard anything like it from this side of the stage. I let Katy go but held onto her hand. I put my left hand up over my head. She took a slight bow.

Mikey jumped onto the stage from the floor. He kissed Katy on the cheek, then grabbed my hand. He stepped up to the mic and said, "Ladies and gentlemen, let them hear..." but the crowd didn't need prodding.

He hugged me. Into my ear he said, "Unreal, man. You are unreal. You still inspire me to want to be better."

I put my Tele in its case and waved one more time. I gave Katy a kiss and said, "I'm sorry. I'll do whatever I can to make it all up to you."

She nodded and gave a little smile. "I know." She stepped toward the edge of the stage. I grabbed her wrist and turned her toward the crowd. The other guys from the band came up and congratulated us.

Too busy trying to hang onto the moment to appreciate it, I watched the crowd scatter, either looking for drinks or the bathroom. I wanted somebody to come up to me and grab my shoulder and tell me how great it was, but I knew the experience meant a lot more to me than it did to most of the kids here. They were ready to move on. Katy bobbed her way back toward the soundboard and her uncle.

I wanted to see Jamie, too. I was sure he had something to say. And I needed the approval. But Dani cut me off on her way to the exit. She looked at me and said, "Very good, Preston. The little boy is all grown up. Pauly was always a lot easier anyway. *Na shledanou.*"

I followed her onto the sidewalk. "Dani!" Going from the room's heat to the night's cold gave me a deep shiver. "Leave Pauly the hell alone."

She ignored me and continued toward the intersection. The red from the stoplight cut through the deep fog and reflected off of the wet street. Patches of snow in the gutter and on grassy spots reflected the red up to the sky. Brake lights cast red sparks onto the faces of the drivers in the cars behind them. The fog was too dense for them to do anything but crawl.

I jogged to try to get ahead of her. "Stop!"

I stepped in front of her. She didn't look at me. Still jittery from the rush of performing, I grabbed her wrist.

She screamed, "Don't you touch me!"

I tried blocking her path, but she made a quick right onto the Westover Bridge to dodge me. "Dani, you listen to me…"

Inflamed with rage I sped ahead of her. Cars stopped at the light on their way up Pleasant, but the drivers ignored us.

I didn't dare touch her again, but was powerless to do anything else. A tiny voice inside me said just give it up and go back inside. "Dani."

She pushed past me. I couldn't see the river below for all the fog, but I heard it washing past the bridge supports. A tugboat pushing empty coal barges rounded the bend by Star City. Its spotlight split the fog like a hatchet through wood.

I ran on her heels. The sound of our footfalls crunching in the old snow and crusted salt was the only other sound until I yelled, "You're unreal, you know that? The difference between me and you is that I was at least loved by somebody. But you're like a tiny little stone that keeps getting pushed downstream, getting passed around from man to man because you feel like you're controlling something. We are not the same. You don't know how to love anybody because nobody's ever loved you." I jabbed the air with my finger.

For the first time tonight she stopped and let me face her. She raised her hand behind her head to slap me. I caught her by the wrist. She smiled, then tried to pull away.

She pushed me with her left hand, then boxed my ear again and again when I didn't let go.

Still gripping her right wrist with my right hand, I tried to block with my elbow. Her nails dug into my forearm. Blood trickled out of burning cuts.

She screamed, "Help me! Please, he's going to kill me," and backed toward the rail that separated the sidewalk from a long drop into the Monongahela River.

I released my grip on her, but she clung to me like a scab to a cut. I tried to twist her off of my arm, but she kept a fierce grip with both hands. She pulled a mask of terror over her face, eyes widened like she was really facing her own death.

I twisted myself out of her grip and she slapped me, her ring cut my cheek. I used my elbows to block her blows and backed away. My ears rang from being hit so many times. Blood dripped onto my white t-shirt. "Fucking stop! You're fucking crazy." I yelled and grabbed her wrist again.

"Preston… I know what it's like for you. Who else can understand?" Her voice wavered and cracked as she wrangled herself free. She said, "*Mám toho plné zuby!* You accuse me of these horrible things, saying I'm the devil. But I'm just a person, like you—a lonely, sad person." Now crying, she said, "I'm just a girl who knows what it's like to have nobody. And now I don't even have you."

She tried to embrace me and I backed away. "Preston," she cried, "I just want to touch you. Please. I want to feel your skin."

She reached her hand out, trying to caress my cheek. "Let's make this work, Preston. We can have our own family."

I stopped fighting and tried to see her as a person again, and not a monster.

"Jump with me. *Nemůžu bez tebe žít.* And I don't want to live without you." She thrashed and struggled. If anybody else had been on the bridge to see, it would've looked like I was pushing her.

Gravity pulled her toward the river. Pulled me toward my wet grave. My prophesied end. I clamped onto her wrist with both hands. She released me. He fingers relaxed but I held on. The weight of her body felt heaviest where my ribs met the railing. I couldn't take full breaths.

I said, "If I jump I'll die. But I bet you won't. You'll pop up somewhere else. Maybe even right back here."

She smiled and said, "I'm sure the large part of me is Danicka Prochazka. Maybe the small part of me must be the devil. "

"All I have to do is let go."

She said, "Do it then."

My fingers relaxed. In that moment her expression changed to a look of self-satisfaction, like she knew all along. She disappeared into the fog without a sound. I stood, waiting to hear the splash her body would make when it hit the water.

I took a breath, but didn't step away from the railing.

"This is when I'm supposed to do it."

Cold water and a muddy grave. Dying in the dark. Just like the song said. I stood up, composing myself. I wiped my hand through the cold water on the rail and patted it on my face. The cold felt good.

Katy called my name from down the street. Her umbrella bobbed in the glow of a green light. I headed down to her, blotting my cheeks with melting snow from the rail.

She held my other shirt folded under her arm. I lifted the bloody t-shirt over my head. She buttoned up my flannel while I pressed the t-shirt against my face.

She brought me under the relative warmth of her pink umbrella and said, "Is that it?"

"That's it." I lied. It wouldn't be over for me until I heard the splash.

I rested my good cheek on the top of her head. She didn't say anything else about it.

I didn't either.

EPILOGUE

The bright May sun poured into the guitar shop through a dingy window and caught Mick square in the eyes. He squinted at Aaron, who stood there with one hand on the door, trying to escape before Mick could talk his ear all the way off. I wanted to tell Aaron it was smart of him to start giving guitar lessons because it would really take his playing to the next level, but supposed he probably had that figured out by now.

I loved summer in Morgantown, which started as soon as the students went home. Traffic moved a lot faster on streets that weren't clogged with an extra twenty thousand cars. And me and Katy had places like Black Bear Burritos all to ourselves. Me and Katy needed neutral territory and a little privacy to really get to know each other after that night at the Stink. It didn't hurt that Black Bear hosted local, live music six nights a week, giving us a place to work on new song ideas in front of a friendly audience. Most importantly, with just the right amount of darkness and noise, it felt like a home.

I pushed my last bite of coleslaw onto a tortilla chip and plopped it into my mouth. I liked the chips that were a little oily and gathered up all the extra salt. On the tiny riser a three-piece string band named *Edgar Allan Pony*— which I thought was awesome—tuned to each other over the sound of Eddie Vedder and his ukulele trickling out of the house speakers. Katy was on the phone with her mom, so I helped myself to her nachos while I eavesdropped.

"Yes. Party tomorrow. I didn't forget," she said, pulling her plate out of my reach. "Pres and I have to get the car inspected so we'll be there a little later. Jamie needs us to pick up some things at Fawley's—strings and a new tailpiece for a fiddle… No, we're at Black Bear now. Preston wants to talk to Mick and Mick doesn't carry that kind of stuff." She looked at me when she said it. Her way of telling me I just needed to get up and do it. "Why's Henry home?"

Her cousin. I reminded myself, trying to keep them all straight in my head.

"So there's drama?" she said, rolling her eyes, amazing me with her ability to be both a woman and a girl in the same moment. "I kind of liked not being involved in any of that."

I gestured that I was going to order something else and she shook her head. I mouthed the question *chips and queso*?

She pushed her plate toward me. "Mom, hang on." She put her phone against her shoulder. "Don't eat it all."

But I ignored her. She never finished her meals anyway.

Across the street Mick pulled his stool over to the register and began cashing out. I knew I had a few minutes before he locked the shop up. My stomach tightened when I tried to think of what I'd say to him. At this point I knew 'I'm sorry' wasn't going to cut it.

Katy watched me wrestle with my nervousness for another minute before finally saying, "Mom, I have to go… We'll be up after lunch tomorrow, okay?" She nodded. "No, we won't ruin our appetites at Taco Bell. Bye-bye." She put her phone into her purse, pushed her plate of nachos aside and reached across the table for my hand. "Preston Black…"

"Katy Stefanic…"

"Stop beating yourself up, okay? Mick will understand. I promise."

"How can you make that promise? I know Mick a little better than you do."

"The guilt is tearing you apart, Preston. Don't you see? There's a cloud over you. Like Eeyore."

I looked across the street at the little guitar shop. All I could do was shake my head.

"Preston…"

"So what do I say? Because there's no way I can act like nothing ever happened."

"Well don't then. Tell Mick I made you apologize. He'll buy it."

But I couldn't move. I looked up at the print on the wall. A pair of black bears dancing a jig. The reason this was Katy's favorite table.

"It's time for closure. You don't have to like it, but you have to do it. We're supposed to go back to Nashville in July and I won't even think about setting foot in that studio again until you get your head on straight. How much tape did we ruin because you couldn't concentrate? April should've been the highpoint of your entire adult life, but your guilt ruined it. For someone who doesn't go to church you sure act Catholic. This is your life, Preston. It's time to take it back."

I slid to the edge of the stool and stood up but couldn't let go of the table. She took my hand and pulled me in for a kiss. She had faith in me, and that was the only reason I had any in myself.

She said, "It'll be fine."

I followed the hand-painted bear tracks on the floor past the other booths, past the band. I nodded at the guitar player as I pushed the door open. I turned, and saw that Katy had switched seats so she could watch. She smiled and scooted me out the door with a flick of her hand.

ACKNOWLEDGEMENTS

I'd like to begin same as I did last time, by thanking Brad Vetter and Jim Sharraden of Nashville, Tennessee's Hatch Show Print for sharing a little of the magic bottled up in all that wood type with me. Their tremendous vision and patience makes me believe a book should be judged by its cover.

I'd also like to thank an important group of people who made 2011 such an amazing year. Releasing *The Devil and Preston Black* on my own was a scary proposition. But like-minded writers and compassionate readers overwhelmed me with support and kindness by seeing the story that lived behind the so-so formatting and home-made cover. They knew, and helped me realize, that Preston's tale is a good one, and this book you are holding in your hands is the result of your encouragement. Chris Stout, Lee Allen Howard, Ron Edison, Tom Mehalek—I owe you all shots.

There are many people responsible for filling my life with music, and I want to thank as many as I can: my uncle, Mike Rega, who showed me there was more fun to be had on the other side of the dance floor, Jeff Sabarese, who put a Gibson Futura in my hands and introduced me to Randy Rhoads, Carl Micarelli, for giving me two years to pay off my first guitar, Lou Rega, for the barre chords, Aaron Barnhart and Jarrod and Josh Schiffbauer of the legendary Phist for my first shot in a real band. And of course I have to mention my little brother, Mike Miller, for strapping on that old bass guitar every time I asked, and Little Mike Rega for being the one guy who knows what I'm talking about when I start comparing *Kid A* to *The Wall*.

And of course, much love to John Lennon, Joe Strummer, Duane Allman, and the rest.

In 2003 I had the pleasure of participating in a workshop on Appalachian Culture and Music with Gerald Milnes, the Folk Arts Coordinator at Davis and Elkins College. He talked about witches, signs, hexes and where they all came from.

Then he broke out his fiddle and invited those of us with instruments to join him. That single evening impacted my writing more than any other over the last ten years, for which I owe him a lifetime of thanks.

And I'd especially like to thank Michael A. Arnzen for being the big brother I never had. In a way, I feel like he went and did all the cool stuff first. But I have no problem sneaking into his room and stealing from him while he isn't home. I got the idea to do a soundtrack for the novel from his *Audiovile*, and he's the guy I most want to impress with my writing. And he's the one who introduced me to the amazing people at Raw Dog Screaming Press.

Speaking of...

What makes Jennifer Barnes and John Edward Lawson so great is the way they show me time and time again that my world is too small. Just when I think I've reached an edge, they change my point of view and make me realize I'm at the beginning of this crazy trek. Writing has never been as easy or as fun as it's been since we all invaded Hagerstown way back in November 2011, and I love being a part of their family.

I don't know what Pattie Boyd did for George Harrison and Eric Clapton, but I know what Heidi, my wife, does for me. She makes me want to see a better version of myself. She inspires me to see the world like a writer would, celebrating its pleasures, wanting to correct its injustices. She makes me realize that my life, as long as she's in it, will never be long enough. But she always reminds me that, through our writing, we will live forever.

ABOUT THE AUTHOR

 Jason Jack Miller hails from Fayette County, Pennsylvania, as in, "Circus freaks, temptation and the Fayette County Fair," made famous by The Clarks in the song, "Cigarette." An outdoor travel guide he co-authored with his wife in 2006 jumpstarted his freelancing career; his work has since appeared in newspapers, magazines, literary journals, online, and as part of a travel guide app for mobile phones. He wrote the novels *Hellbender* and *All Saints* during his graduate studies at Seton Hill University, where he is now adjunct creative writing faculty. He's been a whitewater raft guide, played guitar in a garage band and served as a concierge at a five star resort hotel in Florida. When he isn't writing he's on his mountain bike or looking for his next favorite guitar. He is currently writing *The Revelations of Preston Black*, the sequel to this novel. He lives a stone's throw from Morgantown with his wife, Heidi Ruby Miller. Visit him at http://jasonjackmiller.blogspot.com or on Twitter @jasonjackmiller.

www.ingramcontent.com/pod-product-compliance
Lightning Source LLC
Chambersburg PA
CBHW022045240626

47154CB00007B/2570